Praise for Len Lamensdorf's other works

The Crouching Dragon:

"... unusual, intriguing ... suspense laden ... "
—*Booklist* (American Library Association)

"... Fascinating ... vivid word pictures ... thrilling adventure ... a suspenseful maze ... "
—Fred Wolf, Academy Award and multiple Emmy winning filmmaker

"Unique in my reading experience."
—Stephanie Edwards, KIEV Radio, Los Angeles

"... [Lamensdorf] is a real story teller."
—Fran Halpern, National Public Radio

Kane's World:

"A thriller without crime ... compulsive reading."
—*Durrant's,* London

"... Rare and rewarding ... "
—*Library Journal*

"... Lusty, compelling ... "
—*Chicago Tribune*

Gino, the Countess & Chagall

*To Erika —
fellow art lover*

By Len Lamensdorf

Len Lamensdorf
4/28/07

SeaScape Press™

© 2000 Leonard Lamensdorf. All rights reserved.

No portion of this book may be reproduced or used in any form, or by any means, without prior written permission of the publisher.

SeaScape Press™ 1010 Roble Lane, Santa Barbara, CA 93103
Seascape Press™ is a trademark of Seascape Press, Ltd.

First printing 2000

10 9 8 7 6 5 4 3 2 1

Manufactured in the United States of America

Cover and Interior Illustrations © 2000 by Bleu Turrell
Cover and Interior Design by Lightbourne

Publisher's Cataloging-in-Publication
(Provided by Quality Books, Inc.)

Lamensdorf, Leonard.
    Gino, the countess & Chagall: a novel / by Len Lamensdorf. --1st ed.
    p. cm.
    LCCN: 99-90211
    ISBN: 0-9669741-6-6 (alk. paper)

    1. Chagall, Marc, 1887-1985---Fiction. 2. Artists--Italy--Florence--Fiction. 3. Artists--France--Paris--Fiction. I. Title.

PS3562.A4635G56 2000   813'.6
                                QB100-149

 The paper used in this book meets the minimum requirements of the American National Standard for Information Services—Permanence of Paper for Printed Library Materials, ANSIZ39.48-1984.

Publishers Note: This is a work of fiction. Although real people appear in their natural settings, none of the events depicted in the story really happened, and they are entirely fictitious. Any actions, motivations, or opinions attributed to or about real people in the book are purely fiction and are presented solely as entertainment.

For Erica, Always

Contents

	Prologue	*1*
1	Gino's War	5
2	The Orphan and the Fascist	17
3	The Hero's Return	31
4	Three Monks, a Maestro and a Mystery	37
5	Desire under the Arches	55
6	Too Much Is Enough	79
7	Banished from Paradise	97
8	City of Light—and Darkness	109
9	A New Career	137
10	Rescue and Renewal	153
11	The Battle of the *Biennale*	175
12	Pietro's Fantasy	195
13	Crass Commercialism	207
14	Brave New World	223
15	Commitment	247
16	The Lap of Luxury	259
17	Gino, the Countess & Chagall	283
18	Pietro's Progress	305
19	Civilization and its Discontents	325
20	The High Road	341
21	Separation	355
22	The Twilight Zone	365
23	Life and Transfiguration	387
24	Liberation	405
	Epilogue	*429*

Prologue

Paris, 1969: A Place in the Pantheon

It was becoming more and more difficult to listen to the speeches; Gino was accustomed to acclaim, but nothing like this. His smile was growing tighter and he twisted in his seat—in part because he wore an elegantly tailored formal, and although it fit him perfectly, he was by nature uncomfortable in anything so stiff and artificial. The human heat of the room, billowing up from the audience, didn't help. He was beginning to perspire, dampness on his upper lip, cloying wetness under his jacket. He wanted to pull at his collar, loosen his tie, but that would have been rude. Gino was large and bluff—rarely rude.

He tried to remain politely focused on the speaker, but his eyes occasionally wandered about the vast hall. Facing him, almost surrounding him, were four towering tiers of flamboyantly carved gold balustrades framing scarlet-upholstered walls, draperies, boxes and seats. The first and fourth levels were similar in design, as were the second and third, every inch covered with golden cascades of heraldic and floral patterns, figures and flags, interwoven with breathtaking skill. For a moment, he imagined it was a gigantic gilded web and he was glued in it.

Twenty-two hundred people—women in rainbows of long gowns and bare shoulders, men in black tuxedos, white fronts gleaming: a vast troupe of marionettes, remarkable more for their number than their mobility. From time to time seismic waves of applause rippled across them, and he had to restrain himself from shaking his head in amazement.

Around the auditorium pairs of great fluted gold columns rose at rhythmic intervals, some clutched by cupids, all blossoming high overhead into flowery capitals. These titans upheld a golden circlet encrusted with lights that shimmered like pearls in the faceted glow of the immense, pendulous glass chandelier, an inverted wedding cake wonder of awe-inspiring grandeur.

He would have found the florid, overwrought designs garish, except: above them all soared the dome and on its arching ceiling, the great mural with its brilliant, fragile colors and wraithlike figures, celebrating the city, the arts, life itself. How he had puzzled over the colors and figures, seeking to learn, afraid to be tempted, troubled and yet enlightened. And what a mystical contrast to everything else in the hall.

Another staccato of applause; the marionettes obligingly dipping and lifting their heads, raising their hands and slapping them together, then arranging them in their laps, virtually in unison. The strings were invisible. Where was the maestro who conducted this performance? Hidden in the mural? The chandelier? Another mystery.

The speaker was André Malraux, novelist and art historian, the man who had been President de Gaulle's Minister of Culture until the great leader had resigned only a few months earlier. Wearing the obligatory formal attire, slim, with dark smooth hair, aquiline features; imperious. Malraux! Standing at the microphones and saying: "This is a rare moment in history, when we honor a creative genius during his lifetime—even better, while he is in his prime."

Again the marionettes dipped and swayed in approval.

Gino smiled shyly, head down, unable to believe that this was happening. When he looked up, his eyes caught the eyes of Pietro, who sat in the first row of the orchestra, looking pale and pinched, hands clutching the armrests, eyes blinking rapidly. Despite the glare of the lights, Pietro seemed darker than ever. Gino considered nodding to him, but thought that might seem cruel.

When he looked back toward the dais, he saw Sartre sitting casually, smiling at him. Debonair despite thick black-framed glasses and unruly, thinning hair, he appeared to be the most relaxed man on the stage. No longer young, but still compelling, with lively eyes and a quick tongue. Earlier, Sartre had remarked to the audience that he and Gino shared the same name, Jean-Paul—Gianpaolo. "But Signore Bondone has more hair." That had brought laughter, too.

Malraux continued, praising Gino's innovative artistry, his powerful connection with reality—a new reality transcended by genius. Which made him think of the mural overhead, its translucent, Murano glass colors, the black framing of contorted yet lithesome figures, floating, always floating. What deceptive simplicity! He glanced to his right at Chagall, sitting with his wife, Vava, in the first level of boxes, almost close enough to touch. Small compared to Gianpaolo, bent and more gaunt with every passing year, hair white and sparse, but chin and nose still thrusting, powerful, eyes gleaming with *joie de vivre*. He was smiling benignly and proudly at Gianpaolo—Gino, as if he were his son. Perhaps listening to Malraux, nodding now and then, but never taking his eyes off Gino. His heart swelled with love for this proud, but generous man—teacher, friend, defender, critic. *I am your humble student, Marc, disciple in the high temple of the mysteries of life. Our works have little in common, yet we cherish each other.*

Chagall nodded, as if he had heard.

Malraux pointed to Picasso slumped in a box, and more applause erupted. The great man barely acknowledged it; he was busy murmuring to his pretty, youthful companion. Still, he had come up from Mougins for the occasion, a trip he rarely made these days.

Ariane was there, too. Lovely as ever, regal features flawless, silvery gown swirling below smooth shoulders. It was here, in her company, that he had first been dazzled by the Opera, a callow, ignorant youth, captured by the music, enraptured by a countess. Her escort on this night was young, handsome, attentive. Gino felt no jealousy, only happiness for her.

He wondered if Monique was there. He had scanned the

audience without finding her, but questioned whether he would recognize her after so many years.

The man in the next chair leaned close; the Italian ambassador, whispering something Gino couldn't quite hear. It would have been impolite to ask him to repeat himself, so he merely smiled, he hoped appropriately. Not that he really cared. Gino was honored the ambassador had come, but he had little use for politicians, even handsome, elegant ones with too-perfect teeth.

My birthday, he thought. *Imagine, thousands of people—wealthy, important people from many countries—are celebrating my birthday. I am an ignorant peasant, and they have dedicated a hall to me in a great French institution. It's crazy.*

They were all on their feet applauding him, and he had to stand and acknowledge their cheers. He smiled and waved a hand and then smiled even more broadly. It was a while before they realized he was laughing. *It's ridiculous,* he was thinking, remembering who he was and where he had come from. His laughter had an edge to it, and his audience became uncertain of what he meant, and their applause grew ragged. But he wasn't in that great hall with its cohort of wealthy, powerful and talented people who had come to honor him. He was far away in a dusty town at the very heel of Italy, in September of 1943.

One

Gino's War

The lintel was very low and the door was gone. Even the hinges. Except for the glaring wedge of sunlight that angled from the doorway to the floor, the corridor and the stairs were dark, yet somehow totally visible. They led nowhere. Gino had climbed them once and found a door that opened onto nothingness. Dizzied, he had almost fallen, but with a trembling hand he had pulled the door shut and crept back down the stairs. Why should he mind the creaking? There were no neighbors to disturb.

Again he crouched in the shadows beside the doorway, where he could see a slice of the street and hear everything. His clothes stank, and now that he had a moment of breast-heaving rest, the smell was stronger. But the smell of urine in the hallway was worse. Urine and garbage. Probably dead rats. Even in the shade, the baking heat sent the odors steaming up into his nostrils.

The building shuddered with every blast and the stairs creaked as waves of sound ran up and down them. Each time they creaked, he started. He knew there was no one—could not possibly be anyone up there, but the stairs, groaning under unseen feet, frightened him.

The vibrations grew stronger now, and they came with increasing frequency. The waves rebounded and shattered each other, setting off new waves of sound and motion that seemed to saturate the universe. Out of this trembling cacophony, his ears selected the sound of a vehicle gulping down the narrow street in short swallows as it bounded over the cobbled pavement. Gino leaned back against the wall, trying to merge into it. The vehicle roared past and its echoes were quickly lost in the general clamor. He could breathe again. But then he looked down and realized he had left his rifle lying across the threshold of the doorway, in plain sight. What a soldier! What if they had seen it? And who had they been? What did it matter? He would have hidden all the same. He stared at the rifle. The barrel was smudged and the stock caked with mud. He thought he might be sick again.

It was little more than an hour since General Bellomo had delivered his impassioned speech to the assembled garrison of Bari. When the general announced the armistice, the men had cheered—Gino with them. Three years in uniform and he had never fired a shot in battle. Thank God it was over. But no; the general said they must fight alongside the British and Americans and drive the Germans out. Once more the men cheered. Gino remained silent; it was not over. He might still have to fight. Not that he hated the Germans any less than his comrades. It was just that he had thought he was done with war. Neither killed nor a killer.

The fiery little general ordered the garrison to the south edge of the city where a German column was advancing. The harbor must be held. Italian troops must repel the invaders.

They had dashed off, inflated with enthusiasm, determined to prove their courage. Gino ran with them; reluctant, but with them. His squad trotted down the narrow, deserted streets, every door and shutter closed. Of course, only a fool would be outdoors at a time like this. He was beginning to perspire. In the heat, the dirty yellow walls of the houses seemed to swell outward. The rifle was a damp rock in his hands. Gino glanced at his comrades. Their faces were eager, excited. He was puzzled. How could one be eager to kill—or to die? He slowed his steps and the others hurried past. In a few moments he was at the end of the column. No one seemed to notice.

There was a sudden burst of sound, like a wooden board being ripped from a carton, the nails popping loose rapidly, one after another. Rifle fire. Volley after volley. Gino stopped moving. Ahead, several of his comrades had fallen. Others were running or crouching in doorways, returning the fire. He knew he should do the same, but he stood motionless, his rifle held slackly, pointing at the ground. Gino's eyes snapped shut with every shot, but still he did nothing. Soon, those of his squad who were not hit had scurried to safety in a side street. After a few moments he heard the sounds of gunfire again, deadened now by distance. Gino roused himself and began to run after his platoon.

His boots clattered on the cobblestones. He ran past the motionless bodies of two Italian soldiers, not daring to look at them. He didn't want to know who they were.

Then he was confused. Which street had his comrades taken? The rifle fire seemed to be coming from his left. But where? He stopped running and looked about. Boot steps. Heavy. Thudding down the street ahead. It must be his squad.

A running figure turned the corner and ran toward him, head down, helmet obscuring his face. But the uniform was unmistakably German. Involuntarily, Gino raised his rifle. The soldier looked up. His face expanded in surprise, then wrinkled in anger. A strangely familiar face. The German saw Gino, stopped, and raised his rifle. Gino squeezed the trigger. The German's face exploded in a splatter of blood, flesh and metal. Then more steps. Another German. Once again, Gino shot the man in the face.

The street was silent now except for rifle fire in the distance. Then heavier explosions. A slight shudder of the street. Artillery. Gino sagged against the wall and stared at the two dead Germans. He began to shiver. The rifle fire sounded louder. The battle was swinging toward him. A shell exploded down the street, staggering him.

A few steps away, a door swung slowly open. He ran inside. There was no one there. Gino wanted to close the door, but it had swung outward and he would have to step outside to pull it shut. For a long time, he huddled against the wall, hearing nothing, seeing nothing—except the splattered leavings of the faces he had destroyed.

A shell whined overhead and smashed into the building next door. The explosion blew him to the ground, covering him with debris, yet leaving him unhurt. He should find a safer place or the next shell might kill him. But he didn't want to run. He decided to close the door.

It was gone. Even the hinges.

Gino retreated into the shadows. No more shells fell. He tried the stairs and found the door with nothing behind it. It was not until he had come back downstairs that he realized the explosion had jarred his rifle from his hands. Crouching down, Gino edged toward the open doorway, reaching out a hand to pull at the stock. But within the blur at the corner of his eye he noted a shape and a color; a shape and color that should not have been there. His heart beat so quickly that he could barely breathe. He froze, unable to draw back or move forward, hoping he was not visible; trying to twist his eyes into the side of his skull so as to see this offending shape. It was small and of no particular form, mostly whitish blue or bluish white, with only a hint of red or pink.

It was unbearable; undoubtedly he was being observed. Tensing for the blow that must come, he wrenched his head about, at the same time grabbing his rifle and spinning onto his belly.

He found himself aiming his weapon at a little girl. She looked back with half-lidded eyes, apparently undisturbed by his aggressive posture, his bearded, filthy face, his shaking rifle. She carried a doll: a little blue and white girl doll, with its face turned up to her face. She did not hold it tightly or loosely; simply held it and stared at him while he and the doll stared at her.

Maria, he thought. *She looks like Maria*. Gino stood up, slinging the rifle over his shoulder. The little girl still watched him, motionless. Smiling, he stepped into the sunny street and crossed the pavement towards the child. He towered over her, but she did not seem afraid. When he looked down Gino saw the shadow of his helmet framed on her tiny bodice.

"You shouldn't be here," he said softly. "It isn't safe." As he reached down to touch her shoulder, the bullet hit him.

♦　♦　♦

He never lost consciousness. The bullet sliced through his back, scoring the strings that held up his legs, and they crumpled beneath him. In one shattering second, knifed by pain and cut off from the world of volition, he found himself spraddled in the street, staring up at the girl and her doll. Apparently she didn't know how he had come to settle on the ground before her. She stared at him—curiously—but hardly frightened by the spectacle.

"Go inside," he said, his lips trembling over the words. "They'll kill you."

After a moment, she turned her back and walked away. He heard her little sandals slapping the street. A door opened and closed. Then silence.

A blast in a street nearby brought him back to himself. His hands were still useful and he dragged himself out of the street and back through the doorway.

They found him there some hours later, cradling his helmet in his arms, unaware of the pool of blood in which he sat. As they carried him away on a litter, shivering with pain at every jolting step, he turned to look for the little girl. But he never saw her again.

♦　♦　♦

The hospital was overflowing with wounded men and they kept moving Gino from one place to another. He felt he was a trial to them and often apologized, feeling guilty that these men were repeatedly required to tote him from place to place, like some special treasure, while in reality he was only a crippled man and of no use to anyone.

He cried about that at times, but no one noticed. The hospital was filled with crying men. Contemptuous of those who cried aloud, Gino cried silently. But that made him feel guilty, too. He knew that the sound level of a man's tears couldn't be the measure of the man. Gino hoped they would move him to a hospital in Florence where he could be near his family. But no one suggested this, and it would have been unmanly to ask.

Eventually, the lines of battle having moved north, they moved him by jolting truck to the hospital at Forli. He remembered the town. He had gone there with his father when he was a boy of ten or eleven, but he couldn't recall why they had taken the trip.

Forli was far behind the front, but still a considerable distance from Florence and home. Perhaps that was fortunate. When the doctors operated on Gino, they told him there was very little chance he would ever walk again. The bullet came out easily enough and the doctors said that removing it relieved the pressure, but the nerves were punished severely and very likely would never recover.

When Gino wasn't bemoaning this cruel fate (yet it was better than dying), he thought about what he would do with his life. He could still be a leatherworker; Brother Domenico wouldn't turn him away. After all, what did a leatherworker need with legs? In his few letters home, he did not mention his wounds.

No one suggested that Gino attempt to exercise his legs. In the poorly staffed little hospital there was neither time nor the inclination for such things. Obviously the doctors considered Gino as incurable as the men without legs or arms. No one was helping them.

One day he pulled himself over to the side of his cot to ease his bedsores and his right leg slipped off the bed. Gino looked about for someone to help him put it back, but there were no orderlies in the ward. Sighing, he reached down to pick up his own leg. At that moment, it flexed at the knee. Gino did not recall having willed this motion. He tried to send another message to his leg, but evidently it was not received. Aflame with the thought that the leg could be taught to move again, he sat holding his knee, desperately urging it to bend. Once more it seemed to respond, but perhaps he had moved it with his hands.

"Move, damn you, move!" he screamed at the offending leg, while his wardmates stared at him. "I'm telling you to move, you filthy swine!"

The other soldiers laughed, but Gino's leg moved.

By the time the Germans surrendered, Gino was able to walk with a cane. It was clear that eventually he would regain most, if not all, of the use of his legs and he suspected that his illness had been largely hysterical. The doctors did not suggest this, although they were surprised by his recovery. Surprised, not astounded, for no one in Italy in those days had the inclination to be astounded.

For the first time, Gino was able to think of home without crying. He had told his comrades that he was from Florence. It was almost true. His home was on a small farm outside Fiesole, several kilometers from Florence. But in his heart, Gino was a Florentine. During his army service, he had seen Rome, Naples, and Palermo, and he had happily taken the opportunity to visit their awe-inspiring monuments and museums, stuffed with the great art of the centuries. Nevertheless Florence—his Florence—was the most beautiful city in the world.

He longed to see his mother; to watch her flat, calm features sharpen suddenly into a smile. To feel a fleeting touch from her hand, which was brown and checked, rough and warped on the outside, yet amazingly soft within.

And Maria. His sister's small, dark face framed with long dark hair floated before him. A child. But so kind, so cheerful, so affectionate. She was the one who had begun to call him "Gino," because, as a small child, she was unable to pronounce either his given name or any of the usual familiar versions. The rest of the family had followed her lead.

His father. Gino frowned. He knew he should love his father, but it was very difficult. Carlo Bondone was a large man, not as tall as Gino, but broad-shouldered and thick muscled. His face was strongly horizontal, from the line of his almost flat-topped bald, shaved head (to emulate Mussolini) to the three deep furrows in his forehead, to his square-cut jaw. His brows curled into a continuous gray-black rope, matched by a mustache of only slightly shorter length. His eyes were black and seldom smiled.

Carlo was a careless farmer. The family barely managed to subsist on the meager yield from their few, rocky acres, and he supplemented their income by acting as agent for the brothers at the Monastery of San Felice, marketing their leather products in Florence. He constantly berated his wife, his children, his fields, the monks and their monastery. Also, the sky, the sun, the universe. And God.

At times, Carlo Bondone would disappear for several days without warning. When he returned, he neither explained nor apologized.

Then, a few years before the war, a change came over Carlo. He no longer stalked his fields cursing the unproductive soil. He was too busy praising Mussolini and the "corporative state." Wearing his black shirt proudly, he attended Fascist party meetings religiously. In time, Carlo became some sort of an official. On occasion, he was even called to Florence to join the councils of the mighty.

Carlo told his family that a New World was coming. Italy, of course, would lead that world. And he, Carlo Bondone, would be one of Italy's great leaders. Mama, Gino and Maria listened in perplexed silence, unable to conceive of Carlo as a great leader.

There was one outward sign of Carlo's new importance: the villagers in Fiesole were not as friendly as before. Gino was not certain whether he read respect or contempt in their eyes; it made him uncomfortable. At times, his father returned home wild-eyed and disheveled. There had been violence in the streets. The Black Shirts, Carlo told them, had been forced to battle reactionary elements. His men had triumphed, of course.

Carlo was home even less frequently than before. The fields were neglected and the monks threatened to find another agent. Gino, already apprenticed to the leather factory, feared he would be discharged.

Instead, his father told Gino he must join the army. It was his duty as a son of Italy. Maria and his mother pleaded that he should wait to be conscripted, but Carlo refused to listen to the whining of women. Italy was at war. Gino must fight.

He fought only once, in the streets of Bari. Two shots. Two dead Germans. His father would not be pleased; he had often told Gino of the greatness of the new Germany—Italy's only true friend. Gino doubted his father had changed sides when Italy signed the armistice.

Gino had felt ridiculous, firing his weapon at strangers, killing them, even though if he hadn't they would have killed him. How could he explain his wound to his father? Shot in the back. Carlo would despise him.

Gradually, most of the other patients at Forli were dispatched to other hospitals or discharged. The war was over, the Germans were evacuated, and there was nothing to prevent Gino from going home. He was offered a ride on a Red Cross lorry, but refused it. Something told him to walk home.

It was one hundred and one kilometers from Forli to Fiesole. Although it looked almost straight on the map, the road actually wound through mountainous country. Narrow and ill-paved, it had not been repaired since long before the war.

There were a few tiny towns between Forli and Fiesole, mere outcroppings of the rock, centuries old, far removed from the routes of commerce. That was perfect. He wanted to stay clear of cities; of stinking soldiers and hospitals. Of men. All he took with him was his cane, a packet of dried meat and a round of bread.

For most of the way the road followed a river, the Montone. It was not large, but it had been there a long time. The gorge that carried it was far below the road, crossing under it again and again, so that now the river was on the left, now the right. But always it was somewhere nearby, rushing toward Florence.

The morning he left, a fine June morning, Gino bathed in the Montone. Despite the season, the water was bitter cold. Gino had no soap and no towel. He shivered himself dry, literally shaking his flanks and his shoulders like a dog. He rinsed his clothes as well. It was the first time he had felt clean since the day he had joined the army. His thick, curly chestnut brown hair was clamped wetly around his head, and Gino pressed his fingers—surprisingly slender fingers for so large and strong a man—against his hair to squeeze out the water. Some ran down into his thick brows and long lashes, some into his large, brown eyes. He blinked rapidly and happily, opening his generous mouth to draw the cool draught deep into his throat.

Clambering back up to the road, using his cane as a pikestaff, he grew dirty again. But he didn't smell from chloroform and a dozen other drugs.

By the second day, he had ground his way through his flimsy right shoe. At dawn of the third day he gave up both shoes. But his feet didn't bleed. Not even twenty-one months in a hospital had softened the calluses on his feet.

At noon on the third day, on sudden impulse, he threw away his cane, watching it sail over the bank and splash into the Montone. It sank for a moment, then bobbed to the surface, and was carried by the rushing torrent, bouncing off the rocks, toward Florence.

And then he remembered: when he was ten years old his father had taken him along this very same road to Forli, traveling in a cart behind a donkey, carrying a stock of leather goods from San Felice. The monks had told them there was no market for their goods in Forli, but Carlo went anyway.

Gino begged to be taken along. At first his father refused, but he was in good spirits over the prospects in Forli and eventually agreed. The trip was slow, yet Gino had seldom seen his father so cheerful. That changed in Forli. The monks were right; there was no market. Gino was too frightened by his father's angry demeanor to do anything but huddle in the cart with the unsold merchandise.

The trip back was difficult because it was uphill. The little donkey plodded on, oblivious to Carlo's threats, even to blows with a crop he had cut from a sapling. Then the donkey stopped altogether. Carlo leaped down from the cart, yanking the poor creature's harness and screaming, beating it about the head and flanks with the stick. Finally, in frustration, he flung the stick over the side of the road into the river. Gino watched it bob for a moment, then shoot off in the swift current.

"Look, father," he said. "The stick will get home before we do."

Carlo laughed, reached up into the cart, carried him down, and tousled his hair. "We'll rest a while," he said. "The donkey will move when he feels like it. Then we'll go home." He had put his arm over Gino's shoulder.

It must have been very near here, Gino thought, hurrying along the road. In a moment, he found what he was looking for—a tiny mountain freshet that tumbled down through waving grass, disappeared beneath the road, then spilled out on the other side and dipped into the valley, joining the Montone. He and his father had trailed their hands in the cold water and splashed it on their faces, laughing and talking.

Remembering, he dipped his face and drank straight from the stream as David had done, and felt like David himself. *My father loves me*, Gino thought. *He doesn't show it, but he loves me.*

Gino walked more rapidly, his stride still uneven, but with little pain. Since the day he joined the army, time had seemed to hurry ahead of him, dragging with it the things he wanted, the dreams he cherished. Then, after he was wounded, time ceased to matter. During the first few days of the trip home, Gino felt himself slowly catching up. Now, he had caught sight of time, grabbed its coattail and careened along with it. Finally, in the flush of happy remembrance, he leaped beyond it.

He became impatient and tried to catch a ride on every passing vehicle—of which there were very few. The typically suspicious hill people only glared at him, especially distrustful of his uniform.

He might be a *Fascista*, perhaps even a partisan. Probably a thief who had stripped a dead soldier.

At dusk on the sixth day, Gino realized he was only a few kilometers from Fiesole. He would have to leave the sometimes paved highway and follow dirt roads and cow paths the rest of the way. Wisdom told him to sleep now and wake early, greeting his family on a bright new day. But he yearned to be home, to sleep in his own bed, to feel his mother's soft, hard hands caress his cheek.

The sun slipped away from him in minutes, dropping through the tall pines like a fugitive balloon, leaving only the palest hint of its passing. He quickened his steps, punishing himself until his leg ached again, and he began to limp. Fine way for his mother to see him. Reluctantly, he slowed his pace, deliberately placing his feet in front of each other. It became a painful ritual, and Gino began to wish he had not decided to continue the day's journey.

The view from the top of the next hill resolved his doubts. The lights of Fiesole, few but enough to identify the town, lured him on. He knew the view was deceiving; Fiesole was still two or three kilometers away. But the sight of her was enough to send him hurrying down the road. Thank God, from here on home it was downhill.

Two

The Orphan and the Fascist

Pietro pressed even harder until the stone dug into his chest and face and the stucco seemed to crumble under his curling fingers. Despite the warm night, he was shivering. The cold sweat ran down his forehead and mingled with the dust, making him blink. He struggled to keep his eyes open—as if even a blink could be heard.

Stupid, he thought, *stupid to be here and take such chances. The old monk said it was true. Why should he lie?*

But now the *caribinieri* were passing him only footsteps away, and he was even afraid to think. The air stirred as they passed. Pietro could not breathe until he was certain they were gone. A sound; a shutter dropping against a sill? Perhaps. Every sound was frightening. A cat slithering along the pavement. A cough. A piece of paper flapping in the wind. Any one of these might prove to be a soldier or a policeman.

And the moon was bright—bright enough that he could see what he wanted to see—but so bright that he could be seen as well.

Now, he thought. *Now's the time to get out of Florence*. With great effort he disconnected himself from the wall and edged back the way he had come. Then he hesitated, fighting himself.

This is madness, he told himself. *But I have to know*. He forced himself to turn back, deeper into the city, moving even more cautiously than before. Soldiers and *caribinieri* were everywhere. And they were nervous, too. He was violating the curfew. They might shoot him on sight.

A sound. Fear sent him scrambling over a low wall and into the courtyard beyond. He had not lost the agility that had favored him since childhood. Pietro hurried through a confined passage and onto a narrow street in which he had played as a boy. Somewhere near here had been his home. The word brought a grim smile to his lips. Home. No father—at least no father he had ever known. A mother, dark as he was, but round and smooth. Then she was gone and Pietro was alone. It seemed he had always been alone.

He darted from one arcade to another, hugging the shadows. Soon he approached the ancient convent of the Sisters of Charity, where he had been taken after his mother died. The sisters were kind, but they couldn't protect him from the other children. Pietro had been beaten in that courtyard times without number. Eventually he learned to protect himself. With quickness, because he was not strong. With his wits because he was small.

There was a clatter of cans behind him. Probably a cat, but he could not be certain. Quickly crossing the street, he headed toward the river. Again there were footsteps, which forced him to turn into a side street that angled in the opposite direction from the one he intended.

Pietro had done well in the orphanage school, not because he loved his studies, but because he couldn't bear to be like the others. They were hopeless, despairing, stupid.

More footsteps. Whispered voices. Others besides the *caribinieri* must be abroad tonight. The voices and sounds drove him farther from the bridge. He was angry again. The hours were slipping past.

He knew he should abandon the quest, but couldn't. As his fear grew, his anticipation matched it. Pietro was exhilarated—exhilarated and frightened. If only he could avoid the uniforms.

The Bibliotheca Nazionale rose before him. Two guards lounged on the steps. Then, behind him, voices. He froze in the shadows.

◆ ◆ ◆

The Bibliotheca. How many years had he labored there? The sisters found him the position when he was too old to remain in their school. He spent his days cataloging and filing ancient papers and his nights in a room he had taken on the top floor of a dismal tenement, small and squalid, but his alone.

An old clerk, ancient, bearded, quivering, befriended him. Pietro had never had a friend before. The old man could speak and read several languages and it was his duty to translate state papers. He invited Pietro to assist him, offering to teach him one of the languages he knew. Pietro chose French. Why? There was something intriguing about France—something decadent and alluring. And France shared a border with Italy.

Pietro learned quickly. In a few months he could read French nearly as well as the clerk. His interest in France had grown along with his knowledge of the language. He read books on French history and culture and poured over maps of Paris—old and new, until he had memorized dozens of streets and monument.

He had been studying a map of Paris when Carlo Bondone found him. When Pietro looked up, he was startled by the fierce, hirsute face glaring at him.

A trace of a smile. "I'm Carlo Bondone." A single gold peak glittered in the crumbled mountain range of his teeth. "I hear good things about you, Scegli."

Pietro studied him warily.

"There's no mystery, young man. I'm an official of the party. Highly placed, I might add." A flicker of self-satisfaction smoothed Bondone's grim lips. "I think you could be useful to us. And do much for yourself besides." He glanced around him. "It would be best if we talked elsewhere." Bondone studied the long rows of library shelving with evident mistrust.

Pietro almost laughed.

Bondone led him down the steps and into the streets of Florence. He walked with a swagger, but when he greeted well-dressed people he did so deferentially.

"You see, Scegli, that man is a city councilor. They all know Carlo Bondone."

In a sheltered spot along the Arno, he took Pietro's arm and spoke in conspiratorial tones. "We live in a great era, my boy—a great era for those who foresee the glorious future of our beloved Italy." He paused for breath. "The future of Italy is the Fascist party. I'm sure you understand that."

Pietro nodded, although he didn't understand at all.

"Good. Some of our young people don't see the opportunities. They criticize the State. They criticize Mussolini. Can you imagine that?"

Pietro shook his head.

"Of course not. Since you see the future, you must take hold of it. Fortunately, I'm able to help. You'll thank me for this a million times in the years to come. It's not easy to join the party, one needs references. But my word will be enough. In fact," he paused, "you'll be my personal aide."

It was an order. Still, Pietro was intrigued that anyone as simple-minded as Carlo Bondone had reached a position of power—that is, if he accepted the man's assessment of his own importance. "I'm honored, Signore Bondone."

"Good," Carlo smiled. "We'll start at once."

At first he was an errand boy, carrying messages, making long lists of names of "enemies," attending boring meetings. He was angry. This was no better than the Bibliotheca.

Occasionally there would be a report of the "Disciplinary Committee." The leader would tell them how Black Shirts had taken an "enemy of the state" from his home or his shop and beaten him. The members of the committee were heroes.

"I want to be on the Disciplinary Committee," Pietro told Carlo.

Bondone was surprised, but he arranged it.

They met at night outside Fiesole, about twenty of them. Pietro asked Carlo why it would require so many Black Shirts to pummel a single, unsuspecting individual.

"You think we're not brave?" Bondone whispered.

"I'm told the last time you got in each other's way."

Bondone laughed. "We don't wish to kill anyone—just correct their thinking.

"With a knock on the head?"

Bondone grew angry. "My son is a brave soldier, fighting for the glory of Italy. Each day his life is in danger. Can we permit these criminals to sabotage us at home?"

Pietro shrugged. Carlo stalked away, then gestured to Pietro to follow him.

They stopped before a wine shop and pounded on the door. After a time, it opened and a short, skinny, old man appeared in his nightshirt.

"What do you want?" he asked, in a quavering voice. "My shop isn't open."

They pulled him into the street. "You're accused of cursing the regime."

"I don't know what you mean. I can't sell you any wine now. Please come back in the morning." He turned to reenter his house. None of the Black Shirts moved.

Pietro broke from the group, grabbed the old man by the arm and backed him against the wall.

"Please, sir, I cannot sell you—"

Pietro hit him in the mouth with his fist. The man sagged, immediately senseless, but Pietro pulled him upright and hit him again and again. When he let go, the old man fell face forward into the street. Carlo and his fellows stared at Pietro.

Lights were coming on in houses all along the street. Carlo and the others ran. Pietro slowly wiped his bloody hands on his shirt and sauntered away.

Thereafter, Pietro was treated with more respect. In time, they made him the head of the Disciplinary Committee. Often, he performed the beatings alone. The senior men said he had a great future.

In response to Pietro's discreet inquiry, one of the Black Shirts told him that Bondone owned a small farm outside Fiesole. Pietro wondered why he was never invited there. Otherwise, Carlo treated him well, often intimating that Pietro would play an important role in his plans as soon as Italy—glorious Italy and her glorious Allies—won this glorious war.

The change in Italy's fortunes ended all that. As the American troops inched up the peninsula, as *il Duce's* government fell, conditions in Florence altered. The people were impatient with, then angry at, the Fascists. Partisan bands formed in the countryside. Two city officials, prominent party men, were dragged from their beds and murdered.

Carlo decamped, taking Pietro with him. During the day, they hid in the hills. Some nights Carlo reluctantly brought him to his farm for food and clean clothing. He introduced Pietro to his wife and daughter with evident wariness, telling them he was "protecting" the young man.

The daughter, Maria, attracted Pietro mightily. Her face was finely modeled, a straight, thin nose above full rosebud lips, dark oval eyes and luxuriant, tumbling dark brown hair. And her body was voluptuously formed—high full breasts, tiny waist and ample hips—perhaps, aesthetically too ample, but Pietro wasn't interested in painting her.

When he tried to engage her in conversation, Carlo dragged him outside. "Stay away from her!"

"I didn't mean to offend you."

Carlo's irritation served only to enhance Pietro's interest, and it was obvious that Maria was interested in him, too. He didn't think the simple, innocent farm girl would prove to be difficult.

One night, a messenger brought word of a secret meeting. The Fascists were trying to organize for their own protection against the partisans. Pietro listened disdainfully as the Black Shirts argued fruitlessly for hours.

"I'll form a squad," he said. "We'll seek out the partisans and attack them. If we keep them busy they'll stay away from your homes."

"There are thousands of them," Carlo said. "We'll all be killed. It's better to hide for a while. When the Americans arrive the partisans will disband and we can go home."

The older men agreed with Carlo. The younger ones sided with Pietro. Nothing was resolved.

"I'm not taking you to the next meeting," Carlo told Pietro. "You're a hothead. You'll end up getting us all killed."

"I'll wait at your farm."

"No, in the woods."

Night after night Carlo went off to meet and argue interminably with the Black Shirts. Each night, Pietro went straight to the farmhouse, telling the women Carlo had ordered him to protect them.

Maria's mother retired to the only bedroom early. Pietro remained with the girl, talking. When it grew late, Maria excused herself, pulling a ragged cloth across the corner where her bed stood. Light from a candle outlined her body against the cloth as she pulled her dress over her head. Pietro watched, lips pulled back from his teeth in a ferocious smile. When the light went out, he left.

One night, after the old woman was asleep, he invited Maria to walk with him in the woods.

"Isn't it dangerous?"

"I'll protect you." He patted the heavy revolver strapped to his waist.

They slipped from the house and strolled in the dark.

"I'll take your hand," Pietro whispered, "so you don't trip and fall." He led her to a tree and they sat on the grass beside it. The woman smell of her, sweet and clean, aroused him.

"I'm lonely, Maria. Very lonely. It's good of you to come with me. I know so little of women."

She smiled in the darkness. " I know little of men."

He sighed. "I'm afraid the partisans will find me and kill me."

"Don't say that." She moved closer.

"I need someone to care for me."

She sighed. He moved closer. His hand touched her cheek. "You're so lovely, Maria."

She drew away, but only a fraction. "You mustn't talk that way."

"I understand. Who wants a poor clerk? A hunted man."

"I didn't mean it that way."

"I realize your father is an important man and I'm nobody."

"You misunderstand me."

He didn't speak again as he led her to the house. At the door, he took her face in his hands and kissed her lightly on the lips. Before she could respond, he ran off into the woods.

The next night he led her to the grassy spot beside the tree again. She did not resist when he put his arm about her waist. Her dress was so thin, he could feel her warm flesh through it. She leaned against him. He kissed her hair, then her cheek. She told him to stop, but didn't move away. He kissed her neck, then her lips. When she pressed against him, he could feel all of her through the dress. Soft and firm. Warm and cool. She was breathing deeply, the surge of her breasts sending waves of passion through him. Lightly, his fingers outlined her body. She was trembling, now, twisting her body in his embrace.

"No," she said, "you mustn't." But he was lifting the dress up over her thighs, across her belly, then revealing her breasts, and in a moment, over her head. He was on her now, kissing her face, her breasts, her thighs. She struggled softly, caught between desire and fear.

He hesitated for a moment, enjoying the sight of her smooth, lusciously curved body, luminous in the moonlight. Her stomach contracted. She lay tense and silent, waiting.

Then he took her.

♦ ♦ ♦

For the next several days, Carlo Bondone spent every night debating fruitlessly with his frightened comrades. The only one who profited was Pietro. Deflowering Maria did not disturb him in the slightest. It bothered her only temporarily, because she was in love with Pietro Scegli.

One night as he lay beside her, spent, but still locked in her arms, a harsh bellow tore the air. Before Pietro could move, Carlo was on him, one knee crushing his groin, huge hands at his head, ripping his lips, a thumb searing one eyeball. Pietro never had a chance to defend himself.

"*Bastardo!*" Carlo cried, "*bastardo*," again and again, never ceasing to rain blows upon him. All this against Maria's piercing cries.

Through swollen eyes Pietro saw Carlo raise his revolver by the barrel. The handle crashed against his skull. As he lay on the ground, writhing in pain, blood streaking his face, Carlo leaned close. Pietro could see the gold tooth, inches from his eyes.

"I should kill you, *bastardo*." There was a moment's pause, and Pietro tensed for the bullet that would tear his body. "But you're not worth killing." Bondone's fist slammed his jaw again.

"Stay away, *bastardo*. Stay away or I'll kill you." He gave Pietro one final kick and dragged the weeping Maria away.

Pietro had lain there all night, unable to move. When daylight came, he climbed to his feet and staggered through the forest until he found a stream in which to wash his wounds. Then he rested all day in the shadows.

The next day the pain began to recede. Amazingly, no bones were broken, although his head, his arms, his legs still ached fearfully. During the night he rooted vegetables out of an abandoned field.

On the third day, Pietro took up a position in the woods

overlooking Carlo's farm. Two nights later his watch was rewarded. Carlo left his home and disappeared down the road, Pictro following at a distance. Bondone stopped at the monastery of San Felice, surprising Pietro. What could the old heathen want there? In minutes, Carlo reappeared and continued for several kilometers, eventually reaching a half-burned farmhouse, which he entered. When he had not reappeared two hours later, Pietro assumed he was staying there overnight.

Pietro withdrew into the woods, thinking hard. He knew what to do, but how should he do it? And then his questions were answered. Near him, perhaps a hundred meters away, was a small campfire, and seated around it a group of men, all armed. Partisans. He put his revolver on the ground and covered it with leaves, then walked straight into the midst of them. Startled, they scrambled to their feet, cursing, and turned their rifles on him.

He raised his hands and smiled. "I'm unarmed," he said.

One man covered him while the others scoured the woods. They found no one.

"You've nothing to fear from me," Pietro said. "I have information you want."

No one spoke.

"Have you heard of Carlo Bondone?"

It seemed quite a long time before the leader nodded.

"I can help you find him."

"Why are you telling us?" the leader asked.

Pietro tightened his face and said, haltingly, "Bondone dishonored my mother. I want him punished."

"Do it yourself."

"I have no weapon, and Bondone is armed."

"Where is he?"

"I'll show you, but then you must let me go. Punish Bondone in your own way for his crimes against you. That will satisfy me."

The partisans looked to their leader, who nodded approval.

He led them to the farmhouse. "He's yours," Pietro said, and turned to leave.

The leader gripped his arm. "You stay."

"But we agreed—"

"—Never mind. Come with us."

Together, one partisan covering Pietro, they crept across the clearing, then smashed open the door and rushed inside.

Carlo had been sleeping. When he saw the rifles, he slumped back to the floor. He was alone. Then he saw Pietro. "You!" he cried. "*Bastardo!*"

Pietro kicked him in the face. The partisan leader pushed him aside. Bondone was unconscious.

"All right," the leader said to Pietro. "Go!"

Pietro ran from the house, scrambled across the clearing and rushed headlong into the forest.

♦ ♦ ♦

The guards had moved on. Pietro had been so lost in thought that he had failed to notice their departure. He cursed himself and set out again. Finally he reached the river, then followed the Lungarno towards the Ponte Vecchio, the only bridge still standing in Florence. The street was deserted, probably because of the curfew. He was safe as long as he stayed in the shadows. But there was a lorry parked at the entrance to the bridge, with armed guards flanking it.

How could he have been so stupid? He should have known the bridge would be guarded. Only his fierce determination to cross the river and verify the monk's story had brought him here. *Damn Carlo Bondone. Damn them all.*

Stubbornly, he retraced his steps until he came to a side street, and then ran along it, parallel to the river and some distance beyond the bridge. The sight of the police in the Piazza Santa Croce brought him to a halt. Pietro was beside himself. These crazy Italians guarded old books and churches. He turned into another street and again made his way to the Lungarno, knowing he would have to swim to cross the slow-moving, but very cold river. He darted across the road to the cement abutment. Along this part of the river, there were sandbars. The river was narrower and he would be in less danger of drowning.

He climbed up on the cement balustrade and looked down. Below him, beached on the sand, was a skiff. He was certain now; it was meant to be. Pietro dropped heavily to the sand, the impact sending shivers of pain up his legs. In the skiff was an oar. If he didn't steal the boat, someone else surely would.

As Pietro picked up the oar he heard voices, and he pressed himself back against the embankment. Two men were walking along the street. When they were directly above him, their footsteps stopped.

"Easy, Giovanni," said one, "we'll be home in a minute."

"I'm sick." Then harsh coughing—a horrible belching sound—and Pietro's head and shoulders were drenched in vomit. Pietro dared not move until he was sure they were gone. Then he pulled off his shirt, dipped it in the river to rinse it, and tried to use it to clean his matted hair. *Aagh*. It was terrible. Then he pulled the shirt back on, shivering from the cold wetness.

Fog was rolling over the opposite—the south—bank. Soft, lazy billows that uncurled over the water. Now he would be able to cross the Arno without being seen. He left the shadows, pushed the skiff into the water and climbed in. Carefully angling the single oar, he pulled slowly for the other side.

The skiff bumped the shore. Pietro scrambled over the bow and pulled it onto the sand, hoping it would still be there when he returned. He found a place where he could climb to the Lungarno, near the Piazza Poggi. Somewhere, almost directly above him, was the Piazzale Michelangiolo. But he would have to follow the twisting Viale dei Colli to reach it. Fortunately, the fog would cover him.

The Viale climbed sharply between tall pines. After the first sweeping turn, it leveled out, turned back south again, continued for a while in that direction, then swung east to the Piazzale. He decided to leave the road and climb the steep hill to San Miniato al

Monte. From below the church he should have a good view. Pietro had to pull himself upward by holding onto undergrowth and trees. Branches whipped his face and he stumbled over a fallen log, before reaching a place below the church and above the Piazzale. Perfect.

Not quite. The fog that had protected him also obscured the great bronze statue of David. It was disappointing, but he would wait until it cleared.

Which happened quickly. There was a slight breeze, the mists parted and moonlight poured into the Piazzale. The monument was suddenly revealed, as if the stern eyes of David had ordered the fog to recede. And so it did, forming a halo about the huge green-bronze statue.

David peered steadfastly into the distance. From his sling, where it stretched from his hand to his shoulder, hung a bundle of rags and rope, mottled, shapeless, motionless. In the folds of the bundle slung from the statue, Pietro could trace his own existence—formless, misshapen—a stain, just as the suspended bundle was a stain on the great bronze casting of Michelangelo's sculpture.

Pietro's eyes studied the David. The figure was heroic; smooth, muscular, powerful. Even in the weathered bronze, David seemed light-skinned, his hair blond, tumbling in soft curls about his stern, classic face. A boy. A beautiful boy.

There was no doubt now; the bundle of rags hanging from the statue was Carlo Bondone. His feet hung from the sling of the David, his head touched the base. There were dark stains—blood—on his torn clothing, blood on the base. It was a hideous vision, but Pietro smiled. The filthy beast.

Three

A Hero's Return

To Gino, the night appeared exceptionally clear, even for the Tuscan hills. There was fog in the valley, but he was far above it. Somehow, his bare feet seemed to make an unusual racket when they met the ground. He walked off the hard-baked dirt road into the deep grass.

The smells were all wrong. His peasant nose sniffed for vegetables, but only grass and grain came floating up to him. The people had suffered here. Gino felt sorry for his parents.

It was a new feeling; he had never thought it necessary to worry about them before. What a brute he was. A hulking giant, well over six feet tall and even in his haggard state he must outweigh his father by many kilos. His father; yes, Gino was even able to think of meeting his father without fear.

He came to the rutted track that led to his home. Past the monastery. No lights. The monks were very frugal, but again he sensed something wrong. Should he waken the prior? Surely old Domenico would be happy to see him. But no, just a few hundred meters and he would be home. Let the brothers wait until tomorrow.

The wind came up suddenly, sweeping dust from the ruts into

his eyes and hair. He cursed out loud; thought of the monks and crossed himself. Then smiled at his own simplicity.

He was suddenly aware he would reach home a filthy vagabond. The snarling wind made it difficult to wipe the dirt from his face. He felt like a fool, sweeping at his face with his hands, like a madman driving off demons. Then, through his fluttering fingers, he saw the shadowy farmhouse and a thin strand of light that slipped between the curtains. Breathing deeply, he could smell leeks and potatoes and beans. His family must be all right after all.

A sound touched his ear, disappeared and then returned. Like an animal slithering through the grass. Or a man. Peering through the darkness, he saw a dark figure, either very short or bending low, running along the path. Had he passed this creature on the road? There was no time to guess. Gino broke into a leaping run.

It couldn't be his father; he would have gone to sleep long ago. Nor his mother. It was probably she who had lit the lamp, perhaps to sew or prepare bread for the morning. It couldn't be his sister. Mama wouldn't allow her out alone after dark. A partisan? A thief?

Despite his limp, Gino gained steadily on the running figure, then left his feet and hurled himself against the black shape. The impact stunned him. The creature seemed stunned as well. Gino gathered his senses and returned to the attack. A voice began to cry for help, but Gino's hands closed on its throat, shutting off the sound.

Gino could get no firm hold. It was as if he were trying to grip a mad dog inside a damp canvas bag. Everywhere he reached, the creature pulled away and he was left holding empty clothes.

"For God's sake let me up!" the man cried, but Gino would not let go. They wrestled in the dust. Gino, huge and muscular, the other lean and wiry, neither gaining any advantage. Gino felt himself weakening. Why couldn't he subdue this skinny, slippery creature? Then, once again, he held its throat. The man's nails scratched at his face, tore at his fingers, but Gino held on. In a moment, the black bag would grow limp.

Light spilled from the doorway. Gino looked up, loosening his grip and allowing his victim to pull away. He would have gone after him, but his sister came running out in her shift, crying a name. And the name was not his.

"Pietro!" she cried. "What is he doing to you?" She dropped to the ground to soothe the wounded black shape. Gino watched in amazement. What Pietro could this be?

At that moment his sister twisted around, ready to defend this Pietro. She half rose, saw that it was Gino and fell back to a sitting position on the ground.

"Aieeeee!" her wail mounted in the sky. "Gino? Is it you?"

Before he could respond, his mother hurried from the farmhouse and fell upon him, screaming his name, crying, moaning, and squeezing his face in her hands. Soon Gino, too, was crying.

Now both women were upon him; the black Pietro forgotten. He hugged them both and kissed them (his sister smelled unaccountably womanly), mumbling a hundred repeated greetings, assuring them over and again that it was truly he, that he was safe and well, and thank God they were reunited. Finally, they sat locked together on the ground, rocking back and forth in each other's arms, weeping and murmuring, blissfully happy.

He remembered the intruder. Pietro still sat on the ground watching them, breathing heavily. Gino scowled and raised an arm. "Who is he?"

For a moment no one spoke. Pietro looked from face to face with dark malevolence. Then Maria scrambled to her feet and, suddenly aware of her nightdress, crossed her arms in front in a gesture of modesty which was defeated by the light from the open doorway behind her. She was much rounder than Gino remembered.

"This is Pietro."

"I know it's Pietro!" Gino fairly screamed. "I heard you call him that when you ran out to protect him. But WHO IS HE?" The violence of his response almost sent Maria to the ground again. She stepped back and stared at her brother.

His mother touched Gino's arm. "He's our friend, Gino. He has protected us since the Germans left Florence."

"Why do you need protection? Where is my father?"

"I think," said Pietro, his voice thin and choked, "we should talk inside."

Maria ran into the house to get dressed. His mother took Gino's hand and led him slowly through the door. Pietro followed them, walking heavily, and bolted the door.

Home. The ancient two-room farmhouse, with plaster peeling from the wooden laths. Soft gaslight on the yellow walls. The wood floor—his father's pride—the only one in the district. Simple furniture worn smooth by generations of use.

The four of them seemed to fill the small room. Gino's head was almost lost in the shadows above the lamp glow. Pietro, his clothes wet and caked with mud, was studying him with a cold stare.

"I'm dirty, Mama," Gino said. "I must wash."

"First a glass of wine to celebrate your return."

Pietro cleared his throat gruffly. "This is not a night to celebrate." He paused. "Carlo Bondone is dead."

There was silence, the silence of disbelief.

"It's true, I tell you, he's dead."

"It's not true," wailed Maria. "Not true!"

His mother still had not spoken.

A terrible thought seized Gino. He moved toward Pietro. "You killed him!"

Pietro cringed backward. "No, not I. The partisans."

"How? Why? Are you sure? Who told you this?" Gino grabbed his shoulders and began shaking him.

Pietro twisted out of his grasp and scrambled to the far side of the table.

"Please, Gino," his mother said, "leave him alone."

As Gino hesitated, she spoke again. "Is it true, Pietro? Are you certain?" She was holding Maria against her, to keep the girl from collapsing.

"Yes, it's true. When Brother Domenico told me I didn't believe him, either."

"What has Brother Domenico to do with it?" asked Gino.

"He came here late at night, saying he had to warn us about partisans in the area. He took me outside, alone and told me he didn't want the women to hear the truth: Partisans had captured your father in the woods, dragged him to the priory, told Domenico that Carlo was an agent of the accursed church, and they were going to kill him. The monk pleaded with them, but they wouldn't listen."

"Then you're not certain." Gino's voice was almost a falsetto. "You don't know he's dead."

"I've seen his body."

The women were sobbing now. Gino led his mother to the bed in the corner of the room and Maria sank down beside her.

"Where?" he asked.

"The Piazzale Michelangiolo. They bound him in a wagon filled with hay and took him through Florence in bright daylight. Right under the noses of the police, who didn't even try to stop them. He was still alive when they reached the Piazzale. They tortured him there." The women began moaning again. "They hung him feet first from the statue of David. When they were tired of his groans, they shot him."

The horror of it seized Gino. "You talk as if you were there."

"Not I; the prior. He asked me to try and stop the partisans, but I told him it was impossible. I was a Fascist, too, your father's aide. If I had tried to do anything, they would have killed me. The prior went there alone. It was too late. Bondone was dead. Domenico wanted to cut down the body, but they drove him away. He came back and told me."

"You went there? Why didn't you take him down?"

"You're crazy. I had to hide. If I tried to remove his body . . ." He shrugged his shoulders.

Gino eased himself from the women's arms and stood up. "We must take down my father."

Pietro turned away. "You're crazy."

"Stop saying I'm crazy!" Gino crossed the floor in a few quick strides and grabbed his arm. "I'm going to bury my father and you're going to help me."

Pietro hesitated only a second. "Very well," he said.

When they were outside, Gino said, "Don't try to run away. I have my service revolver. I wouldn't hesitate to use it."

They were not stopped until they reached the Ponte Vecchio, where an officer waved them to a halt. "You're violating the curfew," he said.

"I'm going to bury my father." He handed the officer his papers. "I'm Gianpaolo Bondone, a soldier recently discharged. The partisans killed my father, Carlo Bondone, and left his body in the Piazzale Michelangiolo. I'm going to bury him."

The officer glanced at the papers. "Who is this man?"

"He'll help me bury my father."

The officer wiped his face with his hand. It was cool, but there was perspiration on his forehead. "Very well," he said, "Two soldiers will accompany you. Otherwise there may be trouble."

Gino, Pietro and the soldiers crossed the bridge, followed the Lungarno and turned up the Viale. The night was now clear, and it was very bright in the Piazzale. The domes and pinnacles of Florence gleamed in the distance. The statue seemed huge and ominous.

The sight of his father's body staggered Gino. He reached out to support himself on the cold bronze leg of the David. Involuntarily, he leaned close to his father's face. But there was no face. It had been blown away. A sharp vision came to Gino of the German soldiers he had shot in Bari, their faces exploding into fragments.

He steeled himself, climbed the statue, loosened the rope and slowly lowered his father's body. Then he carried the sack of battered flesh and bones toward the steps that led to the graveyard at the foot of San Miniato.

They buried him without a coffin and without prayers. It was consecrated ground, but there was no one present to object. Gino smoothed the earth flat, without marking it. Yet he knew precisely where his father lay. He would be able to find the grave again.

Four

Three Monks, a Maestro, and a Mystery

The crops were beginning to rot in the field and needed attention. Instead of giving it, Gino slept most of each day, a bitter, restless sleep, filled with throbbing dreams. He saw a German soldier advancing on him, carrying a rifle. When Gino pulled the trigger on his own weapon the face dissolved. The body fell and turned until the feet were higher than the head. It became his father suspended from the statue, dripping blood.

He woke up, hot and damp, aching in every bone, in a room filled with sunlight. He had pulled his old pallet out from under Maria's bed where it was usually stored and shoved it into the far corner of the room. His mother and sister were sitting on a small wooden bench, whispering together. Their words hummed in his ears and in a few moments he was asleep again.

Once more he was in Bari, hurrying down the street. He heard footsteps, not the heavy boots of a soldier, but a whispered slapping on the cobblestones. It was the little girl with her doll, turning the corner as the soldier had done. Once more he raised his rifle.

He didn't want to pull the trigger, but the gun went off and the little girl disappeared. Except for her doll, which stared up at him from the street. He awoke, trembling.

A few nights later he awakened suddenly, frightened and unaccountably angry. After yanking open the curtain that shrouded Maria's bed, he pushed open the door to his mother's room.

The squeaking sound woke her immediately. "What is it, my son?"

"They've run away, mother."

"They haven't run away. They're out in the fields somewhere."

"I'll put an end to that!"

"They're young. It is the way of the young."

He stared at her in disbelief. "You're Maria's mother! How can you permit it?"

"This has been going on for a long time. Your father tried to stop them, without success. If you interfere, she will surely run away with Pietro and I'll be alone."

"But Mama, I'm here."

"Yes, Gino. Please stay here. Sit down beside me and we'll talk."

While his mother murmured to him, he imagined Pietro pressing his sister down upon the earth, kissing her cruelly on the mouth, coarse hands exploring her body. It was agony to do nothing. After a while his mother kissed him and went back to her room. He lay down on the pallet and waited. An hour later, Pietro and Maria eased the door open slowly and slipped inside. Gino turned over on his side and tried to sleep.

♦ ♦ ♦

For several days, Gino barely stirred, sleeping twelve and fourteen hours at a time. When he awoke, his mother did her best to feed him. There was no meat and little wine, no eggs or butter. Mostly potatoes and a few green vegetables.

Maria fussed over him, which he found disconcerting. He had left her a girl and she had become a woman. They had slept in the same room all their lives, Maria on the bed, Gino on the pallet, his large feet extending onto the floor. Although he had turned his head when she dressed, she had seemed . . . well, like a brother. He was relieved that they had put up the curtain while he was away.

It must have been in Sicily that Gino had last lain with a woman. His sister's affectionate caresses only made matters worse. He tried to push her away, but she thought him playful and returned to pull his long hair or pinch his cheeks, not realizing how she affected him.

Eventually, Gino grew tired of lying about the house and decided to go to Brother Domenico and ask for his old position as a leatherworker. It was but a few minutes' walk up the gentle hill and through the pine forest to the Monastery of San Felice.

At first glance, the monastery seemed the same. Pealing stucco walls still surrounded the cloister; the ancient campanile still rose from the northeastern corner. Although the tower was canted a bit, the bells hung straight as a plumb line, strung on ropes that disappeared into the shaft below. You could not see the man who pulled the ropes. When Gino was small, his mother had told him that Jesus was ringing the bells, and he believed her.

But the gates, the ancient iron gates that had arched in rusting dignity before the cloister, were lying twisted on the earth. The yard was open and empty. Inside, the walls of the chapel were intact, but there was no roof, no doors, no stained glass in the window openings. The monastery was a shell, a house of clay cards. He realized he had not heard the bells since his return.

The wind riffled the grass growing raggedly in the courtyard. In the bell tower, he could hear the rope chafing the bell, a vulgar sound, like a man scratching himself. There were tree stumps where once tall poplars had stood. In the farthest corner, under the last remaining arch of the cool walkway, Gino divined a movement, a shape.

"Brother Domenico?"

No answer.

"It is I, brother, Gianpaolo Bondone."

The slight figure burst from the shadows and spun toward him, a tumbleweed sent by the wind.

"Gino, Gino, my dear boy! *Pacem, pacem, pacem!*"

Gino picked up the tiny bird-like creature in his arms—a bundle of dry twigs in a rough woven bag—and kissed him many times before setting him back on the earth.

They stood looking at each other for a very long time. Gino was the first to cry. Then Brother Domenico. They cried in silence. Perhaps it was Brother Domenico who had taught this art to Gino.

Finally, the prior recovered himself, offered a thin smile, and waved a bony arm about the cloister. "Well, what do you think of our home?"

"How did it happen, brother?"

"Partisans."

"But why?"

The tiny man shook his head.

"And the brothers?"

"Some ran away; others I sent away. There was no food, no roof over our heads, nothing we could do. Not everyone hated us, but even those who didn't were afraid to help us."

The thin voice began to crack; the monk's lips continued to form round words, but only ragged, torn fragments came out.

"Please," Gino said, "let's not talk about this any more. Can we sit somewhere? My leg still gives me trouble occasionally."

Domenico led him through the ruined cloister to a corner of what had been the chapter house, where he had built a ragged straw hut against the wall.

"This is where you live?"

"It's not bad, really. It's very quiet here. A monk should live an ascetic life."

He brought an ancient, warped wooden chair from inside the hut. "Sit here, Gino, and tell me why you are limping." The ancient prior squatted in the dust and looked up compassionately, waiting.

Telling the prior was akin to confession, and to his surprise, Gino felt better for it. "As you see, I'm no hero, brother."

"Good. We don't need heroes, Gino—only honest, humble men, willing to do their duty. You did yours, Gino. You needn't feel ashamed."

"But the men I killed?"

"Your own life was at risk; the Lord understands that."

"I was quite fortunate," Gino said, greatly relieved. "I might have been permanently crippled—even killed, myself."

"When a man has had an escape such as yours, my son, he must examine his life. Ask why it was spared? What service does God require of you?"

"I expected to come back home and work at the monastery. To help my father . . . " His voice broke.

The monk touched his hand. "I'm sorry, Gino."

"Pietro and I buried him in the cemetery of San Miniato."

"Pietro?"

"I made him come with me. We buried him together."

"How strange are the ways of the Lord."

"Pietro said the partisans brought him here first. Did the destruction of the monastery have anything to do with my father?"

"The partisans claimed that we protected only the fascists. It wasn't true. But they were angry, you see? They felt the church had failed them."

"They knew you were my father's friend."

The prior looked at him with sudden comprehension. "You're not to blame, Gino."

"The sins of the father!" cried Gino.

Domenico sprang to his feet and shook Gino's shoulders. "You're being foolish, my son. Be a man and go about the tasks that God has set for you."

"What am I suited for?"

"Come, follow me!"

◆ ◆ ◆

Swinging his habit behind him as though it was a mighty train,

Brother Domenico started resolutely out of the cloister. He had passed beneath the entry arch before Gino caught up with him.

"Where are we going, brother?"

The monk waved his hand. "Long way to walk; must save my breath."

They followed the road, really a rut, through flailing, yellow grass and past proud plane trees to the very summit of the hill. There they found the crumbling remains of the road to Florence, with a pale gray serpentine vestige of paving in the center, a frozen river, higher than its banks. The two men walked along the sandy margins of this strange fossil. They were oddly matched—the monk frail and tiny, Gino tall and broad-shouldered. When Gino touched Domenico's shoulder it was as if he held a bent crook in his hand.

They reached the dark, brooding cypresses of the hill of San Francesco, above Fiesole. Below them spread the ruins of the *Teatro Romano*, a playground well remembered from Gino's childhood. He leaned on the rusted metal railing and stared down at the *Cavea*, cut from the hillside two thousand years before; it would still hold three thousand spectators in its curved grasp. His eyes drifted to the baths, the echoing remains of a *tepidarium*; then along a path, past two crumbling altars to the temple, now sliced in two by a street, the stone so worn by the years the marble seemed to have melted.

Brother Domenico picked impatiently at his arm until Gino returned to the road. They passed the Duomo and entered the Piazza Mino da Fiesole. To the west stood the church of San Francesco. The Prior stopped suddenly, grabbed Gino's arm, turned him about and marched him into the Duomo. After the blinding sunshine outside, Gino felt as if his head had been dipped in ink.

Domenico hurried him to the Salutati chapel and pointed to the triptych. "Di Lorenzi," he said; and then, at the tomb of the bishop, "Mino da Fiesole." Gino, bewildered, nodded. The monk smiled, hurried him from the church and led him up the narrow Via San

Francesco. At the pinnacle, he turned Gino and pointed him toward the valley below. "*Firenze!*" he cried as if Gino did not know.

Still, the sight astounded him. His mind was a waiting wineglass, and here was the wine, filling it to the lip. His eyes brimmed with purple hills, green vineyards, melon-toned roofs and the silver Arno. The distance was too great for him to clearly see the segments in Brunelleschi's dome or the Moorish arches in Giotto's Campanile. The tower of the Palazzo Vecchio was only a brown shaft, and the old bridge was out of sight; yet the erratic streets seemed orderly from here, and the yellow-brown walls shimmered.

Presently, the prior dragged him away and they strode down the hill and rejoined the road to Florence.

♦   ♦   ♦

The clamor of the city burst upon him. They reached the Piazza della Liberta, then turned into the Via Cavour, following the tracks of the ancient, wobbly streetcars. People, animals, and vehicles thronged the way, without regard to where the street began or the sidewalks ended or intersections occurred.

Gino was taller than most Italians, and he felt that his head was a melon floating on this human tide. The street was awash with debris—twisted iron, rags, boards, bits and pieces of rusted machinery—which the crowd eddied around. There were many broken windows. Here and there a chunk missing from a wall marked the passing of some missile. Many paving stones were gone. Where, God only knew. Even where stones remained the mortar had washed away, so that they sat like buns in a pan.

They stumbled and hobbled down the Via Cavour, merged in this horde of humanity, moving toward some unknown and possibly mystical goal, like people on a pilgrimage. These were Gino's fellow pilgrims and therefore he smiled upon them.

At the Piazza San Marco, the monk suddenly grabbed his arm and dragged him cross-stream. He stopped before the portal of the monastery, breathing quickly and deeply, almost in racking sobs.

"We're here," he finally managed to say. "Gino, you must trust me. When we go inside, say as little as possible. When required to speak, limit your replies to a few words. This is an important day for you, Gino, and you must promise to do as I say."

Gino found himself nodding assent.

"Splendid," smiled the prior, leading him inside.

A wispy, lisping young monk led them at a pious pace through the cloister. What a contrast to poor Domenico's ruined monastery. The stonework was immaculately clean, the hedges neatly trimmed. Each curve of the Romanesque cortile echoed the harmony and beauty of the place.

They passed monks strolling in the garden. A few nodded to Domenico and he returned their greeting, if somewhat abstractedly. In the chapter house, several novices were reading loudly in Latin—whether to impress each other or God, Gino couldn't tell.

Finally, they reached the open door of a large and spacious room on the highest floor of the priory. From behind a vast desk rose a tall and tonsured monk, who cried a cheerful welcome to Domenico and hurried to embrace him. Gino looked about the room, admiring the high, beamed ceiling and the steep, slender casements. The light from the windows slanted across the tall monk's face, outlining his strong nose and chin, the perfect oval curves of his head.

"This is the young man you have been telling me about."

"Yes. Gino, this is Brother Alberto, prior of the Monastery of San Marco. And this, dear prior, is my cherished young friend, Gianpaolo Bondone."

"Very good. Brother Domenico has been promising to bring you here for a long time. No doubt his prayers and good wishes have helped bring you home safely and thus to San Marco at this propitious time."

Gino nodded and mustered a smile.

"I am sure Signore Patti will be pleased to meet you. Let us seek him out at once."

Gino followed the two priors down the steps, through the

cloisters and then into a large, high-ceilinged chamber. Rich blues, subtle reds and brilliant golds shimmered from dozens of large paintings mounted on screens or painted directly on the walls.

"Fra Angelico," he whispered. His eyes were caught by a movement at the far end of the room. There, a low wooden scaffold creaked sullenly under the feet of a man in a smock who was staring at a partially frescoed wall. Below, at the man's feet, a young boy was grinding colors in a pot.

"Signore Patti," called Brother Alberto, "may we speak to you for a moment?"

The man on the scaffold turned slowly and peered, first at the two monks, then at Gino. His huge bald head sat upon spreading jowls, which reached to his shoulders. He looked as if he had been made in two pieces, the lesser part smashed down on the larger. His nose was tiny, almost lost among the pronounced folds of his face, and his mouth was so small it looked more like a third eye.

"What do you want?" the man snapped in a high-pitched, belligerent voice. Seeing that the boy grinding colors had stopped working, he added, "Get back to work, you moron!"

Brother Alberto spoke mildly, as one might to a recalcitrant child. "Come down please, Signore. We want you to meet your new assistant."

Gino spun around to stare at Brother Domenico, who made an almost imperceptible gesture. By the time Gino looked back, the scaffold was empty and the fat man was approaching him with remarkable speed, his mouth a smiling rosebud, his eyes fiery little peonies shaking in the clasp of his jowled face. Gino stepped back involuntarily, but the man only blinked at him briefly and hurried past to shake the hand of Brother Alberto.

"You promised me a painter and you found one! My God, I'm breaking my back on that scaffold. Who sent him? Who is he? What has he done?" The questions came in quick, high-toned bleeps.

The prior of San Marco laughed. "Wait a minute, Signore. I have not answered one question before you ask another. Our dear friend Brother Domenico has brought this lad from Fiesole. He has only recently returned from army service. Before the war he worked with the friars at the monastery of San Felice, now unfortunately destroyed. Domenico says he is very talented."

"Yes?" Signore Patti, suddenly wary, circled Gino with a measured tread. Suddenly the mountain was at his very nose. "What's your name?"

"Gianpaolo Bondone—but they call me Gino."

"What type of paint have you used?"

"Paint?"

"Yes, paint. When you worked at the monastery, what kind of paint did you use; oil, tempera, watercolor?"

"Uh, mostly tempera and oil."

"No watercolor?"

"Oh no, it wouldn't last."

The face was closer now. "Last? What do you mean, last?"

"It would dry right up. Flake off. You could even wipe it off."

"What on earth are you talking about?"

The man had a faintly feminine smell. "Signore Patti, if we used watercolor on the leather, it wouldn't—"

"—The leather!" he screamed. "What leather?" He made a full circle, screaming at the monks as much as Gino.

"Why, the leather wallets and purses we made. Surely you—"

"—Oh, no!" Signore Patti put his hands to his ears, and began to waddle about the room, muttering imprecations of the vilest sort, directed at the monks, at Gino, the paintings on the wall, and through their ministry, it seemed, at God Almighty. He stopped before a blue-and gold-toned Coronation of the Virgin and raising his arms, hurled a steady stream of questions, malicious in the extreme, at the mild lady's gentle head. It was obvious that he was not satisfied by the response, for he stamped on the floor, shook a fist at her and resumed his pacing.

In mid-circuit, Signore Patti made an abrupt turn and once again headed straight for Gino. The younger man found his arms held tightly in a fearsome grip.

"A leatherworker. A man who paints little flowers on ladies' handbags, curlicues and arabesques at the corners of wallets? Mother of God! I'm commissioned to restore the frescoes of the saintly—the blessed—Fra Angelico, and they send me a shoemaker to do the work. Brother Alberto, have you lost your senses?"

Apparently the prior was accustomed to such outbursts, for he showed no anger. "I think, my good man, that you have been laboring overly hard at this glorious work. We have brought you a fine young man, gifted with the brush, a man who has experience in following the designs of others. It is true that he has never painted a fresco, but he is young, vigorous, intelligent and talented. Surely, so great a master as Lorenzo Patti can teach this youth to do his bidding."

The corpulent painter still held Gino. But now the man's hands slid down across his arms, squeezing the biceps gently, riding along the outside of his forearms and across the hands. Signore Patti's fleshy lips curled into an unpleasant smile.

"Of course. You're right. Forgive me, Brother Alberto. Thank you, Brother Domenico. It's clear to me that this young man is perfect for my purposes. Splendid. When can you begin?"

"I don't know, Signore."

"Today," said Domenico, speaking firmly.

"But my mother and sister—"

"—I'll tell them. They'll be delighted. I'll collect your things and send them to you."

The old monk beckoned to him. Gino pulled away from Signore Patti and followed the prior into the corridor.

"I know I surprised you, my son. You must excuse this small deception. Had I said you were going to be apprenticed to a great painter of frescoes, you'd have thought me mad. But this position is perfect for you, Gino. Even as a boy you sketched and painted when the others could barely sew the leather. Not to say leatherworking isn't an honorable profession. But a painter, Gino! Think of it. Lorenzo Patti is a strange man, but a very fine artist. The Rossini family, one of the oldest and richest in Florence, has hired him to restore the damaged frescoes of Fra Angelico, and to paint a new fresco in the family chapel. This is the first such commission in a hundred years! What Benozzo Gozzoli did for the Medici, what da Vinci accomplished for the Sforzas, as Michelangelo helped Ghirlandaio paint the Duomo frescoes, you will assist a great artist of our time in working for the Rossinis. It's a great honor for a young man."

"But Brother Domenico, I've never painted a fresco in my life!"

"Patti will teach you. You'll live here with the brothers and work for the master. On Sundays you may visit with your family."

"What will my mother think?"

"She'll be very proud. Come now, stop worrying. If the work does not please you, if Lorenzo Patti is cruel or unpleasant, you may leave. The pay is small, but you'll have food to eat, a warm bed to sleep on, a dry roof over your head, a trade to learn, and a few lire in your pocket. What is there to lose?"

While Gino was debating this very question in his mind, the monk turned him gently around and led him back into the hospice. "It is all arranged," he said loudly. "Gino will begin today."

♦ ♦ ♦

Gino was issued a coarse woolen habit like that worn by the friars, which was even less comfortable and no cleaner than his own clothes. He slept in a wooden bunk on a straw-filled mattress in a room with twenty other men, and shared their meager meals of watery soup, pasta and potatoes. Everyone rose before dawn and went to sleep soon after dusk. No talking was permitted at meals or in the "barracks," as Gino called the sleeping quarters. For him, this represented little improvement over his army service.

Lorenzo Patti was surly and a steady stream of inspired invective poured from his lips. If nothing else, he taught Gino an art of swearing superior even to that which he had learned as a soldier.

Patti was a harsh taskmaster. The boy who ground colors and

mixed lime was treated to cuffs and kicks in delicate places and at moments when he least expected them. Gino was spared such physical indignity, but Lorenzo Patti never gave him a moment's rest.

Preparing the walls, applying the scratch and brown coats of plaster was arduous; the first coat was as important as the final. Patti wanted a rough surface, applied in a perfect pattern. Some small leeway was permitted with the second coat, but none with the final one.

Gino learned that the plaster for the final mixed coat had been prepared and stored over a year earlier. In the meantime, the boy had regularly slaked and worked it until it reached just the right consistency.

Once, Gino applied a trace too much of the *intonaco*, the final coat, so that its surface was a minute fraction higher than the adjoining ancient plaster it was supposed to match. Patti flew into a rage, kicked over the pail of lime putty, and personally scraped off every bit of the plaster that Gino had applied. Then he ordered Gino to reapply a fresh coat, which he did with infinite care to the beat of Patti's florid imprecations.

Patti had prepared a set of full-scale drawings based on photographs of the original paintings from the archives of the monastery. The photographs were faded black and white; Patti selected colors based on his knowledge of the painter's palette. And because the set was incomplete it was impossible to be completely faithful to the original conception. Still, to Gino's eye, the invented portions were in perfect harmony with the precious vestiges of the blessed Angelico's creations.

Patti wouldn't allow Gino see more than one section of his beautiful drawings at a time. Despite his contempt—he'd taken to calling Gino "shoemaker"—he was too suspicious to let him see all the drawings together. Gino's open admiration did little to allay the master's fears.

In time, Patti permitted him to help trace the cartoons from the drawings. Gino proved able and quick at this, and Patti gave him a few grudging compliments.

After that, the maestro showed Gino how to roll the wheel along the lines of the cartoon, perforating it and picking a pattern into the brown coat of plaster. Gino was allowed to apply the *intonaco*, but only up to the place the painter had decided might reasonably be completed in a day.

Next, the cartoon was rolled again—this time by Patti—and a bag of pigment shaken across it, so that the spatter would stand out on the final coat. During this process, it was hands off for Gino; Lorenzo Patti applied the watercolors himself. The other apprentice, a scrawny lad named Benvenuto, mixed the colors, and Patti compared them with the samples on his pigment stone. Gino never touched a paintbrush.

However, it soon became evident that Benvenuto could not do an adequate job; at times the colors dried to a different tone from the sample stone. This was a catastrophe, requiring the removal of the entire coat of plaster up to the last dividing line. Patti tried mixing the colors himself, which required him to ascend and descend the scaffold, but he was too old, too fat, and too lazy to continue.

Ultimately the master assigned the job to Gino.

Finally, he thought, *I'll be able to study the great man at work.*

And hard work it was. Each day a segment of the wall must be carefully sized and prepared, the consistency of the plaster prudently checked and rechecked, the colors perfectly mixed and meticulously matched to those applied five hundred years before. The brushwork must match the ancient master's, yet be done in a way appropriate to the modern plaster, because Fra Angelico's ancient formula had been lost. To Gino, copying Patti's splendid drawings on canvas would have been marvelous enough, but to apply them successfully to the treacherous surface of the wet plaster was a miracle.

Gino longed for the day when he would be permitted to touch a brush to the plaster. One night he slipped from his bunk, appropriated some of the lime putty, spread it on a piece of wood, mixed some blue paint and applied it. To his consternation, his single brushstroke left a line that bled in a thousand directions. He might just as well have spilled a bottle of ink. Gino stumbled back to his bunk and did not make another attempt at fresco painting for weeks.

♦   ♦   ♦

On Gino's first Sabbath after moving to the monastery, he struggled from his bunk before dawn, pulled on his "city clothes"—the ones he had worn the day Brother Domenico had lured him there—and left San Marco. He hoped to reach Fiesole at 6 a.m., when his mother would attend Mass at the Duomo.

The hills, as usual, were drenched in fog. Figures materialized out of the swirling vapor. At a distance they seemed to be ominous, filmy wraiths with shrouded faces and fluid strides. Up close they became simple peasants. The highway disappeared a few inches below his knees. He misstepped and plunged up to his waist in wet grass. With a shiver, he lifted himself back onto the road.

The fog lifted and dropped again in a second, like a ragged towel slapped against the earth. In that moment Gino saw that he had reached the piazza in front of the cathedral in Fiesole. Gino waited beside the entrance, hoping to intercept his mother. In a few minutes, he heard the anticipatory echo of the bell as it began to sway, then the first reverberating shock. Little quivers ran through the stones at his feet.

Believing that his mother, never late for Mass, was already inside, he entered the cathedral. Candles flickered in the chapels and on the altar, barely stroking the gloom with brush-tips of wavering light. He scanned the worshippers, but couldn't raise a familiar face.

Disappointed, Gino tried to immerse himself in the ritual. But the simple benches that once seemed warm and friendly, were hard against his knees, hard against his hands. He stopped, realizing that he had no idea what he was praying about.

The man next to him was only moving his lips, his eyes wandering, his gestures as stylized as Gino's. He looked over his shoulder and saw others who rose and knelt without expression. *They're merely going through the motions, just as I am*, he thought.

At last the service ended. He was jostled outside by the crowd, like a seashell pushed along the shore by succeeding waves. Gino waited beyond the towering portal; it was some time before he accepted the idea that his mother wasn't there. He set out for home, moving so rapidly that he didn't notice that he had sliced through a cordon of curious villagers.

◆ ◆ ◆

"I don't understand, Mama. Why weren't you at morning Mass?"

"Please, Gino, stop worrying. Sit down. We have a bit of cake for you. A delicacy."

"Maria, why won't she answer me?"

"Use your head," Pietro said. "It's because the townspeople hated your father."

"Don't they know he's dead?"

"Of course," his mother said, taking his arm and leading him to the table. "They know and they feel guilty. That's why they can't bear to look at me. In time, it will be forgotten."

"I won't forget! I won't let *them* forget. One day I'll find the man who killed him."

"It wasn't one man, it was many'" Pietro said. "You're better off if you never find them."

"Tell us about San Marco," Maria said, changing the subject.

"The monks are kind, the food is simple, and I live in a barracks, not a cell. Monks snore as much as common soldiers."

His mother and sister laughed.

"What work do you do?" Pietro asked.

"I am an assistant to Lorenzo Patti, the great painter. I help him apply the wet plaster and prepare the cartoons. One day, I'll do some of the painting myself."

"You're paid for this?"

"A few lire. But that's not the point. Patti himself is well paid and highly honored. Do you know he was hired by the Rossinis to paint their private chapel? Imagine, their own chapel! Like the Medici."

The women sighed in appreciation.

"It's an honorable profession," his mother said. "Your father would be proud of you."

They were all silent for a moment. Gino looked down at the table. The squeaking slam of the door against its yielding wooden frame brought him upright. Pietro had left without saying a word. Anger flushed through him. "I don't trust that man."

"He's almost one of the family," his mother said.

"Not *my* family." He glared at Maria, who looked away.

"Please, Gino," his mother said. "He tills our fields. He protects us. Now that you're at the monastery, we need someone."

"I'll come home."

"No, you must stay with the maestro. One day you'll be a great painter."

"I'll be back in a while, Mama. I promised Brother Domenico I'd go to see him."

♦ ♦ ♦

"Tell me about Pietro. Who is he?"

"He's an orphan," Brother Domenico said. "He didn't know his father, and his mother died when he was small. As a child he lived with the Sisters of Charity. When he was older, they found him work at the Bibliotheca. That's where your father located him."

"How? Why?

"The *Fascisti* were always seeking to recruit young men."

Gino shook his head. "My father knew dozens of young men in Fiesole. Why would he go to Florence?"

"What's the point, Gino?"

"He knows more about my father than he told us. How he died. *Why* he died. Pietro knows."

"Does it matter now?"

"Yes, brother, to me it matters."

The prior looked at him sadly. "Wait here," he said quietly, then disappeared into the broken shadows of his crumbling shelter. When he returned, he was carrying a small, coarse cotton bag. Silently, he handed it to Gino.

Gino loosened the knot and spread the rim of the bag. Within was a cold, hard shape. When he drew it out he saw it was a wooden crucifix. The anatomy of Christ was rather clumsy; the head a bit too large, the legs too short, the arms too thin. But it was evident the figure had been carved and finished with great care. One might even say the artist had refined its imperfections. The entire work looked as though it had been stained and polished many times. Gino looked at Brother Domenico, his question apparent in his eyes.

The monk reached out and held the hand that held the crucifix. "Your father made this, Gino."

Gino shook his head, violently and involuntarily.

"The night he died, he left it with me. 'When the time is right,' he said, 'give this to Gianpaolo.'"

The crucifix suddenly came alive in Gino's hand. The Christ figure shimmered with ancient agony. Domenico's steady hand kept Gino from dropping it.

"I never knew he had carved or painted anything."

"I think he believed it was a weakness—this desire to be an artist. Carlo knew he was not very talented. Neat, yes. Careful, yes. Even meticulous. But not very talented. Still, he wanted you to know what was in his heart. He was pleased with your skill. Proud of it. Perhaps even envious."

The trembling in Gino's hand subsided. There were no tears in his eyes. Only surprise and wonder.

"We shouldn't ignore his transgressions, Gino, but we must also realize that he was a man."

Gino held the crucifix lightly in his hand. So many coats of varnish. If he could peel each of them away, what might he learn of the man who had been his father?

Five

Desire under the Arches

Some weeks, Gino didn't go home on Sundays, using the opportunity to study Florence, to be a part of it. When he was a boy, a visit to Florence with his father had been a rare adventure, something to look forward to with anticipation. But in those days, Gino had seen only the face and skin of Florence. His father had displayed little interest in art or history, and not much more in religion. They would visit the Duomo, of course, and hear Mass if their timing was right, but for the most part the boy's contacts were limited to his father's customers and friends.

Even so, the centuries-old fairy tale of Florence captivated Gino. Like every other schoolboy, he knew of Leonardo and Michelangelo, Donatello and Ghiberti. His father would stop when they passed the Baptistery, point to the doors that Michelangelo had named the "Gates of Paradise," and say, *"Magnifico, eh?"* He probably meant what he said, but Gino had believed it was more a question of territorial pride than true appreciation. Now that he owned the crucifix, he wasn't as certain.

Gino easily recaptured the delights of those childhood visits. It was true that Florence had suffered from the war, that all her bridges save the Ponte Vecchio were down, that many homes had been destroyed and the streets were still littered with debris. But the Duomo and the Campanile, the Baptistery and the Palazzo Vecchio, the Pitti Palace and the Uffizi were still standing. Although they all bore a thick patina of grime, they had survived for hundreds of years, despite the assaults of man and the elements, and the elements stirred up by man.

Since being apprenticed to Patti, Gino's interest had grown deeper. Merely to observe the facades of the buildings, the winding, twisted streets, the broad and narrow squares was not enough. He wasn't content to bend his knee at one shrine or another. Now he must study the Donatello crucifix and the Brancacci chapel, the OrsenMichele and the Medici Library.

Many monuments and museums were not yet open, or completely open, to the public. Large portions of the great collections had been forcibly carted away to sate the insatiable Nazi *Reichsmarschall*, Hermann Goering. But much remained. Even the Germans had not managed to remove the Gozzoli frescoes from the walls of the Riccardi-Medici chapel.

A few galleries of the Uffizi were open. For the most part, only the works of pre-Renaissance and early Renaissance painters could be seen. But it was a beginning. Gino felt that he was beginning, too. He didn't mind studying the more primitive artists. Even now, he knew he couldn't match their work. He sat before the Cimabue Triptych for several hours. The guards eyed him warily, unable to understand what this ragged young man found so interesting. It was the Virgin's face, beautifully drawn, and full of agony, dominating the panel not because she was five times larger than any other figure, but because she was suffering. The other faces were merely repetitive and perfunctory visages, pasted around the edges of the panel like so many stamps on an envelope.

For months Gino avoided the Accademia. He yearned to see the original marble David displayed there, but he couldn't visualize Michelangelo's masterpiece without seeing the tortured body of his father slung from the bronze copy in the Piazzale.

One day, without thinking, he mentioned the David to Lorenzo Patti and, to his surprise, the master scribbled a note to the Director of the National Archives. When Gino presented this note, the director arranged for a private tour because the Accademia was not yet open to the public.

The ancient attendant examined Gino's pass with evident suspicion and only reluctantly admitted him. The building was filled with dust; and every step sent swirls of it eddying into the air. After a minute of wading through this fog, the attendant began to sneeze.

"Why don't you wait outside?" Gino said.

At first the man demurred, but Gino assured him he didn't intend to cart away the sixteen-foot marble David or any of the other sculptures, and after a perfunctory show of righteous refusal, the attendant gratefully consented.

Gino traversed the long, narrow corridor flanked by great works of the master. The *Palestrina Pieta*, grotesquely shaped, but powerful nonetheless. A captive, once meant for the tomb of Pope Julius, but still imprisoned in his stone cell. He would remain there for the ages; the master would never release him from the roughly hewn marble.

The rotunda. Although the windows at the top of the dome were covered with grime, the David was not diminished by shadows. Gino circled the gigantic figure, his father's tragedy wholly forgotten. He ran his hands over the smooth muscles, the gently swelling veins in the hands. Around and around; over and over again. Then he sat on the floor (there were no benches) and stared up at the mighty Israelite.

What grace may be displayed by a powerful man, he thought. To him, the figure expressed youth and maturity, strength and beauty, power and sensitivity. David frowned slightly, but perpetually. Was it fear, or simply intense concentration on his dangerous undertaking? The eyes were large and staring, but their gaze was direct, level, eternal.

Eternal. He wondered about that. The David was real. Perhaps too real; too solid. There was no illusion. No play of light refracting its way through varying layers of color as in a painting. It was magnificent. Unchanging. The muscles would ripple forever under the translucent marble. The expression in the eyes wouldn't vary—no matter from what angle one studied them.

Gino decided he would never be a sculptor. His decision was both humble and presumptuous, but he wasn't embarrassed, merely relieved. A few minutes with the David made it clear to him that he couldn't hope to match Michelangelo in marble, and he didn't intend to undertake anything without hope of distinction.

The idea gave him pause. When had the thought of achieving distinction occurred to him before? Once he had thought that life would be good if he could work as a leatherworker, raise a family, take care of his mother. Now, suddenly, challenged by the sight of a four-hundred-year-old statue in a dusty museum, he had begun to think of living with distinction. He smiled, but didn't laugh at himself.

In the weeks that followed, Gino followed the circuit from the Convento San Marco where he worked, to green and white striped Santa Croce, to the earth-toned Piazza della Signoria, to the great classic galleries on both sides of the Arno, to the green and white striped Santa Maria Novella, visiting every shrine, religious and artistic, in between and thereabouts. He admired the Medici Chapel at San Lorenzo, but not as fervently as before. The David had cured him of sculpture; he could not be touched by the Medici dukes, nor their naked guardians. Yes, the setting was marvelous; yes, the carving was splendid. But who could exceed perfection? He was still too naive to distinguish the developing artistic power that separated the statue of the Duke of Nemours from the simple (though of course magnificent) shepherd boy.

His taste for the treasures of Florence couldn't be slaked. In the Uffizi Gallery, he studied Botticelli's Venus for hours, in ecstasy over the gentle tones, the elegant drawing, the complex yet beautifully articulated composition. But then he began to see Venus—surprise of surprises—as a beautiful woman. Not Michelangelo's muscular Dawn perched on Giuliano De Medici's tomb with her oddly spaced breasts, but a lovely, graceful young girl. Had she stepped from the canvas, any man in any age would have wanted her.

Gino blushed at the thought. This was art, not pornography, a goddess, not a trollop. Yet it was true that even in mythology goddesses had often been little better than trollops. Ridiculous; this painting was by the divine Botticelli, who had cast his own paintings—those he considered lascivious—on Savonarola's pyre. How had this one escaped? He paced about, cursing himself, as if the pacing would relieve the accumulated heat of many months. Growing suspicious, the gallery guards surveyed the room to see if this agitated stranger had defaced a painting. No, apparently he was just a madman, a breed not unheard of in Florence. Nevertheless, they escorted him out of the building.

Gino wandered the streets, still haunted by this lovely vision. At a *trattoria*, a noisy, dirty one, he ordered a bit of pasta and wine; but the hunger wasn't in his belly, nor the thirst in his throat.

It grew dark and Gino was relieved that his shame was hidden. Unconsciously, he returned to the Uffizi and leaned against a pillar of the arcade, trembling and exhausted.

"Can I help you?" Even in the darkness, his soldier's eyes and ears told him she was a prostitute. "Can I help you?" she repeated. He had only a few lire left from his meager wage.

"I'll give you fifty lire," he said, trying to discern her appearance in the gloom.

She laughed scornfully and turned away.

He followed, took her arm. "You must accept it—very important. Do you understand?"

She was evidently amazed by his vehemence. "I have to make a living you know," she said, a bit uncertainly.

He plunged his hand in his pocket and drew out the few additional lire he had been hoping to save for his mother. "Here! That's all I have."

A moment's pause. "Let's get it over with."

Almost gleefully, he escorted her to her room, which was small and dark but neat, with little lace frills on the chairs, the bed and the edges of tables. There were pictures of the Virgin, of Mary Magdalene, St. Theresa and St. Caterina on the walls.

"What are these for?"

"In this business," she said, "a girl needs all the help she can get."

Gino laughed. "Don't the pictures disturb your patrons?"

"My patrons never seem to notice—except for you." She began to remove her clothes.

"Wait," he said, "I'll do it."

A glaze of makeup fixed a permanent invitation on her face. "Remove it," he said, running a finger across her cheek.

"You haven't paid for that much of my time."

"Then I'll go." He turned to leave.

"Wait," she said, "your money."

He shook his head and reached the door.

"All right," she sighed. "I'll remove it."

Using a basin of dubious cleanliness, the girl splashed water on her face and wiped it with a dirt-stained towel. Her features emerged, strong but not pretty. He smiled anyway, his hands working the buttons on her dress. When he removed it, she was naked. No slip. No brassiere. Nothing.

"You see, it's no work at all," she said, pulling him toward the bed. Her breasts were slack and her thighs were thick. There was no illusion now, only a woman; not very pretty, and a prostitute. When she smiled, he closed his eyes and almost fell upon her. A throbbing moment, an explosion and it was over. He was dazed.

"You're very quick," she laughed.

He rolled away and pulled on his clothes. "Thank you," he mumbled and escaped through the door.

Realizing it was very late and thinking the entrance to San Marco might be closed, he ran through the streets, stumbling here and there, bumping into people and generally creating a disturbance. Happily, the gates were still open. He hurried inside, hoping to find his way to his bed before he was discovered.

"Gino, Gino, where have you been?" It was Benvenuto.

"Hush," Gino whispered.

"Hurry, Brother Alberto is expecting you."

As Gino ran through the corridors, the sound of piteous groans reached his ears. He ran faster until he reached the open doorway of the prior's quarters.

It was Lorenzo Patti. The great man lay propped on the prior's bed, his jowls wiggling in pain at the head of his mountainous body. He groaned aloud, again and again—deep, agonized quavers that were enhanced by the distance they traveled.

Two professional looking men in dark suits appeared from the far side of Signore Patti's resting-place. They had been almost totally obscured by his bulk.

"Signore Patti has taken a hard fall," one said, "the effects of which may have been both accentuated and softened by his, shall we say, scale. We'll have to take x-rays."

Patti moaned.

"We would give him a sedative," the doctor continued, "but we don't know precisely where the damage is and would prefer not to obscure it with drugs." The doctors bowed to each other as if at a dance.

When Gino approached Lorenzo Patti, he bellowed a curse and half rose from the pallet. "You, you beast, you obscene beast! If you had been here, this wouldn't have happened."

"How am I to blame?" Gino was aghast.

"I was on the scaffold, laying the plaster myself, you idiot!"

Brother Alberto spoke mildly, "On the Sabbath, Signore Patti?"

"Yes, on the Sabbath, you insufferable old fool!" (Brother Alberto's expression never changed). "How much of my life do you think I can spend repainting your accursed frescoes?" A yelp of pain accented his words. "If this young jackass had been here to apply my *intonaco*, I shouldn't have fallen. Where *were* you, you ungrateful wretch?"

"He isn't required to work on the Sabbath, Maestro. And you are required not to."

Patti screamed: "I labor like a slave on your pathetic frescoes! I fall and hurt myself desperately, and you dare to complain? Out, I say, every one of you. Out, Out, OUT!"

It was the prior's room, but even he departed. Only Gino remained.

Patti stared after the departed monks in amazement. "You see," he said, "they leave me alone. An old man, grievously injured, and they leave me alone to suffer. What do you think of them now? 'Brothers' they call themselves. Brothers of Satan himself, I assure you."

♦   ♦   ♦

The next day they moved Signore Patti (using a litter of immense proportions and sturdy construction) to the hospital and x-rayed every quivering inch of his body. Whatever else they may have found, there were no broken bones. Patti's right ankle was sprained and he had strained every muscle, but apparently no permanent damage had been done.

When he returned to San Marco, Patti insisted that his bed be moved into the Hospice so that he could return to work as soon as possible. But the days passed, and he seldom rose from his bed. Work on the fresco came to a halt. Gino was disheartened. He wanted to study the master's technique, and eventually learn to do at least simple brushwork on the tricky wet plaster.

Day after day, the prior patiently reminded Patti that he had promised to complete the work within the year.

"I'll go back to work tomorrow," cried Patti one day, "but I can't bear your infernal complaints. Stay away, prior. That will help cure me."

They locked the door of the Hospice, opening it only to receive food, leaving it only to perform normal bodily functions. But they did no work on the fresco.

Gino was exasperated. "Signore, we can keep the doors closed for only so long. Then they'll discover we're stalling."

Patti replied with surprising reasonableness. "Come here, Gino, look." As Gino approached, the painter pulled down the covers and exposed his feet. The right toe was swollen to gigantic size and its color was an unwholesome purple.

Gino stepped back. "What is it?"

"Gout." Patti nodded his head, as if confirming his own diagnosis. "Yes, the ankle's fine, no bones are broken, but the force of the fall activated my gout. The pain is unbearable."

"Why don't you send for a doctor?"

"I don't need a doctor, you fool. I need medicine—Colchicine. Benvenuto has been bringing it to me. The worst is over, but still I cannot step on the toe."

His pig-eyed face, even contorted with pain, did not move Gino to sympathy. Gino withdrew to a corner of the Hospice, studying first the unfinished fresco and then the immobilized Lorenzo Patti. In another part of the room, Benvenuto amused himself by crumbling discarded plaster in his fingers.

After half an hour of internal dialogue, Gino resolved to approach the painter. "Signore, Brother Alberto told me the Rossinis will appear any day now. What will they do when they see how little has been accomplished? Oh, yes, what you have painted is very beautiful—perhaps even more beautiful than the original. But if the Rossinis are dissatisfied, you'll lose the commission."

"Are you trying to make me even sicker than I am?"

"I have an idea. Please don't laugh. If you'll instruct and guide and help me, I believe I can paint the most simple portions of the fresco."

Patti broke out in a coarse bray that wounded Gino, but didn't deter him. He clambered up the scaffolding, and turned to Patti. "Most of this area is sky and clouds and a few columns. If we brought your bed over here, you could mix the colors yourself without getting up. The cartoons are ready. Benvenuto can learn to apply the *intonaco*."

"Ridiculous, you stupid shoemaker."

"What is there to lose?" Gino's voice echoed across the vault of the room. "The doors are locked. No one will see who does the work. We'll swear that you did it." He crossed himself quickly.

"I? I did it? Fresco is for a master, you nincompoop."

"If my work is too clumsy, we'll scrape it off and begin again. Can nothing be worse than nothing?"

Patti rolled on his side and presented his back to Gino. His voice came in muffled tones. "It's too absurd to consider."

Gino jumped down from the scaffold and hurried to the painter. "I tell you, Signore, you'll be disgraced. Everyone will say you bungled the job."

Patti's reply was almost plaintive. "Has a man no right to be ill?"

"Are you afraid of me, Signore? Afraid I'll do the work too well?"

Patti forced a laugh, and laboriously turned about to face Gino. "Fool! No one in Florence is the equal of Lorenzo Patti. But why argue with a shoemaker?"

"Don't argue. Show me how to hold the brush."

Patti stared at him for many minutes. Gino didn't look away.

"Benvenuto!" cried Lorenzo Patti. "Help this madman move my bed next to the scaffold."

♦ ♦ ♦

For three days, the master wouldn't permit Gino to approach the wall. He spent one full day showing Gino how to hold the brushes. Then, two days demonstrating how to make the various strokes—long, short, curved and straight—and a dozen variations. Gino learned to test the paint on his fingers, on his tongue.

Patti was not a patient teacher. Once, he took a pot of ochre and splashed it in Gino's face. The young man patiently washed it off and repeated his questions. They worked through all the hours of daylight and by a single weak bulb at night. Gino's fingers ached from holding a flimsy stick with hair at the end; they shook when he tried to scribe a smooth line.

"Loose, you fool, loose! This isn't a wrestling match. One bit tighter and the brush will crumble in your peasant hands."

Gino couldn't sleep at night because Patti snored unpredictably. Even if Patti had been silent, Gino would not have rested. His mind was busy recalling the master's every word and gesture. Each morning his eyes ached more than the night before. But nervous energy carried him on.

The great moment arrived. Patti permitted him a few practice strokes on a sample plank of wet plaster, then sent him up on the scaffold. It was terribly lonely there. Benvenuto stood at Gino's side, looking up expectantly, eager for once to help. Below, the rolling landscape known as Lorenzo Patti presented a vista of mysterious folds and crevices.

Gino sighed deeply and began. The first color he applied was a deep Phrygian blue. It went on easily. Gino stepped back to contemplate it.

"Don't stop, you fool!" screeched Patti. "The plaster will dry before you're half finished."

Gino dipped his brush and hurried on. It seemed only moments later that Patti told him to stop. Gino reluctantly clambered down to the master's cot and looked up at his tiny section of the fresco.

"Now you think you're Michelangelo."

"No, but I'm proud to be the apprentice of the great Lorenzo Patti."

It was the right answer and it deflected another scathing deprecation.

From that moment forward, Gino grew bolder. Each day he prepared and covered an increasingly larger portion of the wall. He made mistakes—which had to be chipped away—but he worked so assiduously that even Patti was appeased.

Under Gino's fingers, the pale sky spread across the wall. The strokes came easily now. He could blend the lighter tones in the picture into the deeper ones beyond. The clouds were no problem. They curved in soft white billows from horizon to horizon, shadowed below, brilliant above. But he was running out of sky and clouds.

The maestro would not permit him to paint faces or figures, and therefore ugly brown circles of rough plaster punctured the firmament. At night, when the others slept, Gino sketched in pencil on scraps of paper, copying the master's drawings again and again. It was devilishly hard. A face was not a curlicue on the corner of a wallet. The nose must be shaded; just so. The eyes had to seem luminous—alive. The chin and cheeks had to be drawn with hollows in them—hollows, not holes. He drew a cherub a hundred times.

Gino mixed plaster in the half darkness, and spread it on the floor of the Hospice. Next, he quickly prepared the colors before the plaster dried. Only then could he paint. Before the others awakened in the morning, he had to scrape his work off the floor and sweep the leavings away.

An eye. A mouth. A nose. But never a whole face. How would he know if he could do it if he never even tried? He painted a cherub's face in sections, a little at a time each night, then pulled his cot and bedding over to cover his work.

It took him a week. The face wasn't as good as he had hoped, but he was encouraged. However, the floor was damp, and the plaster would soon peel away. He would have to present it to Patti at once.

"I have something to show you, Maestro. Under my bed."

"Roaches? The monastery is infested with them."

"No, not roaches. Please come with me. You can lean on my arm."

"I can't walk, you fool!"

"Very well, Benvenuto and I will carry your bed."

Benvenuto moaned in protest, but Gino was insistent. Slowly, putting the bed down each time the maestro groaned, they moved him close to Gino's bed.

"Now we'll move my bed. Careful, Benvenuto, don't disturb the fresco."

Patti laughed. It was a joke of course. But there on the floor was the face of the cherub. He almost rolled off his bed.

"I've been copying your magnificent work night after night, Maestro. It's nothing compared to what you would do, but with your kind help, I can paint faces and figures on the wall."

Patti stared at him. "You amaze me, shoemaker."

"I'm flattered."

"But you don't know how to build the structure of a face. Bring me a pencil and paper and I'll show you."

◆ ◆ ◆

Each day Gino learned a new secret. Each day he could perform new magic. The maestro still yelled at him, but Gino heard nothing—saw only the brown circles, which he began, slowly and painstakingly, to fill with faces.

After a time, the prior demanded entrance to the Hospice. Gino, with Patti's permission, admitted him. Without preliminaries, Brother Alberto went straight to the fresco and studied it.

"Amazing, Maestro," he said. "Frankly, I thought you were unable to work at all, and look here, you've made splendid progress. Forgive me for doubting you."

"It was difficult," said the master, "with this damaged foot of mine, but it is the will of God that the Rossinis' commission be completed. Of course, I cannot claim it's my best work, but under the circumstances . . ."

"On the contrary, Signore, the work is splendid. If anything, it seems to me even better than before."

Patti began to cough and choke. Gino ran to find a doctor. Strangely, by the time the doctor appeared, Patti was calm and resting easily.

One morning, unexpectedly, a young friar banged his fist against the door of the Hospice, demanding entrance. Patti urged Gino down from the scaffold before he sent Benvenuto to open the door. The friar hurried in with his message: The Rossini family had arrived.

Patti did his best to rouse himself from his bed. Gino and

Benvenuto swung him around and propped him up. When his feet touched the floor, the master winced in pain. They could hear the Rossinis crossing the corridor in slow and measured treads. There were discernible pauses between footfalls and this served to increase the tension. Signore Vasilio Rossini entered first, a miniature version of a Renaissance knight, with perfect, elegant features, slim mustache, curling locks trimmed just above the ears. His nose was remarkably thin—a bit curved, but remarkably thin. Gino wondered how he managed to breathe through it.

Signora Rossini stood at least a full head taller than her husband. His hair was black, hers silver. In contrast to his eagle nose, she presented one that turned up rather abruptly. Rossini was swarthy, his wife, pale. Fortunately, both were thin. A woman with the features of Signora Rossini could be considered elegant as long as she was thin.

By now the room was filled with assorted members of the Rossini clan and a swarm of friars led by Alberto. They all maintained a respectful distance from the fresco, except for Vasilio Rossini, who strode forward and examined it with a proprietary air. Only then did he greet Lorenzo Patti, who sat on his cot leaning forward and watching the millionaire with spinning, ferret eyes.

"*Bene, bene!*" said Rossini, putting forth a slender, beringed hand for Patti to take. The instant the painter touched it, the hand was withdrawn. Patti sat eyeing the slice of space Signore Rossini's hand had previously occupied, almost reverentially.

"Yes," said Rossini. "It is marvelous. One can barely tell—I might say, in fact, it is impossible to tell—where the hand of the maestro, Fra Angelico, leaves off, and the hand of the maestro, Lorenzo Patti, begins."

Everyone nodded; Patti dipped his head modestly.

At the first surge of the critics, Gino had withdrawn to one end of the room. His heart was pounding with a dual fear: first, that someone would distinguish the line between his work and Patti's, and second, that no one would notice.

They were all chattering now, including the monks, gesturing, scurrying about, bobbing their heads. One of the friars even climbed the scaffold to study the masterpiece. Gino smiled. These people preened like pigeons in the piazza.

Except for one: a girl who stood beside Signora Rossini. Instantly, Gino knew she was the Rossinis' daughter. Not that she resembled either of them. She was of medium height, taller than her father, but shorter than her mother. Her hair was golden brown, somewhere between the dark and light tones of her parents. Even her nose was something of a compromise; insofar as Gino could determine from this distance, it was perfectly straight.

She looked at him. The look transfixed him. At ten paces, her eyes were a brilliant blue. Nowhere in Patti's palette could he have found so pure and vivid a color. Gino did not realize this vision had drawn him forward until he found himself standing before her.

"I am Gianpaolo Bondone," he said in a hoarse voice, "assistant to the maestro."

She cocked her head in acknowledgment, but without replying. He could think of nothing whatsoever to say. After a long, silent moment, he nodded, as if in response to some remark she had made, and backed away.

After supper that evening, Lorenzo Patti went to sleep early, greatly pleased by the reception of his work. Gino took Benvenuto to the farthest corner of the Hospice and engaged him in conversation.

"It went well, today," Gino said.

Benvenuto nodded, idly picking a chunk of fish from his mouth with his fingers.

"What do you know about the Rossinis?"

Benvenuto shrugged. It was difficult to work the food out from within the random pattern of his teeth.

"You must know something."

"They're very rich."

Gino stifled his impatience. "What else?"

Benvenuto scratched his ear. He was trying to concentrate. One eye wandered in the effort. He grinned. "They live in a palace."

A palace, Gino thought. *What chance have I with a girl who lives in a palace?* "Where?"

Benvenuto looked at him vacantly.

"Where is the palace?" Gino asked in a gentle voice.

"On the Via Tornabuoni. It's big. A hundred rooms, they say. And a hundred servants." He subsided into silence, except for the irritating click of a black fingernail against his yellow teeth.

Gino looked at his hands. They seemed very coarse to him, the fingers too thick, the calluses hard. *I must trim my nails,* he thought. "There was a girl, a pretty girl with blue eyes. Do you know her name?"

Benvenuto thought for a moment. His eyes brightened, even the wandering one. "Giulia, I think."

♦   ♦   ♦

In the days that followed, the vision of Giulia Rossini remained in Gino's head, as if imprinted on a balloon floating at the very edge of his consciousness. He saw her in his daydreams; even when he worked on the fresco, her face often took the place of the saints he was painting. Her expression was ever the same—cool, remote, except for the fiery blue eyes.

Nights were worse. No matter how Gino twisted and turned, no matter what thoughts he conjured up to distract himself, the Giulia balloon came floating back. He was convinced it was pure love, not a sexual infatuation, because he never imagined her body, only her face.

Gino's work began to suffer. Time and again, Lorenzo Patti screeched at him for missing the pumice-outlined edge of the work, or carrying his strokes too long or too broadly, or letting heavy blobs of paint distort his subject. Gino tried valiantly to shake off the apparition that haunted him, and for hours at a time he would be successful, but then suddenly the Giulia balloon would appear and he would run after it, never quite catching up.

When the maestro complained about his work, Gino protested

that he was very tired—it was impossible for him to sleep in the Hospice with Patti and Benvenuto snoring. Annoyed, the maestro nevertheless asked Brother Alberto to find him a room.

The prior assigned Gino to a tiny cell in a dank corner of the monastery. Gino was delighted; separate quarters would give him freedom of action.

It wasn't difficult to locate her home, known to everyone in Florence as the Palazzo Rossini. Once it had belonged to the Strozzis, famous bankers of another age. Gino was told that only the ancient stone exterior remained. The interior had been ripped out and replaced with apartments and furnishings worthy of Versailles, yet with all the modern conveniences.

At every opportunity, Gino slipped from the monastery and stationed himself at some point from which he could survey the Rossini establishment. He chose a different vantage point each time, hoping that no one would notice him. He came to know the building by heart; he could have drawn each elevation from memory, perhaps every stone on each facade.

Some nights, when he returned from his fruitless mooning, the gates were closed and he slept in a nearby park rather than waken anyone. The priory was such a bustling place that he was usually able to slip back in after matins, when the gates reopened.

Patti viewed Gino's haggard, unshaven face suspiciously, but since the maestro still slept in the Hospice, he had no personal awareness of his apprentice's wanderings.

Every time Gino was sent on an errand, he made sure his path led him past the Palazzo Rossini. After a while, he learned to predict the comings and goings of the family. He seldom saw Giulia; and when he did, he was so struck by the sight of her that often he stayed rooted to the spot, instead of following her as he had intended.

It became a dangerous game. Gino now left the monastery every night; soon his absences would be noticed. Instead of going home on Sundays, he stationed himself outside the Rossini home at dawn, observing every person who came and went. How he envied the visitors, particularly the young men. He was convinced they were all suitors of the beautiful Giulia. His insides seethed as he imagined them kissing her hand, chatting with her, laughing—perhaps even caressing her.

He followed the Rossinis and their retinue to the family church, San Lorenzo, and spent the entire service peering through his clasped hands at the lovely girl. Every gesture she made seemed pure and graceful to him. Her smile was gentle and kindly. Her voice, when he heard her speak to her mother as they left the church, was low and melodic.

All she said was, "I hope we're not having veal again for dinner this evening," but the simple phrase was instantly etched on the spinning wheel of Gino's brain. He played it over and over in his mind, like a record, but it never grew worn. What melody! What charm!

From time to time, the Rossinis revisited the Hospice. Giulia always accompanied them. Gino never mustered the courage to approach and speak to her, but he devoured her with his eyes. Once, Giulia happened to glance his way. Their eyes held for a second, but she showed no expression. Gino swallowed his, and eventually she looked away.

When following her through the streets of Florence, he always maintained a distance so discreet that sometimes he lost her. Once he followed her to midweek Mass at San Lorenzo, waiting outside until she reappeared and then trailing her home. She was alone and he could easily have hurried up and spoken to her, but he was too shy. Gino's feeling of stupidity increased his agitation. What good was all this? It might lead to expulsion from the monastery and separation from his beloved fresco.

One Saturday night when he stationed himself across the Via Tornabuoni from the Rossini palace, he noted that most of the casements were draped and only slivers of light slipped through. Other, higher windows were curtained, and from time to time distorted shadows passed across them. Was that Signore Rossini? Or, God willing, Giulia?

Someone looked out. It was a woman, but he couldn't tell whether or not it was Giulia. Every once in a while people passed him on the street and Gino pretended he was lighting a cigarette, or tying his shoelaces.

"She's not inside." The low voice spun him around, stunned him into silence.

It was Giulia Rossini. She laughed. "You follow me about day after day, Gianpaolo Bondone, and when we finally meet face to face, you're speechless."

"You knew? You saw me?"

"A great, dark-haired man like you can't hide himself."

"But my name—"

"—You told me in the Hospice, remember?" She was only a step in front of him now, looking up with luminous eyes that gleamed brightly, even in the pale lamplight.

Gino felt dizzy. "You're out alone? At this time of night?"

Giulia laughed again. "Yes, I was at my aunt's, and I told everyone our chauffeur was downstairs, waiting to pick me up. Before they could question me, I skipped down the stairs and into the street."

"And your chauffeur?"

"Off for the evening. My father expected my uncle to escort me home."

At the back of Gino's mind a flimsy screen of masculine self-regard was beginning to form.

Giulia began to pout. "Is this all you follow me for, to stare at me with your mouth open and question me like the Inquisition? I thought you'd be more interesting."

"What shall we do?" he asked and then, realizing he had asked another question, he spoke firmly. "We'll take a walk."

"*Bene*," she said, placing her hand on his arm.

Gino, carrying this gentle burden on his sleeve, began to stroll down the Via Tornabuoni towards the Arno.

"Is it not lovely this evening?" asked Giulia in a mocking tone, filling the gap in the conversation.

"Forgive me if I'm poor with words. I'm only a peasant and you've surprised me greatly."

"A peasant?" said the girl, "I thought you were a painter?"

"No, merely an apprentice."

"Merely an apprentice; I must say that, for an apprentice, you paint lovely cherubim."

Gino stopped where he stood. "I paint nothing. I only mix colors and apply the plaster."

"Signore Bondone, you're a poor liar. Surely it was you who painted the *putti* in the lower corner of the 'Adoration.'"

"How did you know?"

"I watched your face when my father complimented Lorenzo Patti; you might as well have yelled out loud that you had painted them."

"Mother of God! Does anyone else know?"

"I don't think so. No one seemed to be as interested in your face as I was."

Her words filled him with an unreasonable surge of hope and joy. *What a gem she is, this girl—beautiful, sensitive, compassionate.*

They said little more as they walked along the Arno to the Ponte Vecchio. The shops were closed, but gold still glittered behind the glass, amazing Gino. *Who, these days, can buy such things?*

At the open arches in the middle of the bridge, Giulia led him to the balustrade. They leaned on it and stared into the river, glowing gold in the moonlight.

Gino had nothing to say. It was enough to be standing there, his rough clothes touching her silken dress, his hands but a few inches from hers. He rubbed his fingers against the pitted railing and, strangely, the stone felt as if it had turned to flesh.

"Will you tell your father?"

"That I was out with you? Of course not."

He was insulted, but that was not what he had meant. "I mean, will you tell him that I've been painting the fresco?"

"Do you want me to?"

"No, I'd lose my job. Besides, I'm grateful to Signore Patti. If not for him, I'd still be a starving farmer."

"If not for you, my father might have cancelled the work. There were rumors the maestro was unable to get up on the scaffolding and paint."

Gino did not want to follow this line of conversation. "Meanwhile," he said, "the fresco is being completed and everyone's happy. Why spoil it?"

"Have you no pride?"

"Apparently not. Otherwise I wouldn't have followed you about like a puppy dog."

She was immediately contrite. "I didn't mean that like it sounded, Gianpaolo. What I meant was, don't you want the world to know what you've done?"

"What have I done? Copied a few sketches by Patti, while the master guides every brushstroke? Why should I disgrace my teacher?"

She did not respond.

They stood that way for a long time, staring into the water, not knowing what to say next.

Finally, Gino spoke. "It's late. Isn't your family expecting you?"

She slapped his hand lightly, "Always so practical, apprentice. Are time and money all you think about?"

Gino flushed in the darkness. "What more *can* an apprentice think of? Surely he can't hope to win the love of a beautiful girl."

Giulia realized they were in dangerous territory. "Come along," she said, "you may walk me home."

She offered her hand and he took it. It was so cool and small, it made him ashamed of his own. Surely she must be able to feel every bump and scar and ridge. He tried to hold her hand as gently as he could without dropping it.

Again the girl laughed. "Hold on," she said, "I'm not a fish." She squeezed his hand and he returned the pressure.

The walk along the Via Tornabuoni was euphoric for Gino. The sky seemed incredibly clear, the street lamps marvelously bright. Even in the darkness, each pavement stone and brick and slice of stucco seemed boldly and powerfully formed. When they reached the corner across from the Palazzo Rossini, Gino paused. Giulia sought to pull him ahead, but he resisted.

Giulia sighed. "All right, apprentice. I'll go on alone."

When she was halfway across the street, he started to ask "When—" but he forced back the words before they left his mouth. Nevertheless, as if he had spoken, Giulia turned and sent a long narrow whisper at him: "Tomorrow night, right here."

♦ ♦ ♦

Gino almost danced back to the monastery. Fortunately, the gate was open. Falling into his bed, he enjoyed the soundest night's sleep he had enjoyed since the day he had entered San Marco. The following morning he bounded about the scaffold like a man possessed, smiling at Lorenzo Patti's insults and finishing the day's work long before darkness.

Which left him a great deal of time to prepare for his tryst. But what could he do besides shave very closely and wash his hands and face until the skin felt raw? Then he slipped out of the monastery and crossed the Arno, not stopping until he found a field of wild flowers. Gino picked them with care and tried to arrange them artfully, fussing with them like a mother dressing her daughter for first communion. Finally, he cast most of them away and prepared a simple nosegay.

Gino waited a long time outside the Palazzo Rossini. As the bells in Giotto's Campanile struck eleven, Giulia hurried from a side entrance. Before he could speak, she pressed her fingers to his lips.

"We're having guests and I was able to slip away for only a second." She squeezed his hand and began to run back to the house. He hurried to catch her, and place the flowers in her hands.

Giulia looked at them and then at Gino, reached up suddenly and kissed him. Before he could respond, she was gone.

Although they had made no arrangement for the following night, Gino was waiting. She did not appear. Again on Tuesday and Wednesday he kept his vigil, but no Giulia. He began to doubt her interest. Perhaps it was only a game to her and she was already tired of it.

He could not concentrate on his work. Repeatedly he swept the brush beyond the outlines. Time and again the blemished work had to be scraped away.

Patti was furious. "You're turning back into a shoemaker!" he cried. "The magic is wearing off!"

On Thursday night, Gino resumed his watch, resolving not to come again if she didn't show up. Fortunately she appeared, warm and lively and filled with chatter. They strolled again to the open arches on the Ponte Vecchio. Once more they stood watching the Arno. This time her hand lay on his, tracing the knuckles and the veins. The force of his pent-up desire emanated from every pore—he could feel it leaving him in waves.

"How warm you feel," she whispered.

Taking Giulia by both shoulders, he kissed her long and hard—not quite directly on the lips. When he released her, Giulia didn't move, standing before him, her expression a mystery. When she spoke, it was in a breathy whisper.

"Not like that, Gianpaolo." She reached up and placed her hands behind his neck, then pulled his head slowly down to hers.

◆ ◆ ◆

Each time they met, their lovemaking grew fiercer, but still it remained unconsummated. Once, he picked up a prostitute only minutes after he left Giulia. The moment he left the woman's bed he wanted Giulia.

A few nights later, Gino saw a flutter at a side door of the Palazzo Rossini. The gesture was repeated. Gino fearfully crossed the street.

At the dark side entrance he found Giulia and despite the risk he embraced her.

"My family is very disturbed," she said. "When I returned last night they were waiting in my room. I told them I'd gone for a walk and they forbade me to leave the palace alone at night ever again. We'll have to find another way."

But there was no other way. Night after night he appeared at the side door, to suffer through a single embrace.

"I can't bear it any longer," he told her. "One kiss each night. What do you think I'm made of?"

She took his hand and lifted it to her breast. Gino felt a surge of desire so powerful he could not contain it. He kissed her deeply, passionately, running his hands along her body.

She pushed him away. "Wait," she said. But she didn't wait. Instead she took his hand and pulled him inside the house. He would have fled, but desire overwhelmed his reason. They kissed again and again in the dark hallway. He began pulling open her dress.

"No," Giulia said, but it was an invitation. She took his hand and led him along the hallway. Even in the semidarkness, he could see the towering tapestries, huge paintings and ornate furniture. Silently, they scaled the curving marble staircase, stepping on thick carpeting held in place by brass rods. It was dimly lighted, but no one appeared. In a moment they had hurried down the hall and passed through a door that Giulia gently closed behind her.

A single glance told him they were in her bedroom, faintly illuminated by one small lamp. Giulia turned it off, but the moonlight pouring in through tall windows was enough to show him his Giulia, slipping out of her dress. It settled at her feet in billowing folds. Then her hands were at work in her hair, loosening it. She shook her head and it tumbled about her shoulders, one long strand across her throat.

Like the Botticelli Venus, he thought. He lifted her out of the shell and carried her to bed.

Six

Too Much Is Enough

Each night the ritual was the same. Giulia would let him in at the side door, and together they would make the dangerous journey to her bedroom. Few words were spoken until they finished lovemaking. Sometimes, they dozed a while. Sooner or later, Gino would reluctantly leave the palazzo and return to the monastery.

But he seldom got back in time and was often forced to sleep in public parks. The more he loved Giulia, the leaner and weaker he grew. His work suffered terribly. He used the scraping knife as much as the brush. Had Patti's gout subsided, he would have thrown Gino into the street.

Finally, the maestro sent Benvenuto from the Hospice on a long errand, bade Gino close the door, and motioned him to his bed for a chat.

"My boy, I'm worried about you. You've been growing thinner and so has your work. I've given you a great privilege. I'm sure you appreciate that."

"I'm very grateful, Signore."

"Then what has happened? Your hand shakes where it used to

be firm. You cover less of the surface each day. Some days your work is entirely wasted. Are you well?"

"Oh yes, Signore, quite well."

"Your mother, she's not ill?"

"Oh no, Signore, she's fine." (It might be true. Gino couldn't be certain because he had not been home in a month.)

"I begin to suspect that it's another problem altogether. Yes, I'd forgotten you're a young man. Other juices are flowing in you."

It seemed that Patti was about to uncover his secret.

"No wonder you're so pale and tired. Probably you're not sleeping well, either. There's no need for that, my boy. Lorenzo Patti is not pure devil, believe me. Please, don't say anything. After all, I'm human, too. I get lonely, too. It's only natural. Surely we can help each other."

Gino was so amazed by the widening circles of flesh created by the smile on Patti's face, he did not even notice the man's hand until it came to rest on his knee. This, in itself, did not set him off as Patti continued speaking in a soothing tone.

When Patti's pudgy palm slipped up inside his groin, Gino leapt to his feet. His mind was racing while his mouth worked. "I'm afraid you misunderstand me, sir. I am in love, Signore. With a girl, Signore. That's all there is to it. You see, it's nothing. Absolutely nothing. Believe me, Signore, I'll do better, tomorrow. Good day."

As he hurried from the Hospice, Gino heard Patti mutter, "Ah well, I'll have to be content with that filthy Benvenuto."

◆ ◆ ◆

But Gino's work did not improve. He continued to spend his nights on silken sheets with Giulia Rossini. And in the daytime, not only was he weakened by loss of sleep, but he continually had the sensation of a hand gliding up his pants leg. Whenever he looked down at Patti, the maestro seemed to be staring up at the bulge of his crotch.

Lorenzo Patti became harsher than ever before. If Gino didn't change his ways, the old reprobate was bound to send him packing. He must do better.

That night he decided to shift the burden to Giulia. While steeling himself to speak, he became intrigued by her undressing. Her robe came rustling down to her feet, then her gown. Giulia came floating toward him, a fragrant vessel of warm flesh and delightful contours. Her arms closed behind his neck, her lips met his before any words were spoken.

Later he said, "I'm an artist."

"Yes. That I can see." Her hand came to rest gently on his thigh.

"No, *Amore*, not in bed—at the monastery. With Lorenzo Patti. I must paint. It's my life."

She sat up. "And I'm not your life?"

"Of course, but in a different way. Try to understand. I must paint, if I'm to respect myself. If I'm to be a man."

"You *are* a man." Her hand was moving again, across his belly.

He took it and held it. "Each night we make love. All night. In the morning I slip back into the Hospice, tired from our lovemaking."

"You don't like it?"

"Yes, I love it, but I'm tired. I can't paint. I make errors. The maestro screams at me."

"I'll tell my father."

"No, you mustn't do that. It would be the end of everything."

"What can I do?"

"Don't let me in."

"What?"

"When I come to the door, don't let me in."

"But why?"

"That way I'll go back to the monastery and sleep—in the morning I'll be able to paint."

"What about me?"

"I'll come to you, only not so often. Not every night."

"You don't love me."

"I do."

"Then why do you want to stay away from me?"

"I don't."

"You do, you do! You're trying to get rid of me."

"No, you misunderstand."

She hurled herself upon him, covering him with kisses from head to foot. He protested, but once again the process began, and once more Gino surrendered. His response evidently convinced Giulia that he would not easily give up such bliss. When he tried to speak again, she pressed fingers to his mouth, shook her head and held him against her breast until he weakly nodded assent.

He tried persuading her on succeeding nights, but with similar results. Giulia began to believe he was playing a game, hoping to spur her to even more passionate lovemaking. When she had this brilliant insight she laughed. "Of course, my dear, I understand," she said, and then engulfed him with her love.

He grew thinner. Almost haggard. He staggered from the Hospice to Giulia's bed, from her bed to the Hospice. It was a struggle to hold his hand steady enough to keep Patti from berating him. At the end of the day he was often too tired to eat, too tired even to wash or to shave. He came to his mistress with paint on his hands, paint in his hair. She seemed not to notice. He was beautiful. Delicious. And she was devouring him.

A few nights later, while he was stumbling out of the monastery, Gino found his path blocked by Brother Alberto. "Good evening, my son."

"Good evening, brother."

"What brings you to our gate at this hour?"

Gino wanted to ask the same question, but dared not. "I could not sleep. I thought I might take a walk."

"But it's raining, my son."

"Oh yes, the rain. Since I was a boy, I've loved to walk in the rain."

"Good. I'll walk with you."

"But, Prior—"

"—I, too, love the rain."

A steady drizzle was falling. Gino believed he could hear the individual raindrops striking the monk's tonsured head as they strolled along the street in silence. The rain began to penetrate Gino's shirt. He was shivering.

"You seem unhappy, Gino."

"Me? Oh, no. I'm very happy."

"You enjoy your work?"

"Very much. I'm learning a great deal."

"And the master is good to you?"

"He has taught me everything."

"I see."

Gino couldn't make out the prior's expression in the darkness. Little rivers of rainwater, stored briefly in his thick hair, were beginning to stream across his face. His ardor for Giulia was cooling.

"You seem thin, my son. And rather nervous."

"Oh, no, brother."

"But you sleep so little."

"I do?"

"So many nights you walk by yourself. It's not a good sign."

"So many nights?"

The prior stopped for a moment. "Let me see. According to my count, the last seventeen nights in a row."

"Seventeen?" Gino was truly amazed by this statistic.

"Of course, that's only since I've been counting. It may have been more."

"How did you happen to observe this?"

"I cannot claim credit for that. Lorenzo Patti put me up to it."

"Oh, no!"

"Ah, yes. He said that your work was deteriorating and therefore he directed Benvenuto to spy on you. Benvenuto reported that you left the monastery at night and did not return until morning."

Gino was suddenly angry. "Benvenuto? That little beast!"

"Please, my son. Do not be harsh with him. He is wholly at the maestro's mercy. Anyway, I took up the count from Benvenuto."

"Seventeen nights! Why didn't you say something before?"

The prior sighed. "I kept hoping it would end."

So did I, Gino thought. He was certain his days at the monastery were over.

When the prior spoke again, there seemed to be a smile in his voice. "This must be an affair of the heart."

Fear tightened Gino's throat. The prior's hand rested on his shoulder.

"I thought so."

"But, brother, how did you know?"

"It is the little shaved spot on top of our heads. It begins to tingle when we are near someone who is in love." The prior stopped abruptly. "Have you walked enough in the rain, my son? Let us return to the monastery."

Gino followed Brother Alberto in silence, trembling. Even in the warm, dry sanctuary of the prior's room, he could not stop shaking. His career was about to end, and he would die of pneumonia in the bargain.

But the prior was smiling. "Here, Gino, wrap yourself in this blanket, before your last shriveled remains quiver away." While Gino dried himself, the prior continued speaking: "You are in love. Splendid. You are young and healthy—a bit thin—but healthy. What is the problem?"

"I'm a man tormented. This girl," he did not dare speak her name, "has overwhelmed my senses. I must be with her every night. Every night, Prior. And then, the next morning, the work goes badly. Signore Patti grows angry and he's right. I spill the paint, I botch the *intonaco*. But I'm helpless, you see? Helpless!"

"Why don't you marry her, Gino?"

"It's impossible. She's very rich and I'm very poor. Her family would never permit it."

"Do you *wish* to marry her?"

Gino hesitated. He did not know the answer.

"I see. I would suggest you give her up, but clearly that is impossible."

Gino shook his head. "Impossible."

"But could you not limit your visits to once or twice a week?"

"I'm too weak, brother." The words began to tumble out of him. "I lie in my bunk and think of her. And then it becomes too much for me. I roll out of my bed and go running out into the night. It's not only seventeen nights. It may well be a hundred and seventeen."

"I promised the maestro something would be done."

"You must help me, Brother Alberto. You must stop me from leaving San Marco."

"Ridiculous, this is not a jail. We cannot simply lock you up."

"That's it! Lock me up!"

The prior was laughing, his long face a lacework of intersecting lines. "Gino, this is absurd."

"It's the only answer."

They argued for some time. Finally, Brother Alberto's logic gave way before Gino's emotion. "Very well," he said, "there is a small room, high in the west wing of the monastery, nearly thirty feet above the ground. The door is heavy oak and I can lock it from the outside. We once used it to hold heretics for the Inquisition."

"Splendid!" cried Gino.

"What about during the day?"

"Daytime is no problem. When I'm working on the fresco, I think of nothing else. Only when the painting is done, then the vision of my love overcomes me."

The prior was dubious. "I don't believe this will succeed."

"It must. Each night you lock me away. I'm safe until morning. You let me out and take me to Patti. I work in the Hospice all day. I eat my dinner there with the maestro. After dinner, you take me to the cell and lock me up. Simple, isn't it?"

"Yes, simple," said the prior. "Very simple."

That very night Gino moved his bedding and clothing to the little cell on the top floor of the priory. It was small and dark, but dry and, most important, when Gino looked down to the street the drop so dizzied him that he had to grip the steel bars on each side of the opening.

The prior smiled," I am not sure why our predecessors believed that the bars were necessary. Surely a leap from here would kill anyone."

"Brother, one more thing. No matter what I say, no matter how I protest, you must lock me away here every night."

"Perhaps once in a while, Gino, you can be permitted a night out."

"Not until I'm cured. A month, at least."

The prior sighed. "Very well, my son."

Brother Alberto gave Gino his blessing and left him in the room. The huge, ancient bronze key scraped in the lock. He threw his weight against the door. It did not yield in the slightest.

Gino smiled. He had conquered his devil. That night, he enjoyed a full night's sleep. In the morning, the prior had to enter the room and shake him awake.

He worked with more enthusiasm and energy than he had displayed in weeks. Patti was so delighted he forgot to abuse him. That evening Gino ate his supper with relish. Then he felt guilty about Giulia. But not for long. He was a man; he had to be strong for both of them.

When they locked him in the room that night, his conscience was perfectly and serenely clear. For several nights Gino slept well, and during the day he worked well.

It was time to paint an Annunciation, and Patti had no cartoon of the angel informing the Virgin of her good fortune. It was a section of the fresco for which no photographs were available in the archives. Lorenzo Patti drew the grouping for Gino, but in fact it amounted to little more than a vague sketch.

"There," he said, "nothing left for you to do but fill in the details."

"With a master such as you to guide me everything is easy."

Both he and Patti realized that Gino would have to create the painting himself. In his cell at night, using an oil lamp, Gino tried to detail a satisfactory Annunciation within the vague outlines Patti had provided. It was impossible. The master's angel was leaning too far forward. In that pose, he would have looked like a farmer sowing a field.

The Virgin was also distorted. Other painters had shown her drawing back in surprise from the announcement, but surely not in horror. Gino decided to bring the figures closer together, straighten up the angel without losing urgency, and bring the Virgin's head closer to his.

He had so little experience at drawing, and surely nothing like this. The figures came stiffly from his rigid hand. He loosened his wrist as the master had told him so many times before, and touched the paper lightly, sweeping across it with long, flowing strokes.

With each new attempt, the lines came more easily, the figures emerged more gracefully. But the scene looked nothing like the one Patti had outlined. Patti seemed not to notice the revision, merely nodding in approval.

Completing the cartoon was just a fraction of the task. The details had to be filled in, colors chosen, modeling decided upon, tones selected. Each night, Gino sketched with a pencil on paper, trying to practice the work he would be called upon to complete the following day. He was secretly quite proud of his progress, and burned to have someone know his true contribution.

◆ ◆ ◆

As the days passed and the pattern of the fresco became clearer, Gino's mind had more time to wander. At night, as he sketched the Virgin, outlining the fluid lines of her figure, his thoughts shifted to Giulia. Staring into the flickering light of the oil lamp, he had no difficulty conjuring up the soft arms and abundant bosom of his love. With one angry gesture, he snuffed out the lamp.

But then he could not draw. And in the darkness it was even

more difficult to keep Giulia out of his mind. The feel of her came up through his fingertips, shivering along his arms and down his body. Her image glowed just behind his closed eyelids, her lips trembled only inches from his.

Finally, one night when the prior came to lock him away, Gino protested. "Not tonight, brother. I must see her."

The prior hesitated, "I have given my word, Gino, both to you and to Lorenzo Patti. Shall we ask the maestro for permission?"

Sadly, Gino shook his head. "No, brother, that's the worst thing we could do."

During the day, Patti never took his eyes off Gino. At night he smiled gleefully when the prior came to collect him. The key turning in the lock was a knife twisting in Gino's heart. He tried to walk out of the Hospice during the day. To his surprise, he found that the door was locked.

Lorenzo Patti was giggling. "Benvenuto locks us in here every morning, then gives me the key. If you want to get out, you must knock both of us on the head."

The only choice remaining was to escape at night through the window of his cell. He found he was able to wedge himself between the bars, but from there it was a sheer drop to the street. The following day Gino told the prior it was very cold at night in his room, and Alberto agreeably provided him with another blanket.

Gino ripped his blankets and bedding into strips, twisted them about each other and knotted them together. Stretched end to end this rope measured close to eight meters, but tied around the bars and dropped over the side, it still dangled some three meters above the street. He cursed himself for not having asked for another blanket.

Pangs of desire were beginning to stir him. He took a deep breath, squeezed himself between the bars and, holding onto the makeshift rope, began to walk down the wall. Sensing his rope was loosening, he scrambled more quickly, but the knot gave way and he fell to the ground. The rope piled like a serpent on top of him.

For a moment Gino was stunned. Then his ankle began to ache.

He gathered up his bedding in a bundle and limped a few blocks from the monastery. There he pulled out his knife, cut a bandage from a blanket and wrapped it tightly around his ankle, discarding the rest in an alley.

Giulia, faithful Giulia, was waiting at the door. As they embraced, he twisted his ankle again and had to smother his own cry of pain.

"My God," she whispered, "what have they done to you?"

The sturdy young woman half carried him to her room, helped him onto the bed, then hurried away to find an ice pack to apply to the swelling.

"The monsters," she said, convinced the monks had beaten him. "First they lock you away and then they do this."

"No," Gino said, and explained his escape.

Giulia gasped. "You did this for me? You might have been killed." She covered him with kisses, then cradled his head to her breast, while she loosened his shirt and his belt. "This will let you breathe more easily," she said. But he was breathing more quickly.

As the ice cooled his ankle, Giulia warmed his blood. His hand was inside her gown, his lips were on her breast. Throbbing desire overwhelmed the pain of his throbbing ankle. Only when both lovers were satisfied did Gino's pain return. Worse still, he didn't dare go back to the monastery.

Giulia told him the Rossinis owned a summer villa not far outside Florence. If Gino could make it there, she would join him the following day. He listened carefully to Giulia's directions and, with her help, hobbled out of the house and waved a woeful goodbye. Not half a mile down the road an old man driving a donkey cart offered him a ride. When they reached the crossroads near the Rossini villa, he thanked his benefactor and climbed down from the cart. After the man disappeared, Gino dragged himself the rest of the way.

He found the house locked up; Giulia had failed to give him a key. There were no open doors or windows, no loose boards or missing panes. Limping around to the rear of the house, he gathered a pile of hay from a flowerbed, burrowed into it, and tried to sleep.

At dawn, moving about as best he could, he searched the grounds. The villa was large and the gardens were extensive, though untended. Vines grew over Grecian statues and reflecting pools were choked with foliage and debris. Evidently, not even the Rossinis had dared to maintain two elaborate households in wartime.

Gino came upon a small fountain in the shape of a cupid, from whose mouth a thin, twisting stream issued forth. He drank voraciously, then held his foot beneath it. Refreshed, he combed the grounds for apples and pears that had fallen from trees.

The sun was still young when Giulia arrived and rushed to embrace him, apologizing for having forgotten to give him a key. She had come on foot, bringing little with her so as not to arouse suspicion.

The interior of the villa was an opulent, almost garish blend of the Baroque and Grecian. It was deep in swirling dust, but well equipped. Giulia unshelved linens and blankets and made up a bed for Gino, who fell into it gratefully. Then she rushed about, wielding a broom and dustcloth fiercely and inefficiently, redistributing the dirt. After an hour or more of this, Gino persuaded her to stop by asking for a drink of water. She hurried away, returning with water and open tins of meat and vegetables. It seemed that the house was stocked with canned provisions of every sort.

By noon, Gino had slept a little and Giulia, exhausted by her labors, sagged to the bed beside him.

"You're marvelous," he told her. "You've saved my life."

Giulia glowed with appreciation. The day was warm, but with the shades and shutters drawn it was cool in the room. Gino put forth his hand and unconsciously stroked her arm. One simple caress was a command to her senses.

Each day was an idyll. Giulia arrived early, carrying as much food as would fit into a small bag and providing the balance of his diet from the vast stores of the villa. She bustled about in the mornings playing house. Afternoons they spent in lovemaking and, as Gino's ankle healed, frolicking among the towering hedges and crumbling statuary of the ruined gardens. They ate when they felt like it, slept when they were tired, made love under the open skies.

♦ ♦ ♦

On Sunday morning, when Brother Alberto found Gino missing, he was neither angry nor surprised. The missing blankets told him how Gino had made his escape. The prior thought that Gino would return that night.

But Gino did not return. On Monday morning, Patti complained to him about Gino's absence and Brother Alberto began to worry. He sent a young monk to Gino's family home. The widow Bondone, bewildered and frightened, sent Alberto's messenger to the aged prior of Santa Felice.

Brother Domenico, of course, knew nothing. Returning with the young monk to Florence, he learned from the prior of San Marco the strange tale of Gino's love affair and his escape from the monastery.

"We have checked the hospitals," Brother Alberto said. "Do you think we should ask the police?"

"Not yet," said Domenico. "Give me a few days."

He hurried out of the monastery and made his way back to the house of the widow Bondone. She and her daughter were frantic. The prior did his best to reassure her, then drew Pietro outside and led him to the cortile of the old, crumbling monastery. There, Domenico told him, "You must find Gino."

Pietro laughed. "That's not my problem."

"Ah, but it is."

"I won't involve myself in Gino's affairs ever again. He made me help bury his father. It was a filthy task and it sickened me. If the partisans had seen me, they would have slit my throat. No, brother, never again."

Domenico stared at him for a long time. His tiny gray eyes

locked with Pietro's black ones. In time, Pietro looked away.

"I hadn't wanted to tell you, Pietro. Somehow I thought it was better if you didn't know. But I was wrong; I should have told you long ago."

The long sermon was coming. Pietro turned away; he had no intention of listening.

"Wait," said Brother Domenico, his voice surprisingly loud and strong.

Pietro waited.

"You must go find Gino," said the monk, "because he is your brother."

Pietro laughed. "Of course," he said. "Are not all men my brothers?"

"Gino is your brother by birth. Carlo Bondone and your mother . . . " He hesitated—the words were not easy to say "They lived together in Florence. You were the child of that . . . union."

The words exploded in Pietro's brain—the foolish, ridiculous words of the foolish, ridiculous monk. "You're a fool, brother. You're old and feeble. The years and the war and the hot sun have touched your brain."

Domenico was shaking his head. "No, it's true. Every word. Your mother and Carlo brought you to me to be baptized. They weren't married. You were Carlo's first child, Pietro, his first son. Unfortunately, your mother died soon after. Perhaps I was wrong . . . "

The prior's voice went on, but Pietro did not hear him. Suddenly he knew it was all true. A great stone forced its way up into his throat and he felt he would gag. The hot sun danced off the barren yard and exploded in his eyes.

It's horrible, he thought, *horrible. That animal, Bondone. My father*. His voice escaped from his throat in a strangled cry. "You're mad, prior, mad!" he screamed.

He did not convince himself. His mother—whoever the bitch was—and Carlo. His father. And he had killed him. His own father. A beast, a pig, but his own father. His blood beat in his ears.

Against his temples. If he had known how, he would have cried.

"I'm sorry, Pietro."

"Sorry? That filthy creature was my father and you're sorry. Oh, no, it's disgusting. Absurd and disgusting."

A terrible cackling laugh escaped him.

Domenico shuddered. "So you see, you must find Gino. He is your brother, Pietro, just as Maria is your sister." The friar waited for Pietro to respond, but he did not. After several minutes, Domenico went quietly into his tiny makeshift dwelling, leaning against the wall of the priory.

Pietro sank to his knees. *I made love to my own sister. I slept with my sister and killed my father.* He sat heavily on the ground, a scream growing in his chest, expanding against his ribs. He held it there, forced it down, but it didn't go away.

Finally, darkness came. Slowly, Pietro got to his feet. He opened his mouth and let the scream escape. It was a long and horrible sound, echoing back to him. He sagged. His body was smaller now without the scream.

Pietro found Brother Domenico and spoke without preamble: "Have you told Gino and Maria what you told me?"

"No."

"Good. You must not do so."

"I think it's unwise to hide this information any longer."

Pietro's voice was a controlled shout: "It would have been wise to carry this information with you to your grave!"

Domenico stared at him. "I don't believe so."

"Of course you don't, but now it's too late. I insist that you leave it up to me to determine when the others will learn the truth. Otherwise, a great disaster will overcome all of us and even greater guilt will be on your head."

♦ ♦ ♦

His ankle restored, Gino was running after Giulia in the garden. She danced away, teasing him, until he caught her, pulled loose the knot in her hair, and spilled the long strands down her back. While she struggled playfully, he loosened her blouse and pulled it from her shoulders.

"Very well," she said, unbuttoning his shirt and kissing him, firm breasts melting into his chest. He raised his hands to touch her hair and she was gone, moving through the garden, bare to the waist, breasts swinging freely. Giulia stopped beside a marble statue and leaned against it, imitating the pose of the naked Aphrodite.

"Who is more beautiful?" she asked.

Gino answered with a kiss, holding her against the statue, her head between the marble breasts. "Four beauties," he said, running his hands across the breasts of Aphrodite and Giulia Rossini. "But these are mine." As he bent to kiss them, she kissed the top of his head, her long hair falling over his shoulders.

His hands were busy undoing her skirt, removing her underthings. She wriggled down beside him. Her soft belly and full breasts slipped past his face. Now the lovers were rolling on the grass and he kicked free of his pants. She was on him, biting his ear, kissing his neck, his chest, his waist, his manhood. Her hands were doing marvelous things and he lay there motionless for a moment, content to be adored, to be manipulated in this delectable way.

There was a loud noise. Perhaps a door slamming in the house. They sprang apart.

Another sound. This time definitely from the house. They leaped to their feet now, running about, retrieving their scattered clothing.

When the door in the garden wall banged open, Giulia screamed. Gino stood statue still at the sight of Brother Alberto, Pietro and Signore Rossini. His manhood slumped.

Rossini yelled at both of them and ran about the garden like a hysterical rabbit, chasing first one and then the other. Finally, he selected Gino as his target, catching up with him just as the young man was buttoning his pants.

"Son of a dog!" screamed Rossini. "Filthy vermin of the street!" He began to leap up and beat his fists against Gino's arms and chest. The blows were so ineffectual, Gino deemed it wisest not to resist.

"Animal! Beast! Dung! Son of dung!"

When he leaped higher and began to strike Gino in the face, he found it necessary to fend him off.

"Aha!" screamed the little man. "You'd strike a man more than twice your age, would you?" He retreated a step. "Help me!" he screamed to Brother Alberto and Pietro.

"Stop, Gino!" cried Alberto. "What are you doing to Signore Rossini?"

"Nothing, brother, believe me."

"Nothing?" screamed Rossini. "You've debauched my daughter, you son of a dog!"

"And you!" Rossini screamed at Giulia. "Whore! Slut! Tramp!" He chased her between the hedges, up one path and down another, yelling wild, incomprehensible epithets at the top of his lungs.

Which then gave out. And when his voice gave out, Signore Rossini stopped. He stood in the middle of the path, spread-legged and panting. Tears of embarrassment and anger streamed down his cheeks.

Gino began to feel sorry for him and ashamed of himself. "I'm sorry, Signore—"

"—Sorry?" The little man's whispery, tortured voice took on an ascending hysterical note. "Will you give my daughter back her virginity?"

Gino hesitated, not persuaded that he had personally appropriated this precious commodity. "I'm sorry, sir, believe me—"

But Rossini would not listen. He slapped Gino and then, catching everyone by surprise, ran to his daughter and caught her wrist before she could get away. He began to cuff her face with his other hand—hard blows, not with his palm, but with the side of his hand.

Brother Alberto ran to Rossini and grabbed his arm. "Stop it!" he cried.

Rossini broke free. His expression was black. "You are a dog, yourself, you filthy priest!"

Alberto stepped back and clapped his hands to his face, staring at Rossini in disbelief.

"Yes, a dog, do you hear? A viper in the bosom of our church. Millions I have spent to support you, and this is my reward. Your masters in Rome will hear of this."

He advanced upon Alberto as if to do him violence.

Pietro stepped before him. "I think you'd be wise, Signore, not to strike the prior. For this, no one in authority would forgive you."

Rossini hesitated, then turned to Gino. "But you—you will suffer. I'll have you clapped into jail for the rest of your days."

Pietro raised his hand. "If I may say so, Signore Rossini, I don't think that will help the name of the family Rossini."

Again the little man hesitated.

"Permit me to be accountable for this young man," continued Pietro smoothly. "I assure you he'll never disturb your family again. Now, I strongly urge you to take your daughter home."

Rossini looked about him. His anger—perhaps even his energy, were gone. He hurried to his daughter, grabbed her arm and dragged her through the garden.

Giulia looked appealingly towards Gino. "Help me!" she cried. "Please Gino, help me!"

But he couldn't; Pietro's hand restrained him.

"Please, Gino, I love you!"

Her father's free hand cracked across her lips. She began to cry. They disappeared through the door of the house.

Beyond the walls, beyond the trees, an automobile motor started and a car door slammed. There was a sound that might have been a girl weeping, although perhaps it was just the wind in the garden. The vehicle rattled and skidded across the gravel. Finally, the sound of its passage dwindled away.

Seven

Banished from Paradise

Gino didn't ask how it had happened that Rossini, Brother Alberto and Pietro had found him with Giulia. All he could think of was that somehow Pietro had dissuaded Rossini from having him arrested. "Pietro!" he cried, "God bless you." He tried to put his arm over his shoulder.

Pietro fiercely slapped it down. "You fool," he said coldly. "Follow me."

Gino hurried after him, out of the garden and onto the road. In moments, they caught up with Brother Alberto, walking slowly along the highway, head down.

"We must accompany you back to San Marco," said Pietro. "I assure you it's vitally important."

The prior shrugged and continued walking. Pietro and Gino fell in behind him. It was very hot and dusty on the road. They all walked with their heads down: three men drenched in perspiration; two in humiliation.

In time, they passed beneath the archway of San Marco and into the cool cloisters. As they entered the Hospice, the prostrate Patti rose halfway from his bed.

"Ungrateful wretch!" he cried at Gino. "In what ditch did they find you?"

Pietro towered above the master's bed. "Hold your tongue, maestro. Be grateful if you're not thrown into a ditch yourself."

Lorenzo Patti stared at him, then subsided into an indignant, pulsating, mound of flesh.

Pietro walked to the fresco and examined it with the calm patience of an art connoisseur. Strolling the length of the room, he inspected portrait after portrait—those painted by the blessed Fra Angelico as well as the ones lately drawn by Gianpaolo Bondone.

He motioned to the prior. "You understand, of course."

Brother Alberto shook his head. "No. What are you talking about?"

A black frown flashed across Pietro's features and disappeared into the corners of his eyes. "Look at the Virgin. Are you blind?"

The prior stepped forward, followed by Gino.

"You fools!" Pietro said. "Gino painted the Virgin with the face of Giulia Rossini." He laughed hideously, and everyone else in the room recoiled. "The Mother of God with the face of Giulia Rossini."

While the walls still rocked with his laughter, he ran to Lorenzo Patti. With a single movement, he upended the bed of the gigantic painter. The man literally spilled from the cot and rolled away. In a moment he was on his feet, running after Pietro, who easily avoided his grasp, roaring with laughter all the while.

"Now you see, Prior," yelled Pietro. "Gianpaolo is the artist. Would the great Lorenzo Patti have painted the Blessed Virgin with the face of Gino's strumpet?"

Patti, enraged and bull-like, lumbered after him. Pietro danced away, scaling the scaffold with all the speed of a monkey. This time his laughter bounced off the curved roof of the Hospice and shattered against them all.

Lorenzo Patti sank down on the corner of his bed.

Brother Alberto spoke in a strained, hollow voice. "Is it true, Signore?"

Patti sat motionless, looking as if he had been sculpted in his own flesh.

"You leave me no choice," said Brother Alberto. "I must tell Signore Rossini."

"Hold, pious prior!" cried Pietro. He slipped from the scaffold to the floor. "What good will it do to tell Rossini? Will he forgive us, do you think? Will the gentle Angelico's fresco ever be restored? And what of the reputation of Signore Patti? Oh, it's true that some of the work was done by my dear friend, Gianpaolo, but who taught him how to do it? Are we to destroy Lorenzo Patti because he has given the world another artist? I hardly think you would call that God's justice."

Brother Alberto paused. "What do you propose?"

Pietro smiled. "I'll speak to Signore Rossini myself. He's certain to give me an audience. After all, it was I who led him to his daughter."

Gino lunged at Pietro, but Alberto restrained him with an arm. "What will you tell Rossini?" asked the prior.

"Trust me, brother. Put your faith in Pietro Scegli."

♦ ♦ ♦

Brother Alberto reluctantly permitted Pietro to stay in the monastery, sharing with Gino the very same room from which he had escaped only a week before.

"Why didn't you warn me?" Gino asked. "You could have saved us all this embarrassment."

"A few hours ago you were grateful I had rescued you from Rossini. A few days ago you pleaded with Brother Alberto to save you from your own passion. I'm doing just that."

"I don't see how."

"You'll see, Gino. But first I must get some respectable clothes in which to meet Rossini. Have you any money?"

"A few hundred lire."

"Not enough. I'll be back late tonight. You'll open the gate."

Before Gino could say another word he was gone.

When Pietro returned he was carrying a bundle. Inside it was a suit in reasonably good condition, a pair of shoes, a shirt, clean underwear and a tie. Gino didn't have to be told the clothes had been stolen.

That night, Gino and Pietro stayed in adjoining cells in the cloister. In the morning, the prior sent one of the monks to Rossini to request an appointment. In less than an hour the meeting was arranged.

Pietro extracted a few lire from Gino, then insisted he accompany him to a shop where he had himself shaven and his hair cut. Afterwards, he took a room—with a bath—in a day hotel, and carefully bathed and dressed himself while Gino watched. The transformation was remarkable. Pietro looked positively bourgeois.

"Wait here, apprentice," Pietro said. "The sorcerer must begin his work."

♦   ♦   ♦

The grandeur of the Palazzo Rossini did not intimidate Pietro. Although he had never been within its ancient walls, the establishment was precisely what he had expected. An unsmiling attendant admitted him to an anteroom and instructed him to wait there until he was summoned.

An hour passed. Pietro remained unruffled, having anticipated this tactic. He used the time to inspect the palace. No one had given him permission to do so; he simply left the anteroom and wandered about. *Obscene*, he thought, *that one man—one family—should own all this*. He admired the Rossinis for having stolen such wealth from the fools of Florence.

He returned to the anteroom at almost precisely the moment that one of Rossini's retainers came to fetch him. The man made a single, disdainful gesture and turned on his heel.

Rossini's office was easily a dozen meters square, and the ceiling was at least seven meters high. Tall windows opened out onto the garden, and the bright noon sunlight bounced off polished flooring and furniture and flashed off the gilt ceiling. The walls were covered with ancient tapestries in fine condition and the rug on the floor was worthy of an oriental potentate. Elegantly carved chests and tables, a marble dado around the walls—all this and more, Pietro took in with one sweeping glance, yet his grave expression did not change. The surroundings served only to sharpen his desire to conquer this merchant lion.

Rossini sat behind a desk over three meters long, easily two meters deep, placed squarely between the windows. The size of it, the reflectance from its polished surface, diminished Rossini physically, but at the same time made him seem ominous. His mustache was waxed, he wore gold-rimmed glasses, and his hands were folded together on the desk before him.

Without waiting for an invitation, Pietro seated himself across from Rossini and folded his hands together on the desk. The two men sat this way for a few moments—knuckles facing knuckles, eyes unblinking.

"You requested this appointment," Rossini said.

"Yes," said Pietro, sitting back comfortably in his chair. "We have a mutual problem, Signore."

"We?"

"It's really your problem. I personally have no deep interest in the matter, except to make certain that the appropriate action is taken."

"I see."

"Do you? That makes everything much easier. Shall we proceed at once to the core of the situation? I know you are a man of important affairs." (Rossini began to work his folded hands against each other, as if he had a nut between them and intended to crack it). "With my help, Signore Rossini, you have learned your daughter is involved with a young man of my village. This man is no friend of mine, Signore. However, I happen to know his family and I have decided to help them settle the matter as quickly and painlessly as possible."

"The matter is already settled."

"If you thought so, you wouldn't have agreed to our meeting."

"State your business."

"Your daughter is in love with this peasant and very likely hasn't ceased wailing since you drove her away in your automobile."

Rossini's hands closed once more with an annoying bellows action. Pietro calmly watched the blood leave the knuckles.

"You still haven't stated your business."

"Forgive me, Signore, but this is not business—it is an affair of the heart and, therefore, more difficult to resolve."

"I believe you exaggerate the importance of this . . . dalliance. It is but a fleeting infatuation."

"Nevertheless, let us assume for the moment, that it's more serious than you suggest. What then?"

"Well, what then?"

Pietro paused again. "I think, Signore Rossini, that if we cannot inoculate the patient, we must dispose of the germs."

Rossini removed his glasses and placed them on the table, where they stared up at Pietro. There was no more expression in one set of lenses than the other. "How do you propose to do this?"

"We must send Gianpaolo Bondone far away."

"How can we be sure he'll go?"

"That will be my responsibility."

"How can we be sure he won't return?"

"I will be with him every second."

For the first time, Rossini's face showed expression. He smiled thinly. "Where?"

"At least as far as Paris."

"At least as far as Paris," Rossini repeated.

Signore Rossini's expression changed again. The situation was beginning to resolve itself into terms he understood. "How much will this pilgrimage cost me?"

"Very little, really. Train fare for the two of us to France, enough to keep us alive until we find employment. Not much more."

"Your terms may be tolerable, Signore, but what guarantee can you give me that you'll do what you say?"

"What is there to lose? A few lire? You'll never miss them. And at the very least, we'll have Gianpaolo out of Florence for a while. Time for your daughter's infatuation to subside. And, perhaps even more important, she will be furious when she learns that you have been able to buy him off—for a handful of coins."

"Please translate all of this into lire."

Pietro stated a figure; Rossini reached into a drawer, pulled out a neat pile of fresh bank notes bound with a strip of paper and spun them across the desk.

"I wager there are other clusters of currency inside that drawer, Signore—several of them—each at least as large."

Rossini frowned, obviously wondering if he should have haggled.

"You need not be concerned, Signore. I'm well aware that what I am offering you is worth more than I've asked. I set this low price so you will understand there is very little in this for me. I want you to remember me with favor."

Rossini looked as if he could barely keep from laughing.

♦ ♦ ♦

"Why on earth should I go to Paris?" Gino raged around the room in the day hotel, while Pietro carefully removed his good clothes and folded them into a neat pile.

"I suppose jail would be better?"

"Who would turn me in? Rossini? You yourself said he would not do that."

"He wouldn't turn you in for seducing his daughter. But trust me, he'd find something. Trespassing on his land, or stealing artworks from his villa. You'd never be able to take a step without looking over your shoulder."

"You mean he can drive me from my own home just because I slept with his daughter?"

"Have you no consideration for anyone else? What about Lorenzo Patti, who taught you how to paint? Brother Domenico who brought you to San Marco and Brother Alberto who sheltered and protected you? What about your mother? Your sister? Are you going to bring shame and dishonor down on all of them?"

Gino subsided under this assault, guilt flickering through him. "It doesn't seem fair."

"Is it fair that Patti should be thrown out of the monastery and the work on the fresco never completed?"

"What has that to do with me?"

"I have Signore Rossini's promise that if you leave Florence, he'll permit Patti to complete the fresco."

"Did you tell him I did some of the painting?"

"No. He hasn't yet recognized his daughter's face and neither has his wife. In all probability they'll never recognize her. When they go to the Hospice they're both too vain to wear spectacles."

"Someone is bound to notice the resemblance and tell him."

"They wouldn't dare. Besides, what does it matter? It could have been Patti, you know? Great painters have often used lovely women as models for the Virgin. It is an honor." He was smiling grimly. "Come on, I'm ready. We'll return to the monastery."

Still very troubled, Gino followed him out of the hotel. "Who will take care of my mother while we're gone?" he asked.

"Signore Rossini has found a place for her in the house of one of his friends. An easy job, more like a grandmother watching her grandchildren, and she'll be living in a fine home."

"Leaving her own home?"

"She'll be better off than she is now."

"And Maria?"

"Maria will work in Rossini's palace."

Gino grabbed Pietro's arm and shoved him against the nearest wall. "I thought you loved my sister? How can you leave her here as a hostage?"

"Do you think this is easy for me? Am I to blame because you've gotten all of us in trouble? Do you think I'm happy to be exiled among the French? We must all suffer because of you."

♦ ♦ ♦

Gino roamed about the corridors of San Marco while Pietro spoke to Brother Alberto. Why was Pietro helping him? What was Gino Bondone to Pietro Scegli? It was clear Pietro was anxious to get out of Florence. What was driving him?

Pietro bounded down the steps, smiling broadly, and clapped Gino a blow on the back. "The prior is very happy to retain Patti, the fresco, and Rossini's money. Now go say your goodbyes to him while I take on Signore Patti."

Brother Alberto sat stolidly behind his desk and did not rise when Gino entered.

"I'm deeply sorry, brother, for the trouble I caused you, Signore Patti and the monastery. I hope you will forgive me."

Alberto spoke in flat, clipped tones. "I forgive you; I hope the Lord does the same."

"Thank you, brother, and thank you for all the kindness you showed me and the opportunity you gave me to learn a wonderful profession."

There was no response. "Will you give me your blessing, brother?"

The prior made a quick sign of the cross. Gino backed out of the room, hurried down the stairs and outside the gates, his head down, feeling even worse than before.

Within the Hospice, Pietro was talking to the maestro. "You should be very grateful that I've saved your commission."

"Thank you." The words were fairly spat at Pietro.

"It's always a pleasure to assist a great man, especially a great artist."

Patti said nothing, impatiently waiting for Pietro to state his true business.

"Still, it's not so good for Bondone. What will he do in Paris?"

Patti shrugged.

"I'm sure a famous artist like you has friends there, people who can help this boy. Gino is very talented as you know. Look at the head of the Virgin. Lovely, isn't it? Hard to believe that anyone so inexperienced could paint such a masterpiece. A veritable Massaccio, don't you think?

"Yes, a veritable Massaccio."

"Surely you must know someone who could help a 'veritable Massaccio.'"

"There's been a war, if you hadn't noticed. What friends I once had are now scattered to the winds. Besides, they're not fond of Italians in Paris these days."

"There must be someone."

"Even if I knew someone, which I do not, what good would that do Gino? They're not painting frescoes in Paris, or anywhere else for that matter. I doubt your friend wants to return to shoemaking."

"Leatherworking," replied Pietro. "Gianpaolo is no more a shoemaker than you are."

"I know no one."

"Strange. Surely you know Pierre Petit?"

Lorenzo Patti's eyes widened, which is to say they expanded to the size of small collar buttons.

"What do you know about Pierre?"

"That he's your brother. That he moved to France twenty-five years ago and changed his name. That he's a painter, a great painter of murals."

"Where on earth did you learn all this?"

Pietro smiled. "From Brother Alberto. According to him, when the war began your brother was in the midst of painting a series of huge canvases in oil to be mounted on the ceiling of the Palais de Chaillot. If the work was resumed after the war—well, surely the perfect place for Gino to work is at the side of your brother."

"How will you get into France? And once there, who says the French will give you a permit to work?"

"That's not your concern. Write us a beautiful letter to your brother, extolling the talents of our young artist. We'll do the rest."

"You'll do the rest. Oh, that is too good, too good. You want a letter from me to my brother. Oh, splendid. Splendid!"

He wrote a letter praising Gino effusively.

"Here," he cried, "here is Gino's passport to fame and fortune. Please extend to my brother my deepest love and affection." He began to laugh again.

"What is so amusing, Signore?"

"I'm so pleased at the thought of Gino working with my brother that I laugh aloud. Would you rather see Lorenzo Patti cry?"

♦ ♦ ♦

Leave-taking was a terrible strain for everyone. The train from Rome was late and the platform was jammed with people and bags. Gino and his mother, Maria and Pietro, stood huddled together, buffeted constantly by hordes of travelers who cursed them with snarls and glares for blocking the center of the platform. They held their position precariously, now withdrawing under the onslaught of a new group of travelers, then reestablishing their beachhead in the midst of this human sea.

It was very noisy—travelers yelling at each other and the world, agents crying out indistinguishable names, a loudspeaker with a deep yawning tone that rode in waves above the crowd, whistles screeching, trains choking and coughing.

Gino said goodbye to his mother and sister a dozen times. But the train did not arrive and the leave-taking grew more and more anticlimactic. How many times could they burst into tears and hug each other?

Pietro sat on a suitcase and studied them disdainfully. Maria tried to nuzzle him once or twice, but he turned his head and stared up at the broken glass vault of the station. Finally, after a number of false cries from train watchers, the wheezing engine dragged herself into the station. She was old and crumbling and the sound of her wheels on the rusty rails was an agonizing wail, but she was in.

Then began the struggle to find a seat in the smelly, third class compartment. Pietro quickly staked out a corner near a window, prepared to defend it against all comers. When the muscular Gino arrived, the others ceased to quarrel with Pietro.

Gino forced his way to the window and looked for his mother and sister. It was not easy to distinguish them among the many shawled heads on the platform. The crowd looked to Gino like a gigantic garden, planted with hundreds of dark flowers, closed against the lowering sky.

A head lifted and he caught sight of a pale blossom that was his sister's face. Then, his mother's. They stood together, hands to their mouths, anxiously scanning the windows. Finally, they noticed his frantically waving arms. He blew them kisses and yelled endearments, which they could not hear. They waved back and touched their fingers to their lips over and over again.

For a fleeting second, Gino thought he recognized Brother Domenico and he tried to yell a greeting, but the monk—if it was Domenico—did not seem to see or hear him.

Eight

City of Light—and Darkness

The train ride was a nightmare. A hot wind carrying dust and cinders blew in over the tops of the open windows. The car was filled with smells, most of them bad: urine, sweat and only God knew what else. The food smells, when mingled with the others, turned rancid and unpleasant. It was worse than a troop train.

They made dozens of stops, sometimes in cities and towns, other times in the countryside. Twice they halted for emergency repairs to the roadbed. Over and again the boilers had to be slaked to avoid disaster. They were not permitted to debark when the train stopped, and then the heat in the cars was even worse.

Gino was sure he was going to be ill—he would almost have welcomed it to be rid of the throbbing queasiness he felt. Unfortunately, his stomach was strong enough to prevent an accident, but not strong enough to leave him in peace. He remained in a kind of peptic purgatory for the entire journey.

Pietro lounged on the wooden seat and closed his eyes as if he were sleeping. *How strange,* he thought. *Gino fears what lies ahead, and I fear what lies behind.* He had a sudden vision of the gold tooth in Carlo Bondone's mouth glaring at him and the crunch of Bondone's shoe against his face. No wonder the beast had been so angry. The misbegotten son and the well-begotten daughter rolling together in the fields.

And Gino. The one man in the entire world to whom he was bound by blood. *I needed him to get out of Florence. Away from Maria. Away from the horrible memory of Carlo Bondone. Now I'm free. When the train reaches Paris, I can slip away. I'm carrying the money.*

There were no difficulties at the border; the papers provided by Signore Rossini took care of everything. Surely it could have been a problem because a large number of Italians were turned back by the French authorities.

In France, the roadbed was a little better. Gino managed to sleep for a few precious minutes during the night. For the rest, he sat in anguished silence, absorbing the jolts of the train, the snores and smells of his fellow travelers. How he envied Pietro, sleeping tranquilly.

On the afternoon of the second day, they reached Paris. The train lurched to a halt in the Gare St. Lazare, and the passengers climbed over one another in their haste to escape. In the immense station, trains filled every siding. Little puffs of steam rose from the cars, and they walked through a misty sea. Whistles shrieked eerily in the half-light, echoing against the towering glass and steel vaults of the dome and sending shivers down Gino's spine.

Pietro pushed ahead. *Now is the time to escape*, he thought. Glancing back, he saw Gino's frightened face bobbing above the crowd, frantically searching for him. He tried to turn away, but couldn't. He felt like he was wrestling with his own body; as if his legs were rooted to the platform and the rest of him was trying to twist around. Gino saw him and waved both hands over his head.

Damn! Pietro thought. *I can't do it. I don't know why, but I can't. Not now.*

♦   ♦   ♦

Paris. Emerging from the station, Gino was terribly disappointed. A thin rain fell from a seamless gray sky. The streets were gray, the buildings were gray—even the people seemed gray. It was as if someone had pulled the stopper, and drained the color from the bottle. This gray was not a color—only a shroud pulled over the city. He turned to Pietro.

"What did you expect?" Pietro asked. "Tulip fields in Holland? This is Paris in September, the grayest city on one of her grayest days. But I love her just as she is."

Gino was amazed that Pietro so easily divined his thoughts and even more surprised to hear him use the word "love." Gino shuddered, perhaps from the rain, perhaps at the thought of someone who loved not a man or a woman, but a city.

Pietro asked a passerby something—in French. Another surprise. "I didn't know you spoke French."

"You think everyone is a peasant like you. Come on. We must find a room before we drown."

They toted their bags through the streets, up the rue d'Amsterdam to the boulevard Clichy, and then through a series of small streets. The green and red lines on the maps of Paris had come alive for Pietro. He smiled with pleasure at each monument he recognized, each street sign that read as he expected. He walked quickly, laughing when Gino took the wrong turn, enjoying the look of bewilderment on his face. Gino, now carrying both satchels, hurried to keep up.

"Tell me where we're going."

"Montmartre, a district where many artists live. You should be happy among your own kind."

The district was shabby, rundown, decrepit. In the persistent drizzle it seemed even worse, and Gino felt a deep longing for Tuscany. There, when it rained, the pale earth turned rich brown, the fields became a dense, vibrant green, and even the stucco buildings took on a warmer, deeper tone. Here, all was dismal gray.

The streets climbed upward—twisting, cobbled streets verged by narrow houses, all with closed shutters. Pietro pointed out the two ancient windmills in the rue Lepic, but they gave no promise of fields and sunshine, only shades and abandonment. And still it rained.

At Number 39 in the rue Lepic, Pietro saw a sign offering rooms. He pulled on the bell and, after a long wait, the door opened a slit. A tiny old lady asked Pietro his business and he pointed to the sign. She did not smile as she beckoned to them.

Inside, the narrow, irregular corridor was dark and damp. They followed the old lady up groaning stairs to the top of the house. At the upper landing, she opened the door to a dingy room. Pietro discussed price briefly, handed her a few francs and took the key in exchange.

The room had a high, sloping roof with exposed rafters, cobwebs clearly visible among them. One large window looked out over the rue Lepic, and a smaller one faced an alleyway next door. The walls had once been covered with some garish floral paper, but much of it had peeled away, revealing the cracked plaster wall. There was no rug and the floorboards were so warped you could get dizzy walking over them. Rain dripped in under the eaves and ran down along the wall next to the window, leaving a small puddle on the floor.

"There should be quite a good view from here," Pietro said. "Wait until the first clear day."

Gino wept inside himself.

♦ ♦ ♦

The morning was marvelously bright and clear. Hardly a cloud marred the sky. Paris stretched away, gray to be sure, but modulated here and there with patches of green and rust, and of course the blue sky.

But where was Pietro? At that very moment, the dark gentleman entered the room, waving a small, scored melon and some rolls—breakfast. Afterwards, they had coffee at a bistro in the rue Lepic, then walked back to the Gare St. Lazare. From there, Pietro permitted them the luxury of a bus. They traversed the boulevard Haussmann, Gino's head swiveling from side to side as he scanned the broad, tree-lined avenue. Leaves were falling from the trees, catching and glinting back the autumn sun. The bus rocked gently. The city was not so austere after all.

They circled the Arc de Triomphe, which Gino found impressive, but hardly beautiful, and with only the briefest glimpse of the Champs-Élyseés, turned into the avenue Kléber. In moments they reached the place du Trocadéro and at Pietro's signal they swung off the bus.

The Palais de Chaillot was filled with people, but no one seemed to know where Pierre Petit might be found. At first, they were directed to the great collection of Gothic murals assembled in the museum. These were most impressive and Gino would have liked to study them, but it was not the place to find Petit, and Pietro hurried him out.

They reached the great inner court of the Palais. Astonished by its size and grandeur, they stopped in their tracks, looked up and saw several workmen holding large panels of painted canvas on a scaffold rising almost to the peak of the vaulted ceiling. The panels swung precariously, and a man, evidently in charge, screamed at the workmen.

"It must be him," Pietro said. "We'll get his attention and introduce ourselves."

To Gino, this hardly seemed to be an auspicious moment for an interview. "Maybe we should return some other time," he suggested.

Pietro spoke scornfully: "Artists are by nature ill-tempered. If we wait for a day when the great man is happy and agreeable, you'll never have a job." Nevertheless, he sat down, cross-legged on the floor, leaned back against a pillar and watched.

Pierre Petit was a slender, angular man with plastered down hair and a pencil-thin mustache, wearing a dark suit, white shirt and dark tie under an open, paint-splattered white smock. Except for the smock, he looked more like a banker. Petit stood near the wall, where the curve began, so tall he had to stoop to avoid hitting the ceiling.

The sullen workmen lifted the panels again, the winch creaking on every turn. Once more the panels edged together. The line of merger was the belt of a soldier's uniform.

"Lower, you fools, lower! That's his belt, not his necktie."

The workmen grunted and eased the panel down a notch.

"Perfect. Now, easy. Together. Easy!"

The soldier racing across the battlefield was a huge distorted figure, his face lean and haggard, bearded like a Hebrew prophet's.

The panels bumped. The bottom edge of the wood frame split away. Petit stood up suddenly, cracking his head. "Mother of God! Look what you've done!"

He ran across the sagging boards. "A hammer!" he said. "A hammer!"

The tool was thrust into his hand. He joined the wood with solid strokes that echoed off the arched ceiling, while the men stood about grumbling. Petit dropped the hammer and its owner sprang to catch it before it bounced off the scaffold.

"My hammer!" the workman cried.

"Your hammer?!" Petit roared. "My painting!"

His tone changed, the words became exaggeratedly gentle. "We begin again. It's simple really. Just two pieces of canvas on wood. We bring them together like this. And then, bang, bang, we attach them to the walls."

He knelt lower to avoid the ceiling. Once again, the winch began to wind. Click, click went the gears. The rope edged downward. The two panels swung closer. The belt matched perfectly. "*Bien! Bien!* Just so. Keep going. We'll have it in a moment. Closer! Closer! Just a few centimeters now."

Suddenly, the panels swung apart. The winch unwound and the men began lowering the panel to the platform.

"Don't stop! It was perfect. Perfect!" He held both hands outstretched, pleading.

The foreman smiled maliciously. "Sorry, Monsieur. Time for lunch."

"Not yet. First the panels."

The men were putting away their tools and climbing down from the scaffold, grinning, almost laughing, at Pierre Petit as they disappeared over the side.

"Stupid, ungrateful idiots!" he screamed. "I'll replace you all!"

The men, ignoring him, climbed to the bottom and sauntered lazily out of the Palais.

Petit sighed and began to clamber down from the scaffolding. Removing his smock, he wiped his forehead as he crossed the floor. Pietro tugged at Gino's arm. He twisted his hat in his hands and moved forward reluctantly. Petit tried to walk around them, but Pietro had hold of his sleeve.

"Excuse me, Monsieur," he began in strongly accented French.

Petit pulled away. "Not now."

"It must be now."

Pierre Petit began to stride away at a very fast pace. But Pietro was running alongside him, while Gino lumbered behind.

"We've come a thousand miles to see you."

Petit stopped. "A thousand miles?"

"Yes," Pietro said. "We come from Florence, bringing greetings from your dear brother."

He held out Patti's letter.

Petit ripped it open. When he had read it, he began to laugh. "A letter of introduction from my brother. You morons. I knew you were morons the moment when I saw you. But this, this!" He could not stop laughing. Gino had been struggling to understand Petit's French, but the meaning of the piercing laughter was unmistakable. He tried to pull Pietro away, but he wouldn't move. "Isn't Signore Patti your brother?" he asked.

"I've been trying to forget that for over twenty years. I left Italy to get away from him. You took this letter and traveled a thousand miles with it. Surely Lorenzo is no friend of yours. He wouldn't have given you the letter if he were. He hates me, and I don't care if he rots in hell."

Gino and Pietro huddled together, staring at him.

"Eat the letter," Petit said. "That's all you'll get from me."

They watched him stalk away down the corridor, neither of them having the courage to follow him. Pietro attempted a smile. It came out thinly, and unconvincingly. "We won't give up. There must be something we can do."

"Maybe we should return to Florence."

Pietro scowled. "We can't go back to Florence. I gave my word to Signore Rossini."

"Never?" The question was almost a scream wrenched from Gino's throat.

"I didn't say never, but not for some time. We've only been gone a few days." He tried to look confident as he began walking briskly out of the Palais.

"Excuse me, Pietro, I have an idea. It's a simple idea, very stupid I'm sure, but maybe it will work."

Pietro said nothing.

Encouraged, Gino continued: "Suppose I come to the Palais every day early—even before the workmen arrive—and remain until they go home. Perhaps I'll have a chance to talk to the master, perhaps not. But if I come faithfully every morning and spend the entire day patiently waiting, he's bound to notice me, eventually to talk to me, and at last to take pity on me and give me work."

"You want to come here every day and beg for work? Petit will have nothing but contempt for you."

"Do you have a better idea?"

♦ ♦ ♦

Pietro awoke long before Gino. Of course. The great, clumsy ox slept like a lamb. *Why not?* Pietro thought. *I'm the one who always has to solve our problems.* He had been certain that Gino would find work with Petit. But the artist's disdainful dismissal had ended that scheme, deeply bruising his pride.

Suddenly he was up and out of the bed, not anxious to see Gino before he had a plan. He would not be embarrassed in front of him again. Gino rolled over in his sleep, but still did not waken. Disgusted, Pietro placed a few francs on the table and slipped from the room.

The Paris that Pietro had studied in old photographs and ancient city plans shimmered before him. He knew this city almost as well as Florence. And this was a true city—not a slumbering village along the Arno. To hell with Florence and its artistic wonders, this was the real world.

Pietro stopped for rolls and coffee, again testing his French. He knew that he rolled his r's too resonantly—not having mastered the correct technique of touching his tongue to the roof of his mouth, but that would come.

On the street again, he stopped at a kiosk. Newspapers were plastered up and down it, journals from all over the world. One paper, tabloid in size, caught his eye. The format was crude compared to the elegant *Le Monde*. Headlines were set in large block letters, printing was imperfect, some of the letters broken. On impulse, he bought it.

Liberté. How appropriate, he thought. *I, too, am struggling to be free.* Pietro soon discovered that all the stories read like propaganda. They were polemics—against the government, against the Americans, against most of the world. Moscow, however, came off rather well.

Communists. A party. Discipline. A cause. This he understood well. What difference if the surface ideology differed from the fascists? Underneath it was all the same. He searched the inside pages for the address of the publisher.

Liberté was located in a nondescript building in a run-down section on the left bank of the Seine near the Sorbonne. On the first floor was a tailor shop. Pietro climbed steep stairs to a cramped, loft-like room divided into open cubicles, partitioned only waist-high. There seemed to be considerable activity, much of it disorganized. This was mildly surprising. He had expected the French variety of communists would be more disciplined than the Italian.

Pietro was greeted with suspicion, particularly when he asked to see the editor. The editor was busy and could not see him now. Very well, he would wait. Pietro sat down in a squeaky, wooden chair with one arm missing. No sooner had he seated himself than a woman stood before him. A short, slovenly woman, wearing no makeup, her hair hanging free in uneven strands, steel-rimmed glasses at the edge of her nose.

"What do you want?" she asked.

Pietro stood up with graceful nonchalance, measuring her ankles, thighs, waist and breasts along the way. Perhaps under that shapeless dress, there was a woman.

"Good day, Madamoiselle," he said. "May I ask who it is I have the pleasure of addressing?"

"The editor."

His eyes widened. "I see. One does not expect to find a young, attractive woman in such a position."

Her eyes narrowed, but she did not seem affronted.

"You're not French," she said.

"Italian."

"I thought so." The words were spoken with a faint touch of disdain.

Pietro was not put off. "Of course," he remarked, glancing about the office, "in this great undertaking a man's nationality is not important. It is the cause that matters." He smiled a bit when he said it, not enough to show contempt, just enough he hoped to indicate his sophistication.

"Yes," she said. "The cause."

All the while, she was measuring him. "What do you want?"

"Work."

"Are you a typesetter, a printer—what?"

"A writer."

"We have no need for writers. Each day we turn away a dozen 'writers' from the university. I doubt your French is as good as theirs."

"No, of course not. But then, I'm not a wide-eyed student; I'm a man. I make up in skill and experience what I lack in literary grace."

The woman was not impressed.

Pietro hurried on. "And I have been, shall we say, in the field? I know what this is all about. I have seen men fight and die for the cause. There is, I think you'll agree, some merit in that."

"Who sent you?"

"No one. I read your paper and realized this was what I wanted."

"Why did you leave Italy?" Her lips were not set as firmly as before.

"Not all the fascists in Italy are dead," he said. "It wasn't safe for me there."

She waited; there was an unasked question.

"I'm not a member of the party. I never was. My comrades thought it was better that way. In fact, I was a double agent—a nominal member of the *Fascisti*. It was very useful, but dangerous. When they learned they had been betrayed, they were furious."

For the first time, she smiled. "I still don't see what you can do for us."

"I speak and read both French and Italian. I know a smattering of Spanish and English. I'm still in contact with my friends in Italy. I can be your resident foreign correspondent."

She laughed, removing and pocketing her glasses. Then she swept her hair back over her shoulders. Pietro managed to look at her approvingly.

"Very well," she said. "You're hired."

"Splendid," Pietro said.

"By the way, Signore Correspondent, what is your name?"

"Pietro Scegli. And by the way, Mademoiselle Editor, what is the salary?"

They both laughed.

◆ ◆ ◆

When Gino awoke, Pietro was gone, having left a few francs on a table, presumably to buy food. Gino decided to walk to the Palais de Chaillot to begin his vigil.

When he reached the great hall, the workmen had already joined the panels which had frustrated them the day before and were struggling with another section. Gino hunched down on the floor and watched patiently, not even leaving to eat lunch. When he finally went home, the master had long since departed, apparently unaware of him.

Pietro was waiting, smiling and cheerful and swinging a bottle of wine in his hand. "Have a drink with me. I've joined the ranks of the employed."

"Really? what kind of job?"

"I'm now a *journaliste* with a Paris newspaper, *Liberté*, a very intellectual journal. They need someone who speaks as many languages as I do." He frowned momentarily. "What did you do today, shoemaker?"

Gino hung his head.

"I see. You begged at the Palais de Chaillot and I presume the great man ignored you. Of course. Come, drink from the bottle and then we'll have a decent meal for once."

They had eaten so little in the past several days that the wine found no barrier between their bellies and their brains. Gino marveled at his companion; to see Pietro laughing freely, even singing, was a revelation.

They ate at a bistro with its storefront open to the street. Pietro's pleasure was so infectious that before long others came to their table to joke and sing with him. Gino smiled and drank and ate, but said nothing.

"Has he a tongue?" one man asked, and Pietro roared with laughter.

"Don't mind him, he's a simple fellow who wouldn't hurt a soul, a shoemaker, kind and harmless."

◆   ◆   ◆

Gino watched each day as Pierre Petit waged a battle with his workmen which was nearly as bitter as the one he depicted in his murals. They made staggering errors. The winch repeatedly shot a gear and had to be repaired. Knots appeared mysteriously in the ropes. Boards that had been smooth and flat the night before were unaccountably warped in the morning. Tools were lost. Time was lost.

Still, he mounted to his battle station each day, ordered the weapons wheeled into position and signaled the assault. The sounds of the engagement echoed through the Palais. The clash of metal on wood, of wood on wood, of wood on stone, all orchestrated with the screams, cries and groans of Pierre Petit.

Gino had begun to bring a small sketchpad with him, hoping to learn something from the great creation taking place above him. He sat on the floor, his back against a pillar, observing and drawing, hunched over so that no one would see what he was doing. However, at times he became so absorbed in his drawing that he ignored the struggle going on above him until some noise or a scream from Petit brought him back to his vigil.

The ropes were taut again. Two more sections were swinging into place. The winch was creaking.

"Look out!" Petit cried. "Higher, higher!" The panel banged the ceiling. "Lower! A bit lower!" The artist gripped the railing tightly. Even at this range Gino could tell he was struggling to restrain himself.

At noon, when Petit descended from the scaffold, Gino was so involved in his sketching that he didn't notice the muralist passing him. When Gino finally looked up, ten minutes later, he was surprised to see the scaffold empty. Panicked for an instant, he quickly realized that Petit and the workmen must have gone to lunch.

That afternoon, Gino's attention wavered erratically between the work on the ceiling and his drawing. It was hard going and he was becoming as frustrated as Pierre Petit. But this time he noticed when the artist left, and he thought the man had given him a long, inquisitive look.

The next morning Gino arrived before anyone. From time to time during the day he had the impression that Petit looked down at him for a few moments. At lunchtime Gino was once again involved in his sketching. He heard the artist and the workmen leaving, but he was too intent on his sketchpad to look up. A hand reached over his shoulder and ripped the pad from his grasp. He scrambled to his feet to find Petit waving the pad at him.

"You've been copying my work in pastels!" He had spoken in Italian.

Gino nodded fearfully.

"This doesn't look like my painting at all."

"I'm sorry, Signore. Believe me."

Pierre Petit smiled. "It's very interesting." He reached up and placed a hand on Gino's shoulder. "What is your name?"

"Gianpaolo Bondone. They call me Gino."

"Who taught you this? Surely not my brother."

Gino couldn't speak.

"But I don't understand: If you have this much talent why did he let you go? My brother has always lived off the efforts of others. And why did he send you to me? He knew I would throw you out. Please explain the mystery?"

Gino shook his head. "I'm sorry, but I, myself, don't understand."

"Very well, we'll have lunch together and you'll tell me about your career with Lorenzo Patti."

Gino was amazed at the change in Pierre Petit. For four days the man had been a vengeful, aquiline-featured hawk, beating his wings and screeching against the sky. Now, walking across the Pont d'Iena toward the Eiffel Tower, he was calm, almost benign.

"Tell me about your friend," Petit said, "the dark-faced man who accompanied you the first day."

"Pietro. Well, there's not much to tell, really. He's from my village, Fiesole. He is the . . . fiancé of my sister, Maria. He brought me to Paris."

"Then he is your friend."

"I hope so."

"You may rely on it. Anyone who brings you to Paris is your friend."

They reached the Eiffel Tower. Petit purchased two tickets and they ascended in the lift. Gino was frightened. It was the first time in his life he had ever ridden in an elevator. This one was particularly awe-inspiring, with its vast platform, fast-closing doors, and windowed sides. What's more, as it traveled at an angle up one steel leg of the tower Gino was presented with a dazzling vision of Paris, seen through the soaring steel framework.

When they debarked at the first level, Petit had some difficulty inducing Gino to approach the railing. "Come now, the gallery at the top of the Duomo in Florence is higher than this and perhaps not as safe."

When Gino finally managed to bring his eyes up from his shoes, he first saw the Chaillot patterned through the iron, then the entire city flaring up to meet him. To the north, as Petit pointed out, one could see as far as the Basilica of the Sacré Coeur and beyond; to the east, almost to Vincennes; to the west, the great park known as the Bois, and the racetrack, Longchamps. At this height and range, the city seemed to be white alabaster carved in an eccentric pattern, interlocking here and there in a mysterious but perfectly harmonious design. Florence, his beloved Florence, was the effort of a clumsy artisan compared to this.

"There's really only one place for a painter, and this is it," Petit said, taking Gino's elbow and leading him around the perimeter. They made the circuit in silence—once, twice, three times, before Petit called a halt.

"Now it's time to dine."

The restaurant was a glass bowl suspended from the steel frame. As he entered, Gino was uncomfortably aware of his ragged clothes. The approaching maitre d'hotel, slender and dressed in black, looked at first like an obsequious question mark. Then he straightened into a disapproving exclamation point. He even tapped his toe for accent. Looking from Pierre Petit to Gino, his expressions ranged from respect to contempt. His reactions flickered back and forth so quickly that both Gino and Petit began to laugh. The maitre d'hotel's hauteur trickled away.

Petit's expression grew stern. "Antoine," he snapped, "give us a table by the glass."

Years later, when he returned, Gino would be struck by the commonplace quality of the food, but that afternoon every sauce seemed subtle, every bite succulent. Of course, he was very hungry.

Petit ordered a sumptuous meal and then left most of it on his plate. He did not ignore the wine. Time and again, he refilled Gino's glass and his own. "I still don't understand about my brother. What really happened? Why did you leave Florence?"

Instinctively, Gino trusted this man. While Petit listened to this chronicle, his mien ranged from somber to amused, and for the first time, Gino saw some humor in the situation.

"Like the painter Fillippo Lippi," Petit said, "you had yourself locked in a room to keep you from your mistress. That's priceless."

Gino felt as if he were playing the lines in Petit's face, as a musician plucks the strings on a lute. He tried to pick the chords which would blend the painter's face into a harmonic smile, playing down the anguish of those days—his doubts and fears.

"What did you do when my brother tried to seduce you?"

"How did you know?"

"It's obvious you turned him down, or why would he send you here? Still I suspect your dark friend had something to do with it."

Gino felt suddenly wary. "Pietro is very clever."

"Obviously. It takes both wit and courage to blackmail Signore Rossini."

"I said nothing about Rossini."

"But you did. Your description of his palace and his villa were perfect."

Gino was silent for a moment. Petit studied him benignly. "It wasn't right of me to tell you these things," Gino said.

"Gino, I suspect you're very honest and terribly naive. You

wish to protect what you believe are confidences, but you're not artful enough to do it."

Petit's expression became serious. He reached in his pocket and pulled out Gino's crumpled sketch, smoothed it on top of the table with care and seemed annoyed when some of the color came away on his hand.

"It shows right here, my boy. You tried to copy me, but you couldn't. I strive to make my colors flow together, to merge. You picked up some of the tones remarkably well, but you couldn't resist defining the shapes. That is your world, young man, a world of clear shapes and distinct forms. This is right; that is wrong. You won't permit them to mingle."

Gino sighed. "Is that wrong, Signore?" Waiting for the answer Gino could not breathe.

"I'm not sure that in art there is a right and wrong. In any event, what I do is not right for you. You were better off copying Lorenzo Patti than Pierre Petit. My morals are better than his, but his art is closer to yours."

Gino thought he would stifle on his own despair.

"In truth, you shouldn't copy anyone. You must be yourself. It's all very well to copy now—now, while you're learning. Eventually you must be unique. Otherwise, you may as well go back to making shoes."

"Wallets, Signore."

"All right then, wallets, purses, briefcases; is that what you want?"

He didn't wait for Gino to answer. "Of course not." He pointed a finger at Paris. "That is what you want. You want to own this city. What a prize! But only for exceptional people. A few may think they own her for a little while. She is given to short affairs. But Paris is not a whore. She is an imperial courtesan, and to be worthy of her continued favors, you must be a giant of a man—virile and strong, but gentle and wise, sensitive and proud. Can you be all those things, Gianpaolo Bondone?"

Gino shook his head.

Petit laughed. "Well, perhaps not in your twenties. Paris demands a more mature lover."

The discussion moved to a level beyond Gino's understanding. He heard the words; in fact he was intent on memorizing them, but they would have no meaning to him until much later.

"Enough of this," Petit said. "We must find something for you to do. It's unthinkable that you should sit on my scaffold all day fitting squares of canvas together. You're an artist, not a carpenter."

"I'd be happy to be a carpenter."

Petit shook his head. "But I won't let you. Besides, this part of the work is nearly done. I've already begun sketching the panels for other sections of the ceiling. In a few weeks I'll be back in my studio."

He stared out the window, obviously deep in thought. "I could discharge one of those insolent workmen and put you on the payroll in his place."

Gino protested, but Petit ignored him. "Yes, that's what I'll do. They're getting in each other's way as it is. It will be a good lesson for them. Perhaps they'll stop trying to smash my work."

"But Signore—"

"—Not to work on the scaffold. That would be absurd. You'll work at my studio. No one will know the difference and that way you can earn a few francs. Yes, that's it—perfect!"

He hammered the table with a satisfied expression, but a look at Gino's face told him the young man did not understand. "Let me explain, my boy. You will work at my studio. Use all my materials, anything you need. From time to time I'll criticize what you've done, perhaps give you an idea or two. The workman's salary will support you until the ceiling is complete. Then we'll have to find something else."

"But, Signore—"

"—Silence! It is decided." Petit smiled. Gino felt that although there was no choice, the choice was good.

♦   ♦   ♦

Gino burst into their room, brimming with enthusiasm.

Pietro eyed him warily. "Why are you so cheerful?"

Gino drew himself proudly erect. "I am employed."

Pietro frowned. "By whom?"

"Pierre Petit."

"I don't believe it."

"You said it wouldn't work, but it did. I sat on the floor until he noticed me. And now I have a job."

"As a carpenter? Working on the scaffold?"

Gino laughed. "No, as a painter."

"Really? Working on the murals?"

"Painting whatever I like. In the studio of the master."

"It doesn't sound right. How did this happen?"

Gino told him. When he reached the part of the story where he had lunch with Petit, Pietro interrupted him.

"I see, Pierre Petit is like his brother."

Gino was puzzled. "What do you mean?"

"I mean he likes you as Patti liked you."

Gino flushed. "It's not like that at all. He saw my drawing and thought it was beautiful. He asked me to lunch because he could see how hungry I was."

"And your appetite could only be satisfied at one of the most expensive restaurants in Paris."

"He's a kind man. He took sympathy on me. Why must you twist everything?"

"You say you have a job, but as far as I can tell you'll be paid for doing nothing."

"I'll work at his studio. I'll draw and paint under his direction."

"Since when does the teacher pay the pupil?"

Gino threw up his hands. "It's hopeless trying to explain. You can't believe there is such a thing as a truly generous man—a man who would help you merely out of the goodness of his heart."

"No, I don't believe it."

◆ ◆ ◆

Pierre Petit's house was located on the rue de Babylone in the Seventeenth Arrondisement. It was quite narrow in relation to its three stories, but it boasted a small garden both beside and behind it. A gray stucco wall screened the garden from the street but not from its neighbors. The building adjoining the garden on the street side presented only a blank wall, but the buildings behind had many windows. These were often open and the denizens shared the blessings of Pierre Petit's fine geometrical little garden.

When Gino first walked into this miniature paradise, its rigid pattern led him to believe that Madame Petit was the family gardener. After all, did not the master choose flowing tones and sometimes indistinct shapes? Here, the hedges were carefully clipped and the flowers ranked in carefully ordered rows. But Gino soon learned that Pierre Petit was the gardener.

"I presume I am in rebellion against Monet and Pissarro and their riotous gardens," he said. "In any event, mine is too small to give the illusion of wild flowers artlessly arranged."

Near the street side of the garden was a patio paved with large irregular shaped, sandstone blocks. There was a small, ornate stone fountain (which did not play), a tall chestnut tree and a bench. At Petit's suggestion, Gino used the patio when he wished to paint outdoors. And generally Gino preferred to work outdoors. Petit's studio, on the top floor of the house, boasted a large window facing north and an artfully constructed skylight, which could be opened to admit a gentle breeze. But the view was limited to steeply gabled roofs and trinitarian chimney pots. Gino felt cold, isolated and constrained there.

The garden reminded him of his native land. It was a bit too formal for his taste, but it was colorful—and fragrant with gardenias, azaleas and camellias, as well as roses climbing a trellis against the blank wall.

When Gino arrived the first morning, Pierre Petit helped him set up his materials on the patio. Then he reappeared with a plate heaped with croissants, a salver of butter, a steaming pot of coffee, and a pitcher of milk. They ate the rolls, sipped the coffee and chatted for a while. Then, Petit sat back to watch.

Gino held the sketchpad in his lap; the pastels lay in a tray on the table nearby. It was delightful in the garden. He smiled at Petit, then picked up a stick of chalk. For a long time, he sat motionless, the chalk poised over the pad, but did nothing.

"What's the matter?" Petit asked. "Does it bother you to have me sitting here?"

"Not in the least."

"But you're not drawing."

It was difficult for Gino to force out the words: "I don't know what to draw."

Petit laughed. "Anything. Draw anything."

"I don't have something to copy. Perhaps if you would give me a sketch or a small painting of yours, I could copy it."

"Why copy? You're in a charming garden. There is a handsome chestnut, flowers, houses and walls. Surely you can find something to paint."

Gino hung his head. "I'm sorry, Monsieur Petit. I've never done that. I always copied someone else's work."

Petit exploded. "I don't believe it! You must have painted something from life."

"No. From the days when I was a leatherworker through my apprenticeship with Patti, I did nothing but copy."

"What about the cherubim—the ones you painted for Patti?"

"I took an eye from one drawing, a nose from another and a mouth from somewhere else."

"But you made faces out of those features."

"Yes; I found it very difficult."

"What about the girl whose face you painted as the Virgin?"

"Oh, that. That was from memory, not from life."

"So. You can put together copied features and you can draw from memory—but not from real objects or people."

Gino shook his head, sadly.

Petit paced about the garden. "I've never heard anything so crazy in my life." He sprang to the table, picked up the coffeepot and set it down before Gino. "Look," he said. "A coffee pot. A simple coffee pot. Round here. Straight there. A spigot here. Brown, the sole color. Draw it."

Gino shook his head.

Petit shook the pot at him. "Pretend it's a picture and copy it."

Gino smiled broadly. "I think I could do that."

Pierre Petit sank back in his chair. "Pretend it's a picture." he mumbled, "and make a picture of the picture."

Gino picked up a brown chalk, narrowed his eyes and began to sketch. First he drew a frame around the edges of the pad, while Petit squirmed. Then with a few quick strokes, he copied the pot.

"*Magnifique!*" cried Pierre Petit. "You see, you can do it." He ran to the nearest flowerbed and plucked a few peonies. "Here," he said, "pretend these are a picture." He pushed the plate of croissants in front of Gino. "And these." He shoved the coffee cups forward. "And these. They're all pictures. Copy them."

"With pleasure," Gino said. "It's really quite simple, the way you put it."

Pierre Petit said no more. He was still shaking his head when he left the garden.

Gino spent the day happily copying the objects Petit had placed on the table. He tried to be as faithful to them in his renderings as he could, but a glimmer of light on a petal would intrigue him and then somehow the flower would turn out subtly different from the original.

When Petit returned, he studied the sketches for a long time. "You are no copyist, Gianpaolo Bondone."

"I'm sorry. I tried very hard to draw these things just as they were."

"But something of you has found its way into each sketch. That's as it should be. Let Gianpaolo Bondone loose on the paper. Let yourself live and breathe—and your art will live and breathe." He patted him fondly on the shoulder.

Each morning, the procedure was the same: *café au lait* and rolls with the master, and then to work.

"I should send you to a good teacher," Petit said, "someone who will help you, particularly with figure drawing. But I'm afraid to let you out of my sight. Instead, I'll give you a few books to study. Eventually we'll hire a model for you—or you may share one of mine. Meanwhile, just sketch. The freedom will be good for you. Your line is very pure and amazingly well controlled for such a novice. Let's see what you can do before we surrender you to some other tyrant."

After the master left, Gino's time was his own. Madame Petit, a tiny, feather-slim middle-aged Frenchwoman, was energetic, but reticent. They could barely communicate in words and did not bother to try. She gave him cheese and bread and a glass of wine for lunch, permitted him to wander through the house and grounds without surveillance. He sometimes forgot she even existed.

It was a peaceful and pleasant life. No responsibilities and no crises. The summer was warm but not stifling, and Gino remained outdoors even when the sun was straight overhead.

He never worried about Giulia Rossini. She was very beautiful and delightfully passionate, but she was intelligent and unbelievably rich. Her family would take care of her. Although he missed her exuberance and generous affection, life in Paris had become too exciting for him to feel regrets.

He wrote to his mother and sister, every week at first, although he did not tell Pietro, and he asked them to respond care of Pierre Petit. When Maria wrote back, her letters were brief but cheerful, and thereafter Gino ceased to worry about his family. He did not want to concern himself about anything.

The best part of each day was the morning session with Petit. The older man would criticize Gino's work of the day before and guide him as he corrected it. Saturday was the best day of all because Petit spent the entire day at home. Gino was careful not to intrude while Petit was working, but the painter's work habits were very informal, not to say chaotic, even though he always wore a suit and tie under his smock and his hair and mustache were carefully brushed.

Petit talked to himself, encouraged himself, even cursed himself, while he worked. He hardly ever stopped speaking, no matter how meticulous the effort required of him, and he was not a mumbler. Occasionally his tirades brought his neighbors to their windows.

One day, while Gino watched, Petit looked up, noted his observers and cried, "Well, what do you think of it?" He spun his easel to afford them a better view.

A pretty young woman on the top floor leaned on her windowsill. Two elderly gentlemen on the ground floor put on their spectacles.

"You see," cried Petit to his audience, "it's positively clumsy! Can you imagine this on the ceiling of the Palais Chaillot?"

All three observers slowly shook their heads.

"I thought so," said Petit with a satisfied smile. He turned about, ripped the drawing paper from the easel and tore it to shreds. The young woman looked down at the two men. The men looked up at the woman. All three shrugged and withdrew inside.

When Petit was not preoccupied with his own work, he gave Gino his full attention, quick to excuse his imperfections and eager to praise him. At times words failed him (not often), and he pulled the pastel from Gino's hand and sketched a few lines. Gino marveled at Petit's ability to emphasize a feature with a single stroke a few centimeters long, or sketch a line that arced boldly across the entire sheet without in the least detracting from Gino's subject.

When Gino remarked on this, Petit frowned contemptuously. "These are nothing but tricks, my boy. Mere tricks. I want you to know that such devices exist and can be used. But they are not art, you understand, they are artifice. You must know the difference."

At her husband's suggestion, Madame Petit agreed to act as Gino's model. She did not pose; Adele Petit was too restless for that. But she would remain in the garden for hours at a time. Gino struggled to believe that this whispery creature with her quick, darting movements was only a picture that he was copying. If he devoted his full attention to his sketchbook even for an instant, he could not hope to look back and find her in the same position as before. The result was that he soon learned to sketch without looking at his drawing. At first, his hand was a bit sloppy; his pastel occasionally slipped off the page. Eventually his touch grew sure. In time, he completely forgot that he had considered himself unable to draw directly from life.

During the fourth week of his apprenticeship at the Hôtel de Petit, the weather turned cooler. When it began to rain Gino was forced inside. He tried to sketch Madame Petit in her kitchen, but the light was so bad that he retreated to the studio upstairs. Even there the sky was so dark that the light was poor. He thought of sketching the clouds above him, but they were too muddy and amorphous to excite his imagination. He was reduced to sketching small items in the studio.

On the second cloudy day, Petit came home early and called Gino down to the parlor for tea and small sandwiches. "Too gray a day," Petit told him. "I could feel the darkness inside the Chaillot and I lost enthusiasm."

Gino had never been in this room, and he looked about as he munched on a roll, finding the furnishings surprisingly ordinary for such a great artist. The couches and chairs were stuffed and comfortable, but they were covered with shabby, floral-patterned fabrics, and the chairs, tables and lamps, were of unmatched styles and undistinguished. A few paintings hung on the walls. Most were views of Paris in shades of dim, not to say dismal, gray and country landscapes dominated by faded sepia tones that seemed to be leaching from the walls.

Except over the sofa itself. There hung an unframed oil on canvas, perhaps one meter square, dominated on the right by a woman in a flowing white gown with a veil over her head that reached to her feet on both sides. She was carrying a small naked boy child—carrying in a formal sense, as a child might be carried in an early renaissance painting, without having any real support from the hand that curved about his lower legs. The head of a male figure, arms around mother and child, was suspended upside down over the woman's forehead. The rest of his body disappeared overhead at the edge of the canvas.

These figures seemed to hang in the sky over a sepia-toned town in the lower quadrant of the painting which looked medieval European except for the glowing candle, many times the height of the tallest building, that rose from the roofs. The area behind the heads of the male and female figures, stretching across the top of the canvas like a theatre curtain being drawn down at the middle, was apparently of golden clouds with strange animal, human and angelic figures—much smaller than the woman, child and man—imprinted on them. There were two small, winged angelic figures in the blue sky, one blowing a golden horn.

This was obviously a painting of the holy family, almost medieval in conception with its outsized Virgin, baby Jesus, Joseph, tiny angels and a smallish town. But where the primitives had striven for reality, but had not known quite how to achieve it, the painter of this scene had virtually abandoned physical realism. The colors were bold and shimmering, colors never seen on a medieval painting, yet the feeling was ethereal, spiritual. Not only the figures, but the very canvas seemed to float on Pierre Petit's wall.

"Chagall," Petit said.

"What?" Gino had been lost in the painting.

"Marc Chagall. A Russian Jew—usually paints in Paris or Provence."

"But—"

"—It's dramatically different from my work, let alone anything else in my home?" He laughed. "True, but when I chanced upon it in a small gallery on the rue de Seine, I couldn't resist."

Gino was indignant. "The perspective is primitive—the drawing is childlike!"

"Precisely," Petit said.

"The size and placement of the figures—it's arbitrary."

"True."

"If you like this work, how can you like mine?"

"I see. We must all draw and paint alike."

"Well, no . . . "

"The colors, Gino, look at the colors."

"They're . . . they're unusual."

Pierre Petit laughed gently. Gino subsided into confused silence.

♦ ♦ ♦

On the third rainy day, Gino was again working in the upstairs studio, when he chanced to glance at the house across the way and noticed a young woman standing at a window—the one who had joined the old men in silently judging Pierre Petit's work. She was watching intently, and even when he surprised her, she did not look away. While he was staring at her, the woman turned her back, reached behind to undo her dress, dropped it to her feet and stepped out of it. When she turned again she was wearing only a slip, nothing under it. Satisfied that she still held his attention, she turned her back once more and, with a slow, graceful movement, pulled the slip up over her head. First her thighs, then hips, then her back was revealed. She held the slip at arm's length over her head, stretched between her hands.

Gino blinked, and she was gone. He wondered if his blink had wiped her off his slate. He wondered whether he had actually seen her at all. Hurrying to the window, he peered through it. In a moment the woman's head appeared around the corner of the casement. She winked and disappeared.

He dreamed about the girl that night, once again watching her remove her clothes—the smooth curves of her body undulating through his vision. She slowly turned around to face him, totally naked, and to his pleasure, he found that her breasts were abundant, the nipples ripe, her belly gently curved, and her vulva inviting. Although it was only a dream, he awoke from it shaken. But smiling.

The next morning, Gino forced himself to remain in the Petit's kitchen. When the sky cleared that afternoon he ventured into the garden. The water had run off through the gravel below, and the patio was nearly dry. Gino set up his easel and went to work.

Towards dusk he noted a figure in an upstairs window and chose to ignore it. He did not want to know whether or not it was the sensual young woman.

The following day was Saturday and the ebullient Petit occupied all of Gino's time and thoughts. On Sunday, Gino went wandering about the left bank with Pietro. Gino was interested in the small galleries and open air stands, but Pietro was focused on the cafes—and the girls. They stopped a couple of times for a coffee, Pietro choosing a table next to a pretty woman or women. But they were disinterested, and Pietro's attempts at conversation were ignored. One slim blonde smiled at Gino, which made him think not about her, but of the girl in the window. The smile, not directed at Pietro, annoyed him, and he abruptly pulled Gino to his feet and dragged him away. The blonde laughed.

By Monday Gino's original spasm had passed. That is not to say that Gino had lost interest. Only that he had mastered the urge to seek out and seduce (or be seduced by) the vision in the window. He was rather proud of this victory over his body. He decided he was gaining maturity.

The following week his idyll ended. Pierre Petit, who had previously paid him on Saturday, returned home on Thursday and paid him a full week's wages.

"I'm sorry," he said, "but the government has cut off my funding and I can't complete the remaining murals. You're free to use my studio, my paints and canvas—anything I have, but I'm simply unable to pay you any longer."

Petit seemed disconsolate, and Gino wanted to tell him he appreciated his kindness, but he himself was too consumed with sadness to speak. Petit patted Gino on the shoulder and went inside to dine. Gino stayed in the garden a long time, fearful he would never be able to return. But the air became chilly. He let himself out through the garden gate and headed despondently towards the rue Lepic.

Nine

A New Career

It was still a few minutes before eight when he entered their room, pulled the shades, threw himself down on his bed. He was a pitiful failure. What had he ever accomplished without the intervention of others? First his father, then the friars, then Pietro, finally Pierre Petit. He was a helpless cork adrift on the sea of life; no rudder, no sail, no motor. He was a tragic misfit.

The slamming door jolted him upright on his bed. Before Pietro turned on the light, Gino wiped his eyes with his sleeve and forced a smile.

Pietro was humming when he came in. At the sight of Gino, he stopped in mid-coda. "My God, man, what's wrong?"

Gino stared down at the faded, unraveling quilt on his bed. "I've lost my job," he mumbled.

Pietro couldn't hide his smile. "Is that all? Well cheer up. You knew it would end. Petit told you so in the beginning. Anyway, I've had a splendid day and I'm going to celebrate tonight. You may come along."

Gino shook his head.

"You're coming, anyway." Pietro pushed him off the bed. "Shave your face, comb that twisted hair of yours, put on your confirmation suit. We're having a party."

The party was being held in a dilapidated apartment building located even higher in Montmartre—or was it lower? They climbed several dark flights of rotting, creaking steps. The banister was no protection—it shivered under Gino's touch and he edged over to the opposite wall.

Through the door of the apartment they heard the murmur of voices and the occasional off-key whine of a poorly plucked guitar. At Pietro's knock, all sounds ceased. The door edged slowly open and a slice of smoke-filled light filtered out. Pietro was recognized and they were permitted to enter. The parlor was almost bare of furniture, but filled with people. They leaned against walls, crouched or slouched on the floor, stood in mumbling groups. Two men sat cross-legged on the floor, using a ragged rug as a blanket around their shoulders. A few people stared briefly at the towering Gino and his powerful physique.

Pietro introduced Gino to a few slovenly looking characters, then disappeared. Someone offered Gino a bottle, and gratefully he took a swig of raw, almost rancid wine. It tasted terrible, but it loosened him up. Still, the smell of cheap cigarettes and bad wine was almost overpowering. Gino excused his way through the crowd until he found a place near a window. It was closed, but occasional gasps of air seeped in around the ancient sash.

Gino wanted to be alone so that he might contemplate the tragedy of his own existence. Little shivers of self-pity slithered up and down his spine. In the fetid, oxygen-deprived air, it was not difficult to feel self-pity. He could have achieved a Buddhist isolation except that the other people in the room fascinated him. Although they talked incessantly and gestured extravagantly, their voices rarely rose above a hoarse whisper. He could not believe this was self-imposed. He wondered whether the smoke acted as a kind of cotton batting which smothered sound.

After a few minutes, he realized that there were women in the room as well as men. Everyone was dressed alike: high-necked shirts, long pants, ragged sweaters or skimpy jackets. But a few bulges here and there told him the occupants were probably not male. He studied the faces with greater care. Even in the murky darkness it was clear that some people were wearing their hair longer than others. A few of these were women.

Pietro reappeared with a woman who clung to his arm, reaching up to whisper into, and then to bite, his ear. The words seem to titillate him more that the physical contact. He did not introduce the girl to Gino, merely mumbled in his ear as he passed: "I must be nice to this woman, top stuff at *Liberté.*" Then he winked and led her away.

Gino was lost. His French was poor and he could understand only the simplest phrases—and then only when spoken slowly. The guests talked rapidly and their words were often large ones. There were two men, apparently Italian, arguing intently in the center of the room. They lapsed into their native tongue occasionally, and Gino felt a tiny prick of chauvinism, but every few moments one would nudge the other, they would look about, and return to speaking French.

A short, dark-haired girl with great round glasses and a similarly shaped bosom approached him, smiling—the same woman who had been with Pietro. She flashed something at him in French.

"*Pardon*," he mumbled, head down, "*Je ne comprends pas.*" And then, as if his intonation had not betrayed him, "*Je suis Italien.*"

She studied him from head to foot, then nodded approvingly. "*Parfait*," she said, took his arm and pulled him through the crowd.

He passed Pietro, who appraised his companion with a single glance. "Very, very good," Pietro said.

There was no chance for further conversation. The woman dragged Gino into another room. From behind a chair she drew forth a bottle and shoved it at him. "Orvieto," she said. There were other bottles hidden behind the chair. Not all were Orvieto, but after a while, Gino ceased to care.

The woman murmured to him in slurred French, very little of which he understood. He replied in thick-tongued Italian, telling her the tragedy of his life. She understood little of what he said, but she could scent an unhappy man when she saw one. At every tortured phrase, she clucked sympathetically.

Encouraged, he put his arm around her. She did not resist when he reached under her sweater and unleashed her ponderous breasts. Now that was real sympathy. For a while, he did nothing more than fondle her, content with this moment of peaceful compassion. After several minutes, she pushed his hand away and rehooked herself, reached down and helped him to his feet, then led him through a long corridor to a small door at the rear of the apartment. In a moment, they were outside. Somehow it did not seem as cold as it had before. She led the way along a porch, then up some sharply angled steps to the roof. The night was glorious with stars, and the lights of Paris sparkled below. But the girl had not brought him there for the view. She lifted his hands to her breasts and sighed in satisfaction as once more he released them. He felt her hands working on his belt buckle. This affronted his masculinity. Gino pushed her away and finished the project himself.

It was almost dawn when Gino and Pietro returned to their room. Pietro had achieved some career triumph that Gino did not understand. Gino had found a woman. She could hardly be considered beautiful, but she was more than adequate.

Pietro kept pounding him on the back and complimenting him, but Gino could not comprehend why. Each time he asked for an explanation, Pietro burst into laughter and praised him again. Finally, no wiser than before, Gino fell across his bed and slept.

♦ ♦ ♦

When they both were awake again, Pietro explained the occasion for the previous evening's celebration: He had been appointed political science editor of *Liberté*.

Gino had no idea what that meant, but he congratulated Pietro anyway. Then, hesitantly, he inquired again as to why Pietro had congratulated *him*.

"All right," Pietro said finally, "I was complimenting you on your conquest of Yvette Chardin."

"Why is that so amusing?"

"She is my employer, the editor-in-chief of *Liberté*."

"God! What have I done?"

"It's splendid! Absolutely perfect. You've accomplished two things. First, now that she has you, she'll stop bothering me. Second, she can't possibly refuse you a job."

This was clearly going to be another of Pietro's enigmatic mornings. Gino resigned himself to it. There was nothing to do but ask the expected questions and receive the unexpected answers.

"What job?"

"Cartoonist."

"Cartoonist?"

"Yes, for *Liberté*."

"I would say you're joking, but every time I say that it turns out you're not."

"I persuaded Yvette to give you a chance to be staff cartoonist for the newspaper."

"But, Pietro, what do I know about cartooning?"

"Any man who can decorate wallets, paint frescoes and sketch to the satisfaction of Pierre Petit, can be a cartoonist."

"It sounds degrading."

"Is it better to be degraded or starve?"

"Give me my share of the money you took from Signore Rossini and let me go my own way."

"The money is long gone, you fool, and my salary at *Liberté* is not enough to support the two of us. Why do you think I found you this position?"

"I came here to be a painter."

"Fine. Be a painter, but on your own time. This job requires only that you sketch a few lines now and then. Mere child's play. And I'll give you the ideas. All you have to do is draw them up."

"It sounds degrading."

"You're repeating yourself. Listen, if you have some other way to support yourself, say so. No? Well then I believe you had better be a cartoonist."

Pietro did not realize how deeply he had wounded Gino. To be a scribbler, to draw caricatures of famous people, insult other human beings, the thought disgusted him. *Degradazione.* But there was little time to think about this indignity, for Pietro put him to work at once.

He showed Gino a photograph of the American President, Harry Truman, and told Gino to caricature his face. It was not difficult. The wispy hair, metal-rimmed glasses, long nose and jutting chin were easy to simulate. Then Pietro told him to sketch Truman draped in a toga, standing on the planet earth. In one hand he would hold a fistful of money; in the other, a clutch of bombs. Gino was to draw a blindfold—half exposing the eyeglasses—with Truman peering out underneath. The caption, as translated by Pietro, read: "The balance of power."

Gino was disturbed. "What does it mean?"

Pietro didn't bother to hide his disgust. "It means what it says."

"You're making fun of the American President."

"All cartoons make fun."

"Why the Americans? Are you angry at them?"

"You fought in the army of your country. You were wounded. Your homeland was devastated, and your family has barely enough to eat. They killed your father. And you're not angry at the Americans?"

"The Americans didn't kill my father."

"If they hadn't invaded Italy your father would still be alive."

"That's not the same."

"Gino," Pietro's voice turned to honey, "you take things too seriously. This is just a cartoon, not a gun or a bomb. It won't kill Signore Truman, or any one else for that matter. And it's true, quite true that the Americans control the world with bombs and banknotes. Correct?"

"In a sense."

"Of course. Your cartoon is very good. I know Yvette will like it. Get dressed and we'll bring it to her."

It was the first time Gino had seen the offices of *Liberté*. The nondescript building hummed with activity. Pietro led him through the basement where grimy-faced men worked grimly on ancient presses, and handed him a copy of the paper, still damp. It was small, magazine size, and poorly printed. Some of the letters completely failed to register. Gino shook his head. There was little honor in being employed by *Liberté*.

"Don't scoff," said Pietro. "What we say is more important than fine type and expensive newsprint."

There were at least a dozen people working in the building that Sunday afternoon. They all seemed haggard, intense and absorbed. Gino recognized some of the faces from the previous night's entertainment.

Once more Pietro seemed to read his mind. "Don't be so stupid as to judge them by their appearance. We employ some of the finest minds in Paris. Of course," he whispered, "we also have some of the biggest fools."

On the second floor they found Yvette, who rose when they entered and kissed Gino on the mouth. He flushed deeply, avoiding her eyes.

Pietro held out the cartoon. Her eyes widened. She chattered something in facile French to Pietro and then looked proudly at Gino. He was hired. There was no escape. He was now the official cartoonist for *Liberté*.

Gino tried to stay away from the newspaper offices, but Pietro insisted he bring his cartoons in himself. Therefore, at least twice a week he was required to visit *Liberté*. And Yvette.

He managed to save but one piece of his dignity; he refused to sign his name to these scratches. Instead he signed them *"Bon,"* which was both ironic and a corruption of his own family name. There was one advantage: he began to learn more French. If only in self-defense. It was unbearable to hear people discuss things without having the slightest idea what they were talking about.

But there were other obligations as well. Some days Yvette was too busy to do more than accept his cartoons and kiss him on the cheek. Other times she insisted that he wait to escort her home. She would cook him a skimpy meal and drag him to bed. It was not totally unpleasant, but it was humiliating. He was a kept man.

Through words and gestures, Yvette finally managed to convey to Gino the idea that she wanted him to move in with her. Her apartment was indeed better than the tiny room he shared with Pietro. It was well furnished and warm, but he was not tempted. Yvette persuaded Pietro to intervene on her behalf. At first Pietro merely tried to convince him of the utility of this arrangement, but when Gino stubbornly refused, he threatened him. If Gino did not accept the offer he would lose his job. Pietro would force him to move out unless he could support himself. If not, he would move to his own lodgings.

"Good," said Gino, "you move in with her."

Pietro's threats proved idle and everything continued as before. If nothing else, the arrangements gave Gino a great deal of free time. He did not spend as much of it at Pierre Petit's, afraid he might let slip the fact that he was employed as a cartoonist on a third-rate newspaper. Instead, he pretended he had taken a job as a construction worker. Petit was unable to offer an alternate solution.

Gino still managed to visit the house in the rue de Babylone two or three mornings a week. Until then, Gino had worked only with charcoal and pastels. Now, Petit began to coach him in the use and application of oil paints—how to stretch and prepare the canvas, how to mix and blend pigments, how to apply and preserve them. It was slow going, but he found working in oil almost simple compared to fresco. And yet painting on a movable piece of canvas was far different than applying pigment on a fixed wall.

For his very first effort in oil, he chose to paint a plain white porcelain coffee pot, with gently sloping sides, a curved handle and an angular spout, sitting on the beige-toned surface of the garden table. In his picture, the light came from the right, facing the canvas, and it threw a black angled shadow from the pot onto the table. The side of the tabletop was a darker tone than the surface. He placed the coffeepot off center on the canvas, and its shadow and the darker tone of the side of the table helped balance the composition. Unwilling to attempt a complex background, he chose a flat light blue color instead, which nicely set off the coffeepot and the table. It was a simple exercise, but Gino was very proud of the result.

Having reached this turning point in his career, Gino decided to sign his work. He had seldom signed his sketches, only occasionally scribbling "G" or "GB" in a corner. When he was a child visiting the Campanile in Florence his father had told him proudly that their family name was the same as that of the great artist and architect Giotto di Bondone. He had not actually claimed that they were related, but the inference was clear.

At first, Gino thought he would sign his work with his full name, Gianpaolo Bondone, but that took up a lot of room and seemed pretentious. G. Bondone seemed vaguely dishonest, and Bondone alone looked arrogant. He decided to use the name that everyone called him: Gino. It gave little information, might even be misleading, but it was natural for him and provided sufficient identity. Pierre Petit didn't even mention the signature when he complimented Gino on his effort. Gino decided he would never sell it. At the moment, that seemed a rather safe decision, since he couldn't think of anyone who would want to buy it.

Petit surprised him. "I'd like to keep it, if I may," he said. "Some day it could be very valuable, but more important, I like it, and I want to mount it in our kitchen. Will you give it to me?" Gino was thrilled.

Paris was growing on him. She was typically gray, occasionally chill, and generally kept her distance, but each encounter offered a new mystery, a new sense of proportion. Her houses were not as colorful as those in Florence, but they were more detailed. Boulevards were broad, the trees delightfully slender. Even narrow *allées* offered a great variety of entrancing views. Paris was subtle without being brittle, inviting without coyness.

He walked the streets for hours on end, climbing every monument and exploring every museum. The art galleries, both public and private, amazed him. At home, he had been exposed to great Renaissance painters—most of them Italian. He regarded them no less highly now, but he learned there were other ways for an artist to express himself. He came to appreciate El Greco and Velasquez, Rembrandt and Vermeer, Rubens and David.

Gino's vision adjusted to the seventeenth, the eighteenth and then to the nineteenth century, even begrudging to the Impressionists and Post-Impressionists a claim on at least a fragment of the truth. His own works began to disturb him. He had felt quite humble in Florence, comparing his art with the paintings in the Uffizi, but at that point he was still a novice. In Paris he told himself the very same things—with less conviction. The realm of art was so vast, the masters of it so numerous and their talents so diverse. How could he hope to find a place among them, particularly since the borders kept widening, the vistas were endless, and the standards fluid? When could he hope to make his own unique contribution? Three things saved him from despair: the inexhaustible optimism of youth, the encouragement of Pierre Petit, and the artists of Paris—not the dead ones, the living.

Most current works displayed in private galleries distressed him. They seemed chaotic, devoid of craftsmanship. There were paintings built up of heavy impasto, one glob of color dribbled on another, with no evident shape or form. There were lacy traceries, lines of color intersecting and recrossing each other without discernible pattern or purpose. There were grotesqueries: objects that resembled human forms, but twisted into frightening shapes. He was certain these were the outpourings of disordered minds. But he dared not totally dismiss any of the contemporary artists. There had been great painters after Donatello, after Michelangelo, after El Greco, after Rubens, after La Tour, after Chardin, after David, after Goya, after Monet, after Van Gogh—why not after Pissarro?

That the works of these contemporary artists were displayed in famous museums, and reviewed with great solemnity by the art critics of the great French newspapers, shook him further. Gino had learned to read a little French, but the reviews were filled with phrases like "abstract expressionism," "non-objective surrealism," "cubist pictorialism," and other concoctions which meant absolutely nothing to him. It was bewildering. Gino was determined to learn to understand and thus to appreciate this new art. He must cast aside his peasant prejudices and see the light that these artists saw. And he would do it the same way he had learned to love the geniuses of earlier ages. He would take his easel to the galleries and copy their work.

The experiment was a failure. He tried to discover the techniques, to emulate the rhythms. It was impossible. The new artists were beyond him. They knew some secret that a simple man like him would never learn. He was doomed to live in the past and to work in a form of art long dead. In an agony of self-doubt he blurted out his fears to Pierre Petit.

"Of course," Petit responded, "that's the point."

Gino bowed his head and turned away. Petit shook him. "Listen to me, Gino. You're right. You cannot copy them. You'll never be able to copy them. In fact, they can't even copy themselves. How could they? Their works are mere accidents. You would have to have the identical accident in order to copy them. And that is impossible."

And so Gino passed the winter drawing cartoons, sketching and painting for Petit, studying the masters and sleeping with Yvette. Once more he had slipped into a pattern. Gino had an affinity for patterns. But he was growing impatient. He could not continue in this mode forever.

◆ ◆ ◆

When spring first touched the city, Gino was already vibrating with it. Now was the time for change, and he hoped Pierre Petit could help him. He found the painter sitting in his kitchen. Petit did not return Gino's greeting, but motioned him to be seated, unrolled a copy of *Liberté*, and shoved it across the table. On the top of the page was a cartoon showing General Charles de Gaulle with a machine gun for a nose and bullets for teeth.

"Did you draw this?" Petit's tone was severe.

"How did you know?"

"I've been watching you sketch for months—do you think I am an idiot? Why did you do it?"

Gino wanted to say it was because they paid him, but he realized this answer would infuriate the master. He remained silent.

"I never suspected that you were a communist."

"I'm not a communist!" Gino's voice trembled with anger.

His vehement denial surprised Petit. He studied Gino warily. "Only communists work for *Liberté*."

"You're wrong. Even Pietro is an editor."

"Then he is a communist."

"I tell you neither Pietro nor I are communists." He was not so stupid as to tell Petit that his father had been murdered for being a fascist.

"You all lie," said Pierre Petit, almost wearily.

"You've been very kind to me, Monsieur, and I'm very grateful. I don't wish to quarrel with you in your own house, but you must stop calling me a communist and a liar."

"Then why did you do this?"

"Pietro got me the job. I draw a few cartoons a week and they pay me enough to live on."

"But these brutal insinuations, these cruel caricatures. How can you draw them?"

"It's a joke, isn't it? All cartoons are jokes. That's what Pietro tells me."

"This Pietro, I didn't like him when I first met him at the Chaillot. He makes me happy I gallicized my name when I came here. But that has nothing do with these so-called cartoons. Frankly, I would never have believed that you could conceive of such grotesque ideas."

"I don't. Pietro describes the cartoon to me and then adds the words. All I do is draw the pictures. I admit that some of them are a bit ugly, but I mean no harm. Really."

Pierre Petit slammed both fists upon the table and glowered at Gino. Then, relenting, he said, "It's difficult for me to believe you, Gino, but I do."

"Thank you."

Petit looked as if he wanted to say more, but could not bring himself to do so.

"Tell me," asked Gino, speaking with profound difficulty, "is what I have done very bad?"

The response was a long time coming. "Yes, my boy, very bad."

◆ ◆ ◆

"You're a communist."

Pietro frowned. "Don't say that."

"I am saying it. You work for them. You're one of them."

Pietro shrugged. "Communist, fascist—what does it matter?"

Gino almost strangled on the words. "Fascists killed my father! To you that means nothing, of course. But he was *my* father."

Pietro's mind was racing. Sooner or later he would have to tell Gino. Perhaps it was better to do it now—now, when he did not expect it. There must be a weapon somewhere in the room.

Pietro sighed and turned his head; what was the point of saying anything? Not now, anyway. "There's no reason to be so angry," he finally said. "I only did this for you. So you could earn a living. So you could eat. It has nothing to do with your father, believe me."

Gino's anger was beginning to ebb. "Why didn't you tell me what we were doing?"

"You mean you didn't know what your own cartoons meant?"

"I thought they were humorous."

"They were."

"But also serious?"

"Yes, of course. Also serious."

"That I didn't understand."

"When you read the newspaper, you must have known."

"I didn't read it. I just looked at my cartoons. If there was anything about art I tried to read that, too. Otherwise I only looked at my drawing—and I won't do it any more."

"Be reasonable, Gino. You need the money."

"Never. I'll never draw another cartoon for *Liberté*."

"All right. If that's how you feel. Do what you think best."

Gino could not believe that Pietro was talking to him in this reasonable manner. It was a triumph of sorts. But he did not understand how he had achieved it.

Gino spoke softly, "Do you want me to leave?"

"Yes, damn you! Leave!"

Gino sadly gathered his things while Pietro watched. He thanked Pietro for all past help, left the room and started morosely down the steps.

Above him the door opened suddenly. "Wait," yelled Pietro from the top of the landing.

♦ ♦ ♦

Fortunately the weather turned warm. The sun shone from early morning until late in the afternoon; there was no need for heat, and little occasion to operate the electric lights. Gino and Pietro resumed the pattern of earlier days. Gino no longer arose at dawn. There was no place to go. When he woke up Pietro was gone and there were a few francs on the table. Fewer than before. He was too ashamed to return to Pierre Petit's studio.

Gino spent many hours along the Seine, sketching and daydreaming, some times working at the lower level, close to the water, occasionally on the terraces above, where the views of the city were expansive. He couldn't afford paints; Pietro's francs were barely sufficient to buy bread and cheese. He subsisted on this diet for weeks. His stomach contracted after a while and he ceased to feel as hungry as before. Neither was he as energetic. It was all Gino could do to drag himself to the Seine, to loll there in the sun and draw a bit when he felt the strength. It was so warm that sometimes he wore his shirt outside his pants, even undoing the buttons to let the sun hit his chest. He would have stripped the shirt off like a peasant working in the fields, but this was Paris, not Fiesole. He became very tan. His coloring belied his weakness, much as a confirmed drunkard might boast a ruddy complexion. Gino knew that Pietro hoped to starve him into submission, but he was determined not to surrender.

Gino was no longer the object of Yvette's attentions; his decision to discontinue drawing cartoons for the paper had alienated her. It was probably just as well. He briefly considered seeking some other form of employment. But that would require a work permit, which would take a very long time and considerable effort.

He finally acknowledged the real reason: he intended to be an artist. Nothing else would satisfy him. It was the first truly independent judgment he had ever made. For some time he had felt humiliated about been manipulated by others. From this time forward he was going to set his own course. On that point his mind was resolved. Thus fortified, Gino suffered discomfort with ragged courage. He was a martyr. One day they would appreciate him.

He passed the summer in this fashion, confirmed in his career, while slowly wasting away. But he forced himself to draw—every day—no matter how he felt. For several weeks he ate almost nothing, using the precious francs Pietro gave him to buy a few opened tubes of paint, cheap used brushes, a small stretched canvas with a tear in one corner, and a rickety easel. Fortunately, his robust body permitted him to starve without collapsing. And having real paint, even though it was old and not very supple, gave him renewed energy. It was better than food. Almost.

Towards the end of August, Gino noticed a few leaves falling from the trees. He was frightened. What if he was forced to live like this in the winter?

Ten

Rescue and Renewal

Pietro traversed the rue Lepic in long strides. This day he would reach home before Gino. Home. Soon, they would leave their dismal room and move on to better quarters. He could afford it now.

For months he had been sending his best columns from *Liberté* to Claude Laurent, the editor of *Paris-Presse*. Not the party line stuff—rather, the tightly reasoned political analysis he often slipped in with the routine propaganda. For a long time there was no response.

Just this morning, Laurent had summoned him. A few minute's discussion and he was on the payroll of one of France's greatest daily papers. It was a minor staff position, of course, but a giant step up from *Liberté*.

The parting with Yvette was acrimonious. Apparently she had expected him to work for her forever. In the end, she called him a traitor. He laughed aloud. It was true; first he had been a fascist, then a communist, and now—with a little luck—a capitalist.

Gino, that mad fool, starving himself slowly to death while he scribbled and painted along the Seine. Would he never break?

Never ask for help? How did he exist on the few francs Pietro gave him? He never complained. During the past few weeks he had rarely spoken at all.

Nevertheless, Pietro no longer thought about abandoning his half-brother. It was not a decision; merely an acceptance of the fact of Gino's existence. Gino was part of his life. If he returned home and Gino wasn't there, he felt distress. Why? Why, why, why? It made no sense to him. The man was utterly useless. Even the few francs he doled out to him each morning had been a drag on Pietro's finances. Why support such a creature?

The door was open. In the middle of the room stood Giulia Rossini and Maria Bondone. Pietro froze. *It can't be*, he thought. *It must not be.*

Maria hurled herself upon him. "Pietro," she cried. "*Inamorata!*" Her arms were around him, her breasts pressed against him, her lips seeking his. He could not speak. He could not move. "Pietro, Pietro. I've come a thousand miles. Can't you give me one kiss?"

Her face was just below his, the rich full lips trembling, dark eyes sparkling with love. He kissed her. Savagely. Not knowing why, not caring about the consequences. But then he started to push her away.

"Giulia!" It was Gino, crying out in surprise as he entered the room. She squealed and threw herself at him. He was too surprised and too weakened by hunger to support her and they collapsed together on the bed.

"My love, my beauty, my only one!" she cried.

"Giulia," he said hoarsely. "Giulia." It was the only endearment he could manage. Over her shoulder he saw his sister and Pietro.

"Maria!" he yelled, disengaging himself from Giulia. "What are the two of you doing here?"

"My God!" his sister said, "look at him—he's a bag of bones. Are you ill, Gino? What's the matter?"

"I'm fine," he answered, glancing at Pietro. "But what are you doing here?"

Giulia hugged him again. "Aren't you happy to see us?"

"Of course. But what about your father?"

"Away at Portofino with mother. As soon as they left, we came here. The servants think Maria quit her job and that I'm visiting my Aunt Flavia."

"And Aunt Flavia thinks you're in Portofino with your parents."

Giulia and Maria laughed. Pietro and Gino did not.

"Stop frowning," said Maria. "We're together in beautiful Paris. Let's enjoy ourselves. What's the matter with you?"

Gino felt foolish. "I'm sorry. I just can't believe it."

He embraced Giulia again. Maria closed her arms about Pietro. He turned his head, but could not avoid her kisses.

"You must take us to see the city," Giulia said.

"You'll have to walk," said Gino, "and I have no idea what you'll eat."

"Don't be foolish," said Giulia. "I have plenty of money." She opened her purse and brought out a thick bundle of French francs. "My father opened accounts for me here many years ago, and now that we're at peace with the French, they've unblocked the funds. I can't take it back into Italy, but surely we can enjoy it here."

Pietro decided not to mention his new job just yet.

♦ ♦ ♦

When they rented an additional room, Gino thought the girls would share it, but Giulia insisted on staying with him. He objected because that meant Maria would be with Pietro. Even Pietro protested, to Gino's surprise. But the girls would not listen, and eventually they had their way.

"Now," said Giulia, "we can devote ourselves to the difficult task of spending my money."

They began enthusiastically—all except Gino. Since leaving Florence, he hadn't written to Giulia and had rarely even thought about her. It was one thing to live off Yvette, for whom he had provided some work, no matter how minimal, and totally different to be enjoying the largesse of Giulia, for whom his contributions had been carnal rather than creative. Of course, Giulia was prettier and he liked her better. But he knew that these were insufficient—not to say dishonest—justifications.

Gino repeatedly debated the point with his conscience, and his conscience always lost. The first night he ate and drank so much he became violently ill and had to be carried home. Giulia complained over his inability to be a proper lover. He promised to do better in the morning, then promptly fell asleep.

In the other room, Pietro sat fully clothed in a chair while Maria slowly undressed. He tried not to look at her, but time and again, unwillingly, his eyes traversed her body. She removed her outer clothing with care and laid it carefully on the dresser. She sat on the bed, dressed only in a cotton brassiere and panties, removing her stockings. He could feel the silk slide down across her smooth thighs, over the knees and then to the floor. He could feel her flesh even now. His palms began to sweat.

"Why do you look so sad?"

He did not answer. His loins were answering and he was struggling to stifle the response. She reached behind her back to unsnap the brassiere. Her breasts swelled against the thin cotton, lush curves spilling over the top.

"It's no good, Maria," he said. "No good."

She smiled. "You've forgotten. It's very good."

The brassiere was undone. She hunched her shoulders as she pulled the straps forward and gently lifted the cups away.

"I should stay with Gino," Pietro said. "I'll get him."

She laughed. "I'm sure Gino doesn't wish to be interrupted." She rolled her panties down over her thighs and dropped them to the floor.

He shook his head. "It's over, Maria. You should never have come. It ended in Fiesole—forever."

His body didn't believe him; the warmth was spreading through him, weakening him. She walked silently across the room, then knelt before him. Her breasts, rounder and fuller than he remembered, were in his lap, the touch of them sending sparks along his legs. He tried to stand up. "I can't, Maria. Really, I can't."

But at her gentle touch he sagged into the seat, while she climbed over him. Her hands entwined behind his head and she pulled his face down between her breasts.

"Of course you can," she murmured.

His resolution melted. He pressed against her, his entire body throbbing. But even as his hands circled her thighs, as his lips sank into hers, he moaned.

Maria smiled. She did not realize he was sobbing.

◆ ◆ ◆

In the morning, Giulia insisted on buying the two men new clothes. Gino protested; Pietro was cold and silent. Giulia carried the day.

Gino was fitted with the first decent suit he had ever owned in his life. The fabric was an English worsted, a subtle gray with a barely visible pinstripe, cut in a classic three-button, single-breasted style. Giulia chose a fine off-white linen shirt with French cuffs, dark shoes and a burgundy silk tie and pocket handkerchief to complete his wardrobe. The cuff links, gold and onyx, cost more than the suit. Gino felt like a prince.

Pietro was somewhat less impressed with his new apparel, a tasteful ensemble in tones of blue, but did not refuse the gifts.

Thus adorned, Gino and Pietro escorted the women to the salons of the famous couturiers of the Place Vendôme. It was a frightening experience for Gino. Not even the Basilica of St. Peter's in Rome had affected him thus. The draperies swinging from wall to wall, the brittle females, all bones, yet boneless, mincing through the showrooms. These women were nothing compared to Maria and Giulia—mere tinsel playthings—but such arrogance! They made him painfully aware that he was a mere peasant.

Gino was delighted to escape to the street again. But Maria and

Giulia were never sated with shopping. Only when the stores finally closed at night were they willing to suspend operations.

They had no interest in museums or art galleries. They exclaimed over the Eiffel Tower (the elevator ride terrified them) and the Sacré Coeur, the flea market (but most things were too dirty to buy), and the Arc de Triomphe, the Champs Élyseés and the place de la Concorde. But they did not stay long. They wanted to be on the move. To see everything; to test everything—lightly— with the tips of their tongues.

Their first elaborate dinner was at Tour d'Argent. Gino had hoped his new clothes and trim haircut would carry him through. But he was too large and inexperienced and too obviously Italian to fool anyone. Giulia and Marie were another matter. Gino might be intimidated by slender French mannequins, but native Frenchmen showed frank appreciation for the young and voluptuous Italian beauties. Style is one thing; pleasure another.

Tour d'Argent; Maxim's; Laperesse. Night after night they dutifully followed the three star selections in Giulia's *Guide Michelin*. They ate delicacies of such subtle flavors they were not certain what they tasted, and in such profusion that it ceased to matter.

After a few days, the joys of dining waned. Yet even in this short time Gino and Pietro grew heavier. Gino's energy, sexual and otherwise, returned overnight. There was a reason to get up in the morning, a reason to go to bed at night—and pleasant dreams in between. He did no sketching and did not even miss it. At least not for a while. But whenever conversation slackened, whenever he had a moment to himself, whenever he saw a tall angular Frenchman, Gino thought of Pierre Petit.

For a few days he managed to fight off this apparition. But it was no good. The vision of the painter, pointing an astonishingly long and accusing finger at him (dripping with paint), was everywhere.

This vision followed him across Paris, from the Bois to St. Germain des Prés, from the twisting streets of Montmartre to the Champs de Mars. Pierre Petit lurked behind every tree in the

Luxembourg Gardens, and confronted Gino every time he faced the statue of Napoleon in the place Vendôme.

"I can't stand it!" he cried.

They stared at him, startled. He was staring at a pond in the garden of the Tuileries when he spoke aloud—evidently to a twin-masted toy boat that a little boy was maneuvering with a long stick. The stick was being pointed accusingly at Gino by Pierre Petit, but of course the others didn't understand.

After a moment, Gino realized where he was. He looked about, noting the perplexed faces of his companions and the blank expressions of the other people in the gardens. His eyes took in the serried trees, the graveled walks, the rusting iron chairs, the Arc du Triumph du Carrousel, the Louvre, the iron gates and the autumn flowers.

"I tell you I can't stand it." This time he looked directly at Pietro.

Pietro shrugged. "To me, it's bearable," he said.

Gino took Giulia by the hand and seated her in a green iron chair. He took another iron chair and placed it before her. He sat knee to knee with her and, holding her hands, said, "Tell me, golden angel, who gave you the idea of coming to Paris?"

"Maria."

"I see. Maria, what made you suggest this to Giulia?"

Maria glanced at Pietro, but did not speak.

"I see."

"No, you don't see," said Pietro. "I never suggested this to Maria. I haven't once written to her since we left Florence."

Maria was staring at the gravel walk. Pietro was in agony. Was he to blame that Maria had come? Once he knew the truth, had he not left Florence immediately? He knew that the moment she first appeared in Paris he should have sent her away. Before this—this thing started again between them.

Gino rose from his chair and walked along the stone margin of the pond. He stooped to throw a piece of gravel through the placid surface. The small boy protested this invasion. Gino followed the circuit in a slow march to throbbing drums. It was very painful. When he returned to Giulia, his mind was made up.

"I'm very sorry, my love, but you must go home."

Giulia laughed.

"Don't laugh. I'm quite serious. We gave our word that we would leave Florence."

"Is this Florence?" Maria asked.

"We took money from Giulia's father on our promise I would not see her again."

"You didn't go to her. She came to you."

"Stop talking about me as if I were a statue!" cried Giulia. "Talk to me."

"I'm sorry, *carrisa mio*, but you must go home."

She burst into tears. "You do . . . not . . . love me!" Her wails rose in the garden. She threw herself upon Gino, pleading with him to let her stay. But his native Tuscan stubbornness sustained him. He led her, weeping piteously, out of the Tuileries.

Pietro was black with anger. *The peasant. The shoemaker. Why must he always be the virtuous one?*

♦ ♦ ♦

During the next two days, Gino continued to insist on the women's departure. Giulia's wailing persisted, and Gino's sympathy was occasionally tinged with annoyance.

Maria tried to argue Giulia's case with Gino. Why not permit her to remain? She loved Gino—that was clear. Signore Rossini was a fool if he thought he could keep them apart. Gino had not promised a lifetime of abstinence. Maria cajoled and reasoned and finally screamed at him.

Gino was unmoved. Until then he had not really known whether he loved Giulia or not. He had never even asked himself the question. The words of love came easily enough, and the lovemaking came even more readily. But there was a difference between love and lovemaking. He knew now that he did not love

Giulia Rossini. He was fond of her, grateful for the pleasure she had given him, the kindness and generosity she had shown him. He regretted that he felt nothing more.

The pilgrimage to the train station was gloomy: Giulia sobbing quietly, Maria comforting her, Gino and Pietro both silent.

Gino could not help crying when he kissed Giulia goodbye. But he knew that his sorrow was not unmixed with self-pity. As Gino and Pietro backed out of the compartment, Maria picked up her suitcase and followed them.

"Where are you going?" Gino asked.

"I'm staying."

"You can't," Gino said, "you must return to Florence with Giulia."

"I'm staying in Paris."

"No," said Pietro. "It's impossible, absolutely impossible."

But Maria was already walking away down the platform, and she did not respond.

Pietro grabbed Gino's arm. "She's your sister!" he yelled. "Make her go back with Giulia!"

"What am I to do?" asked Gino. "Tie her up and throw her on the train?"

Pietro's voice cracked with pain and anger. Gino shook his head. Pietro was still yelling at both of them when the train pulled out.

The final departure of Giulia Rossini went almost unnoticed.

♦ ♦ ♦

When the three of them returned to the rue Lepic, Pietro went directly to Maria's room, gathered her things and brought them to the room he had been sharing with Gino. Then he bundled up his own clothes, carried them to the other room and slammed the door.

Gino didn't know what to think. He hadn't slept in the same room with his sister since before the war and she was no longer a child. Still, he was pleased she would not be living with Pietro.

Maria moved about the room, arranging her clothes. Gino said nothing. It was good to have her there.

"He's much different than he was, Gino."

"I see no change."

"You wouldn't. But to a woman . . . " For a moment she could not speak. "I never believed that he loved me, not when we were in Florence. I loved him, but I knew he wanted only my body."

"Please, Maria."

"You're not a child, Gino."

He was very uncomfortable. He didn't want to hear the things that his sister was determined to tell him.

"Since we arrived in Paris, he acts like he loves me more, yet wants me less. He's not tender. Oh, no. His lovemaking is fierce—almost cruel. It's like it's hard work for him to make love to me, and yet he can't do without it. Then, when it's over, he is gentle. Very gentle."

She shook her head. "Two nights ago he screamed out loud in his sleep. I woke him up. When he realized where he was, he began to cry."

"Pietro? I don't believe it."

"Yes, he cried, and then he asked me to forgive him."

"For what?"

"He wouldn't say."

"How can you love this man?" Gino asked.

"Believe me, dear brother, I wish I didn't."

"But you remain here, nonetheless."

"In Paris I'll see Pietro some of the time. In Florence I have no chance whatsoever."

"I'm ashamed of you."

"Me, too."

She spoke in such a gentle voice and with such a wistful smile, that Gino immediately regretted his words. "I'm sorry, Maria. I suppose that each of us must live his life as best as he knows how."

She kissed him on the forehead and embraced him.

"How will you live, Maria? I have no money, and Pietro won't help us."

She hurried to the door, made sure it was latched, returned to her bed and rummaged through her clothing. With a little exclamation of pleasure she found what she was searching for and presented it to Gino. He was staggered.

"Thousands of francs! Where did you get them?"

"From Giulia. She told me to give them to you."

Gino sat down on Maria's bed. "How can I take this money? After what I've done to her."

"She wanted you to have it, believe me. She made me promise to give it to you after she left."

"Then she knew you were staying."

"Gino, there's enough to support us for a long time. Don't worry about Giulia. She has all the money in the world and any young man she wants—except you. Please share the money with me?" She smiled appealingly.

The temptation was too strong to resist. Here was freedom from Pietro; freedom to paint as he liked. How could he say no? "What about Pietro?"

"We won't tell him." She handed Gino the francs.

"Okay, Maria. I'll tell him Pierre Petit has hired me again as his assistant. But what will you do?"

"I'll find something. Maybe I can get a job that doesn't require a work permit. Or maybe our crafty Pietro can get a permit for me."

◆ ◆ ◆

Pietro had no intention of helping, confident that Maria had little money and would soon be forced to go home. Thus, Maria was left to her own devices, which were few, and only narrowly effective. She found household work from time to time even though she was too pretty for many wives to consider employing. In a few instances, she had to flee for her virtue when the man of the household misunderstood the terms of her contract.

It was some weeks before Gino was ready to see Pierre Petit again. In the meantime, he spent every daylight hour sketching and painting. Finding his room inadequate, Gino arranged with his landlady to hire some unused space up under the eaves. It was dirty and cramped, but a large dormer window provided cool north light and he was satisfied. This was Gino's first studio. He worked assiduously as long as there was adequate illumination and sometimes when there was almost none.

Because of her erratic employment, Maria was often available as a model. Gino sketched her again and again and always in the same position: sitting, hands folded, head straight on. He was trying to capture something, although uncertain at the moment what it was, but he did not want to be distracted by extraneous items in the setting, nor by the problems which a more complex pose would demand. A woman standing or sitting, that was enough. Why confuse the picture with beds, balustrades, tables or bowls of flowers? He was trying to distill something. Not Maria. Not even the special qualities that made him love her.

When Maria was finally allowed to see his first completed portrait of her, she was terribly disappointed. "Gino," she said. "This isn't me."

"Yes, it is. It really is you."

"I don't recognize myself. The face has hardly any features. A line for the mouth, two for the nose, shadows for the eyes. Is that how you see me?"

Gino nodded.

"And my body—a round lump. Hands without fingers. Arms thin as sticks. Your Maria has a better shape than that."

"Of course."

"Then it's not Maria?"

"Yes, it is!" He threw down his brushes and stomped out of the attic. Maria's cajoling voice did not bring him back.

In a sense, she was right. His painting was not of an individual—of a particular Maria. It was all Marias, now and forever. What bothered him was his fear that he had failed to convey his own personal vision of the world. Of course the portrait of Maria was only his first effort, and perhaps it was not as good as he had believed.

Gino painted Maria a dozen times. Each time in a similar pose, but using different colors and tones. He altered the slant of her head. He varied the placement of her hands and the lines of her dress. He refined his brush stroke, avoiding impasto, applying the paint in short even strips of color. Working diligently to reconstruct his sister's face on canvas, Gino sketched a hundred lines for every one he painted. He was not trying to develop a photographic likeness of her features, but rather to extract from the Maria he saw and the ones he had sketched the minimum number of lines and tones which would portray the true Maria on canvas. Maria as he saw her: a beautiful, simple peasant girl, bubbling with affection, deep with expected grief.

When he completed the twelfth "likeness" he knew he had failed. But he also knew that he had improved. Now he would bring all twelve canvases to Pierre Petit. Surely the master would be able to help him.

◆ ◆ ◆

Petit was impressed. "Thank God. I thought you had given up painting and gone home to Florence. And here you have been patiently working. Forgive me, Gino, I should never have doubted you."

"Why not? I still doubt myself."

"There's nothing wrong with that. When you're satisfied you'll cease to be an artist. But these canvases tell a story. The improvement from first to last is amazing. Amazing!"

"Frankly, I feel they're failures. I don't know how to portray my own thoughts. Can you help me?"

"I don't see the problem. Take this final canvas. You have arranged a lovely combination of shapes and colors that leap off the canvas—they provide their own dynamic. Most pleasing." He paused, searching Gino's face. "You don't like what I said. I'm sorry."

"I wanted to do more than merely arrange shapes and colors in a pleasing way. I was trying to paint a portrait."

"Of whom?"

"Not of whom. Of what."

"Very well then, of what?"

Gino struggled to find the words, which might convey the ideas he wanted to show on the canvas. "A portrait of simplicity," he said.

"You know, Gino, some men say that to express the universal, you must paint the particular. In other words, if you want to convey simplicity, paint a simple person, but paint him very well."

Gino shook his head. "True and not true. A camera can do that better. I want to omit all details—that is, all except the ones which will instantly convey my meaning."

"You'll end up an abstractionist."

"No. Well, yes. In a sense. But I want to paint people, not lines. I want to show patterns by means of actual objects. I don't seek camera reality, but I'm not willing to deal only with shapes and colors. People and things are real. I don't want to destroy them. I want to show them on my canvas for what they are—what they really are."

It was the longest speech he had ever made. Petit was surprised. "I think your goals are good, Gino. I know you have the talent to reach them. But I don't know how I can help you. You want to show your own special vision of the world, which is only right. That's what an artist must do. But Pierre Petit cannot creep into your brain and poke around until he finds the elements essential to such an undertaking. That is your struggle and you must fight it alone. But please come and see me often. I can help you with technique (the pigment is too thin on that hand, by the way), but that's all I can do. You must prepare a representative set of your paintings. The twelve paintings of your sister are splendid, but hardly range enough. Paint other people—paint still lifes—landscapes. When you have more variety, come to me.

Perhaps I can persuade a gallery director to show your work."

♦ ♦ ♦

To Gino, Pierre Petit's casual suggestion was inspiring. The master would bring his work to the leading galleries, and one of them would surely find him talented. It was good, very good, to have such a prospect. Every time his hopes or his energy flagged, he thought of Pierre Petit's promise (was it a promise?) and automatically his strength was renewed.

Gino gave up painting Maria and tried other subjects. It was a relief to both of them. Maria had found the posing boring, but she would not have dreamed of complaining. For Gino, this concentration on his sister had been a dangerous and disconcerting exercise. He had worked out his frustrations by delineating them on canvas. But he knew it was best that the sessions ended. He was agitated enough each night by the thought of Maria sleeping only a few feet from his own bed.

Gino could not afford professional models, but that did not disturb him. His models were the memories he called to mind as he required them: Brother Alberto and Lorenzo Patti. His mother and Yvette Chardin. It was difficult but exciting. He thought his memories were quite clear until he tried to copy them on canvas. For an instant he would fix an image on the plate of his brain. Suddenly, it would begin to flutter. He would struggle to retain it, and once again it snapped into place. But then, just as suddenly, the vision dissolved. It might be hours, even days, before he could call it back. Sometimes, not at all.

Although these exercises were frustrating, Gino knew they had merit. His memories of people were as worthy models as the originals. In fact, he enjoyed having the freedom to alter his conception as the thoughts occurred to him. Nevertheless, his subjects were people; real people. If they also represented Gino's conceptions of virtue and vice personified, that did not detract from their clarity as portraits.

When painting Brother Domenico, he didn't have to direct the monk to assume a pious expression. Nevertheless, the completed work radiated religious tension. It was as if the muscles of Domenico's own body had molded the pigment into a pose that betrayed his natural fervor. Gino's painting suggested all this with remarkably few lines. Yet, he was still unhappy. Would anyone have known that this was a monk had he not painted him in a monk's habit? Was he painting only puppets, not people?

Gino found still lifes far easier. After all, they displayed no expression that he must capture, possessed no emotions to illustrate, no character to portray. Yet they were real and very important to him. He had always delighted in the proportions of everyday things. Even as a child he had played with the simple arrangements of bowls and spoons on his mother's table. Every object must have a symmetry—a rhythm—of its own. He knew that this symmetry was the product of someone's design, not of the artifact's volition, but the fact that simple things could be arranged in a pleasing, even expressive, pattern excited his wonder. Why couldn't people achieve such symmetry in the living world?

Each type of subject matter presented a different problem. Plants possess their own patterns, tones and rhythms. They might be arranged in a garden, but this was antithetical to their nature, not a product of it. And "natural" landscapes did not excite him. He loved mountains and streams, trees and flowers. But he loved people more—and the things people made. Humanity was the ultimate achievement. Untamed nature might represent God in all His purity, but Gino, childlike and unsophisticated, loved the God he saw in mankind even more, and, therefore, the God he saw in mankind's creations.

He was constantly distracted. Since he painted visions, he was subject to them. While he drew Domenico, he saw Alberto. When he painted Maria, he saw Giulia. It was not good, not right, not even possible to pin down, to isolate one single human feature of one single human being. He saw the relations and comparisons between things. Each part of the world echoed some other. He sometimes forgot what he was painting and began to illustrate something else. Occasionally the results were attractive. Other times he experienced total failure.

He didn't mind. Life seemed to stretch ahead of him forever, an endless field filled with endless flowers. All of them his to pluck. All his to paint. There was no end of subjects which delighted and enthused him. And yet, he realized he must concentrate on what he was doing. Otherwise he would finish nothing. It was difficult. His joy in the discoveries he made was so intense it almost paralyzed him. He would paint a line and love it, amazed that his hand could place this colorful arc on canvas. In a moment it would be joined by others, eventually it would be lost among the thousands of strokes on each canvas, but for the moment it thrilled him. He, Gianpaolo Bondone, could paint such a line. Marvel of marvels.

The hours of the day were not sufficient. He scraped his palette reluctantly each night and leaped out of bed to prepare it each morning. He ate but little: bread, cheese, wine; bread, cheese, wine. He didn't care. Once he had starved and noted every pang of hunger. Now he starved and noticed nothing. He lay awake late into each night, planning what he would do the following day, seeing each painting complete when it was still a sketch on paper. He lay there with a satisfied smile on his face, contemplating the finished work. It was not easy to match these nocturnal masterpieces. Sometimes he ruined his own dreams. If he painted something that varied from his conception, he couldn't always recapture the original vision. He would be angry and try to remove the offending image from his brain. Without success. The picture painted overcame the image imagined.

Sometimes, while lying in bed he would visualize an error he had made during the day. Impatiently, he dressed and hurried to the attic. There, by the pale, uneven glow of the bald electric light bulb swinging from the ceiling, he made his corrections. But sometimes not. Sometimes the image he had painted was too powerful to adjust. That could be painful—or exhilarating.

He seldom left the rooming house now. Not even Maria could

persuade him to take an evening walk. Pietro didn't interfere. Perhaps he thought that Gino would soon explode and he would be better able to deal with the fragments.

Gino's face paled to a sallow yellow, the same color as the light bulb in his cramped, little studio. Gradually, he took on all the tones of his room: yellow, beige, brown and gray—faded colors, wasting colors. But his canvases were bright with flaming tongues of pigment. It was difficult to believe they came from the brush of this ascetic looking man. Maria worried; Pietro shrugged; Gino painted.

In October he decided to approach Pierre once again, hoping the painter would like his work, fearing he might scoff at it. He selected ten canvases and set out for the house in the rue de Babylone.

Gino stood outside the gate for nearly an hour, unable to pull on the bell cord. He was still standing there when Pierre Petit stepped out of the house.

"Gino, have you just come? I was about to leave."

"All right, I'll return some other time." He prepared to flee.

"What have you there?"

Gino did not respond, but there was no need. Petit took the rolled-up bundle of canvases from beneath his arm and went into his house, Gino trailing behind.

Petit arranged Gino's works about the walls of the studio, propping them here and there. He grunted a few times as he unrolled them, but did not comment until they were all revealed and mounted. The master walked from painting to painting, studying each and then passing on to the next. When he was finished he stood in the middle of the room, slowly surveying the entire lot.

"My son," he said. "You are a painter."

♦   ♦   ♦

The following morning Petit escorted Gino and his works to the Galerie de Nains in the Avenue Matignon, not far from the Palais de l'Élysée. Monsieur de Nains greeted Petit with enthusiasm and expressed an eagerness to see the work of his disciple. They climbed the steps of the narrow building, which was half staircase, until they reached the workshop. There, paintings were secured to stretchers and framed. It was a musty, dusty room crowded with hundreds of strips of wood in assorted sizes and filled with the cloying smell of glue, gesso, oils and varnish.

Gino placed his canvases on an easel that clamped them top and bottom, one by one. First came the painting of Brother Domenico.

De Nains grunted. "Religious painter, eh?"

"Oh no," said Petit. "Show him the *nature mortes*."

De Nains studied them with narrowed eyes, expressionless. Each time he sniffed, it was time to display another. De Nains closed his eyes with a curious slow motion, like a shutter narrowing on a camera.

"Very good, eh?" Pierre Petit filled the silence with his comments. "Fine sense of composition; excellent colors." His words had no visible impact on the gallery owner.

One by one Gino submitted his paintings to this visual guillotine. Each time the blade snapped down, he withdrew the corpse and substituted another victim.

When the executions were over, Monsieur de Nains spoke to Petit as if Gino were not there. "Your young friend has talent. His draftsmanship is good, his sense of color quite interesting. The compositions are a bit static, but not unbearably so."

"I knew you would like his work."

"I do . . . but I could never sell it. It's not the kind of thing that moves these days. It's not classical enough for the old ladies and it's not advanced enough for the sophisticates."

"You can't mean that—you of all people, Henri. You sold Morandi when no one would handle him. You hung Wols when others laughed at his work. You brought Klée and Kandinsky together for the first time in one exhibition. Don't tell me you're afraid to take chances."

"I wouldn't be taking any chance whatsoever. I would just be wasting my time and your friend's. These won't sell. Believe me."

"Now listen, young man." The camera shutter eyes swiveled open, and Gino stared with fascination into the shiny opaque lenses. "Look around in my gallery. Walk down the street and look in the windows of the galleries on the Avenue Matignon. Go into Audrey Goujon's establishment—she's a leader in this community. Examine the works in her gallery, or any other in the city. You'll see what's being done. Believe me, these solid shapes and clear tones are passé. You are in Paris, young man; paint like the Parisians."

"Henri," Petit said. "I think you should reconsider. We'll leave Gianpaolo's works here for a few days so that you may study them. His conception is unique and quite marvelous, really. I'm sure you'll see what I mean after a while."

"Thank you, no." De Nains hurried to the easel and handed the painting mounted there (Maria) to Gino. "It just won't do. Let's not quarrel, Pierre."

But Pierre was in the mood to quarrel. "This is an insult, Henri. You act like I have no taste and no judgment. I bring you this brilliant new talent and you tell him to paint like an uninspired left bank idiot. What kind of nonsense is that?"

"It is the nonsense that sells." De Nains hesitated but a second. "Frankly, if you brought me some of your own canvases—like the ones you painted before doing the Chaillot—I couldn't sell them today, either. The world has run off in another direction, my dear friend. If you don't hurry you'll be left behind."

"Better to be left behind. Come along, Gino." Without a final salutation, Petit hurried down the steps.

It took Gino a moment to bundle up his works. Time enough for De Nains to whisper, "Believe me, young man, I'm telling you the truth. Change your style or give up painting. They won't discover you for a hundred years."

◆ ◆ ◆

"He has grown senile," Petit said with great confidence. "We'll find someone who still retains his faculties."

But evidently all of Paris had lost its wits. Or at least all of the Paris that Pierre Petit knew. Together, they tried six more galleries. In each, the famous French painter was greeted with warmth and respect. But no one would hang the paintings of Gianpaolo Bondone. The gallery owners' comments were reducible to a formula: "Personally, I like it, but it will never sell."

The experience seemed to crush Pierre Petit. He cursed the gallery owners, cursed the heavens, cursed himself.

"Perhaps I should do as they say," Gino offered. "Study the work of the School of Paris. Perhaps in my inexperience I have barely reached the eighteenth century while everyone of talent is in the twentieth."

"No!" screamed Petit, "it's not true. These people are selling anarchy, not art. Don't change what you're doing. Don't copy those illiterate apes. They're going backward not forward."

Suddenly it seemed all of Petit's energy drained away. His fiery cheeks turned a translucent yellow, and Gino was afraid his friend would be ill. He took Petit's arm and led him to a bench in a small, leafy park. They were both grateful for the respite.

"I'm sorry to have shouted at you, Gino. I'm afraid I've not been entirely honest. I do believe you have great talent. I do think these gallery owners are wrong. But mostly I'm afraid for myself. They're saying that I am outdated, too. And it's much worse for me, Gino. I'm too old to change now, but too young to stop working."

"Please," Gino said. "I think they're all fools. They don't appreciate either of us. But people will love our paintings long after their galleries are closed."

Eleven

The Battle of the Biennale

Gino hadn't expected a miracle and therefore he wasn't crushed when one didn't occur. But Petit's loss of faith, not in Gino but in himself, was shattering. How could Gino have confidence in a man who had no faith in himself?

Nevertheless, Gino wasn't blinded. He called to mind the paintings that the gallery owners had told him he must emulate, comparing them in his memory with his own. After considerable and, of course, objective consideration, he reached his conclusion: *I am the better painter,* he thought. *Let them copy me.*

Gino selected four of his best canvases and mounted them on stretchers, and began to tour the galleries himself. In some cases he barely managed to step inside the door before he was dismissed. In other instances, the gallery directors grudgingly permitted him to show his work. Some studied his art for a long time, others for mere minutes. Some were kind, others contemptuous. All rejected him.

He trudged up and down the streets like a peddler, trying to put a foot in every door. He offered to leave a painting as one might leave a piece of yard goods as an inducement to the mistress of the house. He tried humility and he tried insolence. He wore his best clothes and his worst. He appeared for interviews closely shaven and raggedly bearded. It made no difference.

His mood deteriorated from stern determination to quiet desperation. He was unable to believe that not one of these people would have any interest in his work. He told himself that it was because he was Italian, and spoke French so poorly. Yet, in the very galleries where he felt certain this was the explanation, the works of other Italian painters hung on the walls. Perhaps they spoke better French.

One day, still wandering about searching for a gallery—any gallery—he saw a crowd in front of the Musée National d'Art Moderne, and curiosity drew him closer. Some kind of event was in progress, a *retrospectif* for an artist named Marc Chagall. Although the name seemed familiar to him, he would have continued onward except that a splash of color on the poster intrigued him. They would not allow him to carry his canvases into the exhibition and he was afraid to leave them in the checkroom. Stubbornly, he returned to the rue Lepic, put away his work and hurried back to the museum.

Once inside the exhibition rooms he nearly staggered. The colors. Strong, rich, vibrant colors, hues and variations he had never seen before. The subjects hardly mattered, people and things seemed fragile, wistful, incomprehensible, powerful. Until he saw the painting titled *The Birthday*. In a room with much detail, none of it realistic, walked a woman carrying flowers and above her, a man, floating, his head twisted around hers at an impossible angle, kissing her. The pose was absurd, but it was lovely—and filled with love, a cascade of emotion drenched in colors. So much feeling burst from the canvas, he almost fainted.

Next, there was a painting of a violinist, wearing a coat and hat in strange tones of pink and purple. The man's face was green, so was one hand. The name of the painting was *The Green Violinist*. But the hand holding the violin was flesh-toned, and so was one shoe—the other a blackish-brownish hue. And the violinist was standing on the slanting roofs of two houses. He was huge, the town was small. Behind his head were other houses and strange round cloud shapes and a man—or was it a woman?—floating over the clouds. The painting was dated 1923-24; the description on the printed card said there was an earlier version in 1920.

1920, Gino thought, *the year of my birth. The other painting is entitled* The Birthday, *but this one was done in the year of my birth.* The two paintings blended together in his mind, as if the violinist was playing on the roof of the house in which the birthday was being celebrated, playing for the couple within—one of whom was the artist. This Chagall. And then, suddenly he remembered the painting on Pierre Petit's wall. All of the strange and mysterious colors, the natural, unnatural figures, the floating, nebulous world became one.

The violinist sawing away so intently, playing new-old music for a modern-traditional, reborn world. A renaissance riotous with new rhythms and colors, glowing yet serene, instantly recognizable, but filled with mystery.

Is this it? Is this the near past, the shadowy present, the fairy-tale future? I don't dream like this; I don't paint like this. I can't.

Confused and shaken, Gino hurried out of the exhibition halls. Near the exit he saw a group of well-dressed men and women crowded around a man of slender build with thinning grayish hair, but with a lean, powerful face, the chin and nose strong. He was speaking in heavily accented French, but his eyes sparkled, and in one flashing second Gino thought their eyes met and the man smiled. Gino replied with an uncertain grin, but didn't lose stride. Chagall?

Back in his attic, he surveyed his work, feeling in his gut the deep contrast between his vision and Chagall's. He wavered back and forth between despondence and challenge. No longer could he summarily discard all the artists of his time. If there was one painter this powerful, there might be others whose work he hadn't yet seen. Finally, he forced himself to breathe deeply, to relax, to think with less passion.

He is good, no doubt of it. But so am I. He has a vision, but so have I. Chagall does not destroy me. Perhaps there is something I can learn. What is it? Searching his mind he could not find it, but he would neither surrender to it, nor pretend it did not exist.

◆ ◆ ◆

Gino had one consolation: Maria. She commiserated with him, offered to accompany him on his expeditions to the galleries. He turned her down, fearing she would be effective, but only because the Frenchmen would find her high bosom and slim ankles attractive.

"Perhaps Pietro can help you," Maria suggested.

"How?"

"Newspaper people know everyone. This week I've seen Pietro's name over three stories in *Paris-Presse*. I don't really understand the articles, but I'm sure that by now he must be acquainted with everyone who's important in the city. I know it's not easy for you, Gino, but soon we'll have spent all the money Giulia left us."

When Gino reluctantly blurted out his problem, Pietro could not hide his look of triumph. "Having a difficult time, *Signore Artista?*"

"I didn't come here to be taunted."

"Taunted? I don't wish to taunt you. I intend to help you. Bundle up a few of your masterpieces and we'll speak to my friend Le Temps."

How many times had he trailed Pietro through the streets of Florence and Paris? It seemed he was forever trailing in someone's van. When would he be fully a man?

The gallery of Louis Le Temps was a large and elegant establishment on the boulevard St. Germain, a broad concourse lined with birch trees and tall, finely traced apartment houses. The shops below intruded on this elegance, but at least the signs and displays were discreet.

The name "Louis Le Temps" was set in slim, flowing black script not more than a foot high. There was no other designation of the business and the windows were empty. Inside one could see rows of paintings hanging on the walls, each individually lighted from above. As they entered, a man approached from the rear of the gallery.

"Le Temps," Pietro mumbled. He was short and rather heavy, yet his black suit was cut so finely, that one could not smile. Not even his shaved bald head and pearl gray vest betrayed him.

He moved toward them, hands folded chest high, with a priestly look upon his smooth face. At approximately five paces he placed a pince-nez upon his nose and smiled. "Ah, Pietro," he said with great warmth. "How good to see you."

They embraced while exchanging salutations and good wishes. Gino was ignored.

"Perfect that you should be here today, Pietro. I have just hung the latest works of Antoine Lunet. You must observe them with me."

He led Pietro along one wall of the gallery, describing the canvases displayed there. Insofar as Gino could ascertain, the paintings all depicted the same subject: a black amorphous mass, occasionally shot through with muddy purple or turgid blue.

"They are called: *Octave: 1, Octave: 2,* and so on. Each represents a note of the musical scale as it appears to Lunet. *Merveilleux, n'est ce pas?*"

Pietro agreed.

Gino tried to distinguish the notes of the scale from each other; to see why one might be, for example "C", or another "E". But to him the pattern was not evident.

"So lyrical!" cried Le Temps with a fluttery gesture of his hand. "Yet so profound. It's almost impossible to find an artist like Lunet in these times. A man with purpose, with true feeling. I'm so pleased to be able to show him."

"Of course," said Pietro with an inscrutable look, "a true master of the twentieth century."

"Good, very good. I'm so happy that you understand. That's what I like about you, Pietro. You have great insight."

"It's my profession, you know."

"I loved your little masterpiece on art last week, my friend. Quite to the point. Oh, yes, quite to the point. What did you say? He held the bridge of his nose between thumb and forefinger and closed his eyes as he intoned, 'Art without politics is garbage.'"

Gino laughed. Monsieur Le Temps seemed to notice him for the first time; he frowned. "Who is this?"

"My dear friend, Gianpaolo Bondone. They tell me he has talent. I cannot judge. In Florence he was quite highly regarded. Here, Pierre Petit has tutored him until—he now says—there is no more he can teach him. I have brought him to you because your eye is so fine and you are always sympathetic to new artists. I want you to look at his work. Be frank, Louis. Gianpaolo comes of sturdy Tuscan stock. He will bear up no matter what you say."

Le Temps snapped his fingers and an assistant materialized out of the shadows. "Take this young man and his works into the private showroom. Arrange his canvases and call us."

Gino followed the assistant, a dour, incredibly thin fellow, into an inner room, the walls of which were lined with a continuous mounting ledge. The assistant, disdaining Gino's proffered help, quickly arranged his canvases The entire ceiling was filled with spotlights of varying sizes and tones, and there were modulating switches on the wall which made it possible to increase or decrease the level of lighting. To Gino's surprise, the silent assistant seemed to have judgment, choosing appropriate levels of illumination for each work. The assistant retreated, as silently as he had come, returning in a few moments with Pietro and Monsieur Le Temps.

The gallery owner had hardly stepped into the room when he spoke. "You cannot be serious. This is absurd." He turned to Pietro. "What have you brought me? This is the work of a child."

Pietro seemed unmoved. "Come now, Louis. One look is not enough. Study his paintings more closely. I'm sure you'll find something here."

"Impossible. There's nothing to see. One look and you've seen everything—and nothing."

"Come, come. Replace your pince-nez and study Bondone's paintings for a moment longer. Pierre Petit isn't insane."

"Not insane. Obsolete. These, too, are obsolete and clumsy. This is cubism reduced to an infantile level."

Pietro laughed and shook his head. "You surprise me, Louis."

"I'll show you what I mean, Pietro. You're just being stubborn."

During this exchange not one word was directed at Gino. Unshaken, he followed Le Temps and Pietro out of the room.

Le Temps pointed first to the paintings by Lunet. "You see this? True feeling. Modern feeling. The soul in chaos, laid bare on the canvas. And over here—what perception! Modern man entombed in his own machine."

Gino could see neither the man nor the machine. Pietro merely shrugged.

"Open your eyes," Le Temps said. "Look at this." With a grand gesture he pointed to a small canvas marked by calligraphy that appeared vaguely oriental, yet had no obviously literary reference. The signature seemed to read "Mathieu," but even that was vague.

"Ah ha, Pietro! You want to know what it means? It looks like a word or a sign, does it not? Vaguely familiar, eh? I assure you it means nothing, as all of life means nothing. From a distance things seem familiar. Forms appear to have substance. Yet when we study things closely we find they signify—nothing."

Le Temps raised his finger high in a triumphant gesture. Gino looked up, but saw only the dull gray ceiling.

"I see," Pietro murmured. "Yes, now it's clear to me precisely what you are saying. But tell me, Louis, aren't you missing something? Let's take a little stroll together." He signaled to Gino to remain in the gallery.

Pietro took Le Temps' arm and, whispering in his ear, led him outside. Gino could see them through the window, standing along the curb, talking, gesturing. A dumb show. Pietro seemed very intense, bent over Le Temps, pointing a crooked forefinger at his forehead. Le Temps threw his hands up, then down. He turned his back and folded his arms. Pietro stepped around him and began to speak again. The little man tried to return to the gallery, but Pietro restrained him. Suddenly they were both laughing. Pietro put an arm over Le Temps' shoulder and together they returned to the gallery.

"It's settled, Gino," Pietro said. "Louis will hang one of your paintings in the *Biennale*—in a place of honor."

"At the Gallery of Louis Le Temps," the gallery owner said grandly, "every place is a place of honor."

Le Temps permitted Gino to select the painting he wanted to have hung in the show, and the gallery owner agreed to frame it at his own expense. Gino protested that his painting required no frame, but Pietro hushed him and finally it was agreed. Gino's painting would hang in the *Biennale*—in the exhibition known as "Young Masters of Paris," held every two years by Le Temps. He made it clear that this was a great honor for a young painter, and Gino was very humble in his gratitude.

Later, speaking to Pietro privately, Gino expressed his confusion. "I don't understand. One minute he said I was an idiot, the next he promised to frame and hang my painting of Maria in a place of honor."

"As long as you have Pietro Scegli as your mentor you need not understand. He will understand for you."

◆　　◆　　◆

Across the following weeks, Gino learned that Le Temps' *Biennale* was an event of more than passing consequence in the art world. Pietro showed him articles in *France Soir* and *Le Monde*—as well as *Paris-Presse*—reporting on the forthcoming Le Temps exhibit. The stories listed the names of many painters (some known to Gino) who had previously been "discovered" at this event. He was thrilled to learn that the *Biennale* wasn't just another trick that Pietro was playing on him.

As the great day approached, Gino found himself increasingly distracted, unable to paint for more than a few minutes without his thoughts wandering. He imagined his painting hanging in some great museum—perhaps close to a work by Chagall. In these visions he wandered up and down a long gallery, chatting amiably though respectfully with other artists, exchanging elevated conversation with critics and patrons.

The day of the premiere, he treated himself to a professional shave and haircut, had his shoes shined and his clothes pressed by Maria. She was planning to go with him, but when she was dressed and ready, Gino mumbled an apology, promised to meet her later at the gallery and bolted from the premises. Maria ran down the stairs and into the rue Lepic calling after him.

He had melted into a trembling vial of fear. It was autumn—an especially cold and bleak evening. The wind raised lancets of dust from the street, stinging his face and bringing tears to his eyes. That was a release of sorts. Since Gino had hurried away without his coat, he was shivering, but he knew that if he returned to his room, he would never go to the gallery. After an hour of wandering, some of his courage returned. He decided to walk to the gallery. That would take time; perhaps by then most of the crowd would be gone. The worst would be over.

In this hope he was disappointed. Despite his dawdling, the gallery was still crowded, even the sidewalk outside, people chattering, laughing, lifting puffs of cigarette smoke into the air, clinking wine glasses. A steady flow of automobiles arrived and departed.

Gino sat on a doorstoop across the street and waited for the crowd to thin. But it didn't. If anything, more people seemed to arrive than to leave. Finally, the attraction was too much. He wiped his face with a handkerchief (it came away streaked with dirt), straightened his tie and his jacket, pulled a comb through his hair, and crossed the street.

It was not so bad; no one noticed him. They were too busy talking and drinking Le Temps' wine. Inside, it was warm and bright.

People were pressed together in one great mass, pushing and shoving, talking and gesturing.

The first painting he noticed was an angry black slash on a bone white canvas. He realized at once the frowning young man standing next to it must be the artist because he boasted a mustache that weirdly echoed his painting.

This was an interesting and entertaining game, matching the painter with his painting. Sometimes it was quite easy. A dirty young man with an uncombed haystack of yellow hair was the painter of a similarly unkempt landscape—if it really was a landscape. Although most of the paintings confused and perplexed Gino, he didn't laugh, not even at painters whose appearance was as strange as their work. In fact he loved them. They were his brothers and sisters. They, too, shared his search for beauty, the urge to fix it forever on canvas. What if their visions differed from his? Perhaps, like Chagall, they owned some portion of truth he had not yet acknowledged. Perhaps, some day he too would be initiated into these mysteries. His heart expanded with love and pleasure. He could have hugged them all. Two men brushed past him; one was the man who had seemed to smile at him at the museum, and who nodded amiably as he moved toward the exit.

"Chagall," someone whispered, and Gino's heart almost stopped. He wanted to speak to the artist, but the crowd had closed behind him and although he could see over people's heads and follow Chagall's progress out of the gallery, it would have been been impossible to reach him. *One day*, Gino thought. *I'm sure of it.*

Then he saw Maria. Not the living Maria; the one he had painted: A simple girl sitting in a chair (one thick straight line for the back and one for a leg), wearing a geometrically regular green dress, and a geometrically irregular expression. The background was a velvety beige. She was framed in white—simple white as he had imagined her. He loved her. He loved himself. *I have created this*, he thought. *I'm proud of me.*

"You look very proud."

"Maria. I'm sorry, I shouldn't have run away, but I was frightened."

"I knew you would come, eventually."

"The artist I presume." This came from behind Gino, and he turned to see a tall, slender, extremely handsome Frenchman with spiky blonde hair, who was immaculately attired in a pale blue four-button, single-breasted suit, a stiff white, high-collared shirt with a slim black tie and amazingly narrow black shoes polished to a high gloss.

"Yes, I am the artist," Gino responded, smiling.

"Gregory, come here," the Frenchman called to a bulky fellow who lounged against the opposite wall, explaining his painting to a little lady who looked up at him in adoration. "Gregory" flaunted huge black mustaches and an unkempt beard. He was dressed in an open-collared, rumpled white shirt with a brown stain on the front, dark brown trousers that flared at the cuff and a patched leather jacket. Reluctantly leaving his admirer, he moved ponderously across the gallery.

"Here is the artist, Gregory. The man who painted this masterpiece."

Gino said, "Are you an artist, too?"

"Am I an artist, too?" the thin Frenchman mimicked him. "Yes, I am an artist." He stepped aside, indicating by his gesture that the painting behind him was his own.

Gino studied it. At first glance, the canvas seemed to portray a mountain scene with myriad small figures clambering up and down. The lines were very clearly drawn, the colors smoothly applied, and the entire effect quite intricate and controlled. But a closer look revealed the figures were not actually human. They had shapes and forms that reminded one of human shapes, and they struck poses, which at first glance seemed human. But they were not. Just blobs of color, carefully edged and modeled to give the illusion of life and movement without actually depicting it.

"Quite interesting," Gino said politely.

Gregory took Gino's arm and pulled him across the room.

"And what, my educated and learned friend, do you think of this?" he said, speaking in a sonorous accent that sounded Russian to Gino, while indicating a large canvas loaded with chunks of tumultuous color. There were no apparent shapes, no lines—just slashes and lumps built up in a fearsome crescendo of glaring tones.

"Is it yours?" asked Gino tentatively.

"Yes."

"I like it."

"Do you hear that, Marcel. He likes it!" Gregory shouted this intelligence across the room to the tall, handsome Frenchman.

Marcel laughed. "Does he understand it?"

Others were listening. Gino would have slipped away, but Gregory held his arm tightly.

"Do you understand it?"

"Is it necessary to understand it in order to like it?"

"Yes."

Gino hesitated. He glanced about him. For the first time he caught sight of Pietro. Le Temps was standing beside him, his lips turned up, perhaps in a smile, perhaps in distaste. Others gathered on around them. A narrow corridor—a gauntlet as it were—ran from Gino and the tall, untidy Russian to the dapper Marcel. The room was nearly silent, awaiting his reply. He could hear voices receding in waves.

"I said it *is* necessary. Did you hear me?"

"All right, I understand it."

"Very good. Now, what do you understand?"

"It is a painting of a large blob of black paint with many small blobs of other colors."

Even Marcel laughed.

"Silence, all of you!" the Russian yelled, then turned on Gino. "You're an ignorant Italian peasant and you don't understand a thing."

"I am an ignorant Italian peasant, but I understand."

Gregory grew even angrier. "How could you understand? Look at that painting of yours. What is it about?"

Gino smiled. "Another ignorant Italian peasant—my sister."

Everyone laughed again. A voice asked, "What do you see in Marcel's painting?"

"Many ignorant Italian peasants climbing a mountain."

Amid the laughter, Marcel approached him. "Those are not people," he said, his mouth strung in a tight line from cheek to cheek.

"Excuse me, as an obvious expert, I thought I recognized other ignorant Italian peasants."

Now Gregory was laughing at Marcel, along with the rest of the room.

"What are you laughing at?" Marcel asked Gregory. "There is nothing anyone can recognize in your painting."

The Russian let go of Gino's arm and stood very straight. "It is a portrait of the human soul."

Gino tapped him on the chest. "If it's anything like your soul, it must be big and black with purple edges."

"I'll kill you!" Gregory cried.

"Why kill an ignorant Italian peasant? It's your friend Marcel who is laughing at you." Fear had lost its grip on Gino. "Tell me, Gregory," he said. "What do you see in Marcel's painting?"

"A thousand tittering homosexuals."

Marcel stopped laughing.

"Do they look like Marcel?"

"Yes, the resemblance is uncanny."

"Your sister is a whore!" screamed Marcel, pointing at Gino's painting, his face bright red, his hand shaking.

"That's better than a pervert!" cried Gregory.

Gino stepped aside as they leaped at each other. In moments the room was bedlam. Gregory was pummeling Marcel; Marcel was biting Gregory's arm. Others were struggling to separate them. When it seemed that peace might be restored momentarily, Gino grabbed the nearest man by the back of his coat and shoved him into someone else. They both sprawled on the floor.

Others tripped and began to struggle for balance. Women

began to scream. Out of the corner of his eye Gino saw Marcel leap towards him, arms upraised, fingers claw-like. Gino stepped aside and Marcel flew past, lunging face forward onto the floor, skidding into a wall.

Le Temps was screaming for the fighting to stop. Gino pushed him into the melee. Other little quarrels broke out. People rushing in from the street were almost trampled by those trying to get out. Gino slipped through the crowd towards his painting of Maria. As he approached, he noticed Gregory fighting through the crowd trying to reach him. Just as the Russian raised his fist, Gino shouted. "Look, Marcel's painting is laughing at you."

While Gregory was distracted, Gino hit him on the side of the chin and knocked him half way across the room, spectators jumping out of the way to avoid being knocked down. Gino laughed and clapped his hands.

Marcel stood close by, bleeding and sniffling. "You see, Marcel," Gino told him, "Gregory thinks you're a pervert. Apparently that is the message in his painting. What are you going to do about it?"

Marcel stood wavering for a minute, staring at Gregory's blobs of color. He reached up and pulled the painting off its hangers. Then he began to bang it against the wall. The frame fell apart and Marcel began assiduously bending and tearing the canvas.

"My painting!" screamed Gregory. He pushed his way through the crowd to Marcel's painting and drove his fist through the middle of Marcel's mountain, tearing the canvas, but the next instant his hand hit the solid wooden stretcher. When he pulled it back in surprise and pain, it was bleeding and broken.

Gino edged over in front of his own painting. He wanted to remove it from the wall, but that would have subjected it to almost certain destruction. Instead he protected it with his body, blocking anyone who approached it.

Pietro appeared. "Let's get out of here," he said

"No, no, I wouldn't leave for anything. You never told me a gallery exhibit was this exciting."

"Have you gone mad? Look what you started. Come on, before the police come."

"I must protect Maria."

Pietro looked about. "Where is she?"

"The one on the wall, Pietro. You go protect the real one."

A very young, remarkably pretty girl with beige and brown streaked hair was leaning over Gregory, who sat on the floor, a pitiful look on his face, holding his damaged hand as if it was a piece of fine china. The girl was trying to stop the bleeding with a handkerchief, but as she pressed it against his hand, Gregory shoved her away, yelping in pain. The girl toppled onto her backside, looking surprised, but laughing. Gregory stuck out his tongue at her.

A fist struck Gino on the chin; he staggered, but managed to grab the arm of his assailant, who was about to slash his painting with a knife. Gino pulled the knife away (slashing his own knuckle slightly) and smashed the man to the floor with a single blow.

In other parts of the gallery, more paintings were coming down, some by accident as combatants backed or bounced into them, others intentionally, as angry patrons and artists sought to avenge themselves. There was a crescendo of sound: wood cracking, canvas tearing, blows landing, people screaming and crying.

What a festival of the arts! Gino thought. Here indeed was the modern chaos Le Temps had so eloquently described. In the distance he heard the hee-haw of a police wagon approaching.

In a moment the crowd began to scatter. People surged towards the door. A window broke as people crashed into it. Before the police arrived, most of the crowd had decamped, except for the unconscious, the wounded, and Gino, who was defending Maria.

And Le Temps. He was sitting on the floor, still beautifully dressed, but staring at his broken pince-nez. He was crying.

A squad of police hurried into the room, as Gino bent down to question the gallery director. "Are you all right?" Gino asked. Le Temps continued to cry.

The police gathered up many patrons and painters running through the streets and began to herd them into the police wagons.

A policeman approached the gallery owner and helped him slowly to his feet.

"Who is responsible for this?" asked the policeman.

Le Temps pointed at Gino.

Although the police were not particularly gentle with him, Gino felt a profound sense of peace and even pleasure as they dragged him away. The barred rear window of the police wagon gave him a final view of the gallery, almost empty save for the piles of torn canvas and broken wood that littered the floor.

Gino felt a twinge of guilt—which quickly passed. He was serenely confident that little of lasting merit had been lost. No one had been killed or permanently maimed. And Maria, the proud Italian peasant, still graced the wall of the gallery.

But his pleasure was short-lived. Even as the police wagon carted him away Gino saw Louis Le Temps, who had been gravely contemplating Maria, step towards her and grab the frame with both hands.

◆ ◆ ◆

Not until he reached the police station did Gino begin to comprehend that the incident might have serious implications. When the magistrate asked for his papers, he suddenly realized that his actions could be grounds for deportation. The official wore a button, which might very well indicate the Legion of Honor. He would hardly feel merciful towards this recent enemy.

After pleading innocent to the charges, Gino was locked up in a crowded cage with many other men, including a few Italians. Gino was confident Maria and Pietro would soon discover what had happened to him. Whether they would be able to help was a different matter. He picked an unoccupied corner of a bench, leaned back against the damp, rough wall, and in minutes was asleep.

When he awoke a few hours later, he was lying on the floor; apparently he had slipped, or been pushed, off the bench. Every bone ached. The suit Giulia had bought for him was rumpled and torn. He also discovered that his tiepin was gone. Perhaps he had lost it in the battle at the *Biennale*; perhaps it had been stolen during the night by one of his cellmates. He was not in the mood for another fight, so he said nothing.

Shortly after dawn, a guard called out his name, and led him from the cell. He hoped that Maria or Pietro had come to have him released. On the other hand, perhaps he was about to be thrown out of France.

No one was waiting. The sleepy magistrate told him he was discharged and handed him his papers. Gino, too grateful to inquire how this miracle had happened, virtually bolted out of the building and raced towards the rue Lepic. But when he opened the door to his room, Maria wasn't there.

Instead, Louis Le Temps sat on his bed. He leaped up as Gino entered. "Are you all right, Monsieur?" Le Temps asked.

"Yes. I'm fine. I don't—I'm sorry—"

"—Sorry? Don't be sorry. I'm the one who is sorry."

Le Temps took Gino by the arm and led him to the window, examining him carefully in the morning light. "How did they treat you? They didn't harm you, did they? Good. But what a terrible experience!" Le Temps was still dressed in the penguin uniform of the night before, but his suit was rumpled, there were deep bags beneath his eyes and he was unshaven.

"I am deeply ashamed, Monsieur Le Temps—"

"—Please, not again. I've been so upset. So worried."

"Excuse me, Monsieur, but what are you doing here?"

"Waiting for you."

"How did you know where I lived?"

"The police told me."

"When you gave your charges against me?"

"Charges? There are no charges. I persuaded them to let you off. Believe me it wasn't easy. You're not a French citizen and the authorities look unkindly on this sort of thing. I told them you were not to blame."

"But I was. I set those men against each other."

Le Temps fluttered both hands. "No, Bondone, you were not to blame. Those men were trying to provoke you. They received what they deserved. I should never have listened to Scegli, and yet, if I had not . . . " He shrugged his shoulders and wearily sat down on Gino's bed. Gino waited.

"I shall be frank with you," Le Temps said. "It is the only way for us from now on. I myself am very much to blame. I did not want to hang your painting. Pietro persuaded me. He said your work would offer a humorous contrast to the other 'serious' paintings in the show. He thought it would amuse the viewers, perhaps arouse some controversy. Of course, he was more right than he knew. Or perhaps he did know. That Scegli . . . "

"I see," Gino said. He slumped down on the bed next to Le Temps.

"But it was all for the best, was it not?" the gallery owner said, almost pleading.

"I'm sorry, Monsieur, but I don't see how it can be good to have such a riot—and to destroy all the paintings."

"All but one . . . Maria."

"You didn't tear her apart?"

"I confess that I intended to. I pulled your painting off the wall and prepared to break her back over my knee. Then I thought, why should I hurt my knee? I walked about looking for something to smash her against.

"As I held your Maria before me I was forced to look at her face, no more than the length of my short arms away. I said to myself, 'Marcel was wrong. This is no whore. This is a lady.' I propped your painting against the wall, sat down on the floor and stared at her for a long time. What's more, I thought, she is beautiful. And very dignified. How could I abuse this lovely lady? It would be unspeakable brutality, not to mention bad manners. My dear boy, I confess I fell in love with your Maria. Even now in this morning light, hungry, sleepless and irritable, I recall her fondly."

He patted Gino on the knee. "I am truly sorry," he continued.

"Louis Le Temps must confess his own ignorance, his own blindness. You are a fine painter, Gianpaolo Bondone. It took a riot in my venerable establishment and a few blows on my own pate, but I see it now." He bowed slightly. "I shall be very grateful if you will accept my apologies, Signore, and when we are done with apologies, I should like to talk to you about your career."

Twelve

Pietro's Fantasy

Pietro was dismayed by Gino's unexpected triumph. In an absolutely staggering turnabout, Le Temps had become Gino's sponsor, his mentor, his guardian. He purchased the painting of Maria for his private collection at a generous price and advanced Gino another substantial sum against three additional paintings, as yet unsold.

For months Pietro had been unable to find out where Gino and Maria got the money on which they lived. He dismissed Gino's story that Pierre Petit was employing him because he had learned that Petit himself was struggling financially.

Then an irrational fear had seized Pietro. Maria must be selling herself. Following Maria through the streets of Paris, lurking about in dark doorways and narrow passages had both excited and distressed him. Visions of Maria were with him constantly. In one nightmare he surprised Maria in bed with a man, but when he pulled back the covers the man was himself.

After weeks of surveillance and dozens of inquiries, he had uncovered nothing. Maria never went anywhere except to shop for food or occasionally to do some domestic service for an old widow in the 16th Arrondissement. And no one except Gino ever visited her room.

Then, at a moment when he was not thinking about the problem at all, the answer suddenly came to him: Giulia Rossini had left them the money. Of course. How stupid he was! He should have realized it months before. With his fears about Maria now finally laid to rest, Pietro waited patiently for their funds to run out. Eventually they would ask his help and on that day he would demand that Maria return to Florence. That was the price he would exact for saving Gino.

Now? Now all such hopes were shattered. If Gino's works continued to sell he would soon be independent. Maria would remain in Paris, a perpetual accusation.

Pietro did not permit his anxiety over the Bondones to interfere with his work at *Paris-Presse*. Laurent did not give him a standing assignment, but instead sent him to cover specific events. Although these affairs were often tedious—a horse show, the arrival of a foreign dignitary, the opening of the opera season—he did his best to report them accurately and engagingly.

After a few weeks, Laurent called him into the office. "I know you're not happy with the assignments I've given you, but you covered them well and I'm pleased. Now I have more interesting work in mind. Today, Monsieur Tardieu, the Minister of Defense, will speak to the Parliament. When you have written your report, bring it to me."

The assignment proved less interesting than Pietro had hoped. There was considerable aimless argument between the deputies before the minister spoke. And when he did, he was interrupted repeatedly from the floor. Pietro could easily understand why; Tardieu's speech was a dull rehearsal of ancient French history, with little bearing on current French issues. But he remained until the end and diligently prepared his copy.

Laurent read his work silently, then handed it back to Pietro. "I see you're not greatly impressed with our Minister of Defense.

"He's still thinking in terms of the Franco-Prussian war of 1870."

"Scegli, there's more to publishing a newspaper than reporting the news. The press is powerful in France. Powerful enough to bring down governments; powerful enough to bring down this government." He paused. "But we don't wish to bring down this government. Monsieur Tardieu may one day be premier. He is my—our friend. We do not wish to embarrass him. Of course you understand."

"Of course."

"There were some things in your copy I found impressive. Suppose you emphasize those points. Forget about the Franco-Prussian war. Tardieu should have forgotten it long ago, but let us excuse his lapse. He is a good man and he wants only what is best for France."

"I'm certain you're right."

"I was certain you would understand."

Several days later, Laurent stopped at his desk. "I liked your article on the new immigration policy. Quite sound."

"I'm pleased, Monsieur Laurent."

"There is a dinner tomorrow tonight at the Dutch embassy. Why don't you come with me?"

"It would be an honor."

Laurent leaned closer. "I don't mean to offend, but I suspect you may not own formal attire. Visit my tailor, Monsieur Rotman, in the rue de Rennes. I think he may have something that will fit you. While you're there you may wish to look at his fabrics. I think you could use a more fashionable wardrobe. Rotman's prices are quite reasonable—especially for my friends. I'll speak to him this afternoon."

"That would be most kind, "Pietro said. There was a further question in his eyes.

Laurent smiled. "Of course, there will be more francs in your pay envelope this week. No, don't thank me. It's a pleasure to reward merit."

Pietro was not surprised to find that Monsieur Rotman had in stock a fine formal, which, with a few minor alterations, fit him superbly.

"You're most fortunate," Rotman told him. "The gentleman who ordered these clothes was not able to complete his purchase."

Naturally, Pietro also required the proper shirt, shoes, cummerbund, and so on. And he could not help "glancing" at Rotman's display of fabrics. Before he managed to escape, he had ordered three suits in styles and patterns that Rotman assured him were quite *à la mode*—although not in the least ostentatious. Of course he had to buy appropriate haberdashery to match his new wardrobe. When he saw the bill he betrayed no emotion, but could only hope that Laurent's addition to his pay was liberal.

Laurent picked him up at the rue Lepic in his limousine. "You'll have to move out of this neighborhood," he said.

"Yes, but not until I'm out of bondage to your Monsieur Rotman."

Laurent laughed. "You look splendid," he said. "I'm sure you'll find it was worth the investment."

Laurent seemed to know everyone at the party. He kept Pietro at his side and introduced him as his friend. This was flattering, but Pietro was wise enough to permit his mentor to carry each conversation.

A portly gentleman touched Laurent's arm. "Claude," he said, "how good to see you."

"Jacques. I didn't know you would be here. Allow me to introduce my protégé, Pietro Scegli. Monsieur Jacques Debré, Minister of Finance."

"I am honored," Pietro said.

"Your protégé? Well, that speaks highly for you, young man. M. Laurent is unquestionably the finest editor in Paris."

"You are too kind."

"It's true. By the way, Claude, Minister Tardieu was very pleased with your report of his speech. It was the only favorable one in the press. The minister is grateful."

"Tardieu should thank Pietro. He wrote the piece."

"I see. Quite discerning, young man. But then, Monsieur Laurent is noted for the discerning people he employs."

"It is a privilege to work under his tutelage."

"Claude," Debré said, turning to Laurent, "you should be more active in politics."

"I have my newspaper."

"The premier is not unaware of your loyalty to his government. Some day—who knows? Perhaps, a portfolio?" The minister smiled and drifted away. Pietro smiled, too. He was beginning to understand Laurent's ambitions. Everything would be much easier now.

◆ ◆ ◆

Pietro handled each political assignment as if he were in the employ of the government. Laurent was pleased and gave him better and better assignments. With the editor's help, he met most of the influential men and women of Paris: politicians, diplomats, artists, writers—even the last decaying representatives of French royalty, including the so-called Prince of Paris, an almost unbelievably ugly man. Before there could be a Bourbon restoration, Pietro thought the prince would have to be surgically reconstructed. But such ideas did not appear in his columns, as Pietro made his way from embassy to theatre to cafe to salon with growing confidence and awareness.

"It's not enough to meet these people, to attend these gatherings," Laurent told him, "you must become better informed. You simulate knowledge splendidly—sometimes your commentary is almost a *tour de force*. But you must really know what you are talking about. Especially in cultural matters. The French think they are the masters of world culture, and you must be able to meet them on their own ground. I will tell you what to read and what to see."

Pietro read what he was told to read and went to see what he was told to see.

A few weeks later, Laurent said, "Some of your assignments will take you out of the city. Taking trains is inconvenient, and limits you to rigid schedules. I think you should have an automobile—just a small one, of course."

Pietro purchased a Renault—the smallest and cheapest model. It was the single most valuable object he had ever possessed, and he was inordinately proud of it. He hid his purchase from Gino and Maria until he had mastered the intricacies of operating it. Then he could not resist demonstrating his prowess to them.

"An automobile? Your own?" Gino asked.

"My own."

"You must be doing very well."

"This is only the beginning."

"I believe you, Pietro." Gino was impressed. He had never known anyone who owned his own automobile.

♦ ♦ ♦

Pietro first saw the Comtesse de Villon at the Garnier Opera. It was intermission and he was strolling in the Grand Gallery, which to him was merely a great baroque confection of marble, glass, brass and crystal—impressive but inedible. He was amazed at how much at ease he felt—wearing elegant clothes, moving among aristocrats, political dignitaries, and merchant princes. The diamond light sparkled and refracted about him. He felt he walked under a special halo; that his casual elegance was apparent to all. But not to the comtesse. She swept past him, a sinuous ripple of blond hair and jeweled clothes, trailing half a dozen men behind her.

When the intermission ended and he returned to his seat, he had another glimpse of her seated in her box. She noticed no one, neither the man who held her chair, nor those in the gallery who stared at her. He studied her covertly throughout the evening. Her eyes never left the stage. Others might arrange their furs or whisper comments, but her focus was fixed on the performance.

Laurent, whose guest he was, noticed Pietro's distraction. "The Comtesse de Villon. Very striking, don't you think?"

Pietro, crushed at having been observed, merely nodded.

"Don't be embarrassed, my boy. Every man in Paris is taken with her, even I. Of course, I'm too old for her and probably not rich enough. Still, she is a splendid creature."

Pietro could only nod his agreement.

Thereafter, he seemed to see her everywhere: The racecourse at Longchamps, the British embassy, the Élysée Palace—wherever his assignments took him, the comtesse was there. It wasn't until months later that he finally met her in person at a party given by Laurent for an important charity. Laurent made a point of introducing them. The comtesse was gracious, not in the least as remote as he had expected. Quite clear-eyed and direct, disconcertingly direct.

When he spoke, she held her blue-gray eyes fixed on his as if she were probing his brain. He felt quite warm talking to her, but the moment seemed so important that he forced himself to remain calm, to answer her questions lightly, to see that her champagne glass was refilled.

"Then you work with Laurent."

"Not 'with'—'for.' "

"Does that disturb you? Working 'for' someone instead of 'with' him?"

"Not when the man is Laurent."

"A most politic statement."

"Yes, wasn't it?" He smiled at her, but with a certain tightness in his facial muscles. She moved away, with a nod and a warm smile—a smile that seemed to tell him they would meet again.

He saw her at the ballet. From her box, she noticed him, and curled her fingers in a discreet gesture of recognition.

On a later occasion, the comtesse invited him to a party at her Paris apartment. She greeted him warmly at the door, but he had no opportunity to talk to her during the entire evening. When he said his goodbyes she was busy with others and he left feeling slighted.

Thereafter he saw her often, but never spoke more than a few words to her. She was cordial, but reserved. He never saw her alone. Although he would not have dared to ring her up and invite her to spend an evening with him, Pietro thought of her constantly. Until he met the comtesse, women had always seemed casual things to him. Not this one.

The vision of Ariane, Comtesse de Villon, slowly edged the vision of Maria from his mind—like a framed transparency slipped into an old-fashioned magic lantern, shoving the previous one aside. He did not think in terms of love. Such a concept was uncongenial to him, not to say meaningless. All he knew was that a vision of the comtesse was almost always with him, that he wanted to be alone with her, to talk to her, to possess her. His idea of possession was curiously lacking in physical passion. He lusted only to be with her, not to make love to her, although that idea would hardly have proved unattractive to him.

One day, as he strolled the circle of the Vendôme, he noticed a great Silver Cloud Rolls Royce parked before the door of the couturier Cardin. His mind automatically matched the license number to the memorized list in his brain and he knew at once that the limousine belonged to the comtesse. He could hardly take his eyes off the great vehicle. He hesitated, debating whether to go in, to wait on the street, or to let the opportunity pass.

The decision was made for him. A hand touched his arm, a cool voice murmured close to his ear, "You're appraising my Rolls for possible acquisition, I presume."

Pietro did not permit the shock of her closeness to unnerve him. "No, I've decided against it. A bit too large for the city, don't you think?"

She smiled. "Absolutely. Still I'm amazed that a man spends more effort appraising a motorcar than a woman."

"Particularly," said Pietro, "when the investment in the woman would be so much greater, and the expense of maintenance astronomical."

The comtesse laughed. It was a splendid laugh—one that defined her precisely. A laugh neither too loud, nor too soft. A laugh most delicately placed in the throat. A laugh of the proper timbre. An aristocratic laugh.

"I believe you're right," the comtesse said. "The automobile is too big for the city. Would you care to walk with me?"

The comtesse instructed her chauffeur to remain in the place Vendôme until she returned. Pietro had no idea where they were going and didn't care. He walked beside her, matching his stride to hers, barely daring to touch her arm when they crossed the great boulevards.

Imagine, he thought, *Pietro Scegli, the bastard son of a Tuscan whore, strolling along the rue de Rivoli with a comtesse.* Hoping not to be obvious, he observed her from short range, admiring her long pelvic stride, motionless shoulders, long tapered fingers and the play of shadow on her face and chin. *Bones,* he thought, *that's what these aristocrats have. It's not flesh or blood or brains. It's bones.*

She stopped at a shop window, staring at a display of Florentine jewelry while she spoke. "I believe you're awed by us, Monsieur Scegli. You're willing to accept the myth that aristocrats are a unique species." She was off again, striding gracefully along the crowded sidewalk before he could respond.

They stopped for coffee at a street cafe in the place du Louvre. Pietro accepted a cigarette from the comtesse's gold cigarette case, but ignored her offer of a gold lighter and struck a match on the graveled walk.

"I've read your articles."

"I'm flattered."

"Your writing intrigues me. The words skip across the surface of the pond, then gracefully sink from sight."

"How literary."

"But you never drop a rock in the pond. Why?"

"Quite perceptive, Comtesse. You've described my technique—if one can call it that—perfectly. That is precisely what Monsieur Laurent has taught me to do. I'm a pebble-skipper. I don't fling myself into controversy."

"You're afraid to stir the depths."

Pietro frowned. "I've been to the depths, Comtesse. I don't wish to return."

She studied him for a moment. "One day you must return. It is said that we all do."

"Perhaps. I intend to avoid it as long as I can."

After a few uncomfortable moments, she smiled again and rose. "It has indeed been a pleasant afternoon, Monsieur. I hope I shall see more of you."

He would have walked her back to the place Vendôme, but she graciously declined his offer. She did not look back.

Thereafter, Pietro was invited to parties at the comtesse's city apartment and once to her chateau outside Paris, but never alone. Always there were crowds of wealthy and influential people. Surely he was the least important man on her list with the possible exception of the painters and poets. He was unable to judge where they ranked in her hierarchy.

She called him "Pietro"; he was permitted to call her "Ariane." But he learned little more about her. People said of him—he had heard it said—that he was friend of the comtesse. It wasn't true, or at least not true enough. This proximity without closeness, familiarity without intimacy, both irritated and entranced him. And in his frustration, his elevated vision of her began to change; he began to see her as flesh as well as bones. *Lovemaking with the comtesse,* he thought, *would be passion in a porcelain factory—many shattered pieces, but all of them priceless.* He laughed out loud at his own ideas. *She's turning you into a poet, Pietro. I'd never have believed it.*

Once—only once—he had an opportunity to close the gap. The comtesse had driven one of her automobiles—a black Citroen, not the Rolls—into the city to appear at a charitable event that Pietro also attended. When it was over, she offered to drive him to his home. Briefly the picture leaped into his mind of a romantic rendezvous. But that was ridiculous. What could one do with a comtesse in a shabby room on the rue Lepic? He thanked her and refused, explaining that he had driven his own car.

For days—for weeks afterward, he imagined a profound and passionate romance with the comtesse, as it might have developed if only he had a fashionable apartment. After a while, these visions seemed quite real to him.

Another night, having seen her again at the opera, he returned home inflamed with the now ritual vision of their union. As it happened, he entered the building in the rue Lepic but seconds after Maria. In his agitated mind, the figure of the desired comtesse blended with that of the available Maria. Without a word he led her to his room and made love to her savagely, seeing only the comtesse while he tore at the flesh of Maria. When it was over, she left the room, frightened.

Thirteen

Crass Commercialism

A lesser man than Louis Le Temps might have acted at once to exploit the sensational publicity that followed the *Biennale*. But Le Temps was vaguely embarrassed by the affair and he decided not to give Gino a one-man show until the notoriety of past events had died down.

Gino was not unhappy over Le Temps' decision. Planning to paint more and far better works for his personal showing, he went back to work with great enthusiasm. Gino also decided that the time had come to send for his mother. There was no reason now for her to remain in Florence.

To Gino's surprise, Maria didn't agree.

"You're just beginning to make a name, Gino, and earn a little money. But it's quite risky, isn't it—an artist's income? It would be *terribile* to bring Mama here and then be unable to support her."

"Le Temps is very optimistic."

"So am I, Gino, and very proud of you. But are you really thinking of what's best for Mama? She would be uncomfortable living among strangers, people who speak a language she can't understand."

They argued for days, and Maria finally persuaded Gino it would be best to wait a few months. He suspected the truth was that she was afraid to do anything that might affect her relationship with Pietro. But he had no desire to distress his sister, and he wasn't at all certain that his mother would be happy in Paris.

Le Temps suggested that Gino hire a model, an idea that made him feel quite professional. But he didn't know how to find one himself. Obviously the man to ask for help was Pierre Petit. Although he hadn't seen the master in weeks and was embarrassed that he hadn't invited him to the *Biennale*, he couldn't think of anyone else to call. He used the telephone in a nearby bistro; that in itself was an adventure. Even securing Petit's telephone number from the operator was terrifying.

"Gino, is it really you? You promised to come and see me."

"I'm sorry. The last few months have been hectic."

"I saw your paintings at Le Temps'."

Surprised, Gino asked, "What did you think of them?"

"Your work gets better all the time. You need more variety, but the line is stronger than ever, the colors *forte*. I'm proud of you. When will I see you?"

"Soon, *Maître*. But now I need a favor. "Can you help me find a model?"

"Certainly, male or female?"

For a moment, Gino didn't answer.

Petit laughed. "There are two kinds, you know."

"I never thought of using a man."

"I'm not surprised. I'll send you someone in the morning."

Gino rose early and did his best to straighten his attic studio. He swept several weeks of debris into a corner and dusted the ancient table and chairs. Then he realized he would need something on which to pose the model. There was a ragged sofa jammed on end under the eaves, which he eased down and dragged into the center of the room. Seeing it was filthy, he ran downstairs to rip the coverlet off his own bed. When he spread it over the sofa it looked lumpy but presentable.

He was still tidying the room when there was knock on the door.
"Come in," he called.

The door swung open, and in walked a tall, slim and rather pretty girl. "I am Colette."

"Good morning, Colette. Please call me Gino."

Her eyes crinkled. "You don't recognize me?"

"I don't think so."

"How disappointing. But wait a minute." She reached behind herself, unbuttoned her dress and dropped it at her feet. Then she turned her back and slowly raised her slip above her hips and thighs, eventually holding it over her head, so that she was undressed, except for a brassiere and panties.

"The girl in the window!" Gino cried.

She spun around. "The very same."

"What are you doing here?"

"I have modeled for Monsieur Petit for many years. It's pure chance that I'm also his neighbor."

"But—"

"—I saw you in his studio that day, frowning over your work. I decided that you needed a live model so I gave you a demonstration. But I never heard anything—until Petit called yesterday."

Gino nodded, studying her. She was trim and high breasted, without excess flesh anywhere on her body.

"Well then, do with me what you will."

"Uh . . . why don't you arrange yourself on the sofa."

"Like an odalisque?"

"Uh, yes."

The girl removed her bra and panties, although he hadn't asked her to do so, and stretched out on the coverlet. "How's this?"

"Quite graceful."

"Don't you want to arrange me yourself?"

"No, that's perfect." He didn't want to touch her. After all, she was here as a model not as—he shook his head, picked up his pencil and began to sketch.

It wasn't easy. He tried to tell himself the girl wasn't really a girl at all—that she was a picture and that he was drawing a picture of a picture. The trick didn't work. Colette lay quite still, but she hadn't stopped breathing. The rise and fall of her breasts, gentle as it was, distracted him.

"Can I move about a little?"

"Sure."

But when she raised and lowered one knee momentarily, his eyes were drawn unwillingly between her legs. Forcing his eyes upwards across the smooth belly didn't help. And her breasts—he could still see them when he closed his eyes.

Gino made one false start after another, discarding sheets on the floor.

"No good?" Colette asked.

"I've never drawn from a nude model before."

"No wonder you're so nervous."

She rose from the sofa, walked to him, put her arms around his neck and kissed him. He dropped his pencil and pushed her down on the coverlet.

She laughed. "So this is the arrangement you had in mind."

He had stripped off his pants and was between her legs in an instant. She received him with a thrust of her pelvis and welcoming arms. Her firm breasts sweetly resisted the pressure of his body. He wanted to explode, but forced himself to hold back as long as possible. They climaxed together, but he continued on, and she joined with him so that they undulated together in smooth parabolas of passion, again and again.

Later, Colette said, "If you paint as good as you screw, you must be a genius,"

"Who's thinking about painting?" They rolled about the ancient sofa, slipped to the floor, climbed back again, while hands and mouths searched every inch of each other's bodies. The sky outside was quickly darkening when they finally separated and rose from the couch.

Colette's smile was more possessive than coquettish: "When will you require my services again."

He sighed. "I'll call Monsieur Petit."

But Gino didn't call. He made the decision reluctantly, certain that every session would turn out the same way. He would have a mistress, but no paintings. He also decided not to ask Petit for another model. If the girl was homely there would be no pleasure in painting her, and if she was pretty—well, it might happen all over again.

Instead, he went back to the Seine. This time to an upper terrace on the Right Bank, where his view stretched from the Eiffel tower in the west to Notre Dame—even to the Sacré Coeur high in the east. But he did not plan to paint the city, the river or famous monuments. Instead, he used the passing world for his models. He especially liked the very young and the very old. The old were easier to draw. They sat for hours on benches, virtually motionless, as unaware of Gino as they were of the rest of Paris.

The young—if they were lovers—were oblivious, too. He could sketch them without fear of being detected.

Children moved rapidly and were quite alert. They quickly discovered that he was drawing them, but they were tolerant and he did not lack for subjects.

Gino was more interested in mood than in likeness. He had never painted clearly recognizable portraits. Now his work grew more abstract than ever, his forms and colors more basic, rudimentary. At the same time he strove to keep in touch with reality. If his forms were simple, his motifs were powerful. They were fundamental human themes, the same ones that painters had struggled with for thousands of years: joy and sadness, youth and age, love—but not hate. Gino did not hate and therefore could not picture hate. There was no shape or form that represented hate to him, unless it was the form of Pietro Scegli, and he wasn't even sure of that.

One afternoon, an image caught his eye—a dove, almost blinding white, alone and lovely, wheeling in the cerulean sky above the Seine. In the lower corner of his vision, a child, dressed all in yellow, carrying an orange balloon, echoing the colors of the leaves on the plane trees, drifting all around him. The child lost control of the string on her balloon and it floated above her head. She reached and leaped and stretched. For a moment her body was almost parallel to the terrace.

The child and the dove and the balloon floating over Paris.

Gino drew furiously on his canvas, focusing on the real, surreal images the flooded his mind. He had a few tubes of paint, and with them he mixed the colors he needed and began to apply them in long sweeping lines and thick bursts of color. He had never worked as quickly, as fiercely. His blood was pounding so furiously that he felt as hot as if it were summer, and he pulled open his shirt, ripping loose some of the buttons.

The child came flowing onto the canvas, floating over a roughly drawn city, almost riding the dove, whose beak touched the balloon. *Yes,* he thought, *these are the colors I have dreamed of using, these are the images I have been afraid to paint. A new beginning.*

Gino gradually became aware of a man standing very close to him, watching him work. He tried to ignore him, caught up in the magic of creation, of freedom, of beauty.

"Chagall," the man said. "I've seen the original in a museum."

Gino stopped, his hand still holding the brush, the brush still in contact with the canvas—frozen, as if his body had been iced in place and the brush was stuck to the painting. Then the brush began to quiver; Gino's arm began to quiver; his body began to quiver. From deep in his chest came a roar—so loud that the man stepped back in fear, his eyes in danger of lurching from his head. He turned and ran away.

But Gino was laughing; laughing so loud that people a hundred meters away turned to listen, to watch and to listen. The brush dropped from Gino's hand to the pavement. He doubled over from laughter that rang in his own head; laughter so powerful that it turned to pain. But still he laughed, not silently, as he had usually done in the past. Then he backed up a step and sat down on a stone ledge. Men, women, children were watching him with curiosity, a few with concern on their faces. He looked around him with a benign smile and raised his hands in an open gesture to reassure them. Some smiled back, others hurried away, angrily, as if somehow he had cheated them.

After a few minutes, Gino stood up, took the painting from his easel, crushed it with his powerful hands, and stuffed it into a nearby trash container.

Time to go back to work.

♦ ♦ ♦

Le Temps telephoned Gino after the first sale of one of his paintings, a still life. Gino rushed to the gallery and demanded to know the name of the buyers. At first Le Temps refused, but when Gino promised not to disturb the new owners, Le Temps gave him their name.

Gino tracked down the address of the apartment house, verified the name over the doorbell, then returned outside, crossed the street and studied the building. It was a rather ordinary structure, a typical five-story Parisian apartment house on the Boulevard St. Germain, near the Café des Deux-Magots. He determined that the apartment of Monsieur and Madame Elien, his patrons, was on the third floor, its many tall windows fronted with a black iron balcony. The windows were slightly open, but Gino couldn't see inside. Yet, somewhere within those walls was *Still Life with Three Vases*. Was it hung yet? Very likely. In the parlor? Perhaps. He savored this thought for a long time, while his heart swelled with love for this Monsieur and Madame Elien who had shown such good taste.

Later that month, Le Temps arranged Gino's first *vernissage*. Gino had never heard the term. It meant, literally, a "varnishing," the finish a painter puts upon his work. No other painter was displayed in the main gallery. The art of Gianpaolo Bondone would be judged alone, against itself and against the knowledge and imagination of the viewer.

The gallery owner selected carefully from among Gino's paintings, hanging only fifteen and spacing them generously along the walls. This time Gino was permitted to watch, but his opinion of the arrangement was not solicited. If asked, he would have alternated the still lifes with the figure paintings, but Le Temps chose to group them.

Even Gino was surprised at the effect of this selection and arrangement. He began to see elements in his own works he had been unaware of until that moment.

The first evening the *vernissage* was reasonably well attended; Le Temps had informed only a limited number of customers and friends, and a few members of the press. Gino lumbered about, conspicuous and awkward. He held a wineglass which Le Temps kept refilling. The gallery owner seldom left his side. In fact, when a patron required his attention, he drew Gino along. Perhaps he had some lingering fears of a renewal of the hostilities that had in recent memory desolated the gallery.

Monsieur Oriel, the art critic for *Le Monde*, questioned Gino politely regarding his artistic sources, his goals, and his personal history. Le Temps supplied most of the answers, but Gino was permitted a few replies.

"I see, Monsieur Le Temps," said Oriel, "that you consider this wine so precious, you'll only permit us a few drops at a time."

The art critic from *Paris Soir* was a woman who was a bit more aggressive. She pulled Gino away from Le Temps and pinned him against a wall.

"Is the fact that you have used arrangements of three in several of your still lifes intended to establish sexual or religious criteria?"

Before Gino could answer this perplexing inquiry, she burrowed in with another. "Do you hate people?"

"No, why do you ask?"

"Because although your figures are carefully drawn, the faces consists of only a few slashed lines—sometimes merely a blank, flat oval."

"But this is intentional."

"I understand. All true art is brimming with intention. What is yours?"

"To show the world as I see it."

"You mean that to you people have no faces."

"Oh, no! Their faces are so marvelous, so filled with feeling, it's difficult for me, if not impossible, to portray it. I can draw a fair representation of a person's face. It will look very much like him, but will I be able to show his true nature? That is very difficult—perhaps impossible."

"Impossible for you."

"For everyone."

The critic seemed to be impressed. She wanted to ask Gino other questions, but Le Temps rescued him.

The reviews were neither ecstatic nor unkind. *Le Monde* said that Gianpaolo Bondone displayed a talent for composition almost classical, although his figures were somewhat amorphous. *Paris Soir* suggested that the artist nourished a deep-seated fear of people, and that he therefore tried to reduce them all to one indistinguishable level. Nevertheless, the artist's sense of color was good. His line could have been bolder.

These commentaries disturbed Gino. He wanted to seek out the critics and explain his true intentions.

Le Temps dissuaded him. "These are not bad reviews. They indicate you have talent. The writers must criticize something or they would not be critics. Learn to live with it, Gino. You cannot spend your life writing letters and giving lectures to explain your art. The paintings must do that for you."

By the second night of the exhibition Gino was in better humor. The crowd was larger than the evening before. Walking up and down the gallery, Gino was gracious to those who questioned him, even when the questions were absurd or provocative.

"It seems that you have arrived."

Gino spun around. "Pietro!"

"What do you hear from Florence?" Pietro asked.

"I had a letter from my mother today. She's quite well." He did not add that he intended to bring her to Paris in the spring.

"I'd like you to meet a friend of mine," Pietro said, leading him across the room to where a woman stood talking to Le Temps. As Pietro approached, she half turned, presenting her profile to Gino.

He stopped moving. "Bronzino!"

The woman now turned around, and Gino was presented with a full view. She accepted his appraisal with cool detachment.

"I always wondered what you would look like full face."

"*Pardon?*" She appraised him in return. He could not tell what her judgment of him might be.

"I'm sorry," he said. "You remind me of someone."

"You said a name. What was it?"

"Bronzino."

Le Temps, Pietro and the woman laughed.

"That is the name of the woman in question?"

"No, the painter. The work—a portrait of a beautiful Florentine lady—hangs in the National Gallery in London. Until today I'd only seen a print. Now I've seen the original, face to face; Bronzino's painting is in profile."

"I presume you mean to flatter me?"

"No, merely to explain myself."

The crinkle at the corner of her lips told Gino she was amused.

"Comtesse," Pietro said, "this is the painter of the evening, Gianpaolo Bondone. Gianpaolo, the Comtesse de Villon."

As Pietro spoke, Gino saw her eyes turn from lustrous gray to a deep and startling blue. He was fascinated.

"Well, this is a surprise," the comtesse said. "You are so large and dark and healthy. One hardly expects to find that such a man is a painter."

Everyone laughed, including Gino. "I also paint large, dark and healthy canvases." He took her arm and, ignoring the others, led her away. He was surprised by his own audacity, but not in the least embarrassed. Perhaps it was the memory of Bronzino's painting, the comtesse's startling eyes, or the quickening of interest she had betrayed.

They stopped in front of one of Gino's canvases and before she spoke, the comtesse studied it with transparent intensity. "This is neither large nor dark, but rather gay and light."

"Of course, comtesse, but my phrase seemed right at the moment. In this wonderful city everyone seems intent on the right phrase. Who cares whether it fits or not."

She smiled. "I'm told you can be quite violent when aroused?"

"Sheer nonsense, I assure you. An ignorant Italian peasant may sometimes be violent, but an artist—never."

The comtesse stood before a still life. "I like this, although I'm not sure why. The objects are very simple and there is little detail, yet everything seems so important."

"Wonderful. Precisely my intention."

"Why *does* it seem important? A few utensils arranged on a table top?"

"Because these utensils were made by skilled human hands and they have been arranged by skilled human hands—mine."

"Please tell me more."

"Anything created by human beings is by that very fact touched with the divine. I have arranged these simple creations so as to grip and hold your attention. Suddenly they seem important to you although in themselves they are not. Humanity is important." Gino hesitated only a second, and then laughed aloud. "That even impresses me."

They strolled from painting to painting, Gino eagerly awaiting the comtesse's comments and questions. He didn't offer another pontifical explanation. Instead, he phrased his remarks casually, hiding the emotion that had crept over him.

Fortunately, the crowd was large and his admirers many, and he was not required to do all the talking. Others broke in to tell him what his paintings meant, which ones they liked and which they doubted. He listened to all, chatted with many. The swarm seemed to close in on them. He found himself standing close to the comtesse. A delightful fragrance rose from her hair, which looked like burnished gold. He resisted touching it.

"May we leave?" she whispered. He nodded. She took his hand and without saying another word to anyone they left the gallery.

Perhaps someone called or spoke to him. If so, he didn't hear them. It seemed like a fairy tale; he was walking hand in hand with the princess, and as they passed, people naturally fell back to make way.

Even outdoors in the cold autumn night, the illusion did not immediately disappear. His adventure ended at the curb. The princess's carriage, a long silver gray Rolls Royce, was waiting. A uniformed attendant, who should have been wearing a feathered cap and breeches, but instead wore gray livery edged in black, silently opened the door. The comtesse slipped her hand from Gino's and disappeared inside. In a moment, the window came murmuring down, and her lovely face appeared. Her hand rested on the glass.

"It has been a splendid evening. I truly enjoyed your paintings." The expression on her face seemed to change, as if she realized that Gino was trapped in a spell and she felt compelled to break it. "I think I like the still life you first showed me best of all. Please tell Le Temps I will buy it."

"Impossible," Gino replied.

"Impossible?"

"Yes. I've already made a gift of it to the Comtesse de Villon." Gino nodded over her hand, turned and walked away.

♦   ♦   ♦

"You're an ass," Pietro said.

"But why?"

"You gave a painting to the comtesse. Isn't that reason enough?"

"Don't you see the beauty of it? What a triumph for the humble Italian peasant! The great lady tried to buy my painting so she could humiliate me, and I made her a gift of it."

"Stop playing the fool. Ariane de Villon can afford to pay a thousand times the price of your wretched painting. What did you prove when you gave it to her?"

"You forget: I can paint another; she can't."

"She can also turn down your present and then you'll be twice a fool."

"True, but I don't think the comtesse is ungracious."

"You're acting like a child."

"I never understand you, Pietro. Didn't you tell me you brought the comtesse to the exhibit so that I could meet her? Didn't you say she has a great following and if she likes my work, her example will lead other influential people to buy my paintings?"

"Just the point. If she bought your painting it would be one thing. But now she can say that a lovesick young painter gave it to her. *Très amusant.* Believe me, the wealthy only value what they pay for."

"I should think that an incredibly wealthy comtesse might be more impressed that a gift comes from a poor, romantic artist."

Pietro threw up his hands and abandoned the argument. He would not reveal the real reason for his annoyance. The evening of the exhibition, he had attended a dinner party at which the comtesse was also a guest. They had chatted together. Pietro realized that she was bored and, hoping to be alone with her, he had suggested they leave together.

"Where will we go?" she asked.

The words leaped unbidden into his head. "My friend, a young artist, is having a *vernissage*. I'm sure it will be amusing to attend."

The comtesse had agreed, and together they slipped away and drove to Le Temps' gallery. Pietro had intended to remain at the gallery only a few minutes. Then he would manage, somehow, to be alone with her.

"My friend's work," he had told her, "is quite wild, quite incomprehensible. But he's a rather good-natured if a somewhat crude fellow, and I think you'll find it diverting to meet him. Of course we needn't stay long."

Nothing turned out as he expected. Gino had behaved like a gentleman instead of a peasant, and after meeting him, she seemed to forget Pietro completely. In the end she had left without saying another word to him, not even offering a lift home—an incredible breach of etiquette for such a woman. He had watched her car move away from the curb in disbelief. Obviously, Gino was the cause of this disaster. And he would never forgive him.

♦ ♦ ♦

Le Temps delivered the still life to the comtesse on the day following the close of the *vernissage*. A few days later Gino received a brief, perfectly cordial, but impersonal thank you note. From the words the comtesse used, it was impossible to tell that the gift had been a work of art; it might have been a box of chocolates. Gino didn't mention the note to Pietro; it was too humiliating.

"Have you heard from Ariane?" Pietro asked.

"Not yet."

"Not even a thank you note?"

Gino was silent.

"Very strange for such a well-bred lady."

Gino sighed and showed him the letter.

"I told you it was a waste of time and a saleable painting, but of course you're wiser in the ways of the world than I am."

If Gino was disappointed, he enjoyed other consolations. Le Temps had sold ten of his canvases the first night of the *vernissage* and four more in the week that followed. A few others, not even displayed that evening, had been reserved and might yet be sold.

Le Temps was particularly pleased with the prestige of the purchasers, who ranged from wealthy connoisseurs to a nationally known novelist, to a well-known sculptor, even to another gallery owner. Gino's reactions were mixed. He was happy to have his works purchased and hung, that was the only measure of success for an artist. And he had painted them not for himself alone, but to communicate with others. Still, he hated to lose these friends. Each painting held a meaning for him that he believed no one else could fully understood. Each was the loving creation of his hands, a fragment torn from his soul and spread on canvas. He had sold a few paintings before, but now they were going wholesale. He felt more like a street vendor than an artist.

Le Temps had no patience with him. "You've lived with that communist Pietro far too long. Why do you feel guilty when you sell your works? It is your livelihood."

"Yes, but a dozen or more at a time—like wallets at the monastery! As if the money is everything."

"For how much did I sell them? Are you now a millionaire? Count Sforza of Milan paid Leonardo a thousand ducats for a single painting. Would you be a better man if you took less for your paintings? Are your paintings superior if you give them away? Absurd. You're not a philanthropist. This is both your trade and your love. Be thankful of that. And let the others in this world be thankful there is a Gianpaolo Bondone to bring beauty to their lives."

Fourteen

Brave New World

Months passed before Pietro brought Gino the news he had been waiting for: "You've been invited to the estate of the comtesse."

"You're joking."

"No, Ariane is giving a party next Saturday and she asked me to bring you along."

"Oh, a party."

"Were you expecting a private audience?" Pietro laughed. "She's arranging one of her cultural gatherings—artists, writers and the like—to amuse her aristocratic friends. I persuaded her to add you to the list of dignitaries."

It was a lie. The comtesse had told Pietro she planned to invite Gino and he had not dared to protest. Instead, he had persuaded her not to send a formal invitation. "Don't frighten Gianpaolo," Pietro said. "I'll tell him, myself."

"You shouldn't have bothered, Pietro. I won't go."

Pietro hesitated. He really didn't want Gino to attend. On the other hand, Ariane might be angry if Gino did not appear. "Don't be a child," he said. "It will be amusing provided you don't crack any artistic skulls and besides, you'll meet important people. What have you to lose?"

"My honor."

Pietro doubled up with laughter. "Your virginity is long gone. What other honor have you been withholding from the world?"

"You always make fun of me."

"On the contrary, you satirize yourself. It would be stupid not to attend the comtesse's little dinner. She lives near Chartres in a spectacular chateau. Both the drive and the adventure will do you good. No one will pick you out to humiliate; there will be at least a dozen other geniuses there busy humiliating themselves. You'll hardly be noticed."

Pietro's words affronted him. "Perhaps I'll surprise you," Gino said.

♦ ♦ ♦

In the early afternoon they set out for Chartres in Pietro's muddy-green Renault. Despite its tiny size, the car had four doors, and the cramped, miniature seats were constructed of metal pipe with thin cloth stretched over them. Gino was folded and refolded—at the base of his spine so that his upper legs pressed against his chest; at the knees, forcing his lower legs against the upper ones. He was bent again at the neck to avoid hitting the unpadded roof, and his back ached from pressing against the metal pipe.

Fortunately, his attention was captured by the beauty of the season: the countryside was turning green and yellow and pink and red in a cascade of colors that only a Monet or Pissarro, or perhaps Seurat, possibly even Chagall, could have depicted. Such riotous display was not part of Gino's repertory.

The small towns along the road were especially charming in the soft spring light. The refuse of war had long since been swept away, and the warm sun dappled the gray buildings with irregular and dramatic highlights. Children played in the streets and their joyous voices reminded Gino of home.

Huddled shoulder to shoulder, they drove with the car windows pushed back, buffeted by warm breezes and earthy smells. Even Pietro seemed to be in a jovial mood.

"If I don't prepare you for this adventure you'll be overwhelmed. Imagine, if you can, a chateau grand enough for a king. In fact, the Chateau de Villon was originally built as a hunting lodge for Francis the First. When the great king tired of it, he gave it to his steward, Villon, and it has remained in the family ever since, some four hundred years."

"Incredible."

"You'll repeat that word many times tonight. The great architect Lescot designed and built it and the portico is framed with magnificent stone carvings by Goujon."

"You've been there."

Pietro smiled. He had been to Villon once before and then only briefly, seeing little of the chateau and less of the grounds. Most of what he told Gino he had gleaned from others.

Gino turned his attention back to the countryside. In the fields the grain stood high for this early in the year. The smell of the wheat, fanning itself in the soft wind, was almost unbearably enticing. Gino watched men and women working the fields, not on tractors, but behind horses and plows little different from those of his native land. The faces were sharper than at home—keener, more self-absorbed and withdrawn, but otherwise similar. The workers did not stop to watch the automobile, unusual as it was in those days; the grain was more important.

Then, with the swiftness of a slide projected on a screen, a great pale mauve shape appeared, floating over the fields on Gino's side of the Renault. It seemed as if a gigantic ship had suddenly heaved up out of the distant haze. Before he could ask Pietro what it might be, the hull became an angled roof, and the heavy masts turned to towers.

"Can that be Chartres?"

"Yes."

"But we're far away."

"When you come upon the cathedral from the north it seems to ride on the horizon."

Gino stared in wonder at the immense image of the cathedral drifting serenely in the sky "It's so vague and translucent, like a shade rather than reality. The farmers don't seem to notice it."

"It's been there for eight hundred years. Are they to plow their fields or sit in the grass and stare at the church?"

Gino turned his head for a moment. When he looked back, the cathedral was gone. "Where is it?"

"As you approach, the cathedral appears and disappears. I don't know how it happens." Pietro had not seen this vision on his previous, nighttime visit; someone at the party had told him about it.

Gino stared at the horizon, waiting for this apparition to reassert itself. He blinked and there it was. Gino realized he hadn't gone to Mass in months. Feeling guilty he stared at the ghostly cathedral and crossed himself.

Pietro laughed. "I brought you here for a good time, not for a resurgence of faith. Think about the comtesse and forget the cathedral."

When they reached the outskirts of the town there was still some light in the sky, and Pietro insisted on parking along the road until it was dark. "I don't intend to arrive until everyone else is there. It's bad form to be first. Besides, I don't like to park my little car among all those limousines. After dark they may mistake the Renault for a sports car."

"I'm surprised to hear that matters to you."

"Not to me—to others."

An hour later, they drove onto the grounds of the chateau, traversing a broad macadam roadway flanked by towering cypresses. The road turned and turned again, and many minutes passed before Gino saw the expansive glow of the house. Ahead, automobile lights twinkled in a vast glittering plain that arced about the chateau.

"That was once a moat and a small lake," Pietro said. He parked as far as possible from the main building.

Gino simply stared. Pietro's words had not prepared him for the Chateau de Villon, an immense, gray limestone building lighted, as if for a *spectacle illuminé*, by searchlights hidden in the shrubbery. A birch-lined flagstone walk, perhaps fifty meters across, led to a broad, stone staircase, which rose in three stages, rimmed by converging ornately carved balustrades, to the grand triple-arched entrance. Above these soaring portals, the central portion of the building was circular, several stories high and topped with a lavishly ornamented dome.

Two-story, flat-roofed stone structures connected the central tower to rectangular wings, each three stories high with mansard roofs. Glowering stone figures lined the roofs of the wings and surmounted the arches over the main entrance. The tallest appeared larger than life-size, and staring down among the shadows they seemed forbidding.

The parking area was so filled with automobiles that Gino could not estimate the number, and there were many uniformed chauffeurs standing about, smoking and talking. At the middle of the triple entrance to the chateau, two tall bronze doors, wide enough to admit a coach and four, stood open. Once inside, Gino looked up to find that the dome, arching close to twenty meters overhead, roofed the entire foyer. There was a marble staircase at the far end, narrowing and curving upwards to a balcony which circled below the vault. An immense crystal chandelier hung from the lantern, spangling the entry with lozenges of prismed light.

Their arrival was unnoticed. Dozens of people crowded the entrance hall, laughing and chatting. Black-tie-dressed waiters passed among the guests serving drinks and hors d'oeuvres. It was remarkably noisy—even more so because an orchestra was playing in the background. Through half-open glass doors immediately opposite the entrance Gino saw a ballroom filled with dancers. The patterns were not as formal as he had expected. The music was rich but saccharine, and the dancers seemed merely to stroll languidly across the floor, many holding cigarettes and wineglasses.

There were others like Gino here tonight—awkward looking,

clumsily dressed fellows, surrounded by elegantly attired men and women. Clearly Pietro's prediction was correct. The comtesse had put her artists on display. Strangely, in their beards and tweeds and rumpled gray suits, they seemed less self-conscious than the long-gowned women and their manicured men. Pietro, not unexpectedly, had disappeared. It was up to Gino to find his own way in this throng.

From an observation post between two pillars he surveyed the vestibule, frowning at the large but inferior nymph and faun fresco that covered the dome, but approving the beautifully proportioned cream-colored marble columns with Corinthian capitals and the matching dadoed marble wall panels that encircled the room. Apparently, the French artisans (they couldn't have been Italian) had been more adept at stonework than painting. He had noticed this before in France.

A waiter offered a glass of champagne. Two glasses later Gino felt adventurous enough to abandon his sanctuary and wander into the ballroom. The orchestra was exuberant, the dancers less so. The floor itself was a marvel: wood parquet laid in a fleur-de-lis pattern. Could this, too, be four hundred years old? Presumably.

A gray-haired man about sixty, well dressed but corpulent and flush-faced, approached him. "Are you a writer?"

"No, a painter."

This seemed to stop him for a moment, but before Gino could move away, the man launched into a bitter denunciation of Sartre and Camus.

Gino listened without comprehension. "I'm sure what you are saying is profound, but it's wasted on me."

"You mean you have no interest in the other arts?"

Before Gino could confess his disinterest, the man resumed his discourse, twisting his head from side to side incessantly as he spoke. He seemed to be talking to everyone except Gino, apparently trying to draw an audience. After several minutes of rapid discourse, his voice rose. At that moment, a dark-haired man with large ears and wire-rimmed glasses, indifferently dressed, touched

Gino's elbow. "Don't listen to this fellow," he said. "I doubt he has even read my works." He gave Gino a quick grin and walked away.

The corpulent man watched with his mouth open. "Sartre," he whispered. "That was Sartre!"

Not having any idea what or who a "Sartre" might be, Gino nodded and moved away. The corpulent man was silent.

"Enjoying yourself?" It was Pietro.

Gino shrugged.

"Look," Pietro said, taking him by the arm and escorting him to another salon. "Over there, Corbusier, the great architect, is speaking to Jean Dubuffet, the painter. Have you heard of either of them?"

Gino shook his head.

"I thought not. Corbu is the greatest architect in France, one of the greatest in the world. The painter is a leader of the so-called 'School of Paris.' Don't you want to be part of that school? Go over there, introduce yourself."

Gino shook his head, violently.

Pietro was chuckling. "But this is how one makes important friendships, how one builds a great career. You can't just sit in your attic and paint. It won't do."

Mutely, Gino shook his head again. Pietro was still laughing as he strolled away. Gino took one step after him, then held back. He glanced over at the painter and the architect, still deep in conversation. *Someday, perhaps,* he thought.

Gino found other rooms to inspect. Some were occupied by couples talking animatedly in corners, or small groups arguing at peak intensity. He heard names, a few so famous that even he knew them. But none of that mattered to him. He was taken with the elaborate decoration of the walls and ceilings, the hangings, even the paintings—although many of them were dark and mediocre nineteenth century work, distinguished primarily by their ornate framing.

There was a dining room with numerous tables and buffet service from an elaborately carved serving table. The food was stupefying in quantity and arrangement, but there were few people in the room. Beyond, tall glass-paneled doors opened onto the grounds.

Gino found himself outside on the rear terrace. Below was a wide path outlined in the moonlight, leading to a circular pool glimmering in the distance. Gardens stretched away on every side. The air was warm and redolent with smells of earth and flowers. Someday he would like to stroll through this garden. Tonight? It didn't seem right. He should find Pietro.

Reentering the chateau, he felt strangely remote from the sights and sounds around him. No one noticed him; no one tried to gain his attention. It was a splendid adventure, just being there, observing this incredible establishment and the remarkable guests, so busy with nothing. He supposed that was what parties were about. How would he know? The peasant boy from Tuscany.

Gino wandered into a sitting room or parlor, occupied mostly by men smoking and drinking who spoke more quietly than the mixed clientele in the other rooms. They seemed very intense and did not smile. When he approached one group they stopped speaking. Businessmen, he guessed.

Then, he entered a darkly paneled room with hundreds, perhaps thousands, of books on shelves that rose to the high ceiling. The room was dimly lit, except for pools of light on reading tables. In the semi-darkness, he divined a man and a woman in earnest conversation. The man was almost certainly Chagall, and the woman seemed to be much younger, slim and pretty. Their heads were very close, and Chagall's hand rested lightly on the woman's shoulder.

I shouldn't interrupt, but I will, Gino thought. As he strode across the floor, a small group of men and women entered the library, crossing his path.

"Marc! There you are!" one man said. The group hurried towards Chagall, surrounding him, everyone talking at once.

Gino shrugged and left the library by a different doorway that opened into a narrow, darkened corridor. At the end were two massive doors faced with strongly limned landscapes. At first, he thought the surfaces were painted, but on closer inspection he realized it was marquetry. Tiny pieces of wood of varying types and tones had been carefully and brilliantly combined to create the illusion of perspective. He stared for a while, then on impulse opened one of the doors and immediately realized that he had entered a gallery. The room was perhaps thirty meters long and more than ten wide, the walls lined with paintings, each with a light above it. But the lights were not lit. Only a single dim chandelier in the center of the room supplied faint illumination. There must be a light switch somewhere.

"Behind you."

The voice spun him around: The comtesse. He felt like a thief caught with stolen goods.

"I frightened you. Well, little one, I'm certain you'll feel safer in the light." She reached toward the wall and immediately lights glowed; the paintings glowed.

Gino's eyes were drawn to a very large painting hanging in the center of one wall. "*Tiziano!*" he cried. Forgetting the comtesse, he hurried to study the canvas, lush with feminine and earthly abundance.

"As ever, you are more impressed with art than the Comtesse de Villon."

The words stopped him, but her tone was not unkindly. "Forgive me," he said. "The *miràcolo* of these works overwhelms me."

"You are forgiven. It is both fortunate and unfortunate that I have grown up among such things." She waved an almost languorous hand at the room. "I sometimes take them for granted."

"I don't believe you," he said, surprising even himself. "A woman such as you could never take such genius for granted."

She smiled and he felt his confidence return. "You must guide me among these treasures," he said.

"My guests?"

"They couldn't possibly miss you any more than I would."

She studied his face for a moment "You often surprise me, Signore Bondone. Sometimes you play the Tuscan peasant, other times the Italian *nobile*."

"Being a peasant doesn't keep me from speaking the truth."

"Bravo!" She clapped her hands once and smiled.

Gino half bowed.

"We own another Titian, but it's not as fine as this one. In fact, I'm not sure that it truly is an original so I keep it upstairs at the far end of a long corridor."

As the comtesse spoke she led him along the gallery. He had a brief moment to look at her, to admire her burnished blond hair piled high in serpentine coils, her simple dress, black velvet haltered at the neck and cleaving low between her breasts, dipping at the back almost to her waist. A long strand of pearls glowed, translucent at the orbit, about her neck. Except for discreet pearl earrings she wore no other jewelry.

The canvases were large, all by masters of the fifteenth and sixteenth centuries, most of them Italian. There was a lovely Annunciation by Botticelli, a frightening view of purgatory by Signorelli, a fine John the Baptist of Giorgione, an intricate Adoration by Gentile Bellini. The collection was remarkable for the uniformly high quality of the canvases, worthy, he believed, of any museum in the world.

The comtesse spoke to him about each painting, but after a few minutes Gino ceased to hear her. Absorbed by the superb works of art, he moved at his own pace, sometimes peering closely to study the brushwork, sometimes stepping back to gain perspective. From time to time, he stopped abruptly and returned to a painting he had studied previously to examine some detail that had slowly percolated through his consciousness.

After a few of these erratic trips, the comtesse gave up and retired to an upholstered bench in the center of the room. Gino didn't even notice. He continued to study the paintings while the comtesse studied him.

Not until he made two complete circuits of the gallery, did

Gino remember her. "Good Lord!" he cried. "What am I doing?"

"Enjoying my paintings."

"Yes, of course. But my manners, dear lady—terrible even for a Tuscan peasant."

"If you are a peasant, Gianpaolo, then I like peasants. Come with me." It was a command. He obeyed.

At the end of the gallery she opened a door to another, darkened, room. She touched the switch and immediately the glare made him blink. When he opened his eyes, the first thing he saw was his beautiful hostess. He followed the gesture of her outstretched hand to the fingertips and beyond—to the painting he had given her, his *nature morte*. When he had recovered from the shock, he quickly scanned the walls, recognizing works by Picasso and Braque, Matisse and Dubuffet, Rouault and Chagall. While he was not especially fond of some of the works, he understood their prominence in the current world.

"You rank me with these?"

"How do you rank yourself?"

"I'm flattered."

"Braque is at the party, you know. Would you like to meet him?"

"Could you introduce me to Monsieur Chagall? I saw him in the library earlier."

"I'm sorry, I said goodbye to him just before I entered these galleries."

Again! Gino thought. *I keep missing him for some reason.* But then he rallied, not wanting to offend the comtesse. "It's enough that you for place my work in the same gallery with Chagall—and right next to Braque."

"But then, you, too, are a cubist."

He stiffened, uncomfortable with the label. As he was phrasing a response, the comtesse spoke.

"I would have placed your painting in the other gallery, but it didn't go with the marquetry."

"Now you're making fun of me."

"Somehow I find that important where you're concerned."

"But you like my painting."

"I love it."

"Your note was so formal."

"Did you expect a love letter?"

Each time he thought she was growing warmer, she seemed to turn remote.

"Why do you change so? One moment you're friendly, the next you're cold."

"It is the vice of my class."

"I see." Her words seemed to open a gulf between them.

But immediately she moved towards him and took his arm. "You mustn't mind. I know you're not trying to match wits with me, but I'm accustomed to the manners of my friends, which call for cynicism at all times. I cannot surrender this habit easily."

She smiled up at him, which was not a great distance because she was quite tall and for the first time he noticed the tiara plaited in her hair. He had never seen such diamonds before.

"You have only begun to see the treasures of the Chateau de Villon."

She led him back through the large gallery, through the smoking room and into the entrance hall, nodding to those who approached her but not stopping. Gino followed her up the curving marble staircase to the balcony. The walls were lined with paintings, an eclectic selection from Renaissance times to the present—old masters mixed with modernists of the most exotic type; oils, temperas, watercolors, a few engravings.

There was an etching by Daumier, depicting a lone man leaning against a wall, and yet it produced precisely the effect Gino had tried to achieve with a group of card-players, sitting at a table. He realized his painting had been a failure.

The comtesse noted his distress. "Can I help you?"

"Not unless you can draw."

She was wise enough not to respond. Patiently she escorted him around the balcony—once, twice, three times.

"You're very kind to remain with me," he said, more in politeness than appreciation.

The comtesse laughed. "You've grown careful of your manners."

That broke the spell. Before Gino could say anything she began to descend the staircase. It would have been childish to run after her, embarrassing to call out. He followed, but by the time he reached the main floor, she was gone. As he wandered through the rooms searching for her, he bumped into Pietro.

"Where have you been?" Pietro was barely able to mask his agitation.

"Here."

"Did you see the comtesse?"

"Yes, I spent some time with her "

"Wonderful." Pietro's lips were tight, but Gino didn't notice.

"I'm afraid I made her angry. She walked away and left me."

Pietro began to relax. "You find success absolutely unbearable," he said.

Gino was angry. "I only tried to be polite and she became angry. When I was rude she didn't even complain."

"Gino, it would be hopeless for me to try to explain a woman like the comtesse to you. Let's forget it. There's still plenty of food and champagne."

Unfortunately, Gino paid more attention to the champagne than the food.

♦ ♦ ♦

His head ached and his throat was raw, but the rest of him felt cool and relaxed. The pattern above his head was unfamiliar. He studied it carefully despite his aching head, and slowly—very slowly—allowed himself to realize where he was. Obviously, sheets this fine were too expensive for the most elegant hotel. Nor would you be likely to find intricate hunting scenes woven in silk over your head, even in the finest resort.

Gino unsheathed himself from the covers and discovered that he was naked. After a moment of panic he found his clothes, lying pressed and neatly folded on a chest. In the bathroom, spread on the huge green marble washbasin, was a complete set of shaving utensils. Gino washed, shaved and dressed quickly. He must make his apologies and depart as quickly as possible.

Where was Pietro?

The bedroom opened onto a corridor that led to the circular balcony above the foyer. He glanced at the Daumier and hesitated, reminding himself how wide of the mark his own drawing had been, but there was no time for such reflection.

The moment he reached the patterned marble floor of the grand foyer, a uniformed butler materialized and said that Madame le Comtesse was expecting him on the terrace. He would not be able to escape without facing her.

It was delightful outside: clear, warm and almost windless. He sucked in his breath at the sight of the formal gardens in all their sun-swept splendor.

The comtesse was seated at a white, wrought iron table with a glass top. A pleated, blue and white striped umbrella shaded the table, but the comtesse was seated in the sun, her head thrown back, eyes closed. The butler bowed and departed without announcing him.

Her hair was loose; it was the first time he had seen her without a carefully constructed coiffure. In the sunlight her skin was as clear and translucent as it appeared in artificial light. There was a subtle glow to it, like the pearls she had worn the night before. He searched her face for wrinkles, and was relieved to find a tiny one between her brows.

Her lips moved before her eyes opened. "Good morning."

"Good morning, Comtesse. I must apologize—"

"—Let's not bother with apologies. Are you hungry?"

"Why, yes."

"Please sit down, then. *Petit déjeuner* comes with the room."

Her eyes were shockingly blue in the bright light and when she smiled the line between her brows mysteriously disappeared.

Relieved, Gino sank into the nearest chair. *"Alors,"* he said in his best approximation of French, *"le taxe et service sont compris?"*

"That depends on the service required. What do you have in mind?"

He had nothing in mind and was therefore stumped for an answer. He decided a smile was the only response available to him.

A slim, pretty young girl wearing a starched white uniform served him hot rolls and jams and *café au lait*. The croissants were marvelously fresh and melting, the jams bursting with toothsome chunks of fruit. He demolished the rolls with embarrassing speed. A new tray bearing several more suddenly appeared before him. He was too proud to touch them.

"Don't be childish: eat the rolls. If you want something else, please ask for it." The comtesse closed her eyes and once more raised her face to the sun.

"Excuse me, but where is Pietro?"

"He drove back to Paris last night."

"And left me?"

"Like a foundling deposited on a doorstep."

"I must thank you for your kind—"

"—Not necessary."

"Yes, it's necessary." Gino was angry. "I've behaved badly, and I have the duty and the right to apologize. It's wrong for you to prevent me from making a proper apology."

"Very well, then, proceed."

Gino hesitated. "I—I'm sorry."

The comtesse laughed.

Gino laughed, too. He felt foolish, but not disgraced.

"I'll take the next train back to Paris."

"My chauffeur will drive you home."

"That's not necessary."

"We are almost as far from a decent train as from the city."

"I see."

"But of course, you don't have to leave yet. It's still early. Why don't you spend the day here?"

"I'd enjoy that."

"Splendid. In fact, if you like, I'll take you for a drive in the country and bring you back to Paris, myself."

When the comtesse stood up, Gino noticed for the first time that she was wearing a cream-colored skirt and sweater. She looked as perfect and as elegant in casual clothes as she had in her velvet gown.

The comtesse led him to the garage, a huge rambling building, built in the same elaborate style as the chateau, which housed many vehicles, ranging from a tiny Renault to the Silver Cloud Rolls.

"I think we'll take the Jaguar. Do you drive? No. Well, then I shall."

He climbed into the sleek, immaculately clean dove-toned automobile while she started the motor, which growled impressively. The top was already down. This in itself did not awaken his suspicions. Nor did the fact that her clothing looked well with the automobile's color. They pulled onto a gravel driveway and stopped at the *porte cochère*. Immediately, a young man appeared, carrying a large wicker basket, which he deposited on the back seat of the convertible.

"Thank you, Alain," she said with a smile.

It was obvious to Gino that the basket had been previously ordered and prepared and he began to feel wary. People who planned ahead, even for his pleasure, worried him.

She drove the car well, neither fast nor slow, not trying to impress him with her skill, along the way sharing the history of every house, vineyard and shrine in the district. She was cheerful and relaxed. The wind blew strands of hair into her face; she pushed them aside, not seeming to mind that her hair wasn't perfect.

They lunched in a grove of trees at the side of the road, Gino marveling that the comtesse could handle a picnic lunch as graciously as a grand dinner. When they were finished, Gino asked the question he had wanted to ask all day.

"May we go to Chartres? I've only seen the cathedral, or the reflection of it, from the highway."

The idea didn't seem to stimulate the comtesse, but she agreed. They left the convertible at the edge of town and wandered through its streets. As yet he hadn't seen the cathedral—only the tips of its towers as they approached. Once they were inside the town, it disappeared altogether.

Chartres was an ordinary French village; ancient, grimy, houses propped against other houses; more old people than young children; intelligent faces, sharp looks.

"Don't they know you?"

"I never come here."

"I can't believe it. To live so close and never come here."

No response. They turned the last lane and were confronted by the eight-hundred-year-old structure. The square was too small for the church. The little plot of grass fenced with rusted wire was a false note. The two solemn gray towers were mismatched, one squat, the other febrile. Neither matched the rhythmic west portal. Yet there was symmetry here, all the more confusing because it seemed random, perhaps even unconscious. Gradually the facade assumed depth and dimension. The grimy provincial town vanished and the great, austere cathedral floated once again in a field of grain, singular, supreme, eternal. Gino took the hand of the comtesse for reassurance; he wanted to be sure that this was not an illusion.

The great west portal enclosed him. He was enfolded by the soaring tubular forms, the arching figures congealed in stone. His eyes ached and his forehead throbbed as if the very contours were imprinted there. After several, silent minutes Gino gained the courage to enter the cathedral, almost unaware of the woman beside him. He passed through the dark, wooden entranceway, the old but not ancient doors, and then he was inside.

It was near sunset. The great rose window streamed prismatic colors through the thick, cool air. He looked up at the soaring arches, pleating the nave in stone. The cathedral was almost empty. He could hear his own footsteps marring the still air. It was another world, one he had neither seen nor dreamed of before. The lower aisles blended into the arches above, which folded into the windows higher up, then leaped to the vault in simple, subtle, yet necessary curves—not soft curves, but hard ones; not circles but parabolas; not a roof that enclosed man, but an arrow that pointed to God. A series of arrows flung into the sky. There was no ceiling, only heaven. The eye was not permitted to stop at the pinnacle, but forced to press beyond and seek eternity.

He remained there, staring, as long as he could, absorbed by the church, dominated by it, challenged by the soaring edifice. It was too much. He hurried outside, the comtesse following. The remaining sunlight brought him back to himself.

"You're shivering," the comtesse said.

"With fear."

"Of what?"

"Of God."

"You can't be serious."

He looked down at her, so lovely and so real. Yet here she seemed insubstantial.

"If God is not in that cathedral, He is not anywhere."

She took his hand and looked into his eyes. "I think," she said gently, "even Pietro would agree with you."

He pulled his hand away. "What do you know of God, with your grand chateau and your automobiles and your aristocratic friends?"

Suddenly, she looked vulnerable. "Nothing—I suppose."

His anger vanished. He took her hand. "I'm sorry. I'm sure I don't know any more of God than you."

He hurried along the streets, almost dragging her with him. He wanted to leave this place which had disoriented him greatly. He didn't know why; he didn't want to know.

♦ ♦ ♦

On the route back to the chateau the comtesse invited him to dine with her. There seemed no gracious way to refuse, and in fact he welcomed her offer.

Dinner was elegant, served in a large, wooden-paneled dining room with many courses and many wines. The chandelier overhead was almost discreet compared to the one in the vast entry, and the light was soft, yet lambent. They chatted amiably about their day, touching only briefly on the subject of Chartres. There was still much to think about. When they finished dinner, it was late, and he was both tired and at ease. The comtesse suggested he stay the night and of course he agreed.

Awakening at first light in that beautiful room beneath the silk canopy was even more pleasant the second morning. He felt luxuriously lazy and did not hesitate to close his eyes and drift back to sleep.

When Gino arose, he dressed slowly. His clothes had been pressed as before and the shaving things he required were in their expected places.

After breakfast on the terrace, they set off again to explore the countryside. This time the comtesse had not brought lunch, and they dined at an ancient half-timbered inn with sharply sloping roofs and great, carved beams, hidden away on a winding, sandy road. As they waited patiently for their meal to be prepared, the comtesse—unasked—began to tell him about her husband.

"Philippe was tall, quite slender, and very elegant in word and dress and appearance. He was not rich but his family name was good, and he had been well educated. I cannot say that I was wildly in love with him, but he was attractive and he seemed quite right for me. As for money, that hardly seemed important; I had more than enough for both of us. Philippe knew it and I knew it and so did every one else. It was to be expected in France in our class."

"Then why are you explaining it to me?"

She didn't bother to reply. "We reopened an old family

apartment in Paris. Philippe could not bear living at the chateau, not even with dozens of servants and parties every week. It was too far from the *haut monde*—the real world—he used to say.

"Then it was war and the Germans were in Paris. Philippe spent a few hours each day at the banking house my family controlled. If it was not very demanding work, it was considered proper for a gentleman. Philippe always did what was proper. In time, he might have had a dozen mistresses, but nevertheless he would have gone to his office every day. He was a French gentleman, you know, not a rogue."

She sighed, then spoke again. "One day the Germans shot him."

"I'm very sorry. I didn't know."

"It was really quite stupid. He was not a soldier, not a member of the resistance. I'm not even sure he was anti-Nazi. After all, they hardly interfered with his life. His office was next door to the billet of one of the German generals. He passed men in uniform every morning and every noon. As far as I know, he hardly even noticed them.

"One afternoon, as he left his office at the usual time, a guard walking his post next door bumped into him, apparently rather roughly. It was unintentional, but Philippe unaccountably swore at him. The guard either understood or misunderstood what Philippe said. He lowered his rifle and shot him dead."

The comtesse opened a gold case and withdrew a cigarette. She tapped it, then put it down. "Philippe was not a hero; not even a protester. Yet he was dead. The Germans were apologetic. They court-martialed the guard and shot him. Can you imagine? Two men dead over nothing."

"Terrible."

"I didn't really love him."

"But it must have hurt you to lose him."

"Yes, that's true. It was not that I wanted him dead, you see."

"Of course not."

They sat together for a long time, saying little, sipping wine, the comtesse smoking one cigarette after another. She smiled suddenly, and placed her hand on his. "You must stop calling me 'Comtesse'—call me 'Ariane'."

"Ariane. A lovely name. I've longed to say it."

"Gino. Not elegant, but appropriate."

"Not even Gianpaolo is elegant."

"But your paintings are elegant."

"I'm honored."

She looked down at his large, blunt fingers. "Do you know what I thought when we walked from Le Temps' gallery the first time I met you? I said to myself, 'I am a princess and the prince is leading me away from danger.'"

"Is that true?"

"Yes."

"We shared the same vision."

"That's why I ran to my car. I wanted to break the spell. That's why I offered to buy your painting."

"That's why I gave it to you as a present."

"We are foolish children."

"Yes, but isn't it fun?" He laughed and she—well, it seemed to him that she giggled, which was, of course, unthinkable.

♦ ♦ ♦

Gino didn't return to Paris that night either. The following morning, he and Ariane began to explore the countryside on foot, although in fact, they no longer felt any compelling interest in their surroundings. Companionship was what mattered. Walking along country roads, hand in hand, with a breeze blowing and the sun shining, seemed harmonious and right. In the evening, it was pleasant to dine together in warm, gentle light in the great dining hall of the chateau. Wall-sized Gobelin tapestries of gods and goddesses stared down from carved wooden walls, the exquisite chandelier trembled at the footsteps of each servant. Silence was never oppressive, often warm and alive with shared pleasure. The cuisine was predictably superb. Gino had never eaten like this in his life. Beef Stroganoff, squab under glass, trout baked in a shell—he had neither heard of nor seen these dishes before. And the wines, Lafitte Rothschild and Chateau Margaux, local Vouvrays and Sancerres, Heidseick champagnes, were a constant source of surprise and delight. There were even fine Antinori reds to satisfy his longing for the joys of home. Had she routinely stocked them, or brought them in for his pleasure? It didn't matter, it would have been discourteous to inquire.

They strolled through the galleries and the gardens. To Gino, both were lovely and fragrant. Perhaps he preferred the smell of centuries old paint and varnish to that of gladioli and roses. But these were merely refinements of the same phenomena.

His room became familiar. He actually sang when he undressed for bed and again when he rose in the morning. There was time to study the details in the canopy, the pattern in the carpet and the paintings on the walls.

From the windows of his room the gardens displayed graceful patterns worthy of oriental rugs, but walking in them, they were simply lovely and fragrant. It was pleasant to sit at the base of a marble fountain, watching a dolphin spout water at a seated cupid.

It was there, to his own surprise, that he told Ariane about the battle in Bari and his vivid recollection of the little girl and her doll. A brief shudder passed over him. He had not thought about the little girl for a long time. Ariane listened quietly. She did not comment on his tale and he was grateful for that. Nor did she break the long silence that followed.

When he regained his composure, Gino told Ariane about his father. She seemed undisturbed to learn that he had been a fascist. She was not unpolitical, but after the war the maneuverings of men and nations had ceased to interest her.

Gino tried to tell her of his affair with Giulia Rossini. It was improper to discuss a past love, but he felt he should trade confidences with her. However, the story evidently annoyed Ariane, and he switched immediately to tales of Brothers Domenico and

Alberto, the Monastery of San Marco and Lorenzo Patti. These she found interesting and amusing. He was pleased to be able to divert her with stories of his humble life.

Another day passed. Gino learned that the butler's name was Roger, that his chambermaid was Annette, the chauffeur, George. It was a revelation to be served hand and foot by creatures so distant yet so efficient. He began to understand how Ariane was able to behave as if the servants did not exist.

Each day they drove somewhere, or walked somewhere, or picnicked somewhere. Gino's interest in his surroundings was still keen, but it was easy for Ariane to divert him. She had become a wood nymph rather than a fairy princess, yet still infinitely light and lovely and impossible to deny. Once or twice he tried to compare her with women he had known before, but it was impossible. In retrospect, the others seemed unbearably shallow.

It was a strange affair. For Gino, lovemaking had always seemed the inevitable goal of any liaison. Yet he had now spent several days in the company of a beautiful woman and the closest physical contact had been a hand held or lips lightly brushed. Certainly he found her desirable. Ariane de Villon was not as voluptuous as Giulia Rossini, but she was beautifully formed and her skin was wonderfully clear and exciting to the touch. He acknowledged all this with an attitude not of remoteness, but of understanding, leery of damaging their relationship with crude behavior. He didn't think Ariane would repel his advances, but he wasn't certain. Besides, he was fearful the comtesse might be the kind of woman who would embrace him passionately tonight, and have him thrown out the next morning.

At odd moments, he wondered when he would return to Paris and resume his painting. Breaking off this idyll wouldn't be easy. Most of all he didn't want the suggestion to come from Ariane.

He had stayed a week before he was aware of it. Then, one morning when he awakened, his clothes were missing. On the chest lay a beige cashmere jacket and brown woolen slacks, a silk shirt and scarf and other accessories. The feel of them was superb.

He rang for the valet. When the man appeared he asked for the return of his own clothes.

The valet, unblinking, brought back Gino's shabby things. Without bothering to wash or to shave he dressed in his old clothes and left the room. Taking the steps of the marble staircase at a trot, he crossed the great foyer, shoved open the door and hurried outside.

By the time he reached the bottom of the steps, he was deep in doubt, but didn't stop. It took him quite a long time to walk the winding road that led to the highway, and a half hour more to reach the nearest bus stop.

Fifteen

Commitment

For a week Pietro had lived in agony. He had watched Gino getting drunk at the Chateau de Villon and made no attempt to stop him, confident that his loutish behavior would disgust the comtesse and that would be the end of that. When Gino slipped into a drunken stupor—in full sight of Ariane and her guests—Pietro prepared to take him home, satisfied the damage was done.

But the comtesse had surprised him. "The man is too sick to travel," she said.

"He's strong as an ox. I'll take him to his room in Paris. By morning he'll be perfect again."

"I would be better if you left him here, Pietro. We'll put him up for the night."

Pietro didn't dare argue the point further. "I'll come back for him in the morning."

"That won't be necessary," the comtesse said. "My driver will bring him back to Paris."

She might easily have invited Pietro to stay the night and wait for Gino, but she didn't, and her failure to do so offended him. He was puzzled when Gino didn't return the next day—even more puzzled as the days passed with no word from him. How stupid he had been! He should have insisted on bringing Gino back to the city. If the comtesse was truly disgusted with Gino, she wouldn't have suggested he remain overnight. He had been outmaneuvered, not by Gino, who obviously was too drunk to manipulate anyone or anything, but by the comtesse. Why?

Pietro refuse to believe that Ariane was genuinely attracted to Gino. She might find him virile—even physically compelling. Women often did. But how long could such an infatuation last? Still, he was frightened. His life had been cursed by Bondones: the father; the daughter; now the son. He didn't stop to think that he was a Bondone himself.

Then, suddenly, Gino was back in his studio, painting. The romance—if it had been a romance—was apparently over.

"You're the strangest person I've ever met," Pietro said, "a man who runs away from rich, beautiful women."

"I didn't run away from Giulia; you dragged me."

"But when she came to Paris, you sent her home."

"True."

"You see?"

"As for comtesse, there was no romance."

"Oh."

"We didn't make love, although I doubt I'll ever be able to convince you of that."

"Of course. Ariane decided to keep you there for the sake of your towering intellect."

"That's the right word—'keep.' I won't permit any woman to keep me."

"Not even Giulia?"

"That's why I sent her back to Florence. I'm not a pet; I don't want someone to buy a collar for my neck."

"Who bought you a collar?"

"The comtesse. When I saw a silk shirt and scarf in my room I thought immediately of a dog collar."

"You accepted her food, her wine, and her companionship, and then ran out the door like a thief in the night."

"What if the clothes belonged to her husband?"

"Ah, ha! That's what bothered you."

"No, no, no! I told you what bothered me. Don't drag me down side streets."

"What are your feelings toward Ariane?"

"That's not your affair."

"The answer is important."

Gino had been trying to sketch during this exchange, but now he gave up and dropped his chalk. When he spoke, his own words surprised him. "I'm in love with her."

"You're an even greater fool than I thought! You fall in love with a woman, and run away because she gives you a shirt and scarf."

"Pants and a jacket, too."

"What am I to do with you?"

"Leave me alone. Let me paint."

Gino tried to resume his work, but each time he looked at the canvas, he saw glimpses of Ariane. When he looked away, he heard her warm voice and childlike laugh. Images of Ariane filled the room. Every time he drew a line, she seemed to be looking over his shoulder. He wanted to ask her if she liked what he was doing. He wanted to hurry back to Villon.

Pride kept him nailed to the floor before his easel. By a great exercise of will he managed to sketch—not well, but surely he would regain his touch. Some day.

For the next several days he made slow progress, but inevitably, images of Ariane returned, smiling and gently chiding him: "What have I done," she asked, "that you should be so cruel? We are friends, aren't we?"

"Yes," he responded to this wraith, "we're friends. But friends can't own one another. They must be free."

In the vision, the comtesse shook her head. "You're wrong, Gino. What is friendship but a claim on one side and the acknowledgement of it on the other? The one you don't own isn't your friend."

Gino clapped his hands to his forehead. This was stupid, a senseless conversation with a vision. But he continued to see her: Ariane's head turned suddenly, the breeze blowing strands of hair across her mouth; her slim figure gliding through the great entrance hall; a shadow in the garden that must be Ariane's. She seemed closer now than during the week at Villon. He saw her lips on his canvas and gently kissed them.

It was not a complete surprise when she walked through the open door into his studio. He had been expecting her, waiting for her, willing her to come. He had left the door ajar, so that she wouldn't even have to knock. Yet he had made no plans, prepared no speech. Whatever was going to happen would happen spontaneously. He wouldn't try to be clever, not with Ariane.

She seated herself on a chair in the dusty studio and folded her hands. Even this small gesture, this composition of her form on the chair, was achieved so gracefully, so unselfconsciously, that it tugged at his heart.

"You're working."

He nodded.

"Is it going well?"

He shook his head.

"Why not?"

"I keep thinking of you; I can't concentrate."

"Was it the clothes?"

"Yes."

"I wasn't trying to demean you. Afterwards I realized that I'd been very stupid."

"You thought you were being kind."

"No, I was trying to establish my ownership of you."

Her candor astounded him. He put down his brushes and studied her with every sense alerted.

"But I realize that can never be, Gianpaolo Bondone. You are not meant to be possessed."

"Possessed perhaps, but not owned."

"Yes, you're right. Well, what are we to do? Is it impossible?"

"I hope not. But I don't know how to make it work."

She turned in her chair, as if she was growing uncomfortable. "I can promise I won't try to own you."

He could see how difficult this was for her. When she spoke again, her voice sounded hollow. "I'm not certain that will be enough."

"I am an artist." He thought his own words seemed weak and vain.

"I respect that."

"I'm not sure what you want of me."

She lowered her head. "How much must I humiliate myself?"

He moved quickly to her, gently lifted her from the chair and kissed her. "Now," he said, "I presume we're both humiliated."

She said nothing. He kissed her again, then held her at arm's length and stared into her eyes. "Must I say it?" he asked.

She nodded.

"I love you."

"And I love you."

The embrace that followed was so crushing that Ariane struggled within his arms.

"I'm sorry," he said. "I'm still a peasant. "

She smiled. "My peasant," she said.

◆ ◆ ◆

They were married in a small chapel of the cathedral at Chartres. Ariane had suggested the site, knowing Gino would be pleased. The only witnesses were Pierre Petit, Louis Le Temps and Maria.

The cathedral was cool. The vertical rays of noon sunlight barely burnished the soaring glass, so that the great windows glowed with mysterious highlights. Moist air rising from the stone floor tingled Gino's scalp on its way to the arching stone groins. The mumbled words of the young priest were muted in the thick silence.

When it was done, when they had kissed each other and their

friends, Gino took Le Temps aside. "You must do something for me, Louis. If you love me as you claim you do, you must help me."

"But of course, Gino. What is it?"

Gino stepped closer. "A show for Pierre."

Le Temps would have stepped back, but Gino anticipated the move and gripped his arm. "Don't argue, Louis. If you wish to show my works again, you must hold an exhibition devoted solely to Pierre Petit."

The great cathedral constrained the gallery owner. "Now is not the time for this. We'll discuss it later."

"No, now. I'll do whatever you ask. Increase your commission on my works—double it—but give Pierre a *vernissage*."

Le Temps smiled. "If on this occasion, you can think of such a thing, how can I turn you down?"

Gino embraced him. "Bless you, Louis."

As he was driving off with his bride, Gino noticed Le Temps speaking intently to Pierre. Maria stood to one side, alone.

◆ ◆ ◆

When they returned to the chateau, the lights were ablaze and the servants stood arrayed in the hall, beaming with pleasure.

Gino stopped short at the sight. "I had forgotten they were actually alive," he whispered.

"I think you're a greater snob than I am."

Gino laughed, but there was something disturbing about her words. Brushing the thought aside, he accepted the congratulations of the staff.

He had never been in the comtesse's bedroom. The interior was a fantasy of high-arching ceilings, angled and curved walls, tall French windows in curving bays—virtually every surface save the glass covered with plaster floral and cherubic figures, painted and gilded. On the one blank wall hung a gently faded Gobelin tapestry filled with nymphs, satyrs, knights and ladies. Every inch of the domed ceiling was coffered, painted, gilded. Fortunately, the predominant color throughout the room was white and the bounty of figures was brushed in muted pastels.

Resting on the parquet floor, a vast Aubusson carpet yielded underfoot. The furniture was Louis Sixteenth, also painted white with floral patterned upholstery, and the bed was huge, high and canopied in white with sweeping swags and furbelows. Palest of pink satin sheets had been turned down, pillows plumped up.

Ariane had disappeared for the moment and an open door beckoned Gino to a tiled and gilded bathroom. A satin robe and white silk pajamas rode on gilded hooks; he was not in the least offended, but after bathing, he donned only the robe.

When he reentered the room, Ariane materialized, long hair loose and cascading to her shoulders, blue-gray eyes startling against her smooth face, free of makeup. She floated in a diaphanous white cloud, too ethereal to be called a gown. As she approached, the cloud seemed to melt away. Gino slipped the robe from his shoulders, lifted her in his arms and carried her to their bed. He reached to turn off the lamp, but she stayed his hand.

"My peasant god," she murmured and began to trace his face and his body with gentle, but insistent fingers. He wanted to embrace her, but she shook her head, continuing the circuit of his body with a touch both fleeting and unerring that stirred and multiplied every sensation. Her breasts were cool and hot against his chest, nipples hard, legs sliding against his lightly and repeatedly. The pulse in her throat was trembling, and they were both beginning to breathe more quickly and deeply. Ariane's lips retraced the course her fingers had set, while her fingers found new ones, traceries elegant and exciting, surprising and inevitable. His blood roared in his ears, his back arched and the throbbing in his thighs took on a rhythm beyond his control. He could resist no longer. Gino wanted to be gentle, but his hands and mouth, his legs and his loins would not listen. He began to kiss her on the mouth and breasts and belly fiercely, turning her under him, entering her with a sudden thrust that drew a gasp from her, a gasp of surprise and delight. She met him with a thrust of her own, and then they rose beyond passion into a soaring universe of blinding sensation and overwhelming emotion.

♦ ♦ ♦

The following morning, as Gino rested on the terrace after breakfast, feeling pleased and complacent, his bride confronted him.

"I lay awake thinking about you all night."

He smiled at Ariane's exaggeration, but did not contradict her. "Yes my love, what were you thinking about?"

"Our honeymoon."

A chill of fear flickered through him; he had a vision of a cruise ship steaming across the Mediterranean, or a train jolting through Spain.

"I believe," she said, "that these first days are very important for us. I want them to be perfect."

He waited.

"There is only one solution: You must begin to paint again."

"*Pardon.*" He could not believe what he heard.

"Yes, we'll drive into Paris today, pick up your things and bring them back here. There's a large room in the north wing with many windows that will make a perfect studio. You'll paint and if you permit me, I'll watch."

He was astounded by his good fortune. There, on the open terrace, with the entire staff assuredly looking on, he kissed her again and again.

"Are you certain that's what you want?" he asked.

"Absolutely."

Ariane arranged to have George drive into the city in the Rolls, while they rode in a black Bentley saloon. Gino laughed. "What unusual moving vans these are."

It was to be expected that during their many trips from Gino's room and studio to the cars, Pietro would appear. They found him on the sidewalk, leaning against a fender of the Rolls, wearing a grim smile. "Is this permanent or temporary?" he asked. His eyes were on Gino, not Ariane.

"Permanent," Gino said.

"Is it in the interests of art or love?"

"Both," Ariane said.

"Then my congratulations."

"You must visit us," said Ariane.

Gino did not add his invitation. He shook hands gravely with the dark-faced Italian. They parted without a word.

"You were rude," said Ariane, as they pulled away.

"No doubt."

"After all, it was Pietro who brought us together."

"I don't believe he anticipated the result."

♦ ♦ ♦

When the automobiles disappeared around the sloping bend of the rue Lepic, Pietro staggered and almost fell. Why had he spoken to them? One look from his window had told him the full extent of the disaster. But he couldn't resist, even shaking the hand of Gianpaolo Bondone.

The moment they were gone, the immensity of his loss struck him. The sidewalk trembled and melted in his vision. Fingers of blackness moved in from the corners of his eyes. When they interlocked, the rue Lepic became a swamp filled with dark, writhing shapes.

He steadied himself. Yes it was true, Ariane and Gino were gone. Yes, he stood alone in the rue Lepic. Yes, he had brought them together and thus destroyed the greatest dream of his life. But it was senseless to remain in the street, suffering. They wouldn't return. No matter how long and how hard he stared at the winding street he could not force it to roll backwards and thus retrieve the fleeting automobiles. Unconsciously, Pietro brushed off his sleeves, as if he had been splashed by a passing vehicle. He straightened his tie and walked inside. He had never realized there were so many steps. So many steps. And the place smelled fearfully. No doubt about it. It was time to leave this filthy building, this filthy district. He would treat himself to a splendid apartment in the Fauborg St. Germain. There were fine large flats there with great windows looking out on the park.

Surely someone at *Paris-Presse*, perhaps even Laurent, could be helpful in finding an apartment. He entered his room, threw off his jacket, rolled up his sleeves and began to wash his face. The squalor of this place. Why had he remained here this long? Well, now that he was free of that great peasant oaf, there was nothing to keep him.

The knock on his door hardly interrupted his thoughts. He opened it abstractedly, still drying his face with a towel. It was Maria.

"I'm very sorry."

Her words had no meaning to him. "Sorry? For what?"

"About Gino and the comtesse."

"You don't know what you're talking about, Maria."

She smiled sadly. "I know," she whispered. "You love her."

"I love no one!" The words were a scream torn from his throat. She would have spoken again, but his hand was across her mouth and his face inches from her. "I love no one, do you understand? No one!"

He pulled away and folded his hands together, squeezing the blood from them, thinking to himself, *Pietro loves no one; no one loves Pietro.*

"Except for me," Maria said. He spun about. "You think no one loves you, Pietro, but it's not true. I love you. I will always love you."

He stared at her in fascination. She was trying to press closer. Her hands were moving across his chest, sliding over his arms and coming together behind him.

"That was madness, Pietro. The woman wasn't for you. Let Gino have her. You're better off now, beloved, believe me. I'm yours, Pietro. I'm here and I'm yours."

The thin black strand connecting him with sanity snapped. He began to laugh a jittery uneven laugh that bounced from his chest to his throat. He held pulled Maria's arms away from his body and pinned them to her sides. "You want to comfort me? You've waited patiently for this moment. Now you're certain that your rival is gone. Irrevocably gone, married to your brother."

He shook his head, but couldn't clear the blackness of his vision. "So now I'm to be yours—yours alone. We'll live together, happily ever after."

"Please, Pietro—"

"—Shall we be married then, you and I? Is that the destiny you see for us?"

He knew he shouldn't say the words. Once said, they could not be retrieved. But he wanted to punish her; to punish someone; to punish himself. "Do you know who I am?"

She stared at him fearfully.

He whispered the words: "I am your brother." Then he waited. Maria's expression didn't change. She didn't understand him.

He held her arms more tightly and shook her. Then he whispered again, this time fiercely: "I am your brother. You don't believe me? Of course not. Why would you believe me? But it's true. If you like, you may ask your dear friend, Brother Domenico. He will tell you—as he told me—that my father was Carlo Bondone. My mother? Well, who knows who she was, but you see, *I am your brother!* Perhaps, to be technically correct, your half-brother. And since we are of the same blood, it's only natural we should love one another. Only natural."

He was shaking uncontrollably now, trying to laugh, trying not to cry, studying her face, waiting to see it split open in horror, waiting for her scream to rend the air. Then she would suffer with him. Someone would suffer with him.

Under his touch, Maria's flesh retreated a little. He had a strange sensation—that she was turning to ice in his hands. He let her go, but her eyes remained locked on his. They didn't waver. Then she stepped back, still staring at him. She brushed a hand across her breast as he had brushed hands across his sleeves, only minutes earlier.

Her voice came in a whisper, "Oh, my God," she said. "My poor Pietro."

Sixteen

The Lap of Luxury

Gino awoke with a sense of ease and satisfaction. Beside him, his wife slept quietly, her fine small breasts arching the satin sheets. He studied her with pleasure: long blond hair nesting the smooth, pale skin; lips soft and especially full when at rest; her nose cresting slightly an inch from the bridge. He touched the slight imperfection lightly, cherishing it.

Ariane's lids fluttered, then settled against her face. How long and how thick her lashes were. Pride in his patrician bride swelled his chest. He stretched, feeling the muscles ripple in his back, looking at his fingers. *I may even have them manicured*, he thought. Then laughed silently. These peasant nails, trimmed, filed and polished? It was too much.

His eyes followed the curling plaster trellises that scaled the walls and clung to the ceiling, framing cameos of painted cherubs and laughing maidens. A slight breeze fluttered the lace curtains— smell of roses and pines. He breathed deeply. He was at peace. He had never been at peace before. Anxiety and fear had always been a part of his life. Fear of his father, fear of death, fear of Pietro.

Gino remembered the studio. The night before there had only

been time to unload his things. Now, he should be at work. He kissed his wife lightly on the lips. She stirred, whispered his name and wound herself about him. He kissed her passionately, then gently pulled away. She smiled at him uncertainly.

"My studio," he said.

Ariane sighed. "Of course," she said.

For once, the ritual of bathing and dressing in these elegant rooms was interminable and unrewarding. He pulled on a shirt, stuffed it in his trousers and headed for the door.

"But darling," Ariane said, "You haven't had breakfast."

"Bring it to the studio, please." He kissed her on the cheek in apology for his abruptness, then hurried out the door.

The parquet floors angling ahead were a continuous set of arrows urging him forward. He passed doors without seeing them, servants without acknowledging their greetings.

The paned glass doors to the building that would be his studio opened easily under his hands. He stood there for a moment, his tongue tracing his upper lip. Light. Nothing but light. Walls of windows transposing only a thin film between the room and the sun. The floor shimmering with it. The white ceiling checked with even whiter squares sent up by the panes of glass.

Too bright, of course. But a curtain here or there and it would be perfect. Beyond, a splendid terrace. Limestone with a baroque balustrade. And beyond that, the gardens.

The room was a crystal, refracting, reflecting and mirroring the light and he was afloat within it. He hurried to find his canvases, paints, and equipment, and set them against the wall farthest from the windows. It was a long wall, long enough to display his favorite paintings side by side.

Gino set his easel in the middle of the room and placed a blank, stretched, canvas on it—a large one, nearly two meters high, and more than half as wide. It was appropriate to the room. He would make no small plans here.

The canvas canted slightly before him, a wall that must be scaled. What an effort; but he would do it. Then the thought of the effort penetrated his mind, seeped through his body, reached his stomach. He was hungry. Too hungry to scale a wall.

A plate appeared beside him, laden with hot rolls and jams. He grabbed a roll and shoved it into his mouth before he realized the plate was carried by Ariane.

"My love," he cried, through the melting croissant, "you're perfect!" He swept her into his arms, smashing the plate, the rolls and the jelly between them. When he finally let her go, the plate clattered to the floor. Both of them were covered with crumbs and stained with jam. It was several minutes before they stopped laughing.

Gino wouldn't permit Ariane to decorate the studio.

"I love it. It's perfect."

"A few pieces of furniture, Gino. Draperies for the windows. Perhaps some carpeting."

"Nothing. Well, perhaps some curtains on the south glass."

"Why not a few comfortable chairs?"

"This is a place to work, not to rest."

"Must you be uncomfortable?"

"Yes. At least, I think so. After sleeping between silk and satin sheets, this is necessary for me. I may begin to wear a hair shirt to remind myself of my humble beginnings."

"You're not humble any longer, my dear."

"Of course I'm humble. I'll always be humble."

Ariane shrugged.

"I don't require any furniture, but I do need a model. Someone to paint."

"Why not me?"

He smiled. "Later. I'm not ready for so magnificent a subject."

"What about the servants?"

"Splendid. Can I have Annette?"

"Annette?"

"The chambermaid."

"Ah, ha! The prettiest girl in the house."

"Of course. I'm a painter. I have an eye for beauty."

She pretended to pout. "An eye will be enough." But she summoned Annette.

The girl was young, delicately made, with immense dark eyes. Intimidated at the thought of being painted, she kept looking to Ariane for assurance. Ariane could only smile.

"Don't be frightened," Gino said, leading her to a plain wooden armless chair. He seated her and then gently arranged her pose. "Have you ever had a photograph taken?"

The girl nodded.

"This is much the same. Except that it takes a good deal longer."

He sat on a stool for many minutes studying the girl. Annette remained rigid in her chair, beginning to show the strain of his scrutiny. Her eyes flashed toward Ariane.

"Don't be so stiff," Gino commanded. "You may move about on the chair if you wish, just so you come back to more or less the same pose."

The girl's mouth half opened. Then closed.

"What is it?" he asked.

"Why—why do you stare at me, so?"

"I'm trying to see you."

The girl looked bewildered.

"You're very pretty," Gino said. "But that is the outer Annette. Inside, there is a girl who is even prettier."

Gino picked up a stick of charcoal and began to sketch rapidly on the canvas. Under his fingers, the canvas—the wall—became a battle plan: Lines, circles, points of attack. The contending forces were outlined in bold arcs and strong arrows. Very soon the engagement would begin.

Ariane watched in silent fascination, knowing he was unaware of her presence. Perhaps, in a strange way, unaware of the girl. He was struggling on the canvas. His challenge was there. Whatever vision he held in his mind was flowing through his fingers onto the working surface.

At first, the lines and whirls were meaningless to her. Then, she began to see the girl's body, her head, the chair. As they appeared, Gino's arrangement of them was nothing like the pose the girl had assumed. Annette sat at an angle, but the painting was full face. Yet, was it really full face? The lines gave some hint of Annette's profile.

After the sketching was complete, Ariane found it even more interesting to watch Gino apply his paints. He mixed them carefully, very carefully. Oil on canvas was not fresco, but Gino had learned from Lorenzo Patti the importance of finding precisely the perfect tones and textures. His exposure to Chagall's highly original use of color had given him further confirmation of the importance of this focus, although their techniques were radically different. Gino applied the paint smoothly, selecting a portion of the canvas and completing it before he moved on to another. Here again, he carried on the tradition of fresco painting: The artist must work within a rigorously defined area and complete the work assigned for the day.

"Why do you paint in limited areas—a block at a time?" Ariane asked.

"You've used the right word. To scale the wall you must know how it is built."

"I don't understand."

"It's the only way I know how to paint." And then he forgot her and was vigorously at work again, building his wall, block by block; no two alike, the colors in each subtly different, the colors never blending, the strips of paint laid on firmly with infinite care, every joint carefully mortared.

After a few days, it was apparent that Annette felt completely at ease. She entered smiling and confident, took her pose and held it. Her midday meal was served to her in the studio, with the comtesse and the master of the house. She became a celebrity to the staff.

"I think," said Ariane, "we'll soon have a problem with Annette. The honor of posing for you has gone to her head. She may even have led the others to believe she's your mistress. After all, what else would you want with a poor serving girl?"

Gino laughed. "The first day she was frightened and birdlike. Now her face glows with arrogance. The Annette I put on canvas is not the one who now sits before me. I'll tell her I have no further need of her."

The girl was heartbroken. "Have I done something wrong, comtesse? I sit very quietly. I try not to disturb anyone."

"You've done very well, but the master no longer needs a model. We both thank you."

The girl didn't move.

"What is it, Annette?"

"May I see my picture?"

"No," Gino said. "It's not finished."

"Just a look, sir. Please?"

"You won't recognize yourself. You won't like it."

"Oh, yes. I know I'll like it."

Gino smiled. "Very well. Come here then."

The girl's face brightened into a smile as she hurried to the easel. Gino stepped back to give her a full view.

Annette stared for a moment, then burst into tears. "Is that—is that how I look to you?"

"I warned you."

"I hate it!" Then she realized what she had said, and began to cry again. "I'm sorry," she moaned, "please forgive me." But she was more angry than apologetic.

Ariane put a hand on her shoulder. "You've been privileged to pose for a great painter. Your portrait will hang in the home of some very rich and very important family, perhaps even in a museum. Everyone will say, 'What a magnificent painting, the portrait of Annette.' Think of that, my dear. Now, back to the house. You may have the rest of the day off."

"When she was gone, Gino shook his head. " Telling such nonsense to that child."

"In a way she's right. You don't paint a very good likeness, you know. Annette's figure is much better than that. And she does have a face."

Gino took Ariane's arm and seated her in the chair previously occupied by Annette. Then he picked up a pad and pencil and, standing before her, began to sketch. In a few minutes he ripped off the paper and silently handed it to her. She stared at it in amazement. The likeness was startling—almost photographic.

"I didn't know you could draw like that."

"Any competent artist can draw like that."

"But it's me. Really, really me. Still, don't you think the neck is a trifle long?

"That's the point. You're comparing my picture to your own image of yourself. And while you're measuring the surfaces, you've lost what's going on underneath."

"Is that why you don't paint true likenesses?"

"I do paint true likenesses, but not photographic reproductions. I refuse to lose myself in the translucence of your lovely complexion, the delightful fullness of your lips, the startling, shimmering blue-gray-blue of your eyes."

"Gino."

"Those pleasures are for Gino the husband, not Gino the painter."

He leaned down and kissed her.

"I'd like to keep this sketch."

He shrugged his shoulders and kissed her again.

♦ ♦ ♦

Ariane brought him the letter. He knew at once that it was from Maria; he knew at once what it contained: "Dearest Gino, There is nothing for me in Paris. I know that now. I am leaving for Fiesole. I will give Mama your love and tell her of your success. She will be surprised and happy to know you are married. Please send us a photo of you and Ariane. Be happy, Gino. Paint well. Much love, Maria."

He had never done anything for Maria. Never. He had never done anything for his mother. Now, he could send them some money. So what? He had been a poor brother and a worse son.

Ariane touched his hand. "Do you want to visit them, Gino? We can go to Italy."

He shook his head. "No, to go home now would mean little. I'll remain here—and paint. At least, they can be proud of my painting."

Notwithstanding Annette's unhappiness over her portrait, the staff of the Chateau de Villon provided an almost inexhaustible supply of models for Gino. Despite Annette's dismay, all were curious about the comtesse's large, dark-haired husband, and quite willing to sacrifice their household duties for a few hours of posing. They found the master good-natured and jovial. Gino did not demand absolute immobility, at times even encouraging them to wander about the room. But he never permitted the models to see their portraits. The experience with Annette had proved the wisdom of this course.

Old Ferdinand, the ancient gardener, mumbled something about being paid for these extraordinary services. But then, everyone knew he had strong Marxist sympathies.

"If the communists ever take over France," Ariane said, "M. Ferdinand will rush in here with a pitchfork."

The first weeks were idyllic. Ariane shared Gino's days in the studio and his nights in bed. Their lovemaking spurred his art; his art spurred their lovemaking. Gino had never spent so much time alone with a woman—not since those few days at the Villa Rossini—and that episode seemed pallid in comparison.

The unabated ardor of Gino's lovemaking astonished Ariane. He explored her body as intently as he painted his canvases, with the same combination of gentle touch and bold execution. He brought her to flame slowly, with tender caresses at unexpected places. Only when she was trembling with desire, did he take her. And then, when the fires of consummation had flashed through her body, he returned to the tender caresses with which he had begun. Like a painter touching up a masterpiece.

"There's no one like you," she said.

"I hope not."

She put her fingers to his lips. "How can one man be so strong and so gentle? So passionate, yet so kind?"

"We Tuscans are like that. Lovemaking is our local art form."

In fact, he was very pleased by her words and her responses. It all seemed so natural—so necessary—to him. He was gratified to be complimented for what he had always assumed to be merely normal responses. He was gratified, too, by her daily attendance in his studio. He would not have suspected her of having such patience. In this atmosphere, in these surroundings, he knew he was working better than ever before, feeling complete confidence in everything he did. His fingers never hesitated, his mind never cast about for inspiration. It was all there: the ideas in his head; the strength and control in his hands. His only impatience was based on his inability to work even faster. Visions were piling up behind his eyes. They must be stored until he was ready. *My mind is a pressure cooker*, he thought. *God willing, the ideas won't boil off before I can digest them.*

But there seemed little danger of that. He completed canvas after canvas: vast constructions of architectural perfection, infused with his own emotional insights. To others, the portraits might seem faceless, or nearly so. To him they brimmed with tears, quivered with laughter, shimmered with exaltation.

He looked about his studio with satisfaction; the walls were lined with his work. (He turned them face out only when the gallery models were gone.) A great garden of paintings. All his. A dozen large figures, painted in the most vivid colors he had ever used. Primary colors. Strong. Basic. Powerful. He could scarcely believe that he had done them all. Beside him, his wife, aristocratically slim, but softly modeled and warmly appreciative. The smells of wood and canvas, glue, paint and varnish leavening the air. Glorious. Simply glorious. He had never known such sensual pleasure.

"It's an orgy," he told Ariane. "A quiet one." Then he looked at her sharply. "I've been selfish, haven't I? Locking you away here while I work. How could I have been so blind?"

"Blind? Not you, Gino. Never you. I'm quite happy, really I am." She put her arms around him to reassure him.

"No, it's not fair. You've been very patient, but what kind of life is this? A woman like you is entitled to more. What would you like to do, my darling?"

"I don't want to interrupt your painting."

"You won't. The days will be mine, the evenings yours. What do you want to do tonight?"

She smiled. "The opera?"

"Why not? We Italians love opera." In truth, Gino had never seen an opera in his life.

It wasn't easy to find clothes to outfit him for a formal evening. Ultimately, a suitable wardrobe was assembled from among the staff. If Gino looked vaguely like a butler, that could not be helped.

"It's quite proper," Gino said, "that we dress a farmer in the clothes of a servant and send him off to the opera."

"Don't be silly," Ariane said. "You look marvelous."

On the long ride into Paris, Gino began to fidget. The stiff collar was chafing his neck. If he pulled at the front, it rubbed at the back. Pulling from the back was even worse; the points of the collar grazed his neck, which was still tender from a too-close shave.

The pants were of wool and they irritated his legs. The jacket hadn't been cut for Gino's powerful arms and shoulders. Besides, he was worrying about the people he would meet. How would he look to them, stuffed into this outfit? What would he say to Ariane's sophisticated friends?

Ariane's hand touched his. "Everything will be fine, Gino. You look very handsome and my friends will adore you."

They had just alighted from the Rolls, when the first test came.

"Darling!" a female voice cried. "Ariane, my love, where have you been?"

A slight dark woman embraced his wife. She looked over her shoulder and smiled at Gino. She meant to be coquettish, but Gino could almost see her makeup cracking under the strain. In mid-grin, she looked like a stucco wall struck by a hammer.

"I see you've gotten rid of your painter," she whispered loudly to Ariane.

Ariane stepped back. "This *is* my painter, Elaine. Allow me to introduce my husband, Signore Gianpaolo Bondone. Monsieur et Madame St. Quercy."

The thin dark haired lady couldn't hide her surprise. She looked from her husband (also thin and dark) to Ariane and Gino.

"Good heavens, what have I said? My dear Ariane—"

"—Never mind, darling. How could you possibly have recognized him without his paintbrush and easel?"

With an icy smile, she led Gino away. But Gino was laughing. The tension was broken. Ariane's friends could be as crude as farmers. After that, the introductions were easy. Gino, still thinking about the first encounter, greeted Ariane's friends with a faint smile, which everyone found quite aristocratic. He heard none of the names and missed most of the faces, but what did it matter? Most of the men looked just as ill at ease as he did.

The women were a different matter. They found him attractive. Large. Dark. Male. Definitely male. His accent, the rolling "r's," the hesitation between words, was charming. They could see why Ariane was entranced with him. And to think—he was an artist. How fascinating.

Ariane was not surprised and surely not displeased. The women would test him sooner or later. She had always known that. She believed she was prepared.

Gino was far more interested in the Garnier Opera House than in Ariane's friends, even the prettiest ones. He was dazzled by the soaring elegance of the main lobby, the polished brilliance of the split staircase, the delicate convoluted rococo decoration. No doubt it was ornate—redundant. But if it was too much, it was, at the same time, just enough. Enough to confuse his eyes, stagger his usually reliable sense of design and balance. How could such profusion, such an overabundance of form and color, be perfectly right? He shook his head. He was drunk with the grandeur of it.

The interior of the auditorium was less impressive than the great entrance hall and its grand staircase. Elegant? Of course. Ornate? No doubt. But the gold leaf was a shade too bright, the vines intertwined too thickly, the surface detail too intricate to please him.

The opera of the evening was Puccini's *Tosca*, and the program listed several Italian singers. An Italian opera with an Italian cast. He was delighted. He would probably understand more of what was going on than most of the audience.

As a matter of fact, he understood very little. The singers often sang sour notes and repeatedly swallowed the words. The sets looked drab and unconvincing, the lighting weak and inappropriate. As for the orchestra, even he could tell that the singers and the musicians were having difficulty making contact.

The acting was clumsy. The hero walked in a stiff-legged stagger while singing of his love. Tosca swung her train about as if it were dirty laundry. Scarpia, reaching for Tosca, lurched like a drunk aiming for a wine bottle. When the laundress stabbed the wino, he laughed aloud—she looked like she was plumping a pillow.

Gino's laugh, booming out as it did, drew attention to their box. He was embarrassed.

Ariane squeezed his hand. "You're absolutely right," she whispered. "They would all laugh, if they hadn't been trained not to."

The intermission led to another sequence of introductions. Gino passed through it all smiling, pleasant but remote.

"He's really quite handsome," one woman told Ariane, observing Gino's faint smile and speaking of him as though he weren't there. "Rather large, of course, but still quite handsome."

Ariane smiled.

"Tell me," the lady continued confidentially. "Italian royalty?"

Ariane smiled again.

"With that fine head and superior expression, I shouldn't be surprised if you've found yourself a prince."

"No doubt."

"Then he is of royal blood?"

"You're leaping to conclusions." Ariane moved away where the lady wouldn't see her smile.

Within ten minutes the story had spread through the Opera House: Ariane de Villon has married an Italian prince.

The subject of this speculation was beginning to itch in a most unregal way. The collar points and the wool were chafing him. He longed to return to the box where he could give himself a really good scratch. The discomfort arched his back, tightened his smile. He looked more remote than ever.

Yes, indeed, the ladies were saying. There can be no doubt about it. Ariane has married a prince. What fools they had been to believe that she had taken up with a common artist.

"Do you know the story of *Pygmalion?*" Ariane asked Gino.

He shook his head.

"I must tell it to you," she said. "We're recreating it—in reverse."

Gino shrugged.

The evening was a triumph—not unmixed perhaps—but a triumph nonetheless. Gino wore some scars. The red band around his neck, for example, where the stiff collar had rubbed his skin raw, and the blotches on his legs where the woolen pants had chafed them. As for his psyche, it was entirely intact. Inflated, perhaps, by the knowledge that he had passed inspection by Ariane's friends.

Ariane was unmarked physically, except for a sense of exhilaration. Gino had been marvelous. His boisterous laugh had soared out over the galleries on a few occasions. Some of the patrons had frowned, but others had picked up his amusement with an aristocratic giggle of their own. He was right about the opera, of course. His eye and ear were unerring. He could not abide any form of sham.

On the ride home Ariane said, "I'm afraid you didn't enjoy the opera."

"Oh, but I did. When the laundress leaped over the parapet, I thought I would die laughing."

"The laundress? She was not a laundress, and she was leaping to her death."

"Come now. You know she piled her laundry on the other side to break her fall."

They laughed most of the way home.

Thereafter, Gino made no objection when Ariane arranged evenings at the theater and the ballet. Most problems of physical discomfort disappeared when Ariane helped him purchase a formal ensemble, elegant, but cut to fit his massive shoulders and arms, and complete with a collar that looked stiff, but was miraculously soft and comfortable.

In the course of several weeks, Gino met most of Ariane's friends. Obviously those who met him that first night had spread the word, and he was greeted with deference and respect; the French, like all people, nourish a deep-seated awe of royalty. At the ballet, a tall, elegant young woman remarked demurely, "What an honor to meet you, Prince."

Gino smiled. It was obvious to him that she was using the word to be friendly. Touched, he bent to kiss the young lady's hand. It was a simple gesture, one he had seen performed in the cinema. And the response of the lady was the same as in the film: A flutter of her eyelids and a soft blush.

How easy it is, he thought, *to please these simple women.*

Dinners after the theater were a bore. Gino wanted to go home, make love to his wife, sleep well, rise early and paint. But he also wanted to please Ariane, so he didn't refuse. She discreetly supplied him with money so that he could play the host on occasion. He tipped poorly. Other men might give large sums—as much as twenty percent of the bill—to waiters, captains and maitres d'hotel, but Gino thought this was madness. He left only a few francs as a token of his appreciation.

Those of Ariane's friends who saw his penurious behavior were at first appalled and then impressed. Royalty, they thought. Royalty can do as it pleases.

The waiters were resentful. Then, they, too, learned who he

was—or at least who he was supposed to be. Soon they shared the respectful attitude of Gino's guests. One night, however, a waiter at Laperesse berated Gino publicly for his meager tip. The guests were aghast.

Gino only smiled. "You communists," he said, "will never be satisfied."

The man stepped backward. He was indeed a communist, and Gino's words stopped him completely. The guests applauded Gino for his fine comprehension of social and political affairs.

Fortunately, none of this interfered with Gino's painting. Inspirations continued to pile up faster than he could record them on canvas. When the weather grew warm late in the spring, Gino moved his easel out on the terrace. Working under an umbrella, he painted the various views time and again. He was not terribly interested in the formal gardens. They were tempting, but so contrived that he felt trapped in patterns he himself had not designed.

He much preferred the English-style park in the distance. The trees, tall and short, evergreen and deciduous, growing in random array, were a challenge to him. He wanted to preserve this element of caprice and surprise on canvas, but somehow bring order to it. He wanted to reveal the subtle rhythms, the intricate musical processions of nature. As with every artist, he selected what he wanted from what he saw.

But that was not enough. On impulse he painted a farmhouse into the scene, an Italian farmhouse with whitewashed walls and melon-toned tile roof, deep in his invented forest.

The canvas still seemed flat to him. He added a gently curving mountain beyond the trees. The purple Tuscan tones fortified his work and the arc of the peak harmonized the diverse elements of his composition.

Louis Le Temps found him on the terrace, adding a few, last, satisfying touches to the pale blue sky of his landscape. Gino did not see him at once, and Le Temps waited, noting the painter's ruddy complexion, his robust figure, the satisfied smile that curved his lips while he worked.

"Why would anyone who has grown so healthy in France want to paint a scene a thousand miles away?"

"Louis!" Gino cried, and the two men embraced. "You're a shrewd one, Louis. You see that I've turned Ariane's English park into the Tuscan countryside."

"Why not? As long as you realize your home is here."

Gino frowned momentarily. "My home is where I can paint," he said, but happiness at seeing the gallery owner dispelled this uneasy thought.

"I've brought you a check, Gino." Le Temps made quite a show of removing the check from his wallet and flourishing it before him.

Gino stared. "All this? All this for me?"

"Your paintings are selling splendidly, my boy. In fact, I've had to hide the last remaining canvases or I would have none of your works whatsoever."

"Come inside, Louis. Let me show you what I've done." Gino led Le Temps into the studio, where he began to turn the canvases so that their painted surfaces faced the room.

He had hardly begun this process when Le Temps interrupted him. "The girl, Gino—who is she?"

"A servant; Annette."

"How graceful. What a coquette."

"Even without a face?"

"Her sexuality shows in the pose. The arrangement of her body. The tilt of her head. Charming."

Gino laughed. "The girl cried when she saw it."

"She should have been flattered."

"I no longer show my models their portraits. That way they're not disappointed." He continued turning canvases.

"The old man—superb. A suspicious sort, eh? And again you did it without showing facial expression. It's a miracle."

Gino was pleased, but did not respond. To him it was no miracle. Just hard work. Rewarding, joyous, hard work. As he turned each painting, Le Temps responded with increased enthusiasm.

His "ooh's" and "aah's" became a kind of song. He rocked on his heels as he reviewed Gino's canvases. Finally, the entire group was visible.

For a moment, Le Temps was silent. The he rushed to Gino, leaped up and kissed him. "The paintings are wonderful. The colors are the most brilliant you've ever used. The line is as hard as a diamond. Clean and pure. Your work glows, my boy. It glows with genius."

Gino humbly lowered his eyes at these overwhelming words. "You're very kind, Louis, very generous."

"I'm telling you the truth. It's time for a show, Gino. This autumn. Keep painting like this and we'll set Paris on its ear."

When the little man finally left, lugging several canvases with him, Gino returned to the terrace.

He never said that he liked the landscape, Gino thought. *I wonder what's wrong with it.* He stood back and studied the painting. *I like it. Damn Le Temps if he doesn't.*

When Ariane found him out on the terrace, he was still angry over the fancied insult from Le Temps.

"Was Le Temps pleased?" she asked.

He shrugged.

"He seemed so cheerful when he left."

"He didn't like my landscape."

"He told you that?"

"No, he never said a word, and that's even worse."

"Oh, Gino, you're imagining things. I'm sure he loved it. He simply forgot to mention it."

"Louis always knows precisely what he's doing."

She took his arm. "My dear, you're even worse than the actor who is depressed because he hears one "boo" amidst the cheers of thousands. This time, it's not even a "boo," it's one man who failed to applaud."

"Yes, but the man is Le Temps."

"Nonsense, he's applauded everything you've ever done. Come now, stop pouting."

He tried to smile, but the vague pain remained.

Ariane grew animated. "I'm going to cheer you up. Instead of running into town to the theater, we'll have a party. Right here. A few friends, very casual. What do you think?"

"Why not?" But in fact the idea grated on him. A party here, in his refuge from the world? Ariane's elegant friends could be tolerated when one could leave them behind, but how could you leave your own home? Still, he wanted her to be happy. And she asked so little of him.

♦ ♦ ♦

The "few friends" turned out to be fifty. Their dress was "casual," but only when compared to what they wore to the opera. Some of the women's costumes had cost tens of thousands of francs.

Ariane had decorated the terrace in an oriental motif, with Japanese lanterns hung from posts and trees; others stood on legs in the grass. Elsewhere, strange fish-like creatures fluttered in the breeze. He had puzzled over this apparently centuries-old fascination of the wealthy with far-eastern decoration. For him the oriental didn't quite blend with the great western Renaissance structures, but it was fantasy after all.

Gino greeted the guests cordially. Most he had met in Paris on one occasion or another. He did not remember their names and made no attempt to do so. Then, when they had all drifted onto the terrace (exclaiming over the Japanese decor), he mixed himself a Campari and soda and prepared to spend the evening in the shadows observing the guests and thinking his own thoughts. He wandered about, humming to himself, while glasses, plates and laughter tinkled pleasantly about him.

A brief gust swung the lanterns and set them rocking musically. The ladies held their coiffures until the breeze had passed. He stood beside a group of men engaged in animated discussion.

"It's inevitable," one said, "that this regime will fall. For yesterday's vote, the government mustered the magnificent majority of one. Think of it. If Breulliere had spent three minutes longer in the toilet, Auriol would have fallen."

"And who would be next? Mollet? Mendès-France? Bonnet? What choices!"

"I don't give a damn who is in power. What matters to me is the franc. If this government collapses, the next is bound to devalue the currency."

"I doubt it. The workers, the bourgeoisie won't stand for it."

Gino smiled as he listened to this mysterious discussion. He understood not a word, but the anxiety of the group both impressed and amused him.

One of them noticed him. "Well, Monsieur, you seem to find our discussion amusing. Do you think your property won't suffer if there is another upheaval?"

"Property?"

His interrogator man thought he was being intentionally obtuse and he spoke with heavy sarcasm. "Yes, your property. Your assets. What you own."

"Fortunately, I own very little. A few acres in Italy, and then, of course, my paintings. I have little to lose." He smiled and walked away.

When he was gone, the man who had questioned him leaned forward and spoke in a harsh whisper to his friends. "Damned aristocracy. All their wealth is in real estate and art. What the hell do they care about inflation?" The others nodded.

Gino sensed he had upset those men, but didn't understand how. He shrugged his shoulders, walked to the far end of the terrace and leaned on the balustrade. It was a lovely night. A sibilant breeze moved softly through the garden, riffling decorations and foliage, and a full moon hung motionless in the clear, cloudless air. Could he paint this scene? He had never tried to paint a night scene. He loved the daylight too much.

A hand touched his arm lightly. He turned, smiling, thinking it was Ariane.

"Ah, you expected me." A pretty woman, one of his wife's

nameless friends, stood beside him.

Gino was flustered. "No, I thought it was—"

"—Eloise? That flirt. I'm surprised at you."

"Eloise?"

"Then it wasn't she. Well, who might it be?" She posed prettily, one finger to her lips, feigning thought.

"It wouldn't occur to you that it might be my wife."

The girl laughed. "You're so amusing. What a charming thing for you to say."

There seemed no sensible response, so Gino turned again to look at the moonscape. The girl leaned on the balustrade beside him.

"We met at the opera, you recall? But then I was introduced to you as Madame Rousseau. You may not have heard my given name. It's Diane."

"Of course."

"Then you do remember."

Gino straightened up as if to leave.

"Don't go," the woman said. "Tell me about yourself."

"There's little to tell. I'm a simple man."

She smiled slyly. "I wonder."

As he still seemed poised for departure she hurried on. "Tell me about your home."

"You wouldn't be impressed. A few acres in Tuscany."

Ah, she thought. *That's royalty for you. A vast estate, and he calls it 'a few acres.'*

"And your house?"

"A poor thing. Small. Wood. Stone. Stucco. It's crumbling."

Of course, she thought. *An ancient palace. Probably a hundred rooms. My God, how romantic.* "Who lives there?" she asked.

"My mother, except that now she lives in Florence. My sister, perhaps. And of course, I stay there when I'm in Italy."

The woman was wide-eyed, listening to him. *Just the three of them*, she thought, *in that vast rambling, ancient palace.*

"It sounds fascinating." she said.

"Do you think so? I always found it rather cramped."

Diane almost swooned. *A vast estate with a huge palace and he found it cramped.*

Gino was trying to puzzle out why his simple words had such an extraordinary effect on this girl. There was only one explanation. She must be mad, utterly mad. He would have to treat her gently.

Once again, he tried to slip away. She held his arm. "Tell me," she said, "what do you do with your time when you're here?"

He was amazed. Surely Ariane had told her friends he was an artist.

"I watched you at the opera," she went on. "You were quite bored. No, don't argue with me. I could tell. You had a very bored smile. Quite aristocratic, of course, but you couldn't hide your feelings from me. I'm too perceptive for that."

"I see."

"What do you do for amusement? Being buried in the country can hardly be more exciting than your home."

"But it is."

"You needn't say that to me. I understand." She wore a knowing smile. Gino wondered what she knew. She moved closer. He was a bit disconcerted.

"I paint," he blurted out.

"You paint?"

"Yes. Pictures."

"Oh?"

"You doubt me? I'll show you." Anything to get out of this strange conversation. He started to lead her back to the lighted part of the terrace. She held him back.

"Isn't there a shorter way?"

"Not unless you want to climb over the balustrade."

She laughed. "It sounds exciting."

He shrugged, climbed over the balustrade himself and then reached up for her. As he helped her over the stonework she managed to expose one nicely formed leg all the way to the hip. But then he was helping her over and down, and when she had reached the ground she clung to him.

She may be mad or stupid, he thought, *but she smells good*.

He gently pushed her away and turned towards the studio.

"Hold my hand," she whispered. "It's dark here."

Actually, the path was very clear in the moonlight, but he shrugged and took her hand. It was cool and smooth and not unpleasant to hold, although he thought she was gripping him more tightly than the circumstances demanded. They walked up the steps and onto the studio terrace. Gino pushed open the doors and led her inside.

She tried to swing him around toward her. "Don't turn on the lights," she whispered.

"Then how can you see the paintings?" He pulled his hand loose and groped along the wall until he found the wall switch. He sighed with relief as the lights flashed on. Diane stood in the middle of the room, pouting. Gino ignored her, while he performed the ritual of turning the canvases face out.

"Well, " he said, "what do you think?"

"You really brought me here to look at your paintings?" She looked at the long row of colorful canvases and then back at Gino. "Incredible!" she said.

"You like them." Gino's face flushed with pleasure.

She walked over to where he stood, admiring his own handiwork. "Yes," she said. "Magnificent." Her hand was tracing his muscular arm through the jacket while she spoke. Gino hardly noticed.

"I like everything about you." She moved in front of him and was running her hands up his chest, under the open jacket.

She was against him then, breasts pressing against his chest, head tipped up, lips parted, eyes slowly closing. Her body felt very good and it was impossible to ignore the first tingling response in his loins. Her face was pretty, particularly with her eyes closed, nostrils flaring and soft mouth open. He felt himself leaning forward, his arms beginning to encircle her body.

Gino forced his hands higher, until he held her shoulders, then stepped back. His voice was a little shaky. "You're lovely, Diane. Quite lovely. I would enjoy very much painting your portrait."

Her eyes fluttered open. Her mouth opened wider. She stared at him, but could not speak.

"Yes," he continued, "you must come here some time and pose for me. Ariane will help, of course. She's quite good at posing my models. It will be a pleasant day for the three of us."

Diane's mouth snapped shut. Her eyes narrowed. She slapped him once, sharply, across the cheek, said something in French that he could not follow, then turned on her heel and stalked away.

Sadly, he began to turn the canvases back to the wall.

Seventeen

Gino, the Countess & Chagall

Towards the end of July the days grew warmer and the umbrella didn't protect Gino from the sun bouncing up from the terrace. Even in shorts and bare-chested, he was very uncomfortable. Perspiration ran down into his eyes from his thick hair. His hands became clammy holding the paintbrush, and the view shimmered so much in the heat that he felt he was trying to capture a mirage.

In disgust, he moved inside. Until noon the high-ceilinged room was bearable, although his models grumbled about the heat. In desperation, he decided to paint still lifes. It was frustrating to have to paint inanimate objects when there were people and growing things so close at hand, but it was better than nothing.

As always, Gino tried to arrange the objects he painted in combinations that suggested life and action, trying to infuse them with the vitality and the rhythms of living things. He did not entirely succeed, but he was able to imbue his subjects with dignity and architectural strength. He could not paint a careless or random arrangement. The hand of man must show in his canvas, even if the man himself was absent.

By noon each day, however, it was too hot and uncomfortable to work, even without unhappy models. At first, the enforced idleness of the steaming afternoons disturbed him. He fidgeted constantly, even quarreled with Ariane.

"I understand, my dear," she said, "but if you look around the studio you'll soon see how prodigious your efforts have been. You're entitled to rest for a while."

No one had ever taught him the values of idleness. He didn't believe they existed. Ariane tried to distract him by using the cooler hours before sunset to teach him how to drive an automobile. Gino's coordination was excellent and he was a quick study. For a while he found driving entertaining, but it was no substitute for his art.

In August the weather grew even hotter. Heavy clouds hung in the sky, giving little rain, but steaming the already humid air. By nine in the morning it was very hot in the studio; the wall of windows, a blessing in other seasons, was a curse now.

Gino stomped about the chateau in helpless fury. There was almost nothing he could do, and Le Temps was expecting more canvases for the fall exhibition.

He thought of going to Fiesole. If he couldn't work, perhaps he should visit his mother and sister. Of course it would be hot there, too—hotter even than at Villon. He wouldn't take Ariane with him. If he did, they would have to stay in a hotel, which would be formal and uncomfortable. Maria and his mother had moved back to the farm. If he went alone, he could stay with them and dress as he pleased—no more silks and cashmeres. He would be a peasant again, if only for a few days. It would be a grand surprise. He would arrive without warning. How pleased they would be.

The butler brought him a letter. From Maria. His mother was dead. She had died in her sleep. Maria had buried her at San Miniato, close to his father.

"Don't come," Maria wrote. "There's no purpose now."

He couldn't even cry. It was too late to cry. Tears would only have betrayed self-pity. And he didn't deserve compassion.

Gino couldn't sleep. Night after night he walked the corridors of Villon, his mind unfocused, fragments of childhood memories tormenting him.

"You're too hard on yourself," Ariane said. "You didn't cause your mother's death, and besides, she died peacefully, not in pain."

Which was true, but didn't ease Gino's suffering.

"You must rest, Gino—if not for your sake, then for mine. We can go to my place in Antibes. It's hot but lovely this time of year, plenty of sun, but always a cool ocean breeze. You can paint if you feel like it and swim if you don't."

The thought appealed to him. Sun and sea and sandy beaches. It would be good to be away from Villon. Away from Paris. Perhaps he could forget his pain there. Perhaps.

♦ ♦ ♦

Antibes was beautiful: clear blue skies melting into an even deeper blue sea. Mountains tumbling head over heels straight to the sea, separated only by the narrow twisting highway and thin winding strips of white strand.

A breeze blew inland steadily, penetrating every room of Ariane's stuccoed, tile-roofed villa. The road below was often clogged with traffic, but somehow the sounds didn't carry to the villa—as if the breeze had skipped over the highway in order to avoid being polluted with such unpleasantness.

As Gino stood on the balcony of their room, looking out over the sea, he relaxed for the first time in weeks. Yes, it was a perfect place to paint. But first he would explore the coastline. There was too much beauty here for him to remain anchored to the villa.

The next morning, dressed in swim trunks and a loose, open shirt, he set out to inspect this fascinating place. Alone and barefoot, he descended the hillside, ran across the highway and stepped onto the wonderfully warm sand.

There was more beauty than he had expected. It was all physical, but not all of it was rocks and beach, sea and sky. The beaches were busy with hundreds of young people, many of them young women. Most seemed to be blonde, all were clean-limbed and firm-bodied, wearing the briefest of swimsuits as they frolicked in the surf, prowled the beaches or lay on the sand. Where had they come from and who had selected them—weeding out the fat, the ugly, and the old?

It was an exhilarating walk. He swiveled his head from side to side, lingering now and then to stare with frank appreciation at a particularly lissome creature.

He pulled off his shirt. A largely sedentary life had not yet softened his peasant-hard frame. He was an imposing figure as he strode along the beach, with his deep chest springing from a slim trunk, his abundant curly, brown hair spinning into his eyes.

When he returned to the villa, he was more cheerful than he had been in months. Ariane instinctively understood the source of his pleasure. "I think," she said, "that I'll join when you go back to the beach."

That afternoon they set up an umbrella in the sand. Gino looked at his wife with approval. She was not as young as some of the women on the beach, but her body was trim and supple. Even bereft of the adornments of her rank—exposed on this stark landscape of human nakedness—she was exquisite, although her bathing suit wasn't as revealing as those worn by some, nor was she as eager to spill out of it.

Ariane was also too wise to attempt to match the unflagging zest and energy of these youngsters. She remained under the umbrella while Gino patrolled the beach or ran into the surf. Why try to compete with leaping, bounding, sinuous sprites who slithered past Gino in the sand, or fell against him in the pounding sea?

He glowed with admiration for these young women, but his appreciation was so natural, so innocent, that she could not help smiling—even when he described to her the wondrous contours of a young woman lying in the sand, not five meters away.

"If I had my pad, I would sketch her. Have you ever seen such tapered legs, such a tiny waist? And her skin. She must apply tanning lotion an inch at a time to get it so even."

"Yes, she is lovely, Gino. I'm glad your interest is solely artistic."

He laughed and pinched her, then leaned across and kissed her thoroughly. "It's beautiful here, beautiful!" he cried. "I never want to leave."

Thereafter, he brought his drawing materials to the beach every day. He worked in fits and starts, repeatedly distracted by some sight or sound—usually involving a pretty woman. But Gino did not try to sketch her, only to watch her cavorting in sea or sand.

At night, when they dined in fine restaurants or gambled in the casinos, Ariane regained much of her advantage. Few women could match the elegance of her dress, or her regal beauty. Many of her surfside competitors were eliminated by the price of admission. Among those who survived were a number of young and lovely women who nodded in acknowledgment to Gino—and occasionally Ariane. Dressed in long gowns, slashed down from throat to navel and drawn tight against their beautifully packaged behinds, they emanated a disturbing aura of voluptuous sensuality wrapped in civilized trappings. It was clear that Gino was not unaware of this combination. Ariane could read pure enjoyment in his eyes as he stripped these women of their silken coverings.

It was pleasant not to work, not even to think. Gino had never realized such a thing might happen to him, let alone that he would enjoy it. The warm sun and the rippling breezes, the invigorating sea, all relaxed him. After a few days, the behavior of the beach girls took on the pattern of a ritual mating dance that he watched as in a dream. The real show was the sun and sky and sand, the pleasant feeling of sleepy contentment. He would no more have considered laying a finger on one of those girls than he would have tried to reach into the sky and shove the sun along on its way.

When Ariane suggested they return to Paris, Gino was reluctant. Here in Antibes, even Ariane's friends were bearable, their voices lost in the cycle of the waves, the cries of the gulls, even the laughter and chatter of others in the dining and game rooms. But at Villon each voice would be distinguishable from the others even if the words were incomprehensible. He would be asked questions he didn't understand on subjects about which he knew nothing by men who didn't interest him in the least. As for the women—not content to slink around him in a provocative but distant circle—they would back him into corners, their bodies exuding rich perfumes, rather than the smell of sun and sky. Their gems would ruffle the tweed of his jacket; their lips would pout inches before his face; their cold eyes would demand hot acknowledgment of their charm and beauty.

"A few days more," he pleaded. "Many of your friends are still here. Why should we go home yet? Paris must still be hot. And here—here everything is perfect."

"Even so, perhaps you need distraction." She loaded Gino and a picnic lunch into a robins-egg blue Peugeot convertible and drove rapidly but expertly east along the corniche, turned inland just before Nice and raced up the rocky pre-alpes.

"St. Paul," Ariane said, pointing to an ancient town lurking behind crumbling ramparts jutting out on a spur high above the road. In minutes had they passed through an arched gate in the walls and reached a small square, where Ariane pulled up on a sidewalk to keep the Peugeot out of the street. Opposite them was the church, a nondescript Gothic looking structure, which looked to be of considerable age.

"Twelfth or thirteenth century," Ariane said, "but partially rebuilt later. Not bad inside."

They walked between massive pillars and then to a chapel where Ariane pointed out a painting.

"Tintoretto?" Gino guessed. Ariane nodded.

There were other works by well-known painters, but since Gino showed little response, Ariane shrugged and led him back into the square. Across from it was another ancient building that was now in use as the town hall. The walked along a narrow, cobblestone street past some houses, a few with shops on the first floor, but from

Gino's point of view, distinguished only by their age.

"You're not easy," Ariane said.

Then they reached the south gate and mounted the bastion. From there the views were spectacular: the Alps to the north, Cap d'Antibes to the south, and on this very clear day, the Mediterranean coast and the vivid blue sea.

Gino smiled for the first time. "I knew there was a reason you had brought me here—aside from the exciting drive, that is."

She laughed, and after a few minutes drew him down to street level and back to the car.

The road seemed even narrower and the curves sharper, but Ariane with her hair flowing back and her keen profile revealed was charged with energy. She flashed Gino a brief smile that said, "Isn't this fun?," then fortunately turned back to look at the road as it bent sharply. Gino tried to appear nonchalant, but he had never realized Ariane would drive so swiftly and with such apparent pleasure. The roadside overflowed with mimosa, roses and a dozen other kinds of flowers, some carefully cultivated and trimmed, some that looked as though they had been carelessly spilled from houses and farms.

Another promontory and another town. The sign said "Vence," and Gino tried to remember where he had heard that name. But before he could remember, Ariane had pulled to a stop before a plain-looking building with a colored tile roof and an over-sized wrought iron cross. High in the wall were small windows that seemed to be glazed with colored glass.

"An odd church," he said.

"More of a chapel," Ariane responded. "But it's the inside that matters."

White, everything white—tiled walls, ceiling, floor. Except that it wasn't uniformly white. The sun was low in the sky and splashes of color, citron, green, and a bluish green, stippled the floor, and climbed the walls. A succession of images outlined in black scrolled across the white tiles, dappled with color from the stained-glass windows.

"Clever," Gino said.

"Clever?" Ariane said in surprise.

"Don't you think so?" he asked.

"Gino, Henri Matisse claims this chapel is his masterpiece."

"Ah, yes. Matisse. Of course, the squiggly figures are obviously his. Sort of religious, but without God."

"Don't you see Jesus? The Stations of the Cross?"

"Of course."

For a minute, Ariane was stunned into silence. Then, she said, "I thought you would be impressed."

"Well, it *is* amusing. The patterns changing as the sun moves. The figures outlined in black, filling with color, then emptying again. Nice trick. Stained glass images without all the effort."

"You're impossible."

"I'm sorry to disappoint you."

She shook her head. "Now I wonder if the rest of my surprise will mean anything to you."

Gino smiled. "Try me."

She led him out of the chapel and down the street, through the place du Peyra with its sparkling fountain and picture-frame archway, then down a side street and up a hill. A driveway lined with cypresses climbed to a two-story white house with green shutters and a tile roof. Opposite, the rocky carapace climbed sharply to crags hundreds of meters high. At the entrance there was a clump of eucalyptus, a terrace, and climbing vines. Ariane knocked on the door; a few minutes passed without any response, and she knocked again.

The door opened slowly and a thin, young woman with her dark hair in a pageboy, wearing a simple gray short-sleeved dress with a high neckline and a plain, tan apron tied at the waist, looked out cautiously. "Comtesse," she said, in a lilting voice, her strong, even features breaking into a warm smile; she quickly opening the door wide. "Welcome to *Les Collines*."

"Virginia. How nice to see you here."

A small, light-haired boy, perhaps five years old, peeked at them from behind Virginia, and she drew him around in front of her. "This is my son, David." Her accent seemed British to Gino.

"A pleasure to meet you, David," Ariane said. "You're quite a handsome little fellow."

David smiled briefly and looked up at his mother.

"Clever, too," Virginia said, her smile widening even further. "Perhaps even talented." She tousled the boy's hair; he stared at the guests, silent, but with alert, brown eyes.

Ariane was about to introduce Gino when a voice rang out.

"Ariane!"

A slender, stooped, sixtyish man with thin, flyaway hair pushed past Virginia and David. His faintly Asiatic features were dominated by laughing eyes and a generous smile.

"Marc!" Ariane cried, and Gino thought she might embrace the gentleman whom he had immediately recognized as Marc Chagall. Instead, Chagall bent over her hand in a courtly gesture and murmured, "*Une grande surprise.*" He wore a rumpled gray sweater, baggy brown trousers and frayed slippers, but the kiss was infinitely graceful. Then, lifting his head and smiling he looked at Gino. "And the fortunate husband."

"Fortunate or otherwise," Ariane said, "Signore Gianpaolo Bondone, Monsieur Marc Chagall."

Gino took Chagall's hand, small but sinewy for a man his size, and said, "An honor, sir." Gino also nodded toward Virginia, who had withdrawn into the shadows, her son still clinging to her, her arm encircling his slim shoulders.

Chagall's handshake was firm. "I already know this gentleman," he said to Ariane, "and his work. I've seen it at the Galerie Le Temps—first, on the night he set off *Le Carnage des Artistes*."

Gino felt embarrassed, but Chagall was laughing. "They deserved it, young man. I'm sorry I didn't do it myself."

Chagall ushered them into his home. "Virginia," he said, "Tea for my guests."

She nodded and turned away, pulling David by the hand. He looked back at Ariane and Gino, his head cocked at an angle, his eyes curious, a hint of a smile curving his lips.

"A beautiful child," Ariane said.

"Mmmm," said Chagall, leading them through his home. It was a cheerful place with polished wooden floors, the rooms sun-splashed through many windows, filled with charming, mismatched furniture. Over the fireplace in the living room was a large painting with lovers and the Eiffel Tower. In the dining room hung an even larger, rectangular canvas in which the central figures were a man driving a horse cart carrying a cow on it and a woman following it with a calf on her shoulders. The colors and technique was totally different from the Paris scene. Both paintings dazzled Gino.

Along the way, Gino saw a small bronze that he recognized as being by Renoir, and a terra cotta figure he couldn't identify, although he was fairly certain it wasn't by Chagall.

Chagall escorted them to a palm-shaded terrace that overlooked the pre-alpes and the esterel massif; from their hillside perch, a vast green and rock panorama opened to the coast, miles below. Chagall had just seated them around a table with an oval ceramic top of Chagallesque design when Virginia returned—without David—carrying a painted wooden tray which bore a silver teapot, a dish piled high with little cakes, several small plates, and tall glasses. She smiled, placed the tray on the table, and immediately left the terrace. Chagall hardly acknowledged her presence. He poured the tea into the glasses, Russian style, and offered them the cakes. His movements were lithe and quick, and he spoke voluble French with an accent tinged with rolling Russian emphasis.

"Gino was not impressed with the *Chapelle Rosaire*," Ariane said.

Chagall shrugged. "I love Henri and his work. He's very proud of the chapel, you know, and I often stop by, merely to sit and watch the light cross the floors and walls."

Gino blushed in embarrassment. "It's not that I don't like it—" he began.

"—But you don't think it's serious," Chagall interrupted.

"Well, I believe it is. There's a spiritual quality that transcends the simplicity of the glass and the drawing. I like that."

He spoke mildly and with a gentle smile so that Gino did not feel challenged.

"You must have problems with my work, too," Chagall continued, his tone encouraging.

"No," Gino said. "There's no doubt that it's serious, and far more spiritual to me than the chapel. Your colors are unique."

"So are yours," Chagall said. "Strong, solid, opaque. Very human, too. I enjoy what you're doing, distant as it is from my own ideas."

"I thank you for your kind words, *Maître,* especially since your colors are almost the opposite of mine—they seem translucent and yet they are brilliant, as if lighted from within."

"Good!" Chagall said. "Still, I can't quite reach the effect I'm searching for. The colors don't glow as I want them to—with sunlight."

"Stained glass," Gino said.

"Of course. What a miracle the great windows are—those at Chartres are my favorites. But, for the oldest windows, the techniques for both glass and coloring have been lost. Some day I must go to Venice, to Murano, and work with the glass, myself. Try to understand." He gestured as he spoke, his hands describing little circles that, to Gino, echoed the curves he had seen in Chagall's work.

"In painting," Chagall continued, "the material is the canvas and the paints. But in stained glass the material is light itself. The very light of God's creation. What do I bring to the material, to the Lord's earth, the Lord's fire, the leaf, the bark of the tree? One must be humble before the material, the material is natural, and everything that is natural is religious. My work is my prayer."

They sat together silently for several minutes. Chagall's words hung between them, a challenge and a testament.

"In a way," Gino ventured, "we're both trying to bring the past into the present. I with fresco, you with glass."

The older man smiled, but the smile was enigmatic. "We are in France," he said, "this blessed land where, in the past hundred years, the artist has been freed from the shackles of the past. Of course we must learn from our forebears, but the true lesson is one of freedom."

Gino thought he was being criticized, but Chagall sensed his reaction. "I don't find your work derivative," he said. "You are an original. Do not cease to be an original."

"Of course, I can't paint in the same style you do," Gino said. "Everything is so . . . fragile, so mystical. I may not understand it, but it moves me."

"I've never been interested in reality—physical reality. Internal reality, that's something else."

"I confess, I don't always understand your reality."

Chagall said: "We must struggle to understand each other."

"Help me, please," Gino said. A quick glance towards Ariane told him she was listening with pride. "I fear sometimes that I need to soften my line, to let the colors bleed into each other. I can't seem to get beyond my training in fresco."

Chagall reached across and placed a hand on Gino's knee. "Don't try to be someone else. Believe me, that road leads to disaster."

Gino smiled. "I tried to copy you only once—not even aware of what I was doing. Fortunately, I was very bad at it, and I was cured instantly."

They all laughed.

Chagall took them to his studio in the separate two-story structure on the same property, with its marvelous view, even better than from the terrace, of the Mediterranean and the walled city of Vence. Almost unconsciously, he turned on a record of a Mozart piano concerto. Chagall showed them work in progress and explained how he had blended some of his colors. "My secrets," he said, fingers to lips. "You must not tell anyone," but his eyes were laughing within the crinkles and the lines of his strong mouth were upturned.

Gino was pleased by Chagall's openness, but still troubled. "You show such freedom in your work. How can I break away from the fresco pattern of filling in one block of canvas at a time?"

"But I do the same thing," Chagall said. "I outline an area with charcoal, go over the design with a mixture of turpentine and a neutral colored paint, then build up the color within that area painstakingly, layer after layer. My technique is different from yours, but we both build in blocks."

Gino sighed audibly.

"You are too young to worry so much," Chagall said. "Time enough when you are my age, and uncertain what you will do next." And then he went back to demonstrating his brushwork, hands moving with incredible speed.

Finally, near sunset, they took leave.

"I'm going to Vallauris tomorrow to fire some pottery," Chagall said. "Would you like to meet me there, Gino?" Purposefully or not, he hadn't included Ariane in his invitation.

"Of course!" Gino said, thrilled at the prospect.

"I'll be at Madoura—do you know where that is?"

"I'll give Gino precise instructions," Ariane said.

"You're not coming?" Gino asked.

"Dust doesn't agree with me," she said.

And then Ariane did embrace Chagall and Gino shook his hand.

"Tomorrow, at eleven," Chagall said.

When they had walked down the hill and reached their car, Gino swept Ariane into his arms and kissed her thoroughly. "How kind you are to me," he said. "But during the whole afternoon, you said very little."

"I did not want to interrupt my two geniuses."

Gino laughed and kissed her again. "What is Madoura?" he asked.

"The finest studios for the production of ceramics in all of France—among the best in the world."

"I've never had an interest in pottery," Gino said. "But I want to spend as much time with Chagall as possible. It was very generous of him to ask me."

"I'm sure he invites very few people. Chagall can be remote, even brusque where his art is concerned."

"I thought he was brusque with his housekeeper."

"Housekeeper? Yes, in a sense. But Virginia is his mistress—and David is their son."

"I would never have guessed."

"Chagall, as I said, can be remote."

"But he was so warm and friendly to you—to me."

"Chagall is not easily understood, and those who think that either the man or his art are simple, even primitive, are mistaken."

"Why doesn't he marry her?"

"Because she is still married to another man."

♦ ♦ ♦

In the morning, Gino followed Ariane's directions and drove the convertible to the hill town of Vallauris, perhaps two kilometers from the Mediterranean, directly above the Pointe de la Croisette at Cannes. It was a clear day, and as he drove along the chemin des Collines, he caught brief, blindingly beautiful vistas of the sea. Vallauris was an ancient town, with rounded hills, roughly paved streets laid out on a grid, and stone and stucco houses that seemed hundreds of years old, yet were well kept. This was a prosperous place.

On the avenue George-Clemenceau and neighboring streets there were a number of pottery stores and workshops. The bracing smell of burning wood, probably oak, tinctured the air, and little puffs of smoke rose from chimneys, obviously kilns. He had no trouble finding the Madoura studio. Feeling a bit ostentatious in the convertible, he drove a distance away, parked, closed the top and walked back.

Inside there were racks and cases of various kinds of ceramic ware on sale, some of it by Picasso, little of it to his liking, and he quickly waved off the eager clerk and asked for Chagall. A jerked thumb sent him in the right direction, towards a crackle of activity, but he had already heard Chagall's now familiar voice. As he approached, he saw that Chagall was talking to a larger man, bald, ruddy complected, bare-chested and powerful looking. Gino stopped when he realized the man was Pablo Picasso.

Chagall and Picasso were both holding plates of their own design in front of themselves, and from the sound of their voices it appeared there was some risk they might crack them over each other's heads. Other artists and workmen were listening, entranced.

"It seems to me," Picasso was saying, glaring at Chagall, "that this studio is more crowded that it used to be. I find it increasingly difficult to find room to do my work without interference."

"But you work so quickly, so effortlessly," Chagall responded. "A few strokes and you're done. You need little room and little time to increase your already vast inventory. How I envy you."

"Yes, my dear friend," Picasso said, "I'm sure you do. You take a remarkably long time to complete your own rather limited production. It must be very frustrating to work so hard and have so little to show."

Chagall's answering laugh was forced and staccato. *"Bon mot,"* he said. "Trivial, but a *bon mot.*"

"Tell me," Picasso said in a very sarcastic tone, "how can it be that a passionate Russian like you never goes home?"

"After you, dear Picasso." Chagall rejoined. "I understand you're very popular there—not to mention in all the other communist countries."

Picasso's expression hardened. He raised his plate, and Chagall stepped back.

Picasso laughed a loud, grating laugh, delivered with a look that included everyone in the room. "I'm going to fire this piece," he said, "that's the only reason I'm here. You mustn't be so nervous, little man." He was perspiring, despite his bare chest and shoulders, perhaps from the heat of the kilns.

Chagall's eyes were wide and he was red in the face, but then he noticed Gino, and his expression changed. "Gino, come here. I want you to meet the most acclaimed artist in the world."

Gino walked over, smiling tentatively, as Chagall said, "*Maestro*, this is my friend and fellow artist, Gianpaolo Bondone."

Gino put out his hand, but Picasso lowered the plate and briefly touched Gino's fingers with it, almost rapping them. "Signore," he said, in a dismissive tone that was close to an insult, then walked away. He shoved his plate into a wooden cabinet, slammed and locked the door.

"I thought you were going to fire that lovely piece," Chagall said.

"The air is very bad in here today," he said, without turning his head, and soon he had left the studio.

Gino felt extremely ill at ease, but Chagall was now smiling warmly. "That's how he is, the Spaniard. Sometimes friendly, sometimes rude, but he can do whatever he wishes. Anything he does is immediately pronounced a work of the greatest genius."

Gino did not know how to respond.

"Here," Chagall said, "hold this plate, while I check the kiln."

Gino studied the plate, which bore the image of a white-skinned, naked woman with opulent breasts and long legs, reclining on a patch of cumulus cloud, surrounded by a cobalt sky, with a yellow moon arcing over her head and two brilliant red stars. Even in this medium, Chagall had managed to create his signature, brilliant colors. The final glaze would make them even more compelling.

"Good, the temperature is perfect," Chagall said, taking the plate from Gino and handing it to a very young man, really a boy. "Like the others, Armand—exactly like the others—not a minute longer!"

Armand smiled and nodded several times, took the plate and deftly—cautiously—placed it inside the blazing oven.

Chagall clapped Gino on the back. "No need for us to remain here. It will be many, many hours until the plate is properly fired, and Armand is actually better at this than I am." He led Gino out of the studio and along the street to a small cafe with iron tables and chairs and striped umbrellas on the sidewalk. Gino was trying not to show his disappointment; he had expected to spend time in the studio with Chagall, learning something about the art of pottery making.

The minute they seated themselves, a tall, gray-haired waiter with slick hair, a curling mustache and very bad teeth, wearing a weathered white smock approached them. "*Bonjour, Maitre*," he said, bowing slightly. He carried a tray with a ceramic teapot, glasses, plates, and a server with small cakes like the ones Virginia had brought to them the previous day. Obviously Chagall was a familiar patron and his tastes well known.

"*Parfait!*" said Chagall. The waiter retired quickly, and Chagall poured the brewed tea into both glasses. "These cakes are from the patisserie across the street; Virginia buys them for me fresh, almost every day."

Gino took a bite from a cake and smiled. It was too sweet for him, but he would not say so.

"Too rich," Chagall said. "Ah, well, it is one of my many indulgences." Without pausing, he spoke on an entirely different subject. "I suppose you thought I invited you here to see me work, but that's not the reason. I'm happy that we're alone. Don't be surprised. I love Ariane, but I wanted to speak to you, man to man." He smiled encouragingly.

Wary, Gino nodded once and sipped his tea.

"As an artist," Chagall went on, "there's little I can teach you. You're a very good painter, quite inspired, very professional. I admire your craftsmanship and your imagination. Naturally, you'll grow and your work will develop as time passes. That is, I hope so."

At that, Chagall took a bite from his cake, then another, finishing it. He sipped his tea, set it on the table, and looked up at the sky. "I've tried to duplicate this color many times," he said. "Once I got very close, but not quite, and the gap was such that even very close was a great disappointment."

He leaned forward and put a hand on Gino's hand. "For a true artist, disappointment is a blessing. It spurs you to greater effort."

Gino shook his head. "Not always, at least not for me. Sometimes dissatisfaction with my work has nearly paralyzed me."

Chagall smiled. "I thought so."

"How did—"

"—Why did you come to the Riviera?"

"Well—"

"—Picasso comes here to work. To play, now and then, but mostly to work. I go up to Paris regularly to work with my publisher on a set of lithographs, but Vence is not only my home, but also the place I do my best work. Did you know Matisse lives near here—in Cimiez, outside of Nice? The three of us use Madoura for our ceramics. You saw the Spaniard, but you might just as well have met Matisse. Of course, he doesn't get around so well any longer. Much of the time, he is restricted to his home—but he still works there. I love his colors. He loves mine. Actually, Picasso has said some nice things about my colors. But then, he says other things, too. He's not a nice man, the Spaniard. And he's not, in my opinion, as great an artist as he thinks—as most of the world thinks. He works, but not very hard, and he seldom spends more than a few hours on anything he does. Preparing a drawing is for him little more than writing a check. He signs it at the bottom and he can cash it in, almost at once."

Chagall stopped for breath, and to chew on another cake, and drink his tea.

"I came here," Gino said, into the silence, "because my work was not going well at home. Ariane suggested a change might be good for me, and so we came down here, to her villa. I thought I would sketch and paint a little, but as yet I haven't done very much."

Chagall seemed to be musing to himself. "From the chateau to the villa, and then back to the chateau. Lovely."

Gino bridled. "Do you think Ariane spoils me?"

"Of course! But that is as it should be. An artist must be a perfect egoist. His work must come first. Before anything else—before anyone else. I see you are shocked. I'm not sorry. That is how I am, how I must be. How *you* must be, if you are to achieve greatness. The ordinary things of life, the distractions get in my way. I love Virginia, I love my little boy, but if he cries, she must take him away. I can't stand it!"

"You think I should be like you."

"Do as you wish. I'm here as your friend—listen or not, I don't really care. But that's why I invited you. To tell you this. An artist must be free. To be free is to make choices. The choices are not always easy, but they must be made. You can lounge in your chateau, or loll on the beach. What luxurious alternatives you have! I am a jealous man, an envious man, but an artist. First of all, I am an artist.

"I love Ariane—not because she is rich and beautiful—I love her for her warmth and kindness and wit and generosity of spirit."

"Yes, and Picasso loves Francoise and I love Virginia. And we both need these women; in a way we are helpless without them, as you are now helpless without Ariane."

"Perhaps, but I don't think so."

"Choices, always choices."

Chagall lapsed into silence. He drank his tea and ate several cakes, but said nothing for a long time. Gino merely sat there, not eating, drinking or talking.

Chagall stood up suddenly. "I must go back to the studio." He smiled and offered his hand. "This was very interesting."

Gino shook his hand. "Thank you, *Maître*."

Chagall started off along the sidewalk. The waiter appeared and Gino paid the bill. When he looked up again, Chagall was waving to him as he entered the studio. By the time Gino raised his hand to wave back, Chagall was gone.

◆ ◆ ◆

A few nights later, Ariane gave what was intended to be an intimate soirée, and the villa was deluged with guests. It was simply appalling how many of them came—uninvited. And the noise they made. Gino tried very hard to be accommodating, to act the part of the host. He spoke politely to all who approached him and started a few conversations himself; which led nowhere. He thought he might fall asleep on his feet.

Then Gino had an exhilarating idea. He slipped from the house, eased the Peugeot convertible out of the garage and headed for Monte Carlo. It was only forty kilometers, but the corniche road was narrow and required his full attention. In Nice, traffic crawled. It took him two hours to reach his goal.

The opulent elegance of the casino brought a smile to his face. It was a quiet night; perhaps some entertainment in town had thinned the crowd. Nevertheless, the players were fascinating; richly dressed men and women, silently betting fortunes on the flip of a card or the spin of a wheel. Sometimes, at critical moments, their faces briefly assumed almost orgiastic expressions, betraying their true state of mind, then quickly resumed arrogant hauteur. He watched carefully for a while, learning the value of the various colored chips, beginning to understand the rules of the games.

Gino found a roulette table with no players. Perfect. He would discover for himself what this was all about. The chips he bought felt cold but substantial in his hands as he set them on the table. The money was his—the proceeds of Le Temps' latest, large, unexpected check. He could do with it what he wanted. Perhaps make a fortune. The thought dizzied him. He bet cautiously at first, losing steadily, but only small amounts. The croupier—slim, tuxedoed, pomaded, a man of indeterminate age—was bored. Except for Gino, he would have closed down the table. Gino began to win. Small sums. Then he was even. A feeling of confidence gripped him. He bet again. And won. Then bet again. And won. Then he doubled his bet. And won.

He was beginning to feel warm, excited. Yes, clearly, it could be done.

"Are you going to bet, Monsieur?" The flat, dull voice of the croupier annoyed him.

"Of course." In anger, he doubled his bet again. Once more he won. Then he felt cautious, pulling most of the chips from the table and placing only a small bet. He lost. *Ah, ha,* he thought. *My judgment was perfect. I knew I would lose.* He felt quite satisfied with himself. He placed a larger bet, and won.

My God, he thought, *I really could make a fortune. Then I would be free.*

Of what? he wondered. But he knew. Living on his wife's fortune had always disturbed him. It was not manly, not manly at all. He was beginning to earn good money from his painting, but not enough to be truly independent, whole, proud. Chagall's not so subtle warnings had only deepened his discomfort. If he could make enough money here tonight he need never feel that way again. He doubled his bet. Once more he won. The pile was growing before him. The vision of power was growing inside him. In one impetuous movement he shoved every chip he had onto the green cloth. The wheel spun, the ball raced against it, blurring, then hanging motionless, then clicking merrily along the little metal rails.

He lost. All of it. Everything. It couldn't be. But it was. He stared at the wheel, still spinning, with the metal ball still locked in the wrong slot.

"That is all, Monsieur," the croupier said. "This wheel is closed for the night."

When the croupier departed, Gino was still staring at the treacherous wheel.

Eighteen

Pietro's Progress

Pietro studied the porcelain figure. It was a young girl, delicately formed, carrying a parasol, with tiny spots of color in both cheeks and a rosebud mouth. The figure felt cool in his hand. He placed it back on the table and looked about the room, admiring the high ceiling, the huge glass and porcelain chandelier, the ornate waist-high mahogany dado framing the walls. Although dark, the room was large and generously appointed with well-crafted copies of Regency and Louis XVI furniture. The tables and shelves were filled with a strange miscellany of vases, porcelain figures and sculptured glass. On the walls hung large, dark-toned portraits, heavily varnished so that they reflected light from the chandelier and obscured the faces of the subjects. He had no idea who the subjects might be, nor did he care.

Laurent was right. The apartment was perfect. Too large; much too ornate. Perfect. He would have a good address in the Sixteenth Arrondissement. The neighborhood was fading, but elegant. He would need no furniture whatever. Nor silverware. Not even linens. Everything was here. Old, but good. The last occupant had left it all when she had departed this world in her eighty-seventh year. Yes, as usual, Laurent had been right.

"It's a bit dismal, don't you think?"

He turned to face Sonya, who was studying the chandelier with disapproval. Short, dark curls framed her skin, pale as the porcelain he had caressed moments earlier. Her heart-shaped face was as finely modeled as that of the tiny figure, and when she finally looked at him he knew her almond-shaped eyes would be a startling green, as clear and cold as emeralds. The rest of her was opulent. Much too fleshy for a fashion model. Yet that was her profession, from time to time.

"Well?" She was staring at him now, expecting him to agree with her.

"Not bad," he said. "Not bad."

The solicitor sat in a high-backed chair in the corner of the room. He had shown the apartment a dozen times and every prospect had been put off by the address, the furniture or the rent. Evidently this was about to be another wasted evening. He closed his eyes.

Pietro explored the other rooms once more. There was a study filled with cracked leather chairs and cracked bookbindings. The bedroom was nearly as large as the parlor and almost as loaded with furniture. The kitchen was vast, with a cast iron stove that arched almost to the ceiling, and it connected to a small room with windows overlooking the street, where he could breakfast.

"You're not thinking of taking it, are you?" Sonya was behind him, her arms enclosing his waist, her astonishing breasts pressing into his back.

"I might."

"But you mustn't, darling. It's so dark and dreary."

"I'm sure it's quite cheerful in the daylight."

"Yes, but I'll only *be* here at night."

He laughed. "Why don't you move in?"

"I couldn't. What would Laurent think?"

"He brought us together."

She shook her head.

"You still think he'll send for you." The thought amused him.

"One day the great editor may wish to reclaim you, and you don't want to be caught living with a mere correspondent."

She slid around before him. "Don't think that, *Mon chéri*. It's not true." She tried to kiss him.

He pushed her away, walked into the parlor and faced the solicitor. "I'll take it."

The man came awake suddenly, hearing the words and not believing them. "You'll take it?"

"Where is the lease?"

"Wait a minute," Sonya said, looking at Pietro in amazement. "How much is the rent?"

The solicitor closed his eyes again. He knew it was hopeless. For the rest of his life, he would spend two evenings a week showing this apartment. "One hundred fifty thousand a month," the solicitor said.

Sonya gasped. Pietro was stunned. What on earth was Laurent thinking about? He had expected to pay half that much.

"Are you mad?" Sonya asked the solicitor. "A hundred fifty thousand for this ancient wreck? You can't be serious."

The solicitor stared at her, but said nothing.

She turned to Pietro. "You see, it's ridiculous." She had a charming way of fuzzing her "r's." Now both the solicitor and Sonya were glaring at him.

He began to feel angry. "I want this apartment."

"Sixty thousand," Sonya said, "and not a franc more."

The solicitor smiled and shrugged his shoulders. "Impossible."

Sonya took Pietro's arm. "Let's get out of here."

"I might persuade my clients to take one hundred twenty thousand francs," the solicitor said.

"Your clients?" Sonya said scornfully. "Your clients are dead."

"There are heirs, you know."

"Why don't *they* take the apartment."

The solicitor only smiled at her. It wouldn't help to tell these people there was only one heir, an eighty-two-year-old bachelor, confined to a mental institution.

Sonya's cold eyes turned brighter. She had not expected the man to cut his price at all. "Sixty thousand," she said.

"The furniture alone is worth millions and the location is marvelous." He hadn't intended to haggle with them, but there was something about the woman. What was she? Swedish? Russian? Polish? And those breasts. She was leaning forward now and they were almost in his face. She must be wearing a brassiere, but he had the illusion he could see the nipples pushing through light silk. He removed his glasses and wiped them. "Perhaps one hundred ten thousand, but that is my last price."

Sonya leaned forward again. The solicitor regretted having replaced his glasses. He didn't see how he could gracefully remove them again.

"One hundred thousand," Sonya said. "And that's *our* last price."

The solicitor withdrew his chin. Sonya was only a step away from him. It seemed as if those damn nipples were in his eye sockets. Suddenly, he relaxed. "All right," he said. "One hundred thousand." At least he would be sparing showing this barn for a while.

Sonya straightened and smiled at Pietro, who had watched the negotiation in fascination. Now he suddenly realized that he was committed to pay one hundred thousand francs a month for the apartment. He frowned at Sonya. *You'll pay for this,* he thought. *Again and again.*

"Very well," Pietro said aloud. "Where's the lease?"

The solicitor snapped open his briefcase, filled in the rent and handed him the document. Pietro brought it to a table, and still standing, signed the lease without reading it. The solicitor took his copy, handed over the keys and, with a quick thank you, hurried from the apartment.

Sonya kissed Pietro triumphantly. "What would you do without me?"

"It's what I'm going to do with you." His fingers were already undoing the buttons of her blouse.

"What about dinner?"

"You'll have your dinner here." He was already dragging her toward the bedroom.

♦ ♦ ♦

After a few weeks, Sonya moved in with him. It was too restrictive an arrangement, but he was the one who had made the original, thoughtless, suggestion. When she took him up on it he could think of no way to refuse. However, in bed she was more than satisfactory. There was nothing she wouldn't do and she did it all with remarkable enthusiasm.

He wondered why Laurent had given her up. It had been a casual thing. The morning after Maria returned to Florence, Laurent had stopped him in the hall. "You don't look well, Scegli."

"Just tired."

"Not bored, are you?"

"Perhaps a bit."

"I have just the thing."

Laurent led him into his office and placed a phone call. "Sonya? It's Claude. I'm sorry, my dear, but I won't be able to take you to the opera tonight. No. Don't be angry. I have a pleasant surprise for you. I've given the tickets to a friend of mine, a very handsome young man—one of our finest correspondents. He'll pick you up at 7:30."

There was a pause. Laurent frowned slightly. "Don't be silly, my dear. You'll find him quite charming . . . Scegli—Pietro Scegli . . . No, Italian. Of course. Why not? I'll call you in a few days." He placed the phone down and smiled at Pietro. "I'm sure Sonya will cure your ennui."

"Who is she?"

"A model. Polish. Stunning. She works for Entrachat, although she keeps telling me she should be at Balmain or Dior."

Laurent reached into a desk drawer and handed Pietro two tickets. "Enjoy yourself."

"That's what you said to her."

"Yes, she was a bit angry. She wanted to know whether she was supposed to sleep with you."

"And you gave your permission. I suspect I'm doing you a favor."

"That's the trouble with you, Pietro. You always wonder why someone is doing something for you. You don't believe in simple human kindness."

As it turned out, the evening had been extremely pleasant. Sonya was indeed beautiful and she liked him at once. Bored at the opera, they left for an early dinner, then went to her apartment. It was clear he would have no trouble getting her into bed.

Of course, once he had Sonya, he needed an apartment. He called on Laurent for assistance, and as usual it was forthcoming.

Now he had an apartment and a mistress. A good job and an automobile. He was doing better than he had ever imagined. But now and then the image of Ariane and Gino would drift into his mind, and he would feel depressed.

When the chauffeured Rolls had disappeared around the curve of the rue Lepic, Pietro had considered the act final. At first, it seemed as if the fabric of his life had been ripped apart and in the tearing the threads had unraveled. He often struggled to escape this line of thought.

Pietro heard their names occasionally. Claude Laurent would mention an evening at Villon. At times he saw them at the theatre, Gino looking insufferably pompous in black tie, Ariane's hand resting lightly on his arm.

"Who is she?" Sonya had asked, noting his reaction.

"The Comtesse Ariane de Villon."

"Ah, a comtesse. And the handsome man?"

"Her husband."

"Oh, the comte."

Pietro laughed bitterly. "No, an Italian peasant. A painter."

"How romantic. Come, introduce me."

"No."

"Are you ashamed of me with your friends?"

"They're not my friends."

"Too bad. Someone like that comtesse could say a good word for me at Balmain."

◆ ◆ ◆

"You're not listening!"

Pietro snapped back to the present. Sonya was standing over him.

"What did you say?"

"I simply don't understand it. Not even Laurent could get me a job at Balmain."

"You keep repeating yourself, Sonya. What's wrong with Entrachat?"

"It's not first rate."

She was walking about the room, draped only in a towel, fluffing her short hair and drying her body. It was one of her annoying habits. The moment they finished making love she sprang from the bed and ran to the bathroom. She was a fanatic about it. Everything must be clean: her face, her body, her hair. When he heard her gargling, he couldn't help laughing.

She slipped off the towel, held it over her head and stared at herself in the tall mirror. Her breasts rose majestically, her stomach flattened. "I just don't understand it."

"You're not looking."

She came at him, throwing the towel at his head. He caught it, then her, and spun her deftly onto the bed. She struggled, but he held her.

"You don't like my body," she said.

"I love it," he said, nuzzling her breasts. "For love, it's perfect, but for a fashion model?" He shook his head. She slipped away and ran to the mirror.

"What's wrong with me?"

He stood behind her, his hands cupping her breasts. "These," he said. "Have you ever seen a bosom like this at Balmain? Your nipples are bigger than their breasts."

She wrenched away, struck him in the face and ran to the bathroom, locking the door behind her.

"You've already taken your bath," he called. But it was too late. He could hear the water running in the tub.

♦ ♦ ♦

"You look angry," Laurent said.

"Why not? You've saddled me with a big apartment and an expensive mistress. I can't afford either of them and you know it."

"Ah, Pietro. You came here half a communist and now you are almost totally bourgeois."

"Perhaps. But I can't afford to live on my salary."

"You want me to give you a raise, not because your work is good, but because you need it to live on. As a matter of fact, that's not bourgeois. At the very least, it's socialism."

"I'm not interested in a philosophical opinion. I must have the money."

"That's fascism."

Pietro suppressed the urge to strangle him. "Will you give it to me or not?"

Laurent nodded curtly. "Another hundred thousand a month," he said.

Pietro was momentarily speechless. It was exactly the amount of his new rent. How did he know? Sonya must have told him.

"No word of thanks?"

"I'm sorry. Thank you, thank you very much."

"I hope it will be enough. Your tastes are getting quite expensive. Soon you'll want a new automobile and a more fashionable apartment. Perhaps even a more fashionable mistress."

"The one I have will do nicely. Unless you want her back."

"She's not mine."

"I'm not so sure."

Pietro left Laurent's office as quickly as he could. He returned to his desk, totally confused. One hundred thousand a month. Much more of a raise than he had expected. Perhaps more than he was entitled to. No one else in Paris would pay him as much as he was now earning at *Paris-Presse*. No one. He slammed his fist on his desk. Others around him looked up, but Pietro didn't even notice.

It's a trap, he thought. *Laurent knows he has me now. The raise is more than I needed—he obviously expects me to spend it all and more.* He was beginning to see the conspiracy: Sonya; the apartment; the car; Laurent. *They won't do this to me*, he thought. *I won't let them.*

He would watch his step, be careful with his money. They expected him to spend every franc and then go into debt. But he wouldn't. He would put some of it away. The tension began to leave him.

A copy boy placed something on his desk. A clipping of his latest article. His work. He read it avidly, enjoying every word. It was satisfying. Something else on the page caught his eye. An ad:

GALERIE LOUIS LE TEMPS
VERNISSAGE
SEPT. 19
PIERRE PETIT

He crumbled the paper angrily, holding it clenched in his hand as he walked toward Laurent's office.

◆ ◆ ◆

Sonya was frowning, which made it difficult to apply her makeup properly. The creases repeatedly defeated her. She threw down her eyebrow pencil. "I don't see why we have to spend an entire evening at an art gallery."

"I'm covering the exhibition for *Paris-Presse*."

"You never cover art exhibits."

"I want to cover this one."

"But why?"

"Think about it this way, Sonya: There will be many important people at the showing. Perhaps one of them can help you at Balmain."

Le Temps' gallery was more brightly lighted than usual, the glow flaring out from the windows and illuminating the street. It was nearly 10:30 p.m. when Pietro and Sonya arrived, but the crowd was still thick and the sounds carried even farther than the glow.

"Do you see anyone you know?" Sonya was tugging at his sleeve and whispering fiercely in his ear.

"We've just arrived. Be patient. The tall man over there is Prince Beauveau-Craon, the pretender to the throne. Do you want to meet him?"

Sonya frowned. "That ugly man, a prince? Oh, no. I want a handsome one."

Pietro shrugged and helped her through the crowd.

"Who's that?" Sonya whispered.

"Another newspaperman."

Sonya's disgust was audible.

Pietro turned his attention to the canvases. They were immense, many of them several meters long. The figures were heroic, the themes biblical and historical. Huge angry prophets in long capes strode across barren plains, Roman soldiers locked arms with naked savages, a vengeful Christ brought down the heavens on cowering penitents. The colors were bold, the lines heavy. Each canvas had its vortex, and strokes of light and line burst from it. One canvas was mounted on the ceiling. The figures, almost life-size, seemed ready to leap down from the canvas.

"Marvelous, isn't it?" The voice belonged to Le Temps. The little man stood beside him, his eyes distended by heavy lenses, like two egg yolks floating in their own whites.

Pietro slid back his lips in a purposefully close-mouthed smile.

"Marvelous? Yes, it is indeed a marvel that you would hold this exhibition."

Le Temps misunderstood him. "I thought you would be impressed. Pierre has lost none of his old power. Remarkable in a man his age."

"I agree. From the looks of these, he must be over four hundred years old."

Le Temps stared at him. His fried-egg eyes were beginning to twitch and bubble.

Pietro went on: "The last time anyone tried something like this was on the ceiling of the Sistine Chapel."

"You're right, absolutely right. The power of Michelangelo here in the twentieth century. How clever of you to comprehend."

"How could I fail? There's nothing here that isn't derivative."

"You're not serious."

"You surprise me, Louis. Your gallery is famous for recognizing the painters of our time, the *avant-garde*. Yet you give us the last dying gasp of an outmoded and irrelevant academic technique. What on earth are you thinking of?"

Le Temps was angry. "This is not outmoded. It is the rebirth of great draftsmanship and heroic themes. It is as relevant to our time as to any other."

When Pietro laughed, Le Temps hurried on. "Look about you. Watch the others. They're overwhelmed by Petit's genius. Listen to what they say: 'Superb.' 'Inspired.' 'Masterful.' I've heard all that and more, tonight. But why am I trying to convince you? You're not a critic."

"Are we not all critics, Louis? Qualified or not. We'll see whether you still feel the same way tomorrow."

Le Temps was blinking at him, taken aback by his ominous tone.

"Tell the truth, Louis. This wasn't your idea. You would never have hung these works without some—shall we say, persuasion. It was Gino, wasn't it?"

"It's my idea—mine alone. And I'm proud of it. We've ignored

Petit too long. A genius in our midst. Aging, to be sure, but a genius. And now he's been discovered—rediscovered by Louis Le Temps." The gallery owner slapped his chest, nodded almost contemptuously to Pietro and strutted away.

We shall see, Pietro thought.

"Darling," Sonya said. "You didn't even introduce me."

"Le Temps doesn't know anyone at Balmain."

But Sonya wasn't listening. "Isn't that the woman you know? The comtesse?"

Pietro followed her glance across the room. Ariane. He had known she might be here, but for a brief moment he felt like running away. Then his courage hardened. He took Sonya by the arm and began to make his way through the crowd. "It's time, my dear, for you to meet the comtesse."

"He's coming this way," Gino said. "I don't want to talk to him."

"There's no gracious way to avoid him. And after all, once he was your friend."

Gino shuddered. "God save me from such friends."

"Gino," Pietro called cheerfully, waving his hand above the crowd. And then they were facing each other. Pietro held out his hand. "You look wonderful, my boy."

"You look well, too," Gino said, dropping Pietro's hand as quickly as he could.

"Ariane." Before she could move away, Pietro dropped a kiss on her cheek. "This is Sonya Metkoff. Sonya, the Comtesse de Villon and her husband, Signore Bondone."

"I'm honored," Sonya said, suddenly genteel and reserved.

There was a moment of silence—humming with smiles: Ariane's serene; Pietro's cold; Gino's nervous; Sonya's demure.

"How is your family?" Pietro asked.

"My mother is dead. Maria is well."

"I'm sorry," Pietro said.

"About my mother or Maria?"

Pietro didn't intend to quarrel with him. "I'm sorry to hear about your mother, Gino. She was always very kind to me."

"And my sister?"

"You said she was well," Pietro responded mildly.

"No thanks to you."

"Tell me," said Ariane, "what brings you here, tonight?"

"The magic of our old friend, Pierre Petit."

"I'm Polish," Sonya said. "I've lived here since the war."

The men stared at her, surprised by her irrelevant comment, but Ariane responded graciously. "Does your family live here, too?" she asked.

"No, they're all in Warsaw." She was encouraged by Ariane's smile. "I model at Entrachat. He's really a fine couturier. Not in a class with Balmain or Givenchy, but very good."

"Entrachat on the place Clichy?"

"Yes," Sonya said excitedly, "that's the one. Have you shopped there?"

"No, but now that I know you are there, I'll be sure to stop in."

"How kind of you, Comtesse." Sonya glowed with pleasure. "Pietro is covering the exhibition for *Paris-Presse*," she told them proudly.

Ariane turned her smile on Pietro. "I thought you no longer wrote anything but politics."

"Usually, but knowing Petit and Gino's interest in him, I thought, why not? I was surprised, of course, to hear that Louis had arranged this showing. He is truly a generous man, our Louis, but I never imagined that he would go this far."

"I don't understand," Ariane said. "How far has he gone?"

"Why, my dear Comtesse, he has given this elaborate exhibition, invited dozens of important people, all to show the feeble work of this feeble old man."

"You called him your friend," Ariane said.

"I feel kindly toward Petit personally, but it certainly is an affront to display his work in such imposing fashion—and before such an influential audience."

Gino was having trouble containing himself. "Would you like to meet your 'old friend,' Pierre?"

Pietro didn't hesitate. "Why not? Where is he?"

Gino led him through the gallery. When they were some distance from Le Temps, Gino pushed Pietro toward one of the paintings. "Look at this. The figures are more powerful than ever and the composition is harmonious yet dynamic. The faces are masterpieces. You can read the minds of these people."

"Do you really believe that, Gino?"

"I do. These canvases are heroic, noble. No man alive would dare attempt to paint such themes today—no man but Pierre Petit."

"You truly are moved by his work."

"Quite deeply. I knew that Pierre was a great artist, but these paintings have surprised even me."

Pietro stroked his chin. "If that's your true opinion, I will have to give it weight, Gino. I want to be absolutely certain that you aren't letting your emotions influence your judgment."

Gino crossed himself fervently. "I swear they haven't, Pietro."

"Ah," said Pietro, "here is the master."

Pierre Petit, flushed with excitement, was hailing Gino. He didn't even notice Pietro, as he slapped one hand on Gino's back. "It's incredible. They love my work. I haven't heard such praise in twenty years. All thanks to you."

"Pierre, you remember Pietro Scegli?"

The smile faded from Petit's face.

"He's covering the exhibition for *Paris-Presse*. Think of it, Pierre. Every major paper in France is represented here. What a glorious night." He threw one arm over Pierre's shoulder, the other over Pietro's, hugging them as though the three of them were one happy group.

But Petit still glared at Pietro.

"Don't forget the party, Pierre. A celebration at Villon. Don't stand here chatting with us. Back to your public."

Pierre Petit moved away, still staring at the two of them, angry and confused.

"Pietro," Gino said, "You and that juicy Polish pheasant of yours must come back to the country with us."

◆ ◆ ◆

In the morning Sonya was still ecstatic. She wanted to make love again, but Pietro was exhausted from her sexual acrobatics of the night before.

"You're wonderful," she said. "You promised I would meet high-ranking people, but I never believed you. Forgive me, my love."

He accepted her voluptuous embrace, then gently pushed her away. She rose from the bed and stripping off her negligee, spun in an arc. Nerve endings stirred in selected portions of Pietro's anatomy, but he merely shifted his position in bed.

"What a house!" she exulted. "A chateau, a palace! There must be a thousand rooms."

"Probably not more than two hundred."

"A thousand, I'm sure of it! And a thousand servants. Elegant food, splendid wines, brilliant company. A perfect evening, my love, and I have you to thank for it."

"Not now, later."

"Of course, your work. You must write the article."

"It's finished."

"Did you get up during the night?"

"After making love to you? To suggest such a thing is an insult."

"Then when?"

"Yesterday afternoon. I wrote my story and filed it long before we went to the gallery."

◆ ◆ ◆

"He came to our home, accepted our hospitality, then this." Gino was quaking with rage as he read the review in *Paris-Presse*. "Can you believe any man can be so vile?"

"I feel as you do, but what's the use? The newspaper is printed—the copies are in the streets."

"I'll kill him!" Gino roared.

The vehemence of his tone frightened Ariane. She hurried to her husband and took his trembling hands. "Gino, you must calm yourself. Kill a man over a newspaper article? That's ridiculous. I know you don't mean it."

"He toyed with me, letting me believe I was convincing him of the beauty of Pierre's work." He threw the newspaper to the floor, stared at it, picked it up and read it again. When he was finished, another roar escaped his lips. "The dog. The son of a dog." Ariane put her hands to her ears as the expletives rolled out.

♦   ♦   ♦

When Pietro arrived at *Paris-Presse* a note was lying on his desk, instructing him to go to Laurent's office at once. He was surprised to find that Laurent was not alone.

"Come in, Scegli. I want you to meet someone."

A tall, thin, totally bald man with a narrow mustache rose as he entered.

"This is Monsieur Henri Planchard. Monsieur Planchard, Pietro Scegli."

They shook hands.

"Monsieur Planchard is an admirer of yours, Pietro. He has been following your work for some time now. Your latest column on the Petit *vernissage* particularly intrigued him."

Planchard was nodding pleasantly while Pietro expressed his thanks.

Laurent read aloud: "M. Le Temps attempted a feat awe-inspiring at any time, but especially remarkable in this skeptical age: the resurrection of a long dead artist. Sad to relate, the skeleton reappeared, but its flesh was shriveled and rancid. The corpse could not speak, but it certainly stank. We regret to inform you, M. Le Temps, that Pierre Petit is dead, and his art—such as it was—died with him."

Laurent laughed aloud. M. Planchard covered his mustache with his fingers while he giggled.

Pietro permitted himself a small smile. "Unfortunately," he said, "it's all true."

"Of course," said Laurent. "Quite a column. Perhaps the most vitriolic art criticism this paper has printed in years. It has created quite a controversy, you know. No? Well, read the review of the same showing in *Le Monde*." Laurent handed him a clipping.

The review was extremely complimentary to Petit. Phrases like "remarkable rebirth," "penetrating vision," "fantastic inspiration," were scattered through it. Pietro handed it back without a word.

"And now, *France-Soir*," Laurent said.

The *France-Soir* review was also extravagantly complimentary.

"They're all like that, Pietro. They laud M. Petit to the skies. One of the great geniuses of our time, they say. All except you."

"I . . . am . . . surprised, of course," Pietro said. "I wrote what I thought. It never occurred to me—"

"—It is as if," Laurent said, "you had seen a different exhibition."

Pietro was silent, uncomfortable and embarrassed, especially with another person listening. Laurent studied him for a few moments before he spoke. "I don't understand why you look so unhappy. I'm delighted with the column—pleased you have a mind of your own and that you express it so well. A little controversy is good for us, you know? Surprising when it comes under art criticism, but welcome, nonetheless."

Pietro missed part of what Laurent was saying. "Forgive me. I didn't understand you."

Laurent laughed. "I was saying that M. Planchard is an adviser to the Minister of Culture. The minister is about to tour the country, making speeches in several cities. Planchard noticed your work. He thinks you may be able to assist the minister by providing material for his speeches. A few notes, a paragraph here and there."

"The minister is a very busy man," said Planchard. "He's always looking for gifted people who can assist him in his important work.

I showed him some of your work and he liked it. He authorized me to speak to Monsieur Laurent, who has graciously agreed to give us some of your time—that is, if you're willing."

"I'm flattered by your interest, of course, but I never fancied myself as the writer of political speeches."

Planchard waved his hand. "Not political speeches really—rather, talks on cultural subjects of interest to all Frenchmen. The minister writes his own speeches, naturally, but it's useful to have the basic research available. I hasten to add there will be no payment for this work, but if it would give you pleasure to contribute to the culture of France, that perhaps would be adequate compensation."

Pietro looked at Laurent.

"It's entirely up to you," Laurent said.

Pietro recalled the dinner at the Dutch embassy—Laurent's pleasure when a minister had suggested that he had a great future in politics.

"I should be honored."

"Good," Planchard said. "I'll be in touch with you in a few days. My thanks for your cooperation."

As soon as Planchard left the room, the smile left Laurent's face. "You're quite fortunate, Pietro," he said.

"I realize that. Thanks to you."

"You don't understand. This day began badly for you. When I read your review, I was puzzled. When I compared it to the other reviews, I was angry. Then Monsieur Planchard called. Your review had been read by the one man in Paris who apparently hates Pierre Petit more than you—the Minister of Culture. When Petit was painting his murals for the Chaillot, he and the minister quarreled often. The minister thoroughly enjoyed your effort to destroy him."

Pietro was silent, waiting. Then Laurent smiled. "I wouldn't recommend that you give way to your passions in the future."

"I promise it won't happen again."

Laurent appraised him coldly.

"Are you certain," Pietro asked, "that you don't object to my taking this assignment?"

"Not if you use discretion."

"What if it takes time away from my work here?"

"You must not permit that to happen."

"But what if it does?"

"Then you'll have to make a choice."

Pietro hesitated for a moment. "Between a non-paying job as a political hack and a splendid career as a newspaperman? That's hardly a choice."

"Not all political jobs are unpaid. You know, Pietro, you ought to become a French citizen. It could be quite useful."

"With my nationality and background, there's no possibility of my getting anywhere in French politics."

"Perhaps. Meanwhile, working for the minister you'll be exposed to the inner workings of our splendid Fourth Republic. You'll meet influential people. All this should be valuable—unless you intend to devote yourself exclusively to art criticism."

Nineteen

Civilization and its Discontents

"You'd better take me to your studio, Gino," Le Temps said.

"Perhaps some other time."

"Now."

"If I don't return in half an hour," Gino told his wife, "call the Sûreté."

Once in the studio, Gino performed his customary ritual of turning the paintings for Le Temps. "I love this serving girl, don't you, Louis? Her figure is so—"

"—I saw her last spring."

"And here is the gardener."

"I saw him last spring."

"The cook?"

"Last spring."

"Chauffeur?"

"Last spring, last spring! They're all from last spring. Before you went to Antibes, you promised to paint—the sea, the sky, the mountains. Where is your work?"

"I was very tired, Louis. I went away to rest."

"You painted nothing."

"Nothing."

"And since your return?"

Gino shook his head.

"We have a show scheduled for next month and we don't have enough works to hang. What have you been doing with your time? Is this elegant life weakening you? Have you lost all will to work?"

"I'll work, I promise you. I'll start today."

"You'd better, Gino. You have a great talent, but it means nothing if you don't paint."

The moment Le Temps left, Gino changed into his working clothes. It was good to be wearing these coarse garments, to see once again the weird, erratic patterns made by the paint on his smock. He stretched a canvas. The wood felt warm, alive. The muslin was coarse, thirsty, ready to swallow the paint from his brush. He scraped his palette clean and tested his brushes. They were beautiful. The texture was as soft as his cashmere coat, but the bristles sprang back from his fingers, alert, ready to do battle. He drew the south curtains, set his easel, lifted the canvas onto its perch. All was in readiness.

He picked up a pencil and his sketchpad, trying to focus his thoughts. The pad seemed unbelievably large. He drew a line across it—just a line—to cut the problem down to size. Then another line paralleling the first. And another. In moments he had covered half the page with meaningless arcs. He ripped off the paper and stared at the blank sheet below. What should he draw? He thought of the Riviera: mountains, sand, sea. He sketched a mountain. It looked like something a child would draw. He tried to sketch the sea with worse results.

The women. The lovely women on the beach. He began to sketch a female figure reclining on the sand. First the head, then the torso, then the limbs. He studied it and began to laugh. It looked like a soup can with the lid pried open—and pencils stuck in it. Another sheet crumbled to the floor.

It will come, he thought. *It always does*. But he had never had to search for it before.

He waited, his mind clear of thought. He held the pencil and the pad and stared out the windows, without seeing the trees bending in the breeze, the sun racing lower in the west.

"Gino?"

He didn't respond.

"Gino, you said if you didn't return in half an hour I should call the police. It's been over an hour, Gino."

He spun on his stool. "God damn it!" he yelled. "Can't you see I'm working?"

After a while he was contrite. He pulled off his smock, laid his tools aside and went to find his wife, not unhappy to close the door of the studio.

Ariane accepted his apology graciously. "I know you were upset by Pietro's article. Tonight we're supposed to go to the opera. Perhaps you don't feel like going."

The thought of the opera was less than inviting. But he didn't want to be left alone in the house with his empty sketchpad and the blank canvas. "Of course, my dear. I'll be happy to go."

◆ ◆ ◆

Gino realized that the ambience of his life was precisely what it had been before they left for the south, except that the social pace had accelerated, now that the "season" had begun. He was exposed not only to the opera, ballet and theatre, but to elaborate parties in Paris. They went to bed late and rose late, Gino even later than his wife. They breakfasted together, at times in restrained silence, as Gino tensed in preparation for the ordeal to come.

After breakfast, Gino withdrew to his studio. But the pencil would not move, or when it did, the pattern was erratic and uncontrolled. He studied his completed canvases, hoping they would give him some clue, but they told him nothing. He had been in their world before and had no wish to travel through it again. The blank-faced figures stared out at him without compassion, without understanding. The maid, the gardener and the chauffeur refused to help him.

He wandered through the gardens, hoping to find inspiration there. No doubt the flowers and the trees were beautiful, but they didn't inspire him. He wanted to paint a human being, not a plant; something that could move freely, not rooted to a single spot on the face of the earth. The flowers dipped their heads, the trees whispered, but they didn't deceive him. *You can't move yourselves*, he thought, *and therefore you don't move me*.

Saddened, Gino returned to the house. There were rooms he had never seen before, and he decided to explore them. He dawdled away the day, dangling keys on a huge chain, like a jailer, opening doors that hadn't been opened in years. Many of the rooms were empty—large and small cubes unmarked by a single sign of life. He closed the doors quickly and moved on.

Some rooms were filled with furniture, old but very fine, dusty yet elegant when his fingers pushed the grime away. Most of the furniture was covered with heavy cloths, ancient winding sheets wrapped about dead furnishings. Depressed, he moved on.

On the top floor he found a large room, dark and very somber. He would have retreated, but there was something mounted on the wall and he opened the shutters in order to see it better. It was an ancient rifle mounted over the stone mantle. Who had left it there and why? He reached up and lifted it from its mounting.

The cold metal chilled his left hand, the wooden stock warmed his right. As he held it a flicker of remembrance crossed his brain. His eyes began to swim. And then, before him on the wall, he saw the little girl on the street in Bari.

He replaced the rifle on the wall, glad to be rid of it, and hurried to his studio. The little girl's image refused to leave his brain. She stepped backward before him as he strode along the corridor. Pink velvet squared her bodice, a pink bow fluttered in her black hair. She wasn't gone. He hadn't lost her.

A shadow darkened her blue eyes. She held her doll in a loose grip, while the doll looked up at her, arms spread, expression appealing. The little girl stared at Gino without blinking. Her nostrils flared, but her expression remained the same. She wasn't accusing him, she was judging him. He looked down and saw the shadow of his army helmet outlined on her dress.

The clarity of this vision astounded him. He burst into his studio, picked up a pencil and began to sketch. But that didn't satisfy him; he wanted to work directly on canvas. Discarding his drawing pad he took up the charcoal and with a few strokes blocked out the entire canvas. He did not wait to fill in the details, but began to mix colors at once. Chagall had taught him some tricks with pigments, but even so he had difficulty reproducing the blue of the girl's doll, the pink of her bodice. He tried again and again, never quite satisfied. But the urge to paint was great. The colors he had prepared would have to do.

Gino worked feverishly through the afternoon. He was appalled by the approach of darkness and continued working by artificial light, a rarity for him. At seven, Ariane came to tell him to get dressed for the opera. Furious, he refused to leave. Amazed at his fervor, Ariane said with an icy smile that she would attend without him.

But then, just as quickly, he relented. He had regained the little girl. There was nothing to fear now.

The evening was torture. The performance on stage seemed terribly unreal compared to his little girl. The sets were garish, the voices harsh, the action stilted and forced. He closed his mind to it. At intermission, Ariane had to tap his arm to bring him back to consciousness. Refusing to join in the usual chatter, he excused himself and began pacing the gilded halls of Garnier's opera house, avoiding friends of Ariane with mumbled apologies. The mirrored halls with their ornate candelabras and glittering chandeliers were overpowering. Gino couldn't see his painting in the glare of all this metal and glass, so he closed his eyes and tried to visualize it. Someone tapped him on the shoulder and asked if he was ill. Gino brushed him aside.

It was worse in the auditorium. There were no blank walls, no empty spots to stare at, onstage or off. There were no breaks in the music, except for applause. He couldn't focus.

After the performance, he pleaded illness and dragged his wife away. She was concerned for him. "Perhaps you've been working too hard," Ariane said.

"I haven't been working hard enough."

In the morning, when he returned to his studio, he was struck again by the colors on his palette. They were pale and too pretty, not rich enough to convey his true feelings toward the child. But he worked on. He would strengthen his conception by other means.

Gino found it difficult to control himself. He wanted to pour paint on the canvas, to splash it like a house painter emptying dirty brush water.

And then each day, with the coming of darkness, Ariane's social schedule must be faced: parties, shows, salons, while all he wanted to do was to paint the little girl.

Ariane asked him time and again what was disturbing him. Friends inquired as to his health, but he couldn't explain. He thought of returning to Antibes, there to splash cold seawater on his face, split the waves and clear his brain. But that was ridiculous.

Gino struggled with the painting day after day, always unhappy with it, always hurrying on. He felt he was burying something with each strip of paint instead of revealing it, but he couldn't stop adding color.

Finally, the canvas was covered—every inch of it. He was finished. He invited Ariane to view his work.

She studied it for a long while. "I think it's very moving, Gino."

"It's terrible." He took up his palette knife and plunged it into the canvas between the little girl's eyes. Her expression was now lopsided, but her eyes didn't waver. He sat down on the floor and began to cry.

Bewildered, Ariane tried to console him. Once again she suggested he was working too hard; once more he screamed at her.

"Perhaps we should go away," Ariane suggested.

"I must repaint the little girl."

"I'm glad. I love the painting."

"Don't you understand? It's wrong. A terrible, blundering, stupid piece of work. This time I'll do it right."

"Of course."

Gino couldn't bring himself to destroy the mutilated canvas. He turned it to the wall so that the eyes of the child wouldn't stare at him. The vision of the little girl remained bright and clear and unchanged in his mind. Why was it so difficult to reproduce on canvas?

This time Gino worked more slowly, spending many hours blending colors. He worked on the blue first, carefully adding pigment until the tone was clear and strong—cool, yes, but not as recessive as before.

Next, the pink; it must be pale but velvety, the texture rising through the white until it was tactile. Those were his basic colors. All the others, save the black, were shades of blue and pink.

Gino was ready to paint. He attacked the canvas directly, disdaining the use of charcoal, laying the pigments on strongly, filling in the outlines that his eyes sketched on the canvas.

This time the vision and the painting matched. He stood at his easel for hours, feverishly applying colors, hoping to fill in the outlines before they faded. Then, exhausted, he stepped back to examine his work. There was still something wrong. Something missing. He catalogued his problems. The colors: perfect. The composition: precise. The shading: just as he had envisioned it.

As he stared, the canvas seemed to come through the paint. His work was only a surface, a thin, fragile surface. He looked away. If he stared too long it might shatter or dissolve.

I worked too fast. I covered the canvas completely, but not well. I must build up the colors with more care. Gradually, the canvas will be blotted out, the little girl will come to life.

Gino was relieved to have Ariane lead him away to an entertainment. A part of him hated separation from his vision, another part welcomed the escape.

The opening of the racecourse at Longchamps offered an especially pleasant diversion. Despite the fancy clothing he was forced to wear, notwithstanding the dandified men and the women mummified in their own cosmetics, there was a primitive aspect to the races that entranced him: Once each race began, the spectators' masks of indifference cracked, lines of anxiety etched their faces, hands trembled, brows furrowed. The differences were even more extreme than at the gaming tables in Monaco.

At the end—for one amazingly brief moment, the spectators displayed either frenzied pleasure or bitter anguish. Then it was over. He thought that long ago they would have learned to hide their feelings, but something about the sweating horses thundering along the turf unleashed them from convention, and for a brief moment they could suffer—if only for their money.

This excursion provided only brief respite from his agitation. The painting was always with him, taunting and provoking him. The little girl's eyes never wavered. Her challenge never disappeared. Gino would be doing his best to be civil to one of Ariane's friends, when suddenly he would recall the true color of the little girl's eyes, and without an apology he would leave his companions and hurry to his studio.

When he examined the portrait, he found that the color he had painted was not different from the one he had imagined. Once again he would feel defeated.

Despite her confusion, Ariane remained patient, unruffled by Gino's strange behavior toward her friends, oblivious to his occasional discourtesies. She explained to others that he was engaged in painting a major work, and that all his energy was concentrated on it.

In their own relations, she ignored similar indignities. He was often remote, retreating into a private world. She accepted his sporadic, sometimes ferocious lovemaking, believing that he still loved her, and that once he overcame his obsession all would be well.

Gino continued to work on the second painting of the little girl. He tried to alter the expression on her face, but he had already painted her eyes. Somehow those eyes would not permit him to make changes. Every line he painted was directed by this mystic gaze.

Very well, he thought, *this is how it must be. The little girl knows how her own face should look.* He was pleased that she permitted him to make some changes in her dress. He had drawn the bodice improperly before and in this version he corrected his error.

The shadows were more difficult. In the first painting, the shadow of his military helmet had obscured most of the front of her white dress. In this one, he applied a much lighter pigment, which darkened without covering the tones of the garment. That was better; only the blinding sun that day in Bari had made him think the dress couldn't be seen through his shadow. But now the shadow had changed subtly. It looked more like the elaborate helmet a knight would have worn in medieval times rather than the simpler headgear of a modern Italian soldier. Her head, even the bow in her hair had become part of the design—a flaring decoration, perhaps a feather. Somehow that seemed appropriate.

Gino dreamed about her at night, often awakening, feverish and agitated. Why should he dream of a little girl he didn't know, who meant nothing to him? But he knew that wasn't true. Something about her moved him. Her youth? Her innocence? Her indifference to war and violence?

Drifting off again, he saw the little girl fixed on canvas, rotating in space head over heels and receding from him. He awoke in a panic and lay trembling for the rest of the night. The painting wasn't right; he would start again.

In the days that followed, Gino moved through Ariane's social world like a sleepwalker. This was a charade he must play. If he donned his costume and performed satisfactorily on Ariane's stage for Ariane's friends, they would eventually go away and he would be permitted to paint in peace.

As the days passed and her husband remained in this alien state, Ariane grew more deeply disturbed. One night she left him sleeping and hurried to the studio. She turned the little girl—the first one—from the wall and compared her with the other two portraits Gino had painted. Despite the differences, it seemed to her that on every canvas the little girl was trying to express the same emotion. It was an unspoken cry—in darkness despite the bright colors. But Ariane could not interpret the meaning of the child's silent appeal.

When Gino began to paint the child for the fourth time, she sent for Le Temps. The sight of his old friend in the doorway of his studio pleased Gino mightily.

"Come in, come in! What brings you to Villon?"

"You, of course. How are you?"

For a moment Gino felt a twinge of despair. Then he brightened. "I'm fine. How are the sales of my works going?"

"Perhaps too well. As you know, we need more paintings for your show."

"I don't have any new canvases."

"No? On the telephone Ariane told me you've been painting feverishly for weeks."

"Feverishly, but unsuccessfully."

"You completed nothing?"

"A few paintings, but they're not very good."

"Let me be the judge."

Without a word, Gino arranged the four versions of the portrait of the little girl against the wall. Le Temps studied them in silence for close to half an hour. Gino had expected an explosion, but none came.

"Gino, these are totally fascinating—mysterious—brilliant."

Gino looked at him sharply. "Why do you say such horrible things?"

"What is horrible? Your paintings of the little girl are superb. Undoubtedly the most inspired you have ever done."

"Have you gone mad, Le Temps? They're pitiful. Why do you think I've done the same portrait four times? Four times, do you understand? And still I can't paint the little girl. She's destroying me."

"I see this theme has obsessed you, but there's nothing strange about that. Each canvas reveals something the others do not."

"You're blind, Louis." Gino picked up the painting he had slashed and held it only inches from the man's face. "Can't you see? They're all the same. Identical, identical, you hear me? And all wrong!" He threw the mutilated canvas to the floor.

"You don't mean that, Gino. You wouldn't have painted four canvases if you didn't have something important you were trying to convey, but each time in a different way. And you've succeeded brilliantly."

"For God's sake, stop saying that! I can't paint her; I shall never be able to paint her! I'll destroy them all!" As he moved to pick up a palette knife, Le Temps grabbed his arm.

"Don't do it, Gino! Please don't destroy these beautiful paintings. I don't know why you can't see it yourself, but I assure you that your work is wonderful. Trust me."

"You're lying!" Gino screamed, but the urge to mutilate his work suddenly left him. He slumped into a chair and did not speak another word.

♦ ♦ ♦

Weeks passed as Gino continued struggling with the fourth portrait of the little girl. He could have completed it, but was afraid to do so. What would he work on then? What if he was still dissatisfied with his painting? Must he go on and on painting this strange child?

Gino dabbed paint here and there—even scraped some off and reapplied it. He sat for hours studying the canvas, unwilling to acknowledge his fear that he had failed again, hoping that he would yet come upon some stroke—a single swipe of the brush—that would perfect his creation.

Ariane was having another of her parties. He worked until darkness on the portrait. At times, his brush carried only a drop of pigment. When he applied it, the color seemed to disappear. The thirsty canvas was drinking up his art, using up his talent. He began to hate the painting, but he wouldn't permit himself to hate the little girl.

Roger, his valet came to get him; it was time to dress. Reluctantly Gino left the studio, taking one final glance at his painting. Even after the door closed, the calm blue eyes followed him. What did she want, this child of violence?

Gino spent an hour in the bathtub, sloshing water about, slowly soaping and sponging himself. It was relaxing, but he couldn't remain there for the entire evening. Finally, he stepped from the tub, dried himself and began to shave.

Staring at his face in the mirror made him nervous. There were pouches under his eyes and dark lines. He began to wonder if he might be ill. Shaving in this distracted manner, Gino cut his lip. It bled for a long time.

Roger, a prissy little man whom Gino was barely able to tolerate, came in to remind him that the party was about to begin. He chased him from the room, then began brushing his hair over and over again. Usually he merely passed a comb through it once, but this night he couldn't make it lay right. Stray hairs stuck out at the sides. He took scissors from the shelf and began to trim them. This absorbed him for some time. There were an amazing number of strays. Why hadn't he noticed them before? Perhaps he would soon be bald. The thought was ridiculous. Dense curls were piled thickly on his head. But he considered the idea with complete seriousness. *Oh well,* he thought, *there are worse fates than being bald.* He completed his toilette and began to dress, stymied by difficulty with his bow tie.

Roger reappeared with word that guests were beginning to arrive. Once again, Gino chased him out.

His tie was perplexing. He had knotted it easily, even carelessly, many times before. Now the task confounded him; the ends wouldn't match. When he had delayed as long as possible, when the valet had made three appeals for his appearance, Gino finally abandoned his room.

On the way out he hesitated once more, trying to prepare himself for the onslaught of people and noise. The noise was the worst of it. Dozens of voices squeaking and cackling. The clank of plates and glasses. One vast discordant symphony that would irritate him and finally deaden his senses.

He opened the door. Silence. What could they be doing? He walked to the balustrade and looked over. There was no one in sight. Bewildered, he made his way cautiously down the staircase. Could they be in the garden? Even so he would have heard them. And there was always someone in the grand foyer. He crossed the marble floor, stopping every few steps to listen, but the only sounds he heard were the dying echoes of his own footsteps. Then he was opposite the great dining room. The doors stood open.

In the archway stood Ariane, Louis Le Temps and Pierre Petit. "Happy birthday!" they called in unison and hurried forward to embrace him.

He was amazed and delighted. "My birthday? Yes it is my birthday. I had forgotten."

"A surprise party," Ariane said, kissing his cheek. "Just the four of us."

He was deeply touched. "How kind you are," he told his wife. "How kind you all are." He stood with his arms around them, laughing and crying at the same time. "My friends," he said, "my true friends."

They gave him gifts—a small Chagall watercolor of a Paris scene from Pierre Petit, a Daumier etching from Le Temps, an elegant watch from Ariane.

"Come," Ariane said, "we have arranged a feast for you."

A fish course so cunningly prepared that Gino had no idea what he was eating. Pheasant from their own estate. Half a dozen side dishes. A splendid salad. And best of all the champagne. Gino drank it with every course, emptying his glass again and again.

"Be careful," Ariane said, "you know what champagne does to you."

"Not tonight, my love. I could drink your entire stock without noticing it." But he did notice. His head was light at first and then the top of it lifted off entirely. He was floating above the table. They were all floating in a wonderful buoyant sea. *Chagall would understand this*, he thought.

The lights went dim suddenly. Then he saw the flicker of candles. "A birthday cake!" he cried. "In all my life I've never had a birthday cake."

He watched the candles sparkle. The patterns they made entranced him.

"Blow them out," Pierre called, "all of them."

He drew in his breath, then slowly released it. The pattern of the flickering lights was hypnotizing. He saw visions in the shadows, strange and terrifying visions. He staggered to his feet.

"I must get out of here," Gino muttered. His voice sounded strangled, even to him. They were on their feet, moving gingerly toward him. He backed his chair and sprang up. "No, don't come at me, I'll be all right." He waved a hand to keep them away as he stumbled from the room.

He ended up in his studio, turning on all of the lights to hold back the shadows. "Don't flutter," he warned the lights, and wove his way to the center of the room. "And where are your paintings?" he asked himself. "There, over there." He sent himself to the far wall and arranged the paintings of the little girls.

"What did you do to this one?" He pointed to the slashed portrait. "She was nasty to me," he answered. "I had to punish her." He paused for only a moment. "Soon you'll have an entire room filled with little girls."

"No more," he answered in a different tone. "I'm finished with little girls."

The thought struck him as quite funny, so funny he had to sit down on the floor to keep from collapsing. He laughed and leered. "The four sisters," he said pointing to the portraits. "You bear a family resemblance, but each of you has a secret life. I know it. I can't prove it, but I know it. Please. I implore you, tell me your secret?"

There was a sound in the room. He looked around. Ariane was standing there, watching.

"There's a telephone phone call for you, Gino."

"Can't you see I'm talking to the sisters? Leave us alone."

"The call is from Italy. You must take it."

She helped him to his feet. The champagne was buzzing in his ears. Ariane had said something about a call from Italy.

His mother? No, he remembered she was dead. He crossed himself. Maria, It must be Maria.

The connection was bad, but he could understand the words spoken in Italian. How long had it been since anyone had spoken Italian to him? His own language. His own home. Suddenly he ached to be back in Fiesole.

"Gino? Is it you?"

A man's voice. "Gino? This is Brother Domenico in Florence. Do you hear me?"

"Dear friend, God bless you. How good it is to hear your voice."

There was a pause. "My news is not good, Gino. I thought of writing, but I couldn't tell you in a letter."

"What is it? Tell me."

"Your sister, Maria, God rest her soul, has passed on."

A great cry burst through Gino's lips, "It's not true! She's in Fiesole, I know it. She wrote last week. I have her letter."

"I'm sorry, Gino, but it is true. Maria is dead."

"You're lying to me! Why do you lie to me? My sister, my Maria." He was crying now, great sobs that wracked his chest. He could hardly hold the telephone. "I'm coming to Fiesole, brother. I'll prove you're wrong. My sister is alive!" He dropped the phone as if it were a loathsome creature and ran from the room.

Ariane hurried after him. "Where are you going?"

"To see my sister."

"But she's dead."

"She's not dead, she's alive. I'm going to see her."

They were in the great hall now, Ariane holding his arm and

crying, Gino trying to pull away. Pierre and Louis tried to help her, but Gino pushed between them, wrenched free and ran to the door.

"You can't drive, Gino." Ariane cried. "You're in no condition to drive."

She turned to the others. "Someone stop him. Please stop him."

But before anyone could take another step, he had jumped into a four-door Citroen standing outside the garage and raced down the driveway and onto the road.

Twenty

The High Road

Not until he reached the outskirts of Faenza did Gino allow himself to acknowledge he had taken the wrong turn. After Bologna, instead of heading directly south to Firenze, he had taken the route that paralleled the ancient Via Aemilia. *I've lost time*, he thought. *I'll have to make it up.*

At Forli, he turned southwest. The road began to rise again, spinning up through the Umbrian hills in tight loops that pinched and pierced the ancient rocks. Although the pavement was wider, three lanes instead of the previous narrow two, the driving was still demanding. For a while the twisting road held his attention, but he was continually diverted by soaring spires of stone, tumbling waterfalls, and cascades of greenery. With one hand he rolled down the window, drawing in the sharp mountain air, tinted purple and blue and faint pink in the impatient dawn.

He shivered, more from recollection than cold. He had traversed this road before—all one hundred kilometers between Forli and Fiesole, and these were the sights and smells he remembered.

He recalled the stone bridge built across a narrow gorge where the road had once, and again, washed out. He was ten years old the first time he saw it, traveling with his father. Together they had sat on the cold smooth stone, staring out across the pan-shaped valley that had been slapped down in the purple hills. Below their feet the rocks broke away, shattered smooth by their own age and weight and a million storms, disappearing in long yellow grass.

Still lower the trees began, twisting up out of the clutches of rock, and below the trees, the sloping gentle plain and the oddly sliced fields. The smells of grass and trees, stone, earth and sky had mingled in the air. Gino had breathed them in, held them for a second trapped in his youthful lungs and then, reluctantly, let them out.

There had been another sound and it had taken him some time to shake it out and identify it as rushing water.

Then he had seen it—a narrow silver line hardly an arm's length away, flashing through the yellow grass, tumbling down towards the valley. He had realized the water must came from somewhere—somewhere above. He asked his father where it came from and his father had aimed his hand back over his shoulder. Gino leaped to his feet and followed the stream until it passed under the bridge that carried the sandy road they had been following. He hurried across the road.

The ten-year-old boy followed the clear water up its shallow sloping bed, through grass and over pebbles, between boulders and around the stumps of trees. Then there were rocks and a small crevice from which the water issued in a slender stream. He climbed higher on the hillside, but the water did not reappear. He struggled even higher, stumbling, falling, rising again, searching for the water with a growing sense of panic. It was not to be found. Gino realized he would never find it.

He sat down in the grass still damp with dew and cried. Which had made him feel foolish, but better all the same. Then he had lifted his eyes and scanned the valley again from this higher point. It had seemed to him ever so much more splendid than before; particularly since he could not find the source of the water that helped to make it so. When he had climbed slowly down to rejoin his father he was very happy.

And he had been happy again when he traversed the road after his release from the military hospital, not knowing that his father had been killed, or why.

Gino suddenly realized he was driving on the left side of the road. He pulled the wheel violently, scorching the tires and jolting himself back into the present.

There it was: the bridge and the gorge. Not the same bridge, but a larger one, built to accommodate the broader road. Weariness dragged at him. The wheel seemed to have no feel. The car did not respond to his twitching hands.

He touched the brake, slowing the gray Citroen, and edged off the road at an observation platform built beside the bridge. Resting his head against the wheel, the cold plastic felt soothing and he drifted off into a hazy, half-sleep. But he was too overwrought to sleep.

When he got out of the car and closed the door, the metallic sound jarred his ears and echoed out across the valley. Unmindful of his exhaustion, Gino staggered across the road (remembering his youthful panic) and searched again for the water. He found the bed. It was dry. Not grown over, merely dry.

Maria. He had known she was dead even before Brother Domenico had told him, but he hadn't wanted to believe it—had rejected the idea. Now, after more than twenty-four hours of driving, he was too weary to resist the knowledge. Too weak even to cry. He turned to look at the valley. It was as green and beautiful and purple as he remembered it. Yet there was no water.

He sat down in the grass to puzzle it out. The water had dried up but the valley was green. Trying to follow the course of his own logic, he sank slowly back against the hillside, unable to resist the pull of his own gravity. Gino dozed for only a moment. When he was fully awake, his head began to ache again.

A sudden tremor passed over him. Ariane began to clamber up the steps of his mind jarring him with each tread. When she reached the top he slammed the door. Ariane remained outside, scratching at the flimsy portal, but he wouldn't let her in. *Not again, Ariane. Never again.* But why? Why not let her in?

He pulled himself to his feet, stumbled back to his car and began to drive again. The road continued to twist its way through the hills, but the novelty was gone. The road seemed cold, unending, repellent. The narrow strip of chrome on his car hood merged with the stuttering white line of the road.

Stay between the lines, he told himself. But he didn't respond to his own commands. The car continued to career along the highway, weaving from side to side, even though his earlier spinning, alcoholic dizziness had worn off long before he reached the Alps. But now his head was stretching and contracting from a different vertigo compounded of hunger and exhaustion. He should stop and rest, eat something. But he wouldn't. He had stopped once for the remembered mountain stream and it was dry.

Holding the Citroen on the road became an arduous challenge. He narrowed his eyes, fuzzing out all but the highway and the white line, watching it climb hills, dip out of sight, then come rushing up at him in tracer bursts from the black pavement. Occasionally, a vehicle whistled past him in the opposite direction, zooming into the hazy fringe of his vision like a hurtling comet, then disappearing behind him with a release of pressure that sometimes sent his car wobbling.

Gino shook his head to clear it. But it didn't clear, and the movement made him turn the wheel; he came close to the edge of the highway. In a thrust of anxiety his foot pressed harder on the accelerator. Trying to concentrate, he narrowed his eyes and held the wheel ever more tightly, which made him jerk the wheel instead of turning it.

Gino began to be afraid. Perspiration bubbled into his narrowed eyes, blurring the right one completely. He wouldn't, couldn't let go of the wheel to wipe it. He tried to blink it out, but it burned and he barely rocked the car back from the edge of the road with a violent twist at the last second.

He pressed even harder on the accelerator, thinking, *This is ridiculous. I'll kill myself without even reaching Fiesole.*

Gino came up behind an automobile on his side of the road. There were three lanes, ample room to pass, but Gino wanted to ride the stuttering line between the first and second lanes. He spread his thumbs so they reached the horn and pressed it, while he screeched out a hoarse animal bellow at the same time. The other car was going much more slowly than he was, and Gino almost touched its taillight before he braked enough to avoid a collision. He continued to press the horn ring harder and harder. Suddenly the metal gave way and the sound abruptly ceased. The driver in the car ahead pressed over to the very side of the mountain, while Gino sped past, still screaming at the top of his lungs.

Gino retracted his thumbs and stopped yelling. Only then did he notice the fractured horn ring swinging from the steering column. He began to laugh, great gulping laughs that arched his back and turned the wheel in his hands. The car slithered along the highway, rocking and dancing like a toy bounced at the end of a string by an angry child.

Ahead, the road curved out and back in a flat loop. Beyond it was the side road that led to Fiesole. He spun the car around the curve and onto the dirt road, traveling so fast over the uneven surface that the Citroen bounced and landed with a jarring crunch. Shaken, he slowed the car. After a few hundred yards it was obvious that deep ruts and protruding boulders would soon tear out the bottom. He stopped the car, turned off the engine, locked the doors and set out on foot.

For the moment, excitement overcame exhaustion. He was nearly home. Each rock and tree was familiar. The sun was warm overhead, the blue sky as startling blue as ever. For a moment he forgot his purpose, the terrible message which had brought him here. He stopped to breathe in the clean air, the smell of ancient pines and plane trees. Then he moved on. In a moment he had stumbled past the last large stand of forest and he could see the monastery.

The bell tower seemed to slant more sharply than ever, and the bell was gone. The bell and the rope. The tower was a huge empty eye socket staring blindly at the hill.

Perhaps Domenico wasn't there. He hadn't taken the time to ask the friar where he was calling from. There had never been a telephone in the monastery. He had probably telephoned from San Marco in Florence.

He hurried through the arch into the ruined courtyard and very nearly knocked Domenico to the ground. He grabbed the friar's shoulders to keep him from falling, and Domenico's hands gripped his arms. They stood that way for a moment, staring into each other's eyes, rocking with emotions of mingled pain and fondness.

The friar's voice whistled through the cracked pipes of his throat. "You came, Gino, I knew you would."

Gino nodded, unable to speak.

"But so soon. How is it possible? Did you take a train?"

"I drove all the way, brother."

"You're very tired. We must find you a place to rest."

"I don't want to rest, brother, I want to know."

"Of course, Gino. But first, come with me into my little home. The sun is hot and I can't remain outside."

Only then did the two men release their desperate grip on one another. Gino followed the fragile old man into the shadowy warren he had built into a corner of the crumbling cloister. A small fire was burning in a circle of stones, with a crusty white pot hung above it, supported by rusted iron.

"There's coffee, Gino. Will you take some?"

Gino nodded. The coffee, harsh and hot, scalded his throat, but it awakened him. He watched the monk fumbling among his pitiful belongings. Domenico didn't seem anxious to begin speaking.

"Sit down, brother. Sit down and tell me about Maria."

Domenico sighed and eased himself onto a stool before Gino. "There is little to tell, Gino. Your sister is gone. That's all."

"There's more, much more. You've hidden it from me for years, but you're going to tell me, *now*."

"The way you look, Gino, the way you feel at this moment, it would be better to discuss the matter tomorrow."

Gino was on his feet. "Now!" he said through clenched teeth.

The old man sighed. "Sit down, Gino. I'll tell you, but you must listen patiently. What you're going to hear will be very painful. You must remain calm and trust in God."

He hesitated for a moment. Gino waited, fighting down the rising feeling of panic that was twisting his stomach.

"When Maria returned from Paris she was very sad. She took her mother from the house of Rossini, and they moved back into your farmhouse. The fields were grown over, but with the money that came from you and the small garden they planted, they managed fairly well. I suggested they move into town, but Maria didn't want to. She said she was sick of cities and strangers. I thought it odd that such a lovely girl would isolate herself on that lonely farm. Then your mother died."

"I should have come home, then."

"Perhaps, but Maria didn't want you to see her."

"I loved Maria. Surely she loved me."

"You must let me tell you the story. Don't torture yourself about your mother. She went to sleep one night and didn't awaken the following morning. She was content, Gino. She no longer mourned your father and she was proud of your success."

"Even my wife urged me to bring her to Paris."

"She wouldn't have been happy there. Your mother died in her own home. That was where she wanted to die." The friar's voice had become a chant, soft and singsong. "She had asked to be buried near your father in the cemetery of San Miniato. Maria and I arranged it."

"Maria, brother, what then?"

"I couldn't persuade her to leave the land, even though your mother was gone. We often walked together in the woods and she told me many things. One day she gave me a note. 'I want you to read this, Prior,' she said, 'I want you to tell my brother.' I started to open the envelope. 'No,' she said. 'Wait until tomorrow at this time.'"

"When we parted, I walked back to the monastery, feeling uneasy about holding the note unread for so many hours. I decided to return to ask Maria to let me read it at once. By the time I reached the farm, the sun was already behind the hills to the west and it had grown chilly."

The friar drew in a deep breath and Gino trembled. "I knocked, but there was no answer. I pushed open the door and found Maria lying on her bed. It was too late to save her."

The prior gathered himself. "She killed herself, Gino. Her wrists were slashed. There was blood everywhere."

Gino leaped to his feet. "I don't believe it. Maria was so young. She had no reason to kill herself."

"I told you this would be painful. Please sit down and listen to me."

Gino couldn't sit down, but he listened.

"There is no question that she killed herself, my son. It was necessary to call in the authorities. I didn't want to do it, but it was necessary. First I cleaned her body and dressed her in a long sleeved garment, hoping the marks wouldn't show. But the cuts were found. The certificate was made out to show suicide as the cause of death, which meant she couldn't be buried in consecrated ground. In fact, I doubted that she wanted to be. I buried her myself just outside the walls of our cloister."

"She's here, brother? Maria is buried here?"

"Come," the friar said, "I'll show you her grave."

They stumbled across the rocky courtyard to a bend in the wall, just outside the bell tower, to a small fresh mound of earth with a tiny cross. Gino sank to his knees, then fell across the grave, sobbing.

"Please, my son," the monk said, trying ineffectually to raise him, "this isn't right." But Gino wouldn't move. Beneath his body lay the body of his sister. Through the chalky earth he could feel her embrace, her tears joining his. The monk gave up trying to move him.

"I suppose I shouldn't have placed the cross above her,"

Domenico said softly, "but she suffered so much, I can't believe that Christ will blame me." He sat on the ground nearby and waited.

After a while, Gino stopped sobbing. He lay still for several minutes, then slowly raised himself. His big body had made a deep indentation in the grave. He hastened to fill it. The coarse earth felt smooth to him, as smooth as Maria. When he was finished he bent to kiss the ground over her head, crossed himself and stood up.

It seemed to him that the monastery had tilted somehow. The edges had become fluid, the walls melting. He tried to focus, but the tilt was still there, slipping past normal to the other side when he tried to level it.

"Gino, you're exhausted and it's hot out here. Come with me, my son, back into the cloister."

He grasped Gino's arm and began to pull. Gino followed him, stumbling over the gently rocking ground. Another cup of coffee, held to his lips by Domenico, helped to relieve his vertigo.

"You said there was a letter. May I see it?"

The monk reached into his pocket and brought forth a small crumpled piece of paper. Gino took it silently and unfolded it. For a moment, his eyes would not focus, then he was able to decipher the small, tight script.

"Forgive me, Brother Domenico, for what I am doing. Plead with Gino to forgive me, too. Tell him that I have always loved him—more than anyone. Ask him, for my sake, to forgive Pietro. Maria."

"I don't understand."

The Prior spoke in a thin voice. "Maria killed herself because she was going to bear a child."

"Maria was going to have a child?" He wanted to say that was impossible because she wasn't married, but he realized at once how stupid that was. Then, in a sudden shattering instant, he understood: "Pietro—Pietro was the father."

"Yes, my son."

"That animal! I should have killed him that first night when I came home from the army. I had his throat in my hands. If I had tightened my grip a fraction of an inch Maria would be alive."

His anger was so great that he began to shake violently. His hands opened and closed as if he held Pietro's throat in them at that very instant.

"But why did she kill herself? It was her child, too. If she didn't want it, we could have found a home for it. Why did she kill herself?"

"Gino, I've known your family for a long time. Your father—"

"—Why did she kill herself?"

"I'll tell you everything, explain everything, if you'll let me."

Gino was so tired and so angry that he had to struggle to follow the words.

"Your father and mother were married for many years before you were born. For a long time they despaired of having children. At first your father was a good farmer. His fields were small, but he tended them carefully and with great pride. At night, he tried to teach himself to become an artist. It was in those days that he carved the crucifix I gave you.

"When children didn't come, Carlo grew despondent. He no longer farmed with enthusiasm. He began to drink. I talked to him often, trying to convince him that there was still time, that he would yet have a fine son. But he didn't believe me. He began to doubt his manhood. It was then that he began staying in Florence for days at a time, drinking heavily, consorting with loose women.

"Eventually he found a pretty young woman, the daughter of one of his friends. He thought he was in love with her and wanted to leave your mother. I talked him out of it, but he didn't stop seeing the woman. When she became pregnant her father threw her out of his home.

"Your father was both terribly worried and very happy. He had made the woman pregnant. He was . . . a man. When the child was born, a boy, they named him Pietro."

There was a scream—Gino heard it distinctly swelling up and pressing against his skull. He made no attempt to utter the sound, yet he could hear it, loud but distant, echoing, echoing and reverberating. He sat rigidly, eyes wide, corneas completely surrounded by white, hands clenched together pressing down into his lap, as if he wanted to hide them.

"Gino," the monk said softly, "Pietro is your brother and your sister's brother. Or half-brother, but brother nonetheless."

Gino held his lips so rigidly that his words were slurred. "He knew all the time."

"No, Gino, not at first. He didn't know he was your father's son until after Carlo was dead. I was the one who told him. He had been . . . making love to Maria long before that. But until I told him he didn't know. I think that's why he was so anxious to leave Florence. To get away from her."

"But then—in Paris," Gino said. "Again."

"Yes, again. Maria told me he tried to stay away from her. When he could bear it no longer, he told her. That was why she came home. But it was too late. Although she didn't know at the time, she was already bearing his child."

The scream in Gino's brain faded, replaced by a low humming. Perhaps the sound of his own blood, rushing in his ears. He stood up slowly, still holding his hands clenched together, now at arms' length, as if they were bound and dragging a chain. He rocked for a moment, unsure of his footing, then turned slowly and walked from the cloister.

The monk hurried after him. "Where are you going?"

There was no answer. Gino continued to stumble along, rigid, shaking from the tension in his tightened muscles.

"Where are you going, my son?"

"To kill him."

"No Gino, not your own brother. You won't do that."

"I'm going to kill him!" he repeated, breaking into a run.

"Remember what Maria said, Gino. She begged you to forgive him." The monk was running now, but couldn't keep up with Gino, whose long strides carried him swiftly over the rutted ground toward the parked automobile. Domenico staggered and fell to his knees, calling Gino's name again and again.

The wheels of the Citroen spun in the soft earth. Gino rocked the car forward then raced it back in reverse, dug out of the holes and bounced erratically toward the highway. He did not watch for traffic as he roared onto the road. The powerful car shot forward, its tires protesting.

I must concentrate, he thought. *There's no point in killing myself. Not now.*

The road held no magic for him this time. The familiar curves, the arching trees were only landmarks, sufficient to tell him where he was. He sighted on the stuttering white line as his foot pressed down on the accelerator.

Must make as much time as possible before dark. I'll still be in the mountains tonight, but by morning I'll have straight flat roads to Paris.

He hated thinking. It was over. All over. All except the final act, and that would be his.

The sun reflected off the hood and into the windshield forcing him to squint. He began to perspire. *Forgot to open the window.* Keeping his eyes on the road, he rolled it down. A gust of air splashed his face but barely refreshed him.

Tired. But if I stop now, I'll never do it.

The black, bitter face of Pietro grinned at him, just above the hood. *Laugh now, you devil. Laugh while you still can.*

The road was rising again, twisting abruptly again and again. He clutched the wheel more tightly. Pietro's face was gone. Only the flashing white line, the gray rock, the green trees whirling past.

I'm standing still. Only the world is moving. He pressed further down on the accelerator, jolting himself out of this illusion of arrested motion.

From time to time he glanced at the odometer, checking the kilometers as he traversed them. Ten, twenty, fifty. *Making good time. Not much traffic.*

The breeze ceased to cool him. Hot air drove dust into his face, sent his hair spinning into his eyes. His eyeballs ached from the dust, the salty perspiration, the hours of staring at the road.

There was a grinding sound in the engine.

Am I hearing things or is it low on oil?

No answer came from the machine.

There was a shadow on the road. It remained there and it puzzled him. Suddenly he realized it was the shadow of his own car racing first ahead of him, then behind him as the road twisted through the mountains. The sun was to his left now. He glanced toward it, meaning to look away, but he stared for a second too long. When he looked back, little flashes of blue and red sparkled and danced in his vision, confusing but entrancing him. At the next curve he had to wrench the wheel to stay on the highway.

He was perspiring freely. The moisture was spreading under his arms, dampening his palms, making the wheel sticky to his touch. Sweat splashed into his eyes, blurring them. He blinked and then—against his will—saw the face of Maria. She was pleading with him, begging him to turn back. Great tears fell from her eyes, dropping into his own. He screamed, wiping his hand across his face. The vision disappeared. Only the road now. The road and the car.

The white line spun up the mountain, twisting, turning, disappearing and reappearing. Far ahead, it was a ribbon. A twisted ribbon. The ribbon in the little girl's hair. *No,* he thought. *Not you.* But she was there, pink and blue, staring at him.

It's the sun, he thought. *I looked too long at the sun.* He jerked the wheel to one side, then the other, but the little girl remained with him, staring coolly over the hood, beckoning him on.

Every bone ached. His hands were clamped to the wheel, unable to turn smoothly any longer. He wanted to ease up on the accelerator, but his foot was locked there, a lead weight.

A vision of Pietro grinning evilly flickered by. Then Maria pleading. Then the little girl. Then the little girl with the face of Maria.

"That's it!" he cried. "It was always you, Maria!" He drove without knowing he held the wheel. Ahead was the little girl with the face of Maria. He had to reach her. "Wait for me! I'm coming for you!"

But the little girl was retreating from him, sliding back across the road, the face of Maria was fading.

"Don't leave me!"

He took his hands from the wheel and reached for her. The Citroen unhooked itself from the white cable of the highway and shot forward, directly at the vanishing figure.

Twenty-One

Separation

White; everything white. Flat white above and billowing white below. Yet it didn't smell white. It smelled yellow, perhaps green, but not white. Then the flat white above retreated and revealed an eye. A yellow eye without a cornea. Which of course was a light.

He was in a hospital. That was clear now. But where? And when? He recalled the little girl with the shadow on her breast. That was another time, wasn't it? The time the bullet hit him in Bari? Besides, that hospital and the ones that followed were never white. Beige and brown and gray and sometimes yellow (with touches of carmine), but never white. And this was white. Even the smell was different. The sheets never billowed in Bari; they wrinkled and bent and even cut you. Their touch was abrasive, scoring the skin.

It was difficult to think. He rested for a moment, staring back placidly at the yellow eye—which on close examination proved to have a cornea; a tiny black metal one. Gino turned away. The movement was painful, but the eye was so accusing, so blankly judgmental, he couldn't bear to look at it.

While pain raced up and down his arm and side he focused on a chair. It was aluminum and plastic and very new and clean. The curving metal back reminded him of a steering wheel. He realized his hands were clutching something . . . nothing. When he relaxed them, the pain retreated a bit. Squeeze and attack. Release and retreat. It was worth something to be able to make the pain ebb and flow.

Of course he was trying to distract himself. The chair, which reminded him of the steering wheel, had brought it all back. The mountain road from Fiesole, the winding hyphenated road and then the soaring departure. The descent. The grayness, the blackness, and now the whiteness.

How had he managed to survive? He could not imagine. Roaring off the road at over a hundred sixty kilometers per hour. It was unthinkable. Yet here he was. Safe.

Gino began to cry, tears of mingled gratitude and disappointment. Perhaps he was crippled. It hurt to move, but he could wiggle his toes and flex his knees, and then he was able to bring his hands and arms up out of the covers and examine them. Shaking; bone thin. Blood vessels seamed his hands like the spines of dead leaves. Dead white. No, live white. An important difference. The tears came again, wandering down his cheeks, trickling into the corners of his mouth. He felt them in the cracks of his lips; even swallowed.

And thought of wine. And his painting. He raised his hands to look at them again. Too weak to hold a brush; too unstable to follow a line. But even as he watched they seemed steadier. He wanted them to tremble again. They did, but not as rapidly as before. There was no hope. These stupid peasant hands would paint again. Of course.

The whiteness enclosed him again, billowing close, until only the eye of the light glowed in the center of his consciousness. Then it went out.

"You don't need artificial light, Signore Bondone. There's bright sunlight. You see?"

He didn't, but he heard the woman's voice as she walked to the window. She was pointing, demonstrating to him the brightness of the day, as people insist on pointing out what is important to them and, therefore, what they think should be important to you.

When Gino didn't respond, the woman, apparently a nurse, came to his bed. She bent over so that he could not fail to see her. White wimple clamping white face clamping white lips. No teeth visible.

"Well." It was a statement, not a question.

In view of that, Gino felt no need to respond. But she was locked together so tightly, he couldn't keep from smiling.

"I thought so."

The nurse withdrew and from a farther point in the room, her flat little voice skipped across his sheets. "Worrying your wife—about time you showed some life. I'll get doctor." The door hissed shut.

The doctor was shockingly fat and unkempt, a perfect foil for the antiseptic nurse. Gino wanted to take the doctor and wipe him off on her. This thought distracted him while the doctor's pudgy hands worked him over.

"I'm Doctor Antonelli," he said. "How are you?"

The sound of his own voice surprised Gino. Unused for so long, it came out in deep periods which evidently impressed the doctor and frightened the nurse.

"Except for my side and my right arm I feel fine, I think."

"Yes, you feel fine, you think. We scraped you off that mountain and brought the pieces here and sewed you together like Punchinello and you feel fine you think."

A grunt escaped the doctor. Gino suspected it was the same kind of sigh a sculptor might dispense after casting a particularly difficult, but wholly successful bronze.

The doctor slapped him once or twice more and then permitted himself a smile, really more of a leer. "I'm sure you want to see your wife. I'll call her hotel and tell her she may come."

"Where am I?"

"*Ospedale Generale*—Bologna."

Another thought scratched Gino's skull.

"How long have I been here?"

Now the doctor's face cracked open in a cavernous grin. This was what he had been waiting for. He stepped closer to the bed and leaned right over Gino. The words came dripping out from somewhere deep in his tonsils. "Three months."

◆ ◆ ◆

He lay on the hospital bed trying to fit it all together. Three months. The doctor had answered the question with such relish, confident he would astound Gino. He knew that he had been very stupid. But very lucky. He wriggled his legs and his fingers again. It was reassuring. As far as he could tell his mind was clear.

He recalled his conversation with Domenico. Maria. How tortured she must have been. Thank God his mother hadn't lived to see it.

Pietro. He tried to conjure up a vision of that hated face, but it wouldn't come. Nor did the anger. *I'm still too weak*, he thought. *When I'm better, the hate will return.*

The door opened and Ariane came in, smiling, wearing a simple gray suit, her hair knotted tightly in a bun. He tried to rise, but he felt dizzy. "Ariane," he said and stretched out one trembling hand.

She sat down on the bed, eyes wide, took his hand and kissed it. To his relief she seemed unchanged. A bit thinner perhaps, but otherwise unchanged.

"You look fine," he said.

She laughed lightly. "I'm not the one who has been ill."

"I can wriggle my toes and my fingers. My head is as clear as—well, as it ever was."

"Good. Perhaps we can take you home soon." For the first time, he realized that lines of worry circled her eyes.

"Has it been very difficult for you?"

"Not any longer."

"Did I say anything when I was in a coma?"

Her face clouded. "Not much."

"What did I say?"

"You spoke of your sister—and Pietro. You kept mentioning another name: Domenico. I remembered that he was a monk, your friend, and eventually I tracked him down, and talked to him. Of course, he didn't know about your accident. We have been in touch ever since, and last week I brought him here. He's been a great comfort to me throughout your crisis."

"Domenico here? Can I see him?"

"He's waiting outside."

The little monk came in shyly, shambled to the bed and took Gino's hand in his own bony fingers. He could not speak.

"I'm fine, brother. Perfect. Believe me."

"When you left me I thought . . . " Domenico could not go on.

"But I didn't do it, did I?" Gino said, but in fact he was thinking, *Of course, I didn't really have a chance to kill him.* He was afraid to say the words out loud.

"God didn't want you to kill Pietro," the prior said.

At these words, Gino gripped Domenico's hand more tightly and looked at Ariane.

"I know, Gino," she said. "Everything. At first, Brother Domenico didn't want to tell me. He thought—we all thought you might not live and then it would be best if the story passed with you. But after the operations, the doctors said you would survive. They didn't know whether you would recover completely, but they said there was hope. Still, you remained unconscious until now."

"I've been worried, Gino," the monk said, "that when you get well you might still try to kill him."

"I will," Gino said, but his voice came uncertainly.

"No, you won't," the prior said. "You're not a killer, Gino."

"I hate him—I'll always hate him." But then he laughed. "I think it would please him if I tried to kill him. It would prove that I'm as evil as he is."

"Thank God," the prior said.

"I want to get out of here," Gino said. But it took them a long time to locate Doctor Antonelli, and Gino was fuming when he arrived.

The doctor glared back. "I've been patiently caring for you for three months, and now you're angry because I'm too busy with other sick people to come running the very instant you call. If I didn't know better, I'd think you were French."

"Don't insult my wife. "

"I'm complimenting her. One of the magic qualities of the French is their impatience. Despite that, you'll have to remain here at least another week and begin some physical therapy."

Gino decided to treat the doctor with diplomacy. "I'm very grateful—"

"—*Concime!*" The doctor cut him off with a vulgarism. "Doctor Antonio Antonelli is too old and too experienced to expect or even trust gratitude. You don't like me, Bondone, which doesn't bother me in the least. What bothers me is that I'm responsible for you. I have performed miracles to bring you this far, and I don't want you to ruin everything by leaving here before you're ready."

"I'm ready."

"Fine. Stand up and walk out of here."

Gino felt a fantastic surge of joy. He pulled off the covers, rolled out of the bed and stood up.

When he regained consciousness he was lying on the floor face down, staring at the someone's shoes: the doctor's.

Antonelli's voice was almost tender. "You see, you're not ready."

Gino rested on his arms and spoke to the shoes. "That was unfair, Doctor. You knew that if I rose too quickly after spending months in bed, I was bound to collapse."

"Of course. But if I said that, you wouldn't have believed me."

Gino slowly moved himself to a sitting position. Then, after a few minutes he worked his way to his feet, leaning against the bed. When he felt safe, he tried a few steps. He wobbled considerably, and his legs were painfully weak, but he could walk. Feeling faint, he sat down on his bed, but then forced a smile and said, "I'm leaving."

◆ ◆ ◆

It was painful to say goodbye to Brother Domenico. The monk looked more faded than ever; Gino thought he could see his skull through his parchment skin. "Thank you, brother . . . for everything."

The monk touched Gino's face with a trembling hand. "Take care, my son. You have suffered much tragedy, but you're still as kindhearted as when you were a boy."

"Where will you go, brother?"

"The prior, Brother Alberto, has kindly offered to make a place for me at San Marco where I'll live out what time is left to me. Each day I will visit the Hospice and look at the works of Fra Angelico, Lorenzo Patti and Gianpaolo Bondone."

"I'll write to you."

"Of course." He gripped Gino's hands, turning them upward. "You have a great gift, my son. Don't waste it."

◆ ◆ ◆

They reserved a first class compartment on the train for the long trip back to Paris. *I'm always taking the same routes*, Gino thought, *but never in quite the same style*. He was still rather weak and he welcomed the comfortable ride back to Paris.

Ariane propped him against the pillows in the seat next to the window, where he sat quietly, watching the countryside. But the train moved too rapidly to please him. Mountains, valleys, forests, towns flashed past in seconds. The images began to weary him. *A painter must stand in one place*, he thought.

His weariness turned to resentment. These trees and towns were merely markers, setting the distance, measuring the passage of time, narrowing the gap between him and Paris—the place where he must make his decision. He pressed his foot to the floor, as if it was on a brake, as if he could slow the train or even stop it. But nothing happened. The trees, the towns, went flying past him, back out of his sight, out of his control. He looked up into the sky. No clouds. No augury of the future.

This same sky rode over Paris. Over Villon. Over his studio. He shuddered. *I can't paint there.*

He closed his eyes. He was at the opera, wearing elegant formal clothes. Tall, disdainful men sneered at him; elegant, fragile women pulled his arm, whispered in his ear. He couldn't understand the words. The women giggled. The men sneered.

Then he was at the ballet. The theatre. Longchamps. A party at Maxim's. The same men. The same women. The same smiles. The same sneers. The same black clothes.

Ariane. Dressed in gold. Gold dress, golden hair. The black figures were fixed, like statues in a wax museum. Ariane floated past them, between them, nodding here, whispering there. Smiling. Always smiling. Then she was circling him. A light touch. A light kiss. A word. A smile. Circling. Always circling. Tinkle of laughter—or a chandelier. Glasses touching glasses. White wine sliding down white throats. The glasses never empty. The throats never full. Tinkle of wineglasses and chandeliers and laughter. And not a word he understood.

"Are you all right?" The black figures melted into a single black vulture that flapped once and disappeared into the sky. He turned to the single gold figure that remained: Ariane.

"Why do you ask?"

"You were frowning and clenching your fists. Are you in pain?"

"Yes."

"Shall I find a doctor?"

"No doctor can help me. The pain is here." He tapped his chest over his heart.

"I don't understand."

"You've tried very hard to understand, but you cannot."

Jagged lines scarred the golden face. "Help me," she said.

He shook his head. "I can't even help myself."

She took his hand. Her touch was velvet now, not gold. And it was comforting. He was confused for a moment. This woman had done everything for him. Everything. He could not doubt her love. She had been patient and kind. She had ignored his rudeness, his clumsy manners. She had cared for him while he was ill. He visualized her sitting beside his bed, day after day, watching his face, his eyes closed.

"You watched me, Ariane, cared for me. Three months in a coma, while I uttered nothing but wild threats against Pietro. To you I must have looked unchanging. But I was changing. Unconscious. In a coma. But changing. I'm not the same man who drove off that mountain."

"You'll be as good as ever. The doctor said you would."

"I must be better than ever. "

She didn't understand and, therefore, she didn't speak.

He looked outside. The trees were very close to the train and the train moved so fast he could see through them. A small village through the lacework trees. Then a tunnel and blackness.

"I'm not going back to Villon."

The velvet hand tightened. There was gold beneath the velvet.

"Why not?" she asked.

"I can't work there anymore. I'll never paint in that studio again."

"We'll find some other place. There are plenty of empty rooms at Villon."

"Yes, empty."

"Or the small house in the English garden. We could redecorate it very easily."

"It's no use, Ariane."

"You can have a studio anywhere. You can paint anywhere you like."

"I'm not sure I can paint at all. I don't want to paint. Not yet."

"Then it's not the studio."

They were in sunlight again.

"No, I suppose not."

"My friends? I'll give them up."

"Don't be silly. You'd be lost without them."

"I'd be lost without you."

He turned to look at her. "Thank you, Ariane, but it's not true. You'll do very well without me."

"Never."

She tried to embrace him. He was smothered in velvet. It was soothing, but he didn't respond. After a moment, she moved away.

"Why, Gino? Please tell me why?"

He wanted to answer, but he didn't know the answer. Perhaps he could paint the answer. It would well up from somewhere deep in his being and he would spread it on canvas, knowingly, yet somehow unconsciously. But he could not see that painting. And he did not know where to find the channel to the depths of his soul.

Twenty-Two

The Twilight Zone

Gino hurried from the station. Again the gray sky, dripping at the edges. Again the suitcase in his hand, but this time fine leather instead of printed cardboard. Ariane was somewhere behind him, collecting baggage, arranging for the trip to Villon, not realizing he had left. He had tried to explain for many hours, but he wasn't able to express his torment properly, and in any case, she had refused to listen, to understand. She was determined they would work it out, somehow, somewhere. It simply could not be over.

She would soon realize that he had gone on without her, and she would be stunned and hurt. But he couldn't chance saying the goodbye that might fade and become a surrender to all that had ensnared him for so long.

At first he walked rapidly. He didn't see Paris, but he sensed her, and despite the nagging drizzle, he had a feeling of anticipation. A new adventure. A new life. He dodged traffic in the streets with accustomed if unconscious skill. A few people glanced at him. He was too well dressed to be carrying his own large suitcase. Where was he going? He stopped abruptly, causing the man behind to bump into him. The man uttered an obscenity. Gino didn't bother to respond. He realized he had walked a long way. The street was beginning to bend upward.

The rue Lepic. He was following the same route he had traveled with Pietro years earlier. Very well. He would find a room in Montmartre. Gino struggled up the winding, narrow sidewalk, the suitcase banging against his thigh. He paused at No. 39. It wasn't a good idea to start a new life in precisely the same place. He passed No. 54; he had heard Van Gogh had lived there, but he kept walking.

The rain had stopped and the place du Tertre was filled with activity. Artists lined the walks, producing postcard pictures of the narrow streets, the cafes, large-eyed children, and peasant-bloused girls. Several artists, standing in a single row, were painting the Sacré Coeur, viewed along the same street as Utrillo's masterpiece. Each painting was in a different state of completion, but they would be virtually identical when finished. A production line.

How easy it was for these men. How similar they were to the leatherworkers at San Felice. Perhaps he should have remained a leatherworker.

In a tiny garden off the square he found a building with a room for rent. The landlord viewed him suspiciously. His expensive clothes and finely barbered head didn't suit the decor. But Gino paid a month's rent in advance and the room was his, a tiny one with a window overlooking the square. A stove, a bed. A desk. Dust in the corners, webs on the ceiling, holes in the bedding. But he didn't care. Suddenly he was quite tired. Without opening his suitcase, without loosening his tie, he fell across the bed and slept.

When he awoke it was dark. Sleep had not refreshed him, and he felt edgy, thick in the tongue, exhausted. *The walk was too much for me. I should have taken a taxi.* But he didn't have that much money with him. And the money he had might have to last a long time if he didn't contact Le Temps; and he didn't plan to. He slipped into sleep again and when he awoke it was morning.

He leaped from the bed, took one step and staggered, dizzied. He sagged to the bed again. *I'm not well yet*, he thought. *I left the hospital too soon. I should have stayed at least another week. Why was I in such a hurry to return?* The dreary room provided no answer.

After a while he roused himself. The dizziness was gone, although he felt unaccountably tired. The faucets coughed into the grimy basin as he splashed water on his face. Even in the faded mirror he could see that his growth of beard was heavy. That pleased him. He hadn't gone a single day without shaving (even in the hospital, in a coma, they had dutifully shaved him), since he had married Ariane. He glanced down at his rumpled clothes, then stripped off the expensive jacket and rolled up the sleeves of his shirt. Now he looked thoroughly disreputable. Good. He was ready to face the world.

The place du Tertre was drowning in sunlight. It prickled Gino's beard and made him feel vaguely irritable. He found a bistro on the far side of the square and went inside. It was dark and cool and empty. A rather slovenly woman took his order for rolls and coffee. He ate quickly, then slapped his money on the counter. But when he stepped outside he realized he had no plan, no place to go. He shrugged his shoulders and began to walk through Montmartre, wandering aimlessly, seeing little, hearing nothing. From time to time he stopped to rest on a bench or the steps of a church. His mind was barely functioning. It was long past sunset before he realized that darkness had fallen.

He made his way back to the bistro, ate a frugal meal, and returned to his room. There was really nothing to do so he went to sleep. Gratefully.

Each morning Gino awoke with a surge of anticipation, but then felt dizzy or tired or irritable—at times all three. *Not yet*, he told himself. *Not quite yet.* Therefore, he spent the days in his room, leaving only to take meals and an occasional stroll.

I'm regaining my strength, he told himself. *A man who lives through such an accident can't be too careful. Soon. Soon, I'll start to work.*

One afternoon, ambling along the street, he came upon an

artist's supply shop. The sight of these familiar utensils arrayed in the window stopped him. He stared at the easel, the brushes and the tubes of paint with growing hunger. In the corner of one window was a set of used equipment, "priced for quick sale." He dragged himself away from the window and walked a few steps, but then, against his will, turned back. He stood staring into the window for many minutes, unaware that the proprietor had come to the open doorway and was watching him.

"A nice set, eh?"

"What?" Gino wasn't happy to hear his own thoughts voiced aloud by someone else.

"I said, 'That is a nice set.' "

"Yes."

"And priced very cheaply."

"Oh."

"You can have them all for only five thousand francs."

Gino smiled, relieved. "I'm sorry. I have only three thousand with me."

"Done," the proprietor said, "they're yours."

"But . . . " It was too late. The man was leading him into the store, removing the items from the window, wrapping them quickly in newspaper, expertly cinching the package with twine. The shopkeeper held the package before him. Gino, reluctantly, reached into his pocket, and handed over a wadded bundle of notes.

"But there are three thousand five hundred francs here," the shopkeeper said. "You're a better haggler than I am."

The five hundred-franc note hung in the air before Gino. Then it was withdrawn.

"Wait," the shopkeeper said, "You'll need canvas, won't you?"

Gino nodded numbly. In seconds, the shopkeeper had yanked two small and rather tired looking stretched canvasses from a rack and handed them to Gino. "There, you have everything you require to be another Picasso."

It was done. But after all, it would have happened eventually.

An artist couldn't paint without paint and canvas and brushes. And it was a good buy. Gino could barely suppress his excitement. Clutching the parcels to his chest, he hurried to his room and ripped open the packages, unmindful that he had scored his fingers deeply on the twine. Then he set up the easel, mounted a canvas on it and laid the paints and brushes on the table alongside. The easel wobbled a bit, but he propped it with a piece of cardboard.

Gino fingered the brushes lovingly. They were old, but still supple. The fur tips felt like a woman's skin to him and he was aroused accordingly. Still holding a brush, his fingers stroking the tip, he backed onto his bed. From there he admired his acquisitions.

Now, all I have to do is begin painting. The thought deflated him and he sat motionless for a long time.

I'm too tired to begin today. He lay back on the bed, still holding the brush. After a while he slept. In his dream he was making love to a beautiful woman, someone familiar, although he couldn't remember her name. She had long, lustrous hair and he couldn't stop caressing it. When he awoke, he found he was clutching the tip of the brush tightly in his hand. He laughed weakly, then threw the brush onto the floor. When he turned on his side he was face to face with the blank canvas.

Stop accusing me, he thought. *I'll get to you soon enough.* He rolled onto his back and stared at the ceiling. *I'm afraid*, he thought, then shook his head angrily. *No, I'm not afraid. No one needs to tell me when or when not to paint. I am my own man. They all tried to rule my life. Brothers Domenico and Alberto; Lorenzo Patti; Pietro; Pierre Petit; Ariane. All of them. But not any longer. Now I decide.*

Gino ran the same thought through his mind many times, convincing himself it was true. *If I don't paint, it's not because I can't. It's only because I don't want to. No one can tell an artist when to paint. An artist must tell himself.*

He sat up suddenly. "I'm not afraid!" he said aloud. But the sound of his own voice, issuing unexpectedly, surprised him. This time he mumbled, "I'm not afraid." And then, in the sanctuary of his own mind: *Soon I'll be ready. Then I'll paint. What I want to paint. When I want to paint.*

He wondered why he was shivering.

◆   ◆   ◆

One morning, Gino reluctantly faced up to his need to enter into a commercial transaction, something that agitated him almost as much as the thought of painting. *I'm almost out of money,* he thought. *Not enough for this month's rent; soon not enough to buy food. I could go to Le Temps; he would give me an advance, but criticise me for not painting. I couldn't face Pierre Petit and couldn't bear asking Pietro.*

He dug into the bottom of the large, black suitcase he had brought with him from the hospital in Bologna. There, in a sensual, felt-covered box, was the watch Ariane had given him for his birthday. It was a gold Piaget, with a simple rectangular face etched with interlocking pyramids, narrow black hands but no numbers, and a flexible gold band the same width as the face. The entire watch was only a few centimeters thick. *Simple, lovely,* he thought. *I wonder how much I can sell it for. Who can I sell it to?* He decided to ask the owner of the bistro, Madame de Renne.

She was clearly surprised by his question, and when he produced the Piaget for her examination, her eyes widened. "This is very valuable," she said. "Are you certain you want to sell it? Perhaps you should go to a *prêteur sur gage.*

"What is that?"

La Renne smugly explained about pawnbrokers and the process of pawning one's belongings. "That way, you can get it back some day."

"I don't think I'll want it back."

She shrugged.

"But please tell me where I can find such a person."

The bistro owner informed him that there was a street of such businesses on the Right Bank, and she directed him to it. He had actually hoped she would buy the watch herself, and he would be done with the transaction, but it was clear that the watch was much more valuable than he had thought. He thanked her and set out for the street she had named.

The rue Monge was not as narrow and the shops were not as decrepit as he had expected. Among the antique shops and ancient bookstores were a few with the symbol La Renne had told him to expect, the three balls. He ignored the largest shop and the smallest, and chose one with a clean window, but a dim interior.

Inside, there were shelves and showcases jammed with a vast variety of items bearing inscrutable tags, some of which actually seemed to have a discernible purpose. The proprietor sat on a stool behind a high counter, a corpulent, but clean-shaven fellow with glasses perched low on his nose and a black skullcap on the back of his largely bald head. His smile was warm, although his teeth were irregular.

"Good morning, Monsieur," he said. "May I be of service?"

Gino took the Piaget from his pocket and silently placed it on the deeply scored wooden counter.

"Lovely!" the man said. "And very new, I would guess?"

Gino nodded; he didn't actually know how to carry on this conversation.

The man picked up the watch and examined it, turning it this way and that, smiling now and then.

"How much can I get?" Gino blurted out.

"Italian?" the man smiled. "The Italians are the most warmhearted people on earth," he said. "Next to my own, of course."

Gino said nothing.

"Are you always this quiet? Or is this just a new and perhaps unpleasant experience for you?"

Gino smiled. "Everything you say. The lady who sent me to this street said I must haggle with you. How do I do that?"

The man laughed. "Fortunately, you have come into the pawnshop of Saul Gumbiner, which is absolutely the best place for a virgin like you to begin, Gino."

"How do you know my name?"

"It's inscribed on the back, as well as what I would guess to be your birth date, young man."

Gino was surprised. He did not recall turning over the watch when Ariane gave it to him, and he had not looked since.

"Unfortunately," Gumbiner said, "the personal inscription decreases the value."

Gino nodded and reached for the watch, but the pawnbroker held on to it. "But that doesn't mean it isn't quite valuable. I'll give you sixty thousand francs for it."

"Good," Gino said.

Gumbiner laughed. "Your friend told you to haggle. When I say sixty thousand, you must say one hundred thousand. We go up and back, and then we finally compromise at, say, seventy-five thousand. Okay?"

"I was happy at sixty thousand."

"I know. That is why one must be gentle with a virgin." He quickly wrote up a pawn ticket, opened his cash box with a key and counted out seventy-five thousand francs and pushed them across the counter to Gino.

"You are a kind man," Gino said, shoving the money into his pocket.

Gumbiner shrugged. "Few people understand that," he said, and put out his hand.

Gino shook it firmly, then turned and hurried from the shop. Before starting back up the street, he looked into the pawnshop window, smiled and waved his hand. It was too dark inside to tell whether the owner had waved back.

♦ ♦ ♦

Even before he opened his eyes, Gino knew it was dark. The night felt cool on his eyelids and his lips bent in a satisfied smile. For a moment he kept his eyes closed. Another day was over;

another sunny afternoon used up. He sighed with relief.

Gino permitted the world to intrude very slowly. His eyes followed the string of light that stretched between the shutters and across the ceiling, bending down at the wall and ending vaguely on the door.

Gino shook his head: Not yet. He would perhaps have gone back to sleep, but the opening, which admitted the light, brought with it a shaft of cold air that darted across the room and struck the bottoms of his naked feet. He retracted them under a cover, but it was too late. The cold vibrated up through his body. He turned onto his belly, hoping to escape or at least to smother it; without success. Now he was uncomfortable—and chilled. The pleasure was gone.

Still, the afternoon was also gone and that was satisfaction enough. Gino struggled off the bed and walked gingerly across the clammy, cold tile floor to the window. He pushed open the shutters, bravely facing the cold-eyed street lamp that stared up at him reprovingly. It was chillier at the window, but a full-faced, frontal cold, much easier to bear than the sneaky draught which had slithered up his legs.

The street was almost empty. A few children scrambled about in the square, playing some variant of hide and seek, dodging among the trees, covering their faces (ah, yes, faces), and gesturing in an elaborate and incomprehensible style. But no tourists. No street artists.

A few shambling shapes flickered in and out of the lamplight. Local shapes, amorphous, undistinguished, but indigenous. Now the cold gripped him, prickling the hairs on his naked chest. He put his arms across his chest, hugging himself like a woman surprised in her bath.

Gino looked down below his arms where his belly (once proudly flat) rippled languidly above his belt. He shook his head. *Ugly*.

The staring street lamp began to annoy him, an eye without a face. Gino shuddered under its contemptuous scrutiny, took one last look at the empty street, and retreated behind his shutters. It was a mistake. He had to grope in the darkness for the light switch. He laughed when the light went on. The light from the small bulb screwed into a socket against the high ceiling had all the effect of an eyedropper of lemon colored medicine squeezed into a tall glass of water, barely tinting the gray-walled room. But enough for him to find the stove, light a match to the gas jet and start it into flame with a miniature volcanic thud.

He left the filthy iron door open for the moment, washing his hands in the fluttering heat. That was the trouble. The days were shorter now, the afternoons difficult to traverse, but the nights were cold. *I'll have to sleep in a shirt*, he thought, picking up the collarless madras he had cast aside earlier that day, when warm light still cascaded through the room.

There was a pool of heat now around the stove, slowly spreading through the room, filling the air so lightly tinctured by the yellow bulb. He drew on his socks and his shoes. They still showed their aristocratic origins, although he hadn't cleaned them in many weeks. The shirt was stiff and grimy. Someone might guess that it had once cost thousands of francs, but never suspect that Gino had been the original purchaser. The pants? Well, he had always worn baggy old pants. At least when he was working. Or trying to. But now?

He walked to the window and pushed open the shutters, fortified by the light, the heat, and his worn shirt. Over the houses across the square he could see the dome of the Sacré Coeur glowing whitely under the searchlights. *Good*. It was past seven (the lights went on at seven, October through April, and at nine, May through September; a kind of celestial clock). *Time to eat*.

But not quite yet. It wasn't wise to rush the hour. Not wise to arrive at the bistro too early—too soon after the proprietress, Madame de Renne, had swept the crumbs onto the floor and covered the tables with yellow paper. Gino usually had difficulty busying himself. But now the pressure was gone. The sun was down and who could blame him if he pulled the oil stained cloth over his easel?

The hallway was dark. The landlord seldom turned the lights on before nine (his clock was set perpetually on a summer schedule). Some nights he never turned them on at all. Gino groped his way down the stairs, following the curving wall (peeling plaster), and the creaking steps to the bottom. Light and voices leaked out under the doors as he passed. He stepped in the puddles, feeling as though he had stepped on the speakers' tongues as well. And once in a while he received a scream in return.

The front door had no window, but it was so warped and cracked that light penetrated at a dozen points. He pulled it towards him, not without effort, and stepped around it onto the sidewalk. After the hall, the street seemed terribly bright. The ornate double lamps dripped yellow light onto the buildings and the plane trees. In the breeze, the light seemed to drift with the leaves. Illusion. All was illusion.

A figure brushed past him. A girl. In a trenchcoat. Gino watched her hurrying down the street, her hips swinging the coat out as if it were a skirt. Unconsciously, unwillingly, he imagined her. *She's pretty*, he thought, inventing her face, which he could not actually see. *Long black hair and black eyes, a flaring, sensual nose, and pouty lips. Slim ankles, slim waist, high breasts. Not large, not full, but high. You see how observant I still am? Even in the dark?*

He turned to follow her to the end of the street, where it met the steps rising from the city. She was far ahead of him now, hurrying somewhere to somebody, unaware that he was almost running behind her. Her shape was vague, merging with the evening mist, dropping below his visual horizon as she took the steps.

When he reached the railing she was gone. Into the underworld. He looked up, but couldn't see beyond the first row of housetops. The city was gray-black down there. But when he turned he could see the lighted dome.

Here, we are above the mists of the city, he thought, and watching the pure white dome floating above him, he felt secure. Well, anyway, it wasn't too early to eat now. The short run had given him an appetite.

He reached inside his jacket (suitably heavy, suitably old, suitably worn) and squeezed the roll of flesh through his shirt. *We'll get rid of you yet, old fellow.*

He walked purposefully down the street, across the plane-tree-framed square and onto the sidewalk before the bistro. "Bistro," the sign said, and Gino nodded in approval. So plain, so simple, so honest, so accurate. The letters all block, no script, drawn to the full height of the lintel. No nonsense. No pretense.

All the panels were closed but one. In summer, they stood open, with a fine orange canopy above (Cinzano), and three white iron tables with chairs filling the walk. But it grew too cold too early these days, and Madame de Renne had stored the tables in the basement. The orange canopy was gone, too. Other shopkeepers might keep theirs out all year long, but not La Renne. You only got one free from the Cinzano people—they made you pay for a replacement.

The portable store panels were in place, except for the last. Later in the season, Madame de Renne would hang the door there. Now, there was nothing.

Gino stopped for a moment, enjoying the sight of the bistro, brown and orange outside, brown and yellow inside. Fine, clean rectangles, hung on the night. There was no one visible inside. By the time Gino crossed the narrow street, mounted the curb and slipped inside, Madame de Renne had appeared behind the counter. She was flogging the top with a ragged brown cloth, attacking the surface so intently and so angrily that she did not acknowledge Gino's entrance.

Gino preferred it that way. Once, weeks earlier, she had greeted him by name in front of a room full of patrons. Several had turned to stare at him. Probably they didn't recognize his name. But he had flushed with anger, turned and hurried out. She had come to his room to apologize the following day. Gino answered the knock without curiosity and without expectation. It couldn't be anyone who would interest him. It was La Renne. Suddenly, as he stood in the doorway, bare-chested and dirty, perspiring from the steaming day, he realized she was pretty. Forty, perhaps, and a bit sloppy, frizzle-haired and slack-skinned, but her nose was neat and her mouth was full. She smiled hesitantly, parting her lips and flicking her tongue across them. Gino had shivered with a fleeting pleasure, feeling utterly certain that her body was suitably full and respectably trim beneath the shapeless brown dress.

He didn't invite her in. She stood in the hall, looking down the stairs nervously from time to time and mumbling French phrases to Gino, little murmurs that he didn't understand. His French was not that good anyway, and he wasn't concentrating. But he enjoyed the vision of her unseen breasts rising and falling somewhere beneath the million creases of her lumpy bodice. In imagination he ran his hands around her naked hips. He smiled.

"Then you'll come back?"

He tried to focus on her face, lips parted in anticipation, eyes luminous with anxiety. He smiled again and nodded. Gino turned from the door, expecting her to follow him inside. But when he looked back, she was gone. He heard her footsteps rocking down the creaking steps. An opportunity missed.

What had he agreed to? The words still hung in the air, unused but fading. He stopped them, turned them over and examined them before they melted away. Oh, yes. He had agreed to continue taking his meals at the bistro. But surely, she had expected more than that. Ah, well, this was no time for involvements—surely not with the owner of the bistro. It would complicate his life. The taking of every meal would become an adventure. Each day he would have to worry whether or not the widow still loved him. Each day he would be forced to set a smile on his face when he met her. Otherwise, his cuisine, and consequently his liver, might suffer. Better this way.

Thereafter, she didn't even acknowledge his presence when he entered her place of business. Gino was pleased. This was no more exciting than walking from the living room to the kitchen in his own home (he had no home now; and this thought flickered only briefly through his brain before he quashed it). Gino passed Madame de Renne without speaking, nodding his head although he knew she was not looking, relishing this closeness, this courtesy without intimacy, this grace without kindness.

He stopped. His favorite table was taken. He couldn't believe it. From outside the bistro had seemed empty. Where had this person come from—slipping into the bistro and taking his table while his eyes were averted? He turned, intending to protest to La Renne, then changed his mind. The thought of protesting, of arguing with the occupant of his place was unpleasant. A quarrel. He shuddered at the thought. No, it wasn't worth it. He would take another table. What did it matter? This was but one night out of a thousand.

Gino sat down, discreetly leaving two unoccupied tables between him and his enemy. He couldn't resist taking the chair facing the interloper. A girl. Until that moment, it had not occurred to him that this creature might have a sex. She was leaning against the wall, face lowered, long hair cascading onto her arms and the table. Slowly, she raised her head, her hair parted, but only slightly, and Gino could barely make out her face, screened by beige and brown hair. Her hands flicked upward, remarkably white and graceful, and drew back her hair, like curtains parting. Gino felt that he was staring into a strange, new world.

He wrenched his eyes away, stared across his shoulder at the back of the bistro counter, busy with the reflections of plates and glasses. It should have been impossible for him to see her there, but he did. Fragments of her face. An eye on one section of glass; a pair of lips on another; strands of hair, patches of luminous skin. Like some grisly cubist painting. Then, unconscious of the effort, his imagination fused them into one brilliant portrait, so compelling that against his will he turned to match it against the original. Perfect. The vision and reality were identical.

The girl seemed to be looking through him, unaware of his intense scrutiny. Gino felt as free to examine her as if she was a painting in a gallery. He relaxed, feeling the tension draining from his body. His eyes scanned her face, side to side and top to bottom. Where were the brush marks of time? He could discern no wrinkles on her forehead, no lines leaving the corners of her eyes. Perhaps at closer range he would find the flaws. But that was impossible, and besides, something told him that even minute examination would not reveal imperfections.

Gino had no intention of exploring this question any further. He remembered himself—remembered the monastic orders under which he served. As if to punctuate his thought, La Renne set a carafe of wine and a glass before him. Saved from the soul by the flesh.

Gino spilled sparkling red wine into the plain glass tumbler, and drank half the glass before he was aware of it. The strange feminine vision had completely destroyed his routine. Gino never allowed himself more than one carafe at dinner, and now he had drunk more than half a glass without tasting a bite of his food.

"Are you all right, M'sieu?" It was La Renne, looking down at him with remote concern.

Gino gave her a small smile. "I'm fine," he said, but his voice betrayed him, issuing as a sharp gasp, as if he had spat out a jagged stone trapped in his throat.

"*Bien.*" The widow showed no expression as she set a steaming bowl of potato soup before him. Gino tried to soothe his raw throat with the smooth soup. The first swallow was painful, but gradually, as the warmth of it spread through his body, he felt the rhythm of his life returning. He held his eyes on the bowl, staring blankly to prevent images from forming on the flat, creamy surface of the soup. But it was impossible to sit through an entire meal without looking up.

Gino prepared himself for the moment with extreme care, composing his thoughts and his face. He placed his hands against the table and slowly raised his head. She was gone. His brain told him he should be relieved. But he wasn't. It was all right to deliberately blot out the vision; to erase it; to wad up the sketch and spin it into the wastebasket. But the vision ought not to disappear of its own volition. For Gino to triumph it was necessary that he conquer the temptation himself—by his own restraint; his own courage.

Grudgingly, he conceded that she had appeared without his permission, and there was no apparent reason she should not disappear without consulting him. He forced himself to continue his meal as if she had never been there.

After a while the old harmonies returned. The simple basic rhythms of moving one's hand (with a fork attached) from plate to mouth and back. Wine curling down his throat in cooling draughts. La Renne's fish and meat and small cakes, the green salad (discreetly brown at the edges), all following one another in orderly procession.

The bistro was less crowded than usual, and La Renne served him rapidly. When he took the last sip of wine, he realized that he had been seated less than thirty minutes. He pushed back his chair and rose to go.

"Is everything satisfactory?"

It was, of course, La Renne. *Damn the girl. It was she who had started this unpleasantness. Or was it the other girl—the one who had disappeared down the steps*? Two disturbing visions. Both female. No, three: La Renne. "*C'est tout. Bien*," he muttered, leaving his money on the counter and stalking out.

There were more people on the street than before. Tourists, drifting in clouds of alien perfumes; the locals, shambling like wrens in ever decreasing circles until at last they settled on their own stoops—hunched, domesticated, waiting. A few nodded to Gino, not knowing him, but accustomed to his presence. These abstract greetings proved he had a place in this world and that he was in that place. They marked his passage without describing his life, like animal tracks in the snow.

Gino slowed his pace, hoping to use up the time he should have spent in the bistro. Insofar as he could tell, no permanent damage had been done to his life. The adventure was over and he had preserved his insular existence. In fact, it was important that he be tested in this way. If he could learn to live with minor irritations, he could learn to live with larger ones.

The thought pleased him. This had been a victory, not a defeat. He climbed the steps to his room and threw himself down on the unmade bed, still dressed, and fell asleep.

The following day passed easily. It was raining, and even if his shutters had been wide open, the room would still have been far too dark for work. Gino read a book he had picked up in a secondhand shop because he liked the colors on the cover, glancing out now and then to see if the sky was clearing, but the clouds, distinct earlier, had merged by afternoon. The wind changed, and it became impossible for Gino to leave his shutters open at all. He closed them with satisfaction.

The book, some kind of mystery story, bored him. The words began to melt into each other; the lines grew wavy, and the letters proved to have shadows. *My eyes,* he thought. *I can't read without glasses any more.* By his own standards this discovery should have evoked pure pleasure—one that boded even greater release from pain in the future. But he couldn't master the fear (irrational, of course) that gripped him. He shook his head angrily and to his surprise found that the words on the page had grown clearer. He felt a shiver of pleasure, which was obviously perverse. With a single anguished motion he flung the book against the shutters. It struck with a loud report, almost like a pistol shot, and for several minutes, Gino sat on the edge of the bed, almost rigid with fear that his landlord would appear and spoil the languid day.

No one came. Gino collected the broken binding and the scattered leaves. For a few minutes, he tried to reassemble them in numerical order. But somehow he kept putting the pages in the wrong progression. Next, he tried to assemble the book by following the order of the sentences on succeeding pages. There were obvious mismatches and others not so obvious. Only when he read for more than half a page was Gino able to be certain that the order was wrong. He had heard that someone had written a book this way, forcing pages together in random order. That was supposed to show the chance nature of life. Perhaps. To Gino it merely seemed to demonstrate the perverse nature of people.

Gino sat pondering this profound philosophical problem, a sheaf of unmatched papers in each hand, the book covers lying between his feet on the floor. He shook his head, shoved the torn pages between the covers, carefully folded the covers shut, lined up the edges of the pages, and dropped the whole mess into the wastebasket. *Thus does the barbarian triumph over civilization*, he thought. *Besides, it's a bad book and deserves its fate.*

Gino had heard it said that a man's life starts, ends, and is most ecstatic in bed. It certainly wasn't ecstatic for him these days. At best boring, at worst an excruciating travail. Ah, well, perhaps there were other men who suffered through their lives as he did, waiting for the interminable days to pass, only to be confronted by interminable nights they half hoped would not end.

As a matter of fact, it's very peaceful here, he thought, again watching the yellow finger of light point at the door. *I have become the master of myself.*

But then he remembered the book. The thought drove him from the bed, hurrying to the wastebasket as if the remnants might have flown away. Stumbling in the half-darkness, he dragged it out of the basket (along with some slimy, moldering food), brushed it clean and set it back on the shelf. A bit of food, perhaps egg, dripped from a corner. Still, Gino was proud. *You see, I'm not an evil, destructive person.*

Having successfully traversed another day, he permitted himself to leave his room and go out into the night—a night even damper and mistier than the one before. The yellow street lamps barely managed to poke holes through the night shroud. Gino stayed close to the buildings, fearful of stepping off into the void beyond the curbs (*A good sign. See, I don't want to die*). He felt like a small boy playing hide and seek as he edged his way along the walk. A man hurried by. Gino had to fight down the urge to yell "Boo" at him.

Am I going mad? Before he could answer the question, the glowing shape of the bistro materialized in the near distance. Ah, he could feel La Renne's hot, thick soup oozing down his throat.

She was there. The girl. Sitting in the same place. His place. A snarl of anger began to unwind itself deep in his belly and force its way through the imagined soup, still thick in his throat. Then he was frightened. He stepped back as if to flee. The girl looked up—stared at him—through him. He couldn't move.

"Come in, Monsieur Bondone, your dinner is waiting." La Renne was laughing at him. And she had used his name. He sagged and dog-like shambled to a table. The same table. Facing the girl. *Is this the new pattern?* he asked himself. *The girl has dislodged me. That is no longer my niche in life. This is my new niche. Who will push me out of this one?*

His soup came and he spooned it. The meat came and he ate it. He drank his wine and slopped gravy with his bread. A feeling of beatific resignation came over him. Once again he had bested the world, which constantly tried to taunt and provoke him, but once again it had failed. He smiled. The girl smiled back. He rose from his place, spilling the chair behind him, and lurched to the table where the girl sat.

Unaccountably, he slipped into the chair on the opposite side of the table. He had thought he meant to strike her and for a moment he could not speak. Cascading hair, luminous skin, glowing eyes—green, deepest green—transfixed him.

"Who are you?"

"Monique."

"A pretty name. Have you any other?"

"For us, Monique will be sufficient."

"How is it you know that for us Monique will be sufficient?"

She smiled. Her nostrils flared and the tip seemed pinched. "I've thought it out very carefully."

"You know me?"

"Gianpaolo Bondone."

"La Renne told you."

She shook her head. The long hair waved across her face, following the movement of her head a fraction of a second later. It was very graceful. "I've seen you before," she said.

"Where?"

"The gallery of Louis Le Temps. I went to the *Biennale* with the Russian painter, Gregory Potofski."

"The big fellow with the enormous mustaches. Were you the one who was trying to help him with his damaged hand?"

"Yes."

"It seems everyone in Paris was at the gallery that night. I remember he shoved you away—I didn't see you after that."

"You were too busy fomenting revolution."

Gino laughed. It was a clear and healthy laugh. He had not heard such a sound come from his lips in many weeks. He wanted to laugh again; to listen to himself. "But why are you here?"

"I was looking for you."

"Impossible."

"True . . . well, half true. I saw you walking the street a week ago and I followed you to this bistro."

"What do you want of me?"

She shrugged. For the first time, her clear eyes seemed clouded.

"Where do you live?" he asked.

"Close by."

"Come," he said rising from the table, "I'll take you there." He threw the required number of francs on the table and took her arm. He did not look at La Renne as he left.

"Which direction?"

She pointed.

"That's where I live," he said.

"That's where we're going." She spoke in a level voice, and even in the darkness he could tell that her expression was serene. She took his arm.

It was pleasant in the cold night to feel her young body moving alongside him. He hadn't enjoyed such a moment for a very long time. Ariane was an affectionate woman, but there was little trace of the animal in her. Ariane was beauty and dignity. Beside him was desire.

He slowed his pace. What was this all about? What new obligations would he be assuming?

"Come along," she whispered. "You needn't fear me."

It was a strange thing to say, but it reassured him.

Once in his room, he searched about until he found a bottle of brandy. She shook her head. Gino poured himself a drink and savored it.

"Have you any family?"

"Yes, but they moved to Marseille a few years ago. I've lived alone in Paris since I was seventeen."

"And now you are what, eighteen?"

"Nineteen."

She propped herself on his bed, her legs tucked underneath, long hair falling in a single cascade almost to the top of his comforter.

"Monique, who is nineteen." He shook his head.

"Gianpaolo who is thirty."

"You seem to know a great deal about me."

She shrugged. "Your age was listed in the catalogue."

He settled into the only chair in the room, opposite from her, and filled his brandy glass again.

"For courage?" she asked.

"Yes."

"Why are you afraid of me?"

"Why should a lovely French girl named Monique who is nineteen seek out an Italian painter who is thirty and whose name is Gianpaolo Bondone? Oh yes, and who is married."

"To a beautiful and gracious woman. That was the next time I saw you—at the Chateau de Villon. I was talking to Chagall when you walked into the library."

Gino was stunned. "Were you . . . ?"

She laughed. "No, I wasn't there with Marc. He is a friend of my family, and of the man I came with, Jean-Paul Sartre."

Gino was still frowning.

Monique shook her head. "You think such evil thoughts. Sartre is a cousin, a distant cousin, but he and my father have been very close since childhood. Jean-Paul sometimes invites me to be his companion at cultural events, especially at fashionable houses. He wants to find an eligible young man for me. I don't know whether he would have considered you eligible or not—even before you married the comtesse."

"You know I am married to a beautiful comtesse and still you are here."

"Yes. But she isn't here." She stared at him for a long time. He looked away, unnerved by her clear eyes. She smiled. "We're wasting time," she said. Standing up before him, she began to undress.

Monique had already taken off her blouse and skirt and removed her brassiere when she realized that Gino hadn't budged. "What are you waiting for?"

He didn't answer, but she continued undressing, stripping off her panties. Naked, she looked exactly as he had expected—firm-bodied, high-breasted, slim-hipped and athletic. And nineteen, with pellucid skin to match.

"I know you're not shy, but I'm not planning to do all the work." She took his arm and pulled him to his feet, with surprising strength. There was no use resisting any longer. He pulled her to him, feeling her lithe body burning through his clothing.

"Finally," she said, as she felt him surge in response, and kissed him hard on the mouth. Then she pushed away and wrinkled her nose. "You shirt stinks—when's the last time you washed it?" Without waiting for an answer, she began to tear it off, popping buttons.

He laughed and grabbed both of her hands in one of his. "I'm not totally helpless," he said, and ripped his shirt the rest of the way with the other.

Twenty-Three

Life and Transfiguration

In the morning Gino awoke early, feeling remarkably fresh and vigorous. It was impossible to remain in bed, sleeping late, or methodically planning meals and other meaningless rituals.

The girl still slept; he moved about carefully so as not to disturb her. She wore nothing, and in the night she had flung the sheets from her body. She lay on her back, one arm over her head, one hand cupped under her breast, as if offering it. Smooth, flawless skin arched down from her breast, rising gently at her waist even as it narrowed and then flaring into rounded, but tightly drawn thighs. One leg was raised at the knee, the foot touching the other. He smothered the urge to caress her. Then he smothered the urge to sketch her.

Gino found the brandy and would have drunk from it, but suddenly the idea seemed distasteful. He sank into a chair and waited for the girl to waken. She moved. Her hand slid along her side and he could feel the flesh it passed over. Her eyes opened slowly. She curled onto her side and smiled at him. Gino stood up, walked to the bed and gently pushed her onto her back.

Afterwards, they slept again, and this time she awakened

before Gino. When he opened his eyes, she was sitting in a chair, regarding him. "Something tells me," he said, "we should find other diversions."

They stopped at a tiny restaurant with a counter open to the street where they stood while they ate rolls and drank coffee—ravenously. They spoke little, smiled often. After draining their cups for the third time, they strolled to the Sacré Coeur. "Here we have the paramount example," Gino said, "of a building that is hideous and yet quite lovely."

"But of course. That's her secret."

They ambled down the steps to the terrace that overlooked the city. It was an unusually clear day and the lines of the city seemed firmly drawn. He looked at everything, but saw nothing. Again and again his gaze swept the city, and although he marveled at the clarity of his vision he did not recognize a single landmark. After several minutes, they began to descend the steps into the city.

"What do you do?" he asked.

"I? I do nothing."

"I'm serious. What do you do?"

"I hope to paint."

"Is that why you're in Paris?"

"I'm in Paris to be with you."

She had said a foolish thing, but Gino wanted to believe her.

In a market, they bought apples and munched them as they strolled. Later, Gino bought a loaf of bread and they ate great chunks of it sitting in a small park. It was absurd to be sitting with a young woman in a park eating bread, but it was enchanting. Gino decided he wouldn't explore his feelings at this moment. Instead he would relax and enjoy the day—and Monique.

They resumed wandering through the streets, hand in hand, smiling contentedly at the good citizens of Paris, who had no time for, nor any interest in, their beatitude. Gino and Monique were not disturbed; the Parisians were performing precisely as expected. When a particularly frowsy woman carrying two heavy paper bags frowned at them, they waited until she had passed and burst into laughter.

After a while, they reached the Seine. At the Pont Neuf they took the steps down to the quay. There was the usual amount of foot traffic along the bank, the usual number of lovers fondling each other on the benches, the usual number of small boys sitting along the edge, kicking their dusty shoes against the slowly yielding stone. Barges moved along the river, placid as ever, and the white and glass sightseeing boats passed them serenely. Sunlight bounded up from small, patterned waves and made them blink. Above, on the boulevard, they heard trams and motorcars forcing their way implacably towards the west.

It was astounding how many sunny hours there were in an autumn day, Gino marveled, wondering how he had managed to use up days like this—perfectly lovely, unhurried days that only reluctantly turned into blue-gray twilight. But it was not yet twilight. Below the Louvre the quay ended and they were forced to mount to the street. An idea caught Gino, and he took Monique by the hand and hurried her along. They passed beneath the Arc du Triomphe du Carrousel into the Tuileries.

"Thank God, he's still here!" Gino laughed aloud and hurried to the gnarled little man who rented toy sailboats for the pond. They weren't typical customers and he eyed them with suspicion. Ignoring him, Gino studied the wooden boats, which were of good size, solidly built, with broad hulls and deep centerboards. Gino chose one with square rigging and a red and white horizontally striped hull, handed over a few francs and started toward the pond.

"Wait," said the little man in a peevish voice. "You're entitled to a stick."

"Of course," said Gino. "How stupid of me. Every man is entitled to his stick."

"You haven't much time," the man continued. "I leave in half an hour."

Gino ran to the edge of the circular cement pond, dropped to his knees and carefully set the boat in the water. It didn't even bob when he released it, nor did he require the round wooden stick. The minute the boat touched water a gust of wind caught the sails, sending it hard over and driving it toward the center of the pond. For a moment, Gino narrowed his eyes so that he could see only the tiny ship within hazy margins.

He sighed. "Ah, to be aboard my little schooner, heading for . . . " His voice trailed off.

"For where?"

"I don't know."

"What a navigator."

"I don't claim to be a navigator, only a sailor."

"Well, I know where."

"Where?"

"To the other side of the pond. Hurry before someone takes our boat."

She began to run around the edge of the broad, shallow basin and Gino jumped up and followed. It was a longer run than they expected. The boat didn't steer a straight course, but instead, caught by each gust of the capricious breeze, rocked back and forth in a zigzag path that sent them scurrying round and round the basin.

"That's all very well," said Gino, "but please tell me: Where is the other side?"

The girl shrugged. By the time they finally recaptured the boat, they were exhausted

"You see," said Monique. "This is what comes from not setting your rudder."

"What makes you think I have a rudder."

They began to laugh.

"Your time is up," the little boatman said, coming up behind them.

"But of course, Monsieur. Thank you for the trip."

The man said nothing. Gripping the little boat firmly against his chest, he strode back to his cart.

"You know," Monique said, "I believe he loves those little ships."

"You're very sentimental," Gino replied. "To a Frenchman all possessions are sacred, particularly those which turn a profit." He gestured towards an elderly lady moving along the pond, gathering the ancient iron chairs. "Here in the park everything is rented: the boats, the chairs, everything. I'm surprised the French don't charge for the trees."

"We would," Monique answered, "but it's too difficult to replant them every morning."

It was darkening rapidly as they left the park. Through the triple arch, the ancient Louvre glowed in the distance. Streetlights had come on and yellow auto headlamps flashed along the boulevards. The wind had died and the sky remained clear, so that even after sunset the mansard roofs of the Louvre were clearly outlined against the sky. They crossed the Seine, lingering to study the light patterns in the water. Eventually they found a bistro that looked reasonably clean. The food proved to be passable, the wine bitter, but the place was quiet and they savored it. If the owner hadn't stared at them repeatedly, they would have remained a long time.

♦ ♦ ♦

They slept a great deal, Gino less than Monique. He didn't mind. The sounds of her gentle breathing were a delight to him. The very sight of her was a source of unending pleasure. Even when he should have felt thoroughly satisfied, she would make a graceful movement, or twist her body in an unconsciously provocative manner, and he would begin trembling again. He had only to touch her, even when she was deep in sleep, and she would come awake, enfolding, caressing, kissing him, and once more the game was on.

During the days they ate, strolled, sat, talked, did nothing. They regretted neither dusk nor dawn nor the passing of a day or night, barely noticing the difference. They didn't master time; they ignored it. Of course, time and the city ignored them. It was a polite, if somewhat ambiguous arrangement.

When they were back in his shabby room, and had made love

again, Monique dozed off. Gino rose, pushed the shutters open a crack, and stared down the ancient lamplight. It didn't frighten him now, it was no longer his enemy. The square seemed very close, as if he was sitting in it, as if the trees were all around him, as if he could reach out and touch a leaf. A leaf touched him.

Not a leaf; Monique.

"I thought you were asleep."

"The light woke me up." She leaned her arms on the sill.

"What do you see?" she asked.

"Out there, nothing. In here, everything."

"Very gallant." She kissed his hand.

"It's true."

"And what do you feel?"

"Contentment."

"Is that good?"

"At times."

"And at other times?"

"Very bad."

"When will the bad time come?"

For some reason, he shuddered. "Why do you ask?"

"I want a favor." She seemed more intense than he had seen her before.

"What do you want?"

She stared straight into his eyes. "A painting."

He drew back. "One of mine?"

"Yes, I want you to paint me."

"But I don't paint any more."

She took his arms in her cool hands. "Yes, you do. You've never stopped."

"Monique, I swear to you, I haven't mixed colors in months."

"But you paint all the same. I see the way you look at things. I hear the way you describe them. Everything is a composition."

He thought about that for a long time. "Seeing is not painting."

"If you don't paint what you see, you die. If you paint it, the canvas may not be as good as what you see."

He moved away. "You talk like Le Temps."

"But I'm not Le Temps." She stood before the window and pushed the shutters open wider. She stretched her arms overhead and her magnificent body was outlined against the light from the street lamp. She moved toward him. "If I'm good enough to love, I'm good enough to paint."

"Perhaps," he murmured, drawing her to him.

◆ ◆ ◆

They spent the following day in their usual random fashion, neither of them referring to the previous night's discussion. Monique was a determined woman and Gino had expected to hear more on the subject. Perhaps he wanted to hear more.

Something Monique had said stirred him: her reference to his visual compositions. It was true, although he had been only half-aware of it. Now, each time he focused on a scene, each time he framed out the nonessential factors and rearranged the rest, he was conscious of what he was doing.

When they returned to his room that evening he sat on the edge of the bed watching Monique undress. Usually this was a pleasant and stimulating procedure that tuned his mind and body to the adventure ahead. But this time Monique's body took on a formal, sculptural quality. Without willing it, he began to select features he would emphasize, to choose the pose appropriate to her grace.

He sighed. "Very well, Monique. You must be responsible for what follows." He carried her to the bed and arranged her on it. In that moment, she ceased to be a paramour and became an odalisque.

"Isn't it rather dark for sketching?"

"Be silent. This was your idea."

Gino took up his sketchbook and found a pencil that suited him. He stood spreadlegged, the pad crooked in his arm and began to draw.

"Are you making notes, or drawing?"

"The model doesn't speak."

"I'm not a landscape; I'm a woman."

"When I'm done with you, you'll wish you were a landscape."

She spoke from time to time, but he hardly heard her and didn't bother to reply. The lines came hard at first, but after a while Gino could feel control returning to his wrist and fingers. Trying to capture the long smooth curve that carried from her head down her back along her thighs and into her slim legs, he found it necessary to distort the legs to carry out the line. That did not disturb him; he was satisfied that the completed arc was both elegant and feminine.

The single incandescent lamp offered poor illumination, but in a sense it was useful, forcing him to concentrate on the basic elements of his model, while fusing her skin tones in a gentle chiaroscuro. The gradations of light and color began to fascinate him more than the lines. He thumbed the pencil line until it blurred. But this was unsatisfactory, substituting indistinctness for form. He would have to use paint rather than pencil or chalk to gain the right effect.

Gino was tiring, but the harmony of curves drew him on. Each line echoed another, each shape balanced its counterpart. The rhythms of Monique's body danced across his pad. Then he was too aroused to continue. Time now for lovemaking.

But Monique was asleep.

◆ ◆ ◆

In the morning Gino awakened early, dressed and left the room. He knocked at the door of the Bistro La Renne, awakening the surprised proprietress, from whom he demanded rolls and coffee. A few minutes later he hurried back to his room with a pot of coffee and a bag of brioche and butter.

Monique was still asleep. Gino pushed open the shutters, allowing the cool morning light to sweep her face. After gently removing the thin blanket he had pulled across her naked body the night before, he began to sketch. She moved in her sleep, assuming poses that emphasized the very details of shape and volume that he was trying to fix on paper.

"You never sleep," she said, bolting upright with a surprised expression on her face.

"Of course I sleep, but now I'm awake and at work. You may have thirty seconds to pour yourself a cup of coffee and select a roll which you will bring back to bed."

She lifted her eyebrows, but did as she was told. On the way back to the bed she pinched him in a private place. He did not respond. She rearranged herself on the bed and relaxed.

He drew furiously, as if she were melting snow, about to disappear. The hours passed. Monique grumbled, but stayed in place. "At this rate, I'll spend my entire life in the nude."

He laughed, but in fact only a small compartment in his mind was free to receive messages from the outside. Nothing was available with which to answer.

At noon, Monique protested that she was hungry again. Once more he left the room and purchased a few sandwiches and some cheap wine from La Renne. When he returned, Monique was pacing the room. She reached for the food, but her loveliness overcame him. He shook his head and led her to the rumpled bed.

"Very well," she said later. "Have I earned my dinner now?"

"Much more than that. Unfortunately all I have are La Renne's ham sandwiches and cheap wine."

"That's better than starving here in the harem."

By afternoon, his drafting was complete and he was ready to paint. Too impatient to go out and buy the pigments required, he mixed the colors he had and began to apply them to the canvas. The joy that filled him was almost inexpressible. As he stood at the easel, laying on color, tears ran down his cheeks.

"Is it that bad?" inquired his model.

"No, it's that good."

In the days that followed, Gino painted with a fervor beyond any he had ever experienced. It was as if he had discovered painting for the first time, recalling the joy of his first days working for Lorenzo Patti, blending in the confidence he had learned after his first show at Le Temps' gallery, and adding a technique for mixing colors he had learned from Chagall. His colors sparkled on the canvas. Reds and yellows replaced somber grays and purple blues. The lines were freer now and flowed together in slender tributaries that merged into the great stream of his exploding consciousness. He surrendered the rigid battle lines that had margined his earlier work and found a softer modeling of shapes that formed a soothing enchantment for his soul. Before, the world had seemed two-dimensional. Now he was intrigued with the sculptural quality of things, the depth and fullness of objects, and particularly of the human form.

His model was calm when required and fiery when he demanded it. They abandoned only the sightseeing phase of their existence. They still ate, drank and made love, but in the intervals Gino sketched and painted. Monique surprised him. She was so young, so energetic and restless, that he had been certain she would make a fidgety model. Yet, she proved to be patient—sitting or standing where he placed her for hours on end, seldom complaining and always cheerful when the ordeal was over.

He allowed her considerable freedom of movement, but she did not often take it, and he worked hard to portray on canvas this contained energy, this vibrant serenity. They abandoned the regimen that required them to take their meals in the room. Now that he had regained his confidence he didn't insist on working until he dropped from fatigue. He could work for a few hours in the morning, break off for a meal and rest (and lovemaking) at midday, and return refreshed to his easel.

After a week of this, Monique took up one of Gino's pads and began to sketch. At first he was surprised to find himself playing the role of male model and asked to see her drawing. It was fuzzy, the portraiture a bit distorted, but undoubtedly Monique had talent. He had no intention of helping her, but he was not displeased to find that she displayed some virtuosity. It seemed to tie them more closely together.

Before he had even finished one canvas, Gino began another—one in which Monique was only one of several figures, although all had their origins in her. This time he had to buy a much larger canvas from the dealer.

As usual, Gino used his model only as a starting point. His figures, although clearly feminine, were not clearly Monique. She became the source of multiple portraits and figure studies, each of different women. Later, he grouped some of these figures with others, some male, some female. This, too, was a new departure. Until then, Gino had seldom painted a large canvas containing more than a single figure. Never had he combined men and women on one canvas. Gino was aware of walls tumbling down within his mind, images flowing together, a freedom and ease of composition opening up to him. All things seemed possible. No subject was beyond his skill or interest. No technique seemed unavailable. He was intense yet elated. His temperament was pitched at a peak of creative frenzy tempered only by joy in the results and the deep affection he shared with Monique. He couldn't help but contrast the contentment he now felt with the false ease that had perfumed him in Antibes.

◆   ◆   ◆

A snowstorm in early February made Gino realize he had been living with Monique for more than two months. He studied the pattern of flakes against the plane trees, then circled the room to weigh and measure his artistic production. There were a dozen large unframed canvases, and since the room was too cramped to display them properly, they were propped haphazardly. He studied each intently, searching for the flaws which had often disturbed him in the past—the clumsy brush strokes, the awkward shapes that others seemed not to notice, but which had sent him into paroxysms of anguish. He found no trace of such imperfections. *Have I gone blind*, he wondered, *or am I truly painting better?*

"What do you see?" she asked.

"In every shape, in every line—you."

"You're in love."

"It's true. You're the inspiration for every painting. Your form, your smile, your gaiety, your beauty infuses them all. I'm very grateful."

She kissed him lightly on the very point of his chin. "You're becoming very sentimental, you great Italian peasant."

"Yes, very sentimental, but not, I hope, maudlin."

She looked about the room. "These are not maudlin. There is, you know, great power in real human sentiment."

"Have I ever denied it?"

"Yes."

"Absurd."

"Then why do you paint without faces, or only a hint of them?"

Gino was silent. He turned away and once again circled the little room. There was no place to go. "Do you think I can't express the human condition without showing the particular expression on the face of some particular human being?"

"I don't know."

"Then why do you quarrel with me?"

"My love, I'm not quarreling. Merely asking."

"Look at my paintings. There is your answer. Have I not expressed human grace, human beauty? Of course. Once, long ago, I painted faces, but they began to haunt me. It's not the feelings of any single individual that I want to portray, but the nobility of all people."

"Then why no faces?"

"Shall I paint one face for everyone? It's the same as no faces."

"I think you're afraid."

Gino screamed his reply. "I am *not* afraid," and in the hollow silence that followed he heard his own voice echoing back his own fear. He shuddered and sat down. Monique hurried to him.

"I'm sorry, Gino. So sorry."

He shook his head. "What you said was cruel, but it's true. I still see the little girl."

"What little girl?"

He looked at her sharply, then smiled. "I often think you know everything about me. The little girl was a child of six or seven in a town in Italy during the war." He told her about the battle, about shooting the German soldiers.

"You shot them in the face."

"I didn't want to shoot them at all, but yes, I shot each of them in the face." The memory sickened him.

"And then you saw the child."

"I was hiding in the doorway, trembling with fear. I thought it was another soldier and that I would have to shoot him, but it was only the child."

"Only the child."

"She was very pretty. Silent, sad, but pretty. She wore a blue dress and a pink bow in her hair. And she held a doll. I told her to go back inside. It wasn't safe on the street. Then, the bullet hit me. I was in the hospital for months, until long after the end of the war. When I could walk again, I went home. But I kept seeing the child. I've seen her ever since. I tried to paint her, not once but four times. I couldn't do it the way I wanted to. I couldn't get her face right. I was rather hysterical—insane if you like—at the time."

"You feel guilty about killing the Germans."

"I knew it was my duty—I had to do it to save my life, but yes, I felt guilty."

"You destroyed their faces and then couldn't paint a face, at least not as you wanted it."

"I've aware of that." But in truth, he had never allowed the idea to reach full consciousness. He had never discussed the subject this openly with anyone before, not even Ariane.

"Having destroyed a face, you found it difficult to create one."

He was silent.

"But the little girl. What does she mean to you?"

"I've tried to understand that. Once, just before I drove off the mountain, I thought I understood."

He had almost forgotten that last moment before oblivion, but now it was quite vivid in his memory. He spoke excitedly. "I saw the child, but with the face of my sister, Maria. Suddenly it seemed right. The child should have the face of Maria. Maria was the child. But then I drove off the road and the image disappeared."

Pain twisted his face. "It's difficult to be a man, Monique. The things a man does are often very bad. Like killing other men. It's better to be as innocent as a child."

Monique smiled. "Then you understand."

"I suppose I do. The child was Maria and if Maria was a child then I was a child. And if I was a child, I would be innocent."

"The little girl couldn't have killed the Germans with her doll."

He nodded, beginning to feel the stirrings of relief. Perhaps he would no longer have to face this mystery, to try to erase the vision from his mind even as he was struggling to fix it on canvas.

"You needn't be afraid any longer. You can express the full scope of your humanity—the real power of your manhood."

"Because I made love to you? Forgive me, but any boy could do that."

She smiled. "You make love to me as a man, not as a boy. But that's the smallest part of it, and you know it. Everything you've said tells me you're just beginning to be aware of your true genius."

"I wonder whether I'll ever feel completely free and open when I paint a face."

"You must. Otherwise, any time you paint a blank circle, the little girl will fill it in. Every blank face will still be her face. You'll go on diminishing yourself."

Suddenly the demands of his life and his art seemed daunting—overwhelming. He didn't want to hear any more. He pushed her away and headed towards the door.

"Stop running, Gino."

He stopped. She ran towards him and planted herself between him and the door. "Look at my face, Gino. Is it so bad?"

He shook his head.

"Then paint me."

He found the process slow and difficult. With his pencil, he could follow the fullness of Monique's mouth, the curve of her chin, the slant of her eyes, the narrow, flaring lines of her nose. But when he was finished, he had sketched only a lifeless collection of straight and curved lines, shadows and highlights. A stone Monique stared at him—expressionless, remote.

He wanted to catch the shape of her mouth when she frowned, the glint in her eyes when she smiled. These fleeting expressions must somehow be fixed on the paper, yet without tyranny. He feared that if he didn't succeed with Monique, he would never succeed with anyone. Her features were so clearly cut, yet her face was so mobile, that in the course of a day she expressed a vast range of emotions and always with depth and charm and grace. Everything was revealed in her face, except hate and fear—emotions she did not know and he did not wish to remember. Still, merely recording a series of masks was not at all what he wanted. There must be the illusion of motion—of life.

None of the techniques familiar to him, not one of the tricks he had learned from Pierre Petit, worked. Then, almost by chance, he caught the mischievous cast of her smile with a few strokes. More important, he immediately understood what had happened. Previously, he had tried to capture her smile when it was already a smile. This time he had internalized the process: She was *about* to smile, *beginning* to smile, and it showed in the hint of a glint in her eye, the subtle, anticipatory, curve of her lips. Was that Leonardo's secret?

"Your soul. I have your soul right here on paper."

"Please," she said, "don't erase it before I look. I've always wanted to see my soul."

"You're laughing at me."

"Only on the drawing pad—because you made me laugh."

"Yes, I can make you do what I like—on paper. You see, if I turn this line, you'll be about to frown."

"My God, there goes my happy, smiling soul."

He drew a thousand sketches of her. None satisfied him, but none repelled him. And each was undeniably Monique. Not the little girl in Bari.

The disturbing vision of the little girl began to dissolve. Now he was obsessed with faces. Every circle must be filled. Every human expression must be shown.

"I've been learning, little by little," Gino told Monique. "Patti taught me to copy, Pierre Petit made me work from life. But from them I learned only the forms and outlines of things—the colors and the surfaces. The accidents. Now I've begun to penetrate the skin. For the first time my people are really alive. I believe I've gone even farther than Chagall. My work isn't as mystical, but it has a spiritual quality I know he would admire."

Emboldened, he painted an oil portrait of Monique.

She marveled. "It's me."

"Well, not precisely."

"Of course. I'm not precisely anything. But in the heart of it, I am."

He gave her the painting as a present. She was immensely pleased, almost overwhelmed.

Gino painted her again and again, each time with greater confidence. He was able now to weld the abstract forms he had commanded before with the fleeting expressions on her face, and he felt confident enough to model his compositions in soft tones and melting lines.

"No more fresco," he said. "No more hard lines, sharp squares and perfect circles. I can do what I want. Anything. I'm free."

"Yes, Gino," Monique said softly. "You're free."

"It's time to see Le Temps. You and I both love what I've done, but only Le Temps is dispassionate. Do I dare go to him?"

"You dare."

Gino lashed a half dozen canvases together, kissed Monique and set out for Le Temps' gallery. He had intended to take a taxi—a rare luxury for him—but once outside a twinge of fear touched him. It was a cold day, and he wasn't dressed for winter, but he did not want to arrive too quickly. He decided to walk.

This resolution lasted only a few blocks. The paintings were bulky and difficult to carry. More important, Gino was suddenly very anxious to see Le Temps. For months he had avoided the man. Now, seeing him, hearing his opinion, seemed a matter of life or death. He hailed a taxi and piled in his canvases.

When he reached the gallery, Le Temps wasn't there. Gino's anticipation turned to despair. He slumped disconsolately into a chair, his paintings resting against his knees.

Eventually—it seemed like hours, although it was really only a few minutes—Le Temps returned, elated at seeing Gino and the stack of canvases.

"Quick. Arrange them around the wall. I won't look until you have them mounted."

But when the paintings were ready, Le Temps couldn't bring himself to look. Gently, Gino took his shoulders and turned him around.

For a moment, Le Temps stared. No expression crossed his face. Then he began to cry. Inevitably they both cried. Then they laughed. Le Temps circled his own gallery clapping his hands, laughing and crying, literally dancing with delight. He called on an assistant to bring champagne. It was warm and when Le Temps removed the cork, it poured over the lip onto the floor.

They laughed at the expanding puddle. Together, they drank the warm champagne, wrinkling their noses at the wry taste and coughing, but unwilling to abandon their celebration.

Gino told Le Temps about Monique.

"She's very beautiful," Le Temps said.

"And very young," Gino said.

Le Temps smiled benignly.

"I think I . . . love her," Gino added.

"Why not?"

"For God's sake, help me."

"I can sell your paintings, but I can't deal with your women."

Gino sighed.

"I have a confession to make," Le Temps said and then rushed ahead. "I gave an exhibition of the paintings I took months ago from Villon. I tried to find you, but Ariane couldn't tell me where you were. I gave the show anyway, last month."

"Was it a success?"

"I owe you a considerable sum of money."

"Wonderful, I've been living like a beggar."

"But you look well."

"Because I'm happy."

"There's something else. I entered one of your works in the competition for the *Prix de Paris*. I hope you don't mind."

"Not if I win."

"I don't know yet. The judges will announce their decision any day."

Gino could hardly wait to tell Monique about his meeting with Le Temps. Tonight would be a night of true celebration for them. He banged on the window of the taxi and urged the driver to go faster and faster.

He took the steps in great leaps and banged open the door.

She was gone. He looked about, but he knew it was useless. She was not there. Nor would he try to find her. He knew that would be fruitless. She had taken only her clothes and the first oil portrait he had painted of her. There was a note. No apology or explanation, just, "Thank you, I love you."

He studied the note over and over again, searching for deeper meaning in the youthful scrawl. The letters were boldly drawn, vibrant and feminine, with no hint of hesitation. She had said it all.

He was grateful. Not with the feeling of guilt he had felt so many times before when he had recognized a debt, but with deep appreciation of the transcendent gift she had given him.

Twenty-Four

Liberation

The same day Planchard offered Pietro a position with the Minister of Culture, Pietro quietly investigated the problems of obtaining French citizenship. It would be a time-consuming, complex procedure and he wouldn't get far without informing Laurent, since he would need the editor's help in securing certain essential affidavits. On the other hand, his new association with the government would probably ease the way.

Planchard put him to work investigating provincial museums in Brittany. Pietro, who had no intention of traveling through the countryside, found most of the data he needed at the Bibliothèque Nationale and learned the rest from other newsmen.

Pietro compiled the data in a single afternoon and sent his notes to Planchard. A few days later, Planchard reported that the minister was pleased with the thoroughness of Pietro's report. Thereafter, the assignments Planchard gave him were more interesting, most of them relating to events and institutions in Paris. On behalf of the minister, Pietro prepared research studies on the Opera, the Opera Comique, the Salle Playel, the Gobelins, and a dozen lesser establishments.

The work amused him. He enjoyed thoroughly the respectful—if suspicious—manner in which the directors and managers received him. They were intimidated because he represented the government and thus the source of the subsidies that supported them. A few of the directors were proud, intelligent and capable. Others seemed bombastic and authoritarian, but he was certain that underneath they were greedy, weak and timorous, anxious to buy his approval by any means possible.

In his reports, Pietro added personal assessments of the directors to his comments on their operations. Planchard told him the minister found these "personnel studies" especially useful and encouraged him to continue this type of investigation.

Fascists, communists, capitalists, socialists—all men are the same, Pietro thought. He didn't dare use information he acquired working for the minister in his work at *Paris-Presse,* except when the minister specifically requested such coverage. However, through his association with the ministry, Pietro gained access to other departments of the government, which was immensely useful to him in his work.

"Politics is making you a better reporter," Laurent told him, "and reporting makes you a better politician."

Pietro didn't meet the minister in person for the first several weeks. When he did, he found him to be a quite ordinary, bourgeois individual.

"I'm pleased with you, Scegli. Your work is very accurate. Most useful."

"*Merci, Monsieur le Ministre,*"

"I need more of your time."

"I'll have to ask Laurent."

"Don't bother, Planchard can arrange it."

"Would it be agreeable if I were to speak to Laurent myself?"

"As you wish. I am going abroad—England, the United States, Canada. I want you to accompany me."

"I'm honored."

"Two weeks beginning next month, plus time for reasearch."

"My English is limited, you know."

"You should improve it."

"I'll do what I can."

"Good. Planchard will give you our itinerary and the subjects you must investigate."

Pietro was exhilarated. England, America, Canada. This work was going to prove far more exciting than he had expected.

Laurent was not pleased. "Several weeks of research, two weeks out of the country. I don't like it."

"I'm sure I'll acquire information useful to my work here."

"You don't speak much English."

"I'll learn."

"In a few weeks?"

"I'll begin."

Laurent shook his head.

"Shall I tell the minister I am unavailable?"

"That's impossible. You've compromised me, you know?"

"I'm sorry." Of course, he wasn't sorry; he was annoyed. It was Laurent who had encouraged him to undertake the assignment in the first place. Well, it couldn't be helped. Perhaps he would leave *Paris-Presse*—not now, but when his position was stronger with the government.

He enrolled in a language school, taking an intensive private course in English that required several hours every day. It was difficult work. *What a barbarous language!* he thought. Nights he spent in the library researching the subjects that Planchard had assigned to him. This, too, was difficult because the most important sources were in English.

Pietro learned that Le Temps was holding an exhibit of Gino's work. Despite his busy schedule, he was determined to see it. Neither Le Temps nor Gino would be happy to see him, but they could hardly throw him out. He decided not to take Sonya.

The show was well patronized, but then so were all of Le Temps' shows. Even before he looked at the paintings, Pietro searched for the little red dots that would tell him whether or not the works had been sold. To his disgust, more than half the paintings bore red dots.

The paintings surprised him. He had expected to see the same subjects, the same treatment that Gino's earlier work had made familiar to him. These were different, disturbingly different. They demanded his attention. He didn't judge whether they were good or bad; he didn't care. What mattered was that they were different and they were selling.

Perhaps he has no limits, Pietro thought, with considerable distress. He looked about for Gino, who was nowhere to be seen. Le Temps was avoiding him so Pietro questioned one of the assistants.

"I'm sorry, Monsieur, but the artist is not here and is not expected."

"You mean Bondone won't attend an exhibition of his own work?"

The assistant shrugged. "Strange, isn't it?"

What arrogance, Pietro thought.

The reviews Pietro read were ecstatic. Some hailed Gino as the coming artist of the century. Pietro was angry, but relieved that he had been prudent enough not to write a contemptuous review.

A week later, his work for the minister brought Pietro to the Museum of Modern Art. He had barely stepped inside the lobby when he came face to face with a painting by Gianpaolo Bondone mounted on a freestanding easel. A card beside it read, "*Prix de Paris*, Acquired for the Permanent Collection."

Pietro felt a pang of deep pain. Soon Gino's works would hang in major museums all over the world. He would be feted, renowned, admired. And so arrogant that he didn't attend his own show.

I should never have brought him to Paris, Pietro thought. He tried to reassure himself. *I'll surpass him yet. The Minister of Culture needs and values me. Gino has everything but power. One day I will have power.*

Sonya was unhappy. "I seldom see you. Always you work—*Paris-Presse*, the Ministry. Now these stupid English lessons."

"It's all essential to my career."

"Two weeks abroad. Why can't I go?"

"My dear, I don't think the minister would consider it appropriate for me to bring my mistress."

"What will I do with myself? Night after night in this wretched apartment?"

"When I return we'll spend more time together."

"You promised to help me find work with one of the great couturiers."

"I never promised."

"You did."

"I'm busy. Can't you see I'm busy? Damn you and damn your great couturiers!"

"Laurent never said such a horrible thing to me."

"Then ask him to help you."

"I will!"

◆ ◆ ◆

Pietro enjoyed London. His intensive language training helped, especially since his hosts spoke an abominable brand of French that baffled him. It was stimulating to visit a strange country, to live in elegant establishments, to dine at important tables. He soon learned that the research notes he had prepared for the minister were hopelessly out of date, but no one seemed to notice. At least Pietro had given him the correct names of the museums, galleries and theatres.

In a few days they were off to the United States. Their group took up the entire first class section of the aircraft and was treated with great deference by the airline personnel, who scurried about seeking to satisfy their every wish. They arrived in Washington filled with champagne and good will. At the gate an attaché of the French embassy was waiting, looking embarrassed.

"Where is the Ambassador?" the minister snapped.

"I am sorry, *Monsieur le Ministre*, to inform you that he has been called back to Paris. If you will come with me I'll explain everything."

"I want to know now."

"I think it would be best—"

An American newspaperman had forced his way to the minister's side. "—Your government has fallen. Have you any comment?"

The minister paled. "Get us out of here immediately," he told the attaché.

Thus ended Pietro's quasi-political career. He spent one bitter night in his Washington hotel room cursing the French and their political institutions. *I wasted my time*, he thought. *Damn the Fourth Republic—and the Fifth, if there is one.*

Laurent was condescending. "I'm afraid you took the assignment too seriously."

"You said you thought I had a flair for politics."

"I still do, but now you understand the risks a bit better."

"Yes, well, I think I'll cover the Chamber of Deputies today. The debate should be fascinating."

"Don't bother. I'm sending Renaud."

Pietro frowned. "Who is Renaud?"

"Bright young fellow." Laurent rang for his secretary. "Surprised you haven't noticed his work. Reminds me a bit of your articles when you were at *Liberté*."

A swarthy young man entered the office. Pietro could barely cover his surprise. *He looks like me*, he thought.

"Pietro Scegli, Jean Renaud. It's time you got to know one another. You'll be working in the same fields—politics mostly. You both have a feel for it."

"I've read your articles," Renaud said. "I admire your work."

"I'm sure I would say the same if I had read any of yours."

Renaud smiled. *One point for you,* the smile said.

"Well," Renaud said, "I'm quite pleased to meet you. If there's nothing more, Claude, I'll be off to the Chamber."

"Be careful. The atmosphere is bound to be tense there. We

don't want to lose you."

Renaud laughed and waved goodbye.

"I don't see why I can't have that assignment."

"You've been busy with your minister. I'll wager you didn't even know a crisis was coming. Of course not. Renaud has been on the story for weeks. It would take you time to catch up."

"I have plenty of time now, and frankly I don't like it when someone else takes my assignments."

Laurent looked at him coldly. "They're *my* assignments. Renaud is ambitious, aggressive and capable." Then he smiled. "The world is moving ever faster. There's plenty of work to keep everyone busy. You, for example. The opera season opens tonight. Why don't you cover it?"

Pietro knew better than to protest.

♦ ♦ ♦

Pietro wheeled his svelte Lancia, successor to the little Renault, through the heavy rush hour traffic with cool skill. The motor purred smoothly, the fine suspension system glided easily over the imperfections in the pavement. It should have been reassuring, but it wasn't. The fiasco with the minister; nothing to show for his time but a red face. And now that bright young man.

I don't like him, Pietro thought. *He looks like me and he probably writes like me. Laurent is a sadist. Putting the pressure on. How the resemblance must amuse him.*

He would have to fight for his position. Renaud would see to that. A man like Renaud wanted to be first.

Well, he won't get there without a battle. But for what? What is the struggle about? A few lines of print in a newspaper—something people wrap garbage in? Where am I going? Nowhere, possibly down. And Gino is going up, out of reach, beyond me. It's absurd. That peasant. Stupid, so stupid. How can these fools admire him?

Sonya was not in the apartment when he arrived. Nothing was

going right. He wanted a woman to take the edge off his despair. Pietro opened a bottle of wine; he had drunk several glasses when Sonya came in. He stood up to greet her, smiling. In a few minutes, ecstasy.

"Pietro," she said, "I didn't know you were back."

"No kiss?"

"Of course." But she didn't respond as he had expected. When he ran his hands over her thighs, she pulled away.

"What's the matter?"

"I must go back to the shop."

"Since when? Entrachat never works at night."

She smiled at him triumphantly. "Ah, but you see, I am now at Balmain, not Entrachat."

He was speechless.

"A surprise, eh? My bust is too big, is it?" She ran her hands up along her sides and cupped her bosom.

Pietro fervently wished they were his hands. "I don't believe it."

"You wouldn't, but it's true. Balmain at last."

"How did you manage it."

"Not I, Laurent."

"I see. And what is the price?"

"You think everything has a price. Well, this was just a small favor, from one friend to another."

"Why didn't he do it before?"

"I don't know, I don't care. Now, with your permission, I'll take my bath."

He hurried to intercept her. "Congratulations, my love. I'm very happy for you."

She began to move away. He held her wrist. "Perhaps—before your bath?"

"Oh no, Pietro. I simply don't have time."

She didn't emerge from the bathroom for nearly an hour. By then, Pietro had opened a second bottle of wine.

Sonya wore no robe. She paraded past him with her stomach

drawn in, breasts held high. She touched her nipples. "My God," she said, "how they stand up after a cold shower."

He put out his hand, but she danced away, laughing. "You're too drunk."

Sonya seated herself before the mirror and began to apply her makeup. "I've seen your comtesse," she said. "She came into the shop yesterday. I never saw her at Entrachat, but Balmain? Ah, that is different."

"Ariane?"

"She was gracious enough to say she remembered me. My customer, Madame Rousseau, knew her. They chatted for a moment and when the comtesse left, Madame Rousseau told me all about her."

Pietro wanted to concentrate but it was difficult,

"Her husband's not really a prince, you know?"

Pietro laughed. "When I told you that, you didn't believe me."

"He's very rich it seems, but not a prince, although there may be royal blood somewhere. He spent three months in Italy administering his estates."

Pietro knew it was useless to disagree.

"But now, there's a mystery. No one has seen the husband recently. The comtesse hasn't given a party in months and she seldom goes to the theatre. Madame Rousseau was surprised to see her shopping."

Pietro struggled to form the words. "Where—where is her husband?"

"No one knows. There's a rumor he's living alone in Montmartre, but Madame Rousseau doesn't believe it. Why would a wealthy Italian live in Montmartre?"

"And the comtesse. How does she seem to you?"

"Sad, thin. Madame Rousseau thinks she's very unhappy. She says she cannot understand why a beautiful young woman would lock herself away in the country—at the very height of the season."

Pietro had many questions, but thought it wise not to ask them. Sonya finished her toilette and disappeared into the bedroom. He continued to sip the wine, growing more despondent every minute.

Sonya stood before him fully dressed.

Pietro's eyes narrowed. "Aren't you a bit overdressed to go to the shop?"

She laughed, and kissed him quickly on the cheek. "Nonsense," she said.

Pietro awoke repeatedly during the night. His head ached from the wine, but even more from the nightmarish impressions that assailed him whenever he slept. The visions were absurd. Gino, barechested, wearing a crown, sitting on top of a mountain; Laurent and Renaud, arm in arm laughing at him; Sonya's breasts, bigger even than in life, pressing against his face, smothering him. The night dragged on. Sonya didn't return. At the shop, indeed.

Towards morning, Pietro slept. When he awoke, Sonya was sleeping beside him. He leaned close, watching her breasts rising and falling, yearning to touch them, but afraid. He inhaled deeply, trying to calm himself. The scent of Sonya disturbed him. The aroma of—what was it? Sex? *I see, my love*, he thought. *After Laurent you don't feel the need to bathe.*

He dragged himself from bed, washed and dressed. Sonya was still sleeping when he left. He had always known that Laurent could have her back whenever he wanted. Laurent held a lien on everything he owned—or leased: His job, his apartment, his mistress.

Instead of going to the office, Pietro drove to Montmartre, stopping in front of No. 39, rue Lepic. The memories came back to him: Gino, gaunt and starving, Maria, full bodied and passionate.

He hadn't thought of Maria for weeks. Not a word since she left Paris. Not that he had expected to hear from her.

"My poor Pietro," she had said.

How dare she feel sorry for him?

Gino was not at No. 39, but the landlady thought she had seen him the week before in the place du Tertre. He left his Lancia in front of No. 39 and walked up the hill.

In the place du Tertre, Pietro asked after Gino. No one seemed to know him. At noon, Pietro stopped in a bistro for a cup of coffee. He had not eaten since the night before. When he asked the proprietress about Gino, she studied him suspiciously.

"I'm an old friend," Pietro said soothingly, "a fellow countryman. I'm visiting France and I want to see him."

When the woman still hesitated he thought of offering her money. But after a moment she began to speak. "I suppose it's all right. He seems to be seeing his friends these days, anyway." She accented the word "friends."

"Where does he live?"

"Around the corner at No. 72. On the third floor, opposite the landing."

"Thank you. Would he be there now?"

"Perhaps. Unless he's out with that woman."

"What woman?"

"I don't know. It's none of my business. Some young thing he picked up—right here in my bistro." She seemed affronted.

"Well, thanks again."

"It's nothing. But don't tell him I told you. He prefers not to have me give anyone his name or his address."

"I understand."

Pietro waited for hours in the shadows across the street from No. 72. It was after midnight when he saw—and heard—Gino and the woman walking down the street, arm in arm. They were laughing and singing. The woman was very young.

Women come so easily to him, Pietro thought bitterly. *All ages, all types.* He waited until the light went on in Gino's window, then went home.

Sonya was out again. He was not surprised. He returned to Montmartre early the next morning and took up a different post. Gino and the woman came out, as they had gone in, arm in arm. The woman was beautiful. Not more than twenty. Tall, long-haired and shapely.

Gino was clean-shaven and looked lean and fit. In fact he looked no older than the woman. Pietro had seen enough. As soon as they turned the corner, he hurried to his car and drove to his apartment.

Sonya was not there. All day at Balmain. All night with Laurent. He went to the phone and dialed a number. "May I speak to the comtesse, please?"

"May I tell her who is calling?"

"It is quite personal."

There was a long pause. Then Ariane's voice. "Hello."

"Hello, this is Pietro Scegli."

The phone banged in his ear. He sighed and called again. This time he was told the comtesse was not there. He called several more times during the day with the same result. Finally, he gave up calling and left his apartment. He would have to drive out to Villon and, if necessary, force his way in.

There's hope, he thought, *if only I can get to see her. Whatever Gino has said about me doesn't matter now. She liked me once, found me amusing. I've learned a great deal since then. Perhaps she was angry because of my article on Pierre Petit. I'll apologize. Good thing I didn't write a column on Gino's show. No matter how she feels toward him, that wouldn't help.*

The closer he came to Villon, the more excited he felt. *This may be the way out of this trap. Out of the hands of Laurent. Of Sonya. All of them. If not now, never.*

He parked his Lancia before the great portico of Villon. *To have all this and to give it up for a longhaired girl*. Pietro shook his head. *Gino is a fool.*

Before ringing the bell, he scribbled a note. When the butler answered, he handed it to him. "Please give this to the comtesse. I'll wait here."

It was a long wait. Once or twice he despaired of seeing her at all. After almost an hour the butler admitted him. His courage began to return. He was inside. The first step.

The butler led him down long corridors, opened a set of tall doors and admitted him to the library. Ahead, before the mantle, stood Ariane. He advanced across the parquet floor and tried to kiss her hand. She pulled it away.

"Your note says that you have word of my husband. What is it?"

"May I sit down?"

She did not respond. He remained standing. His admiration for her had never been greater. To have such a woman—

"—Please say what you are here to say."

"I've come here with good intentions. I'm surprised you treat me so rudely."

Her eyes wavered for a moment. She seated herself in a chair and motioned him to take the one opposite.

"Thank you," he murmured. "I've known Gino for a long time. It was I who brought him to Paris, to Pierre Petit and to Le Temps."

"And to me."

"In a sense, yes. I knew him when he was a simple Tuscan peasant, happy to mix paints in an ancient monastery. And, of course, I see him today, acclaimed as a great artist, called 'The Prince' by your friends."

"A harmless joke. What are you leading up to?"

"A simple fact, obvious to all: he has changed."

She laughed drily. "Yes, he has changed."

"Not, I think, for the better."

"You wouldn't think so."

"Nor should you."

"It's not your privilege to tell me what I should think."

"I thought I could speak freely."

"Up to a point."

"What is that point?"

"I will tell you when you reach the limit."

"May I say that once he was dear to us both."

"You may say it. In my case at least, it was—perhaps still is—true."

"True in my case, also. You smile. Ask yourself a question: Why did I do all I did for him? You might answer that it was for my own benefit. But not always. No, not always."

"I don't pretend to understand your motivation."

"But you must admit I helped him. Whether Gino thinks so or not, he is forever in my debt."

"You are incredible."

"Your tone has grown harsh. I regret that. Still I must go on. I did much for Gino. He would still be decorating wallets were it not for me. And how has he repaid me? At best with indifference. He pretends I don't exist."

"I think he is happier that way."

"Yes, but I'm not. I saw him today. In Montmartre."

Her face betrayed concern. "Is he well?"

"He's quite well. He looked like a boy of twenty." Pietro hesitated, waiting to emphasize his point. "But then, why not, he was walking arm in arm with a girl of twenty."

The comtesse's expression did not change. *Remarkable*, he thought. "That doesn't surprise you?"

"I didn't suppose that Gino would live apart from me for many months without having a woman."

"I don't think this is just 'a woman.' I'm quite certain he's in love with her."

Ariane said nothing.

"If you will permit me the liberty of making this comparison: Gino is betraying you the same way that he betrayed me. The pattern is identical. You, too, have done great things for Gino—even more perhaps than I. Yet he repays you as he repaid me."

"I reject the parallel."

"I don't claim that it's perfect. Nevertheless, I assure you that the effect of Gino's ingratitude is as painful for me as it is for you. I think of him—although I have never told him—as a brother."

"As a brother. And of course, I'm still his wife. You are then, in a purely poetical sense, my brother-in-law." She was smiling now, a cold golden smile that perplexed him.

"Yes, it's possible to think of me in that way."

"What way do you want me to think of you?"

He was too nervous to remain seated. The conversation was

now at a critical point. He stood up and walked to her chair. "As a friend, Ariane." She was about to speak, but he hurried on. "We spent many pleasant evenings together before you met Gino. You enjoyed my company. I know you did. You found me amusing. Then Gino came between us, destroying that friendship. We have both suffered from Gino's ingratitude. But instead of being bitter, we can profit from it. It can bring us together."

His voice had reached a trembling pitch. He held his hands out toward her.

Ariane began to laugh, harshly, bitterly. "This is what you offer? Yourself?" She laughed again, a jarring sound that unnerved him. Ariane stood up, too. "Your friendship? Your love? Your hand in marriage? Of course, we will have to dispose of Gino somehow, but that's a mere technicality. One that would never bother you. I'm sure you would be willing to do it yourself. How? A gun? A knife? Which do you prefer?"

"I . . . I would never harm—"

"—Your brother. Yes, he *is*, in fact, your brother. How kind of you to feel like a brother toward your brother."

"You don't know what—"

"—I know precisely what I'm saying. You are indeed his brother—his bastard half-brother. The bastard son of his father and some slut off the streets of Florence."

"Don't say that."

"It's true. You knew it, but never told him. You couldn't tell him. Not even when you were sleeping with his sister. Your sister."

"I'm not going to listen to you."

"You'll listen to every word. Your own sister. What man could be lower than that? Only a murderer. And you are a murderer as well."

"No."

"Yes. You killed her."

"You don't know what you're talking about. Maria is in Florence."

"She killed herself."

"Maria? It can't be."

"Yes, she killed herself because she was carrying your child."

He was dizzy now, dizzy with disbelief and suffering. "Is this true?"

Ariane nodded.

"I didn't know. I heard nothing."

"She's dead. Your unborn child is dead. And you are dead—if you ever were alive."

"Believe me, Ariane—"

"—I could never believe you. For you there is no truth, only one lie or another. There's no one like you in the world, Pietro. No one as cold, no one as vicious, no one as cruel. You came here today—as you always come—to take advantage of someone's misfortune. Mine. The loss of my husband—your brother. Do you know him—this brother of yours? Is there anything between you except blood? Nothing. Nothing at all. Gino is kind, you are cruel. Gino is generous, you are selfish. Gino is a genius, you are a fool. There is nothing to you but a cold, hard, dark surface. I would hate the touch of you. It would make me ill. The sight of you makes me ill. Do you think that a woman who has loved Gino could ever love you? Get out, Pietro. I can't stand having you here for another second."

◆ ◆ ◆

Gino looked about the dismal room with fondness. *I was reborn here*, he thought. Nevertheless, he would be leaving soon. He didn't know where he would go, but he wasn't concerned. Carefully, he piled his sketchbooks together and rolled the few remaining canvases into a loose bundle. His books he would leave for the next occupant.

When he had packed his few possessions, he stopped for one last survey of this magic place. The shutters were wide open. Bright sunlight scorched the room.

There was a knock on the door. *Monique*, he thought. He ran to the door and yanked it open.

"Pietro!" he cried out in surprise.

Walking in from the dark hallway, Pietro recoiled from the brilliant light. He looked very thin to Gino, pale and unshaven. His clothes were badly wrinkled.

"Close the shutters," Pietro said, "I can't stand that bright light." His voice was hoarse—little more than a harsh whisper.

"Are you all right, Pietro? You look as if you haven't slept for a week."

Pietro uttered a choked laugh. Gino put his hand on Pietro's shoulder. "Perhaps you need a doctor."

Pietro pushed his hand away roughly. "No doctor can help me. Only you."

"I want to help you. As others have helped me. I'm grateful to the world, Pietro. Sometimes I've doubted the world's good intentions, but not any longer."

Pietro studied his brother. He had not been this close to Gino in a long time. He observed his firm skin, unlined brow and clear, smiling, guileless eyes. "Sit down, Gino, I must talk to you. " The strength, the depth was returning to his voice. He straightened his jacket, pushed his hair out of his eyes.

Gino sat down on the bed. Pietro stood before him, his back to the windows. "I've been to see your wife, Gino."

"Oh." Gino didn't seem particularly interested.

"You can never go back there, you know. Never."

"I know. I suppose that's sad. I loved Ariane very much at one time, and although I wasn't always kind to her, I don't believe apologies would be very useful."

"I told her about the woman."

"Monique? How did you know?"

"I've been here before, watching you."

Gino laughed. "And you said nothing. How like you, Pietro. You should have let me know. You would like Monique."

"Your wife doesn't like her."

"No? Ariane doesn't even know Monique. I'm sure that if she did, she would like her."

"You don't know what you're talking about. Do you think your wife would like your mistress?"

"I see. Of course not. So you told her. Was she angry?"

"Very."

"That's too bad. I'm sorry to distress Ariane, but it hardly matters, as I have no intention of going back to her, anyway."

"You couldn't if you wanted to," Pietro said angrily. "She wouldn't have you."

"Are you sure you're all right, Pietro? Why don't you sit down?"

"I'm fine. You've lost your wife, Gino. Do you understand? And I am in large part responsible, because I told her. Doesn't that make you angry at me?"

"You shouldn't have disturbed Ariane. That was unkind. I can never understand why you do such things, Pietro. It's pointless."

"Pointless? No, it's not. I'm trying to hurt you."

Gino was puzzled. His look was perplexed—a look Pietro had not seen for years—a look so childlike that it very nearly sent him through the ceiling. "Why would you want to do that? But, of course, you don't. You're just saying it."

"I mean it."

"It's pointless. Especially in this case, when I've lost Monique, too."

"What do you mean?"

"I've lost her. She walked out. Disappeared."

"Then you, too, have been punished."

"No, Monique did it to be kind. I'm grateful for her kindness."

Pietro began to tremble. "You're mad!" he said. "The things you say make no sense at all."

Gino shrugged. Pietro moved closer. "Do you realize what has happened to you? You've lost your wife *and* your mistress."

"Yes, of course. I understand perfectly. I've lost my wife and my mistress."

"And that means nothing to you?"

"It means a great deal. It saddens me."

"You don't look sad. You don't act sad. You look insufferably happy."

Gino laughed again. "I am happy—happier than I have ever been. I would like to share my happiness with you."

"With me?"

It was almost a scream. Pietro tottered for a moment. Gino leaped up to steady him. Pietro shoved him back down on the bed.

"You want to share your happiness with me, after all I've done to you?"

"Why not? After all, you are my brother. I have no other. Once I feared you. Later, I hated you. But not any more. When I saw you in the doorway, I realized I don't hate you any more. I'm happy to be free of that hatred. It was a poison in my blood."

"You know I made love to your sister. My sister."

"Yes, that sickened me. But then, in the beginning, you didn't know she was your sister."

"Later I did. When she came to Paris, I knew. But I slept with her anyway."

"How horrible it must have been for you. To know, yet to have been unable to control yourself."

"I didn't want to control myself."

"Yes, you did. It was a terrible sin and you must have suffered greatly. I see that now."

The anger was growing again in Pietro's mind. "I made her pregnant. She killed herself. Do you understand she killed herself because of me. I'm responsible for her death. I killed her!"

"No, she killed herself, although you must share the responsibility. For a while I was inflamed with hatred for you. I wanted to kill you—"

"—You still want to kill me."

"Not any longer. I've had time to think. Maria is dead. There is nothing I can do for her now. But you are alive—alive with the knowledge of the terrible things you did. Poor Pietro."

"Don't say that!" he screamed. "*She* said that."

"You see? Even Maria. We both learned to understand how tragic this has been for you."

"Tragic for me? I dishonored your sister. She killed herself. And you say it was tragic for me?"

Gino spoke softly, hoping to calm him. "Your sister, too, Pietro. You mustn't forget that."

"And you'll do nothing. I dishonored your name and killed your sister, but you'll do nothing. What kind of man are you?"

"A man like any other, I think."

"I see. Very well, since none of this moves you, I'll tell you something that will."

He took a small table and pushed it into the center of the room. He placed a chair, so that the table was halfway between the chair and the bed where Gino sat. Then he reached into his jacket, removed an object from it and carried it to the table. When he lifted his hand, Gino could see that it was a gun.

"What are you doing?"

"Be patient. I want to tell you a story."

He was smiling as he sat down in the chair.

"Put the gun away, Pietro. I can't see what it has to do with us."

"You will when my story is finished."

Gino made a movement toward the table. "Not yet!" Pietro cried, "not yet."

Gino settled back onto the bed.

"You know I worked with our father in the Fascist party. I was his assistant. He recruited me, knowing I was his son, but he didn't tell me. I followed his orders and I performed the vicious deeds that he assigned me. I learned to hate him. He was a stupid man, our father, a petty, vicious, narrow-minded man."

"Why say such things? He's dead."

"Yes, he's dead, and I think it is time you learned how he died."

"He was shot by the partisans."

"Tortured, shot, hanged."

"I know all that. I buried him."

"Did you ever wonder how the partisans were able to find him?"

"No."

"I'll tell you. Our father tried to keep me from your home. He didn't want me to meet his family—his real family. I wasn't good enough. But when the Germans pulled out, the fascists were frightened, certain the citizens would exact retribution for the terrible things they had done. So we fled. Carlo and I hid in the woods by day, and went to your house for food at night. Carlo didn't want me there, but there was no choice.

"Then he made a bad mistake. When he went off to meet with the other fascists, I was free to do what I pleased. And what I pleased was to seduce Maria. It was very easy and very enjoyable."

"Please, Pietro, there's no need for that."

"Very easy and very enjoyable. But then, Carlo came home unexpectedly one night and found me fucking Maria in the fields. He was very angry. He beat me with his hands and his gun. He called me *'bastardo,'* although I didn't understand the true significance of the word. When he left me, I was more dead than alive. And I hated him. I hated him as I had never hated anyone. I waited in the woods outside your house. When Carlo left I followed him to his hiding place. Then I searched for the partisans. I found a band of them and, in return for my own safety, I led them to Carlo. I knew very well what they would do to him."

Gino stared at him, knowing the story was true, but unwilling to accept the horror of it. "You betrayed my father, knowing they would kill him."

"I *wanted* them to kill him. I hated him. I didn't know he was my father, but even if I had I would have done the same thing."

"Except for you, my father would be alive."

"Except for me, both Carlo and Maria would be alive."

"Oh, my God!" Gino said. He rocked from side to side on the bed. "You killed them. You killed them both."

Pietro was standing now. "That brings us to the gun." He smiled. "Do you understand how much I hate you? You've taken everything from me. My birthright, my name. Everything."

"Not I. I've done nothing to you."

"Yes, it was you. Had I been you, I would have had everything, perhaps even your talent." He took a deep breath. "Stand up."

Gino shook his head.

"Stand up, I tell you."

Gino stood up.

"One of us must die, Gino. There's only one bullet. The man who has the gun will kill the other."

"No," Gino said. "I won't do it."

"You will. If you don't, I'll kill you."

"This is madness. I refuse to take part in it."

Pietro was standing very close to the table, and his voice, piercing and strangled, moved a notch higher. "You have no choice. It's your life or mine. Now, Gino. Now! Go for the gun."

For a brief moment, they stood poised, leaning forward. Then Pietro moved. Uttering a cry, Gino leaped for the gun. Both men crashed against the table. The gun bounced off and slid along the floor. They scrambled after it.

Pietro reached it first, but Gino was on him, smashing his forearm into the back of his head. Pietro dropped the gun. Gino reached for it. Pietro spun around and drove his fist into his face. Gino rocked with the blow, then grabbed Pietro by the shoulders and slammed him to the floor. The gun lay a few feet away. Pietro's knee came up in Gino's groin. He toppled over, but twisted toward the gun. Pietro dove toward it. They struck the floor, hands outstretched—four hands almost touching the gun.

Gino threw his shoulder into Pietro, then leaped on top of him. He smashed his fist into the side of Pietro's head—once, twice. For a moment, Pietro didn't move. Gino hesitated. Then Pietro shoved violently, knocking Gino to the floor, but Gino grabbed his shoulder and still Pietro couldn't reach the gun.

They were on their knees now, locked in a wrestler's embrace. Pietro banged his head into Gino's face, drawing blood from his nose. Gino's grip only tightened. He forced Pietro onto his back, then freed one hand and hit his face. Blood spurted from Pietro's eye. Gino hit him again. And again. Both fists now—pounding into that face. He could see only blood and matted hair and a loose tooth lying on Pietro's chin. But he didn't stop. Pietro wasn't moving, but Gino couldn't stop hitting him.

Then he was sick. He climbed to his feet, stumbled to the window, and pushed open the shutters. He vomited into the street, taking no notice of the outraged cries from below. Then Gino turned and picked up the gun. Pietro still lay motionless.

Gino waited. After a while, Pietro moved. His eyes opened. He brushed the hair and blood from his face and sat up.

"You look terrible," Gino said softly.

Pietro's eyes, vague until then, sharpened suddenly. Gino detected a flicker of fear. Only a flicker, soon gone.

"You have the gun," Pietro muttered, spitting blood as he spoke. "Use it."

"That would satisfy you, wouldn't it? Then I would be as evil as you are."

"Don't talk. Use the gun."

"I enjoyed beating you. I suppose I always wanted to. Now I've done it and the pleasure is over. I never want to repeat it."

"Stop talking!" Pietro was trembling again. "Pull the trigger!"

"Very well."

Gino leveled the barrel at Pietro's head and carefully pulled the trigger. There was a click. Pietro screamed. There was no report.

Gino began to laugh softly. "I removed the bullet," he said, "and threw it into the street."

A bellow escaped from Pietro's mouth. He climbed to his feet and started toward Gino.

Gino stood up. "Don't do it, Pietro. I'll only have to beat you up again. And I don't want to."

Pietro wavered. "Why?" he asked.

"I don't hate you, my brother. I don't hate anyone. I've found myself, here in this dingy room. That's what I was saying, but you wouldn't listen. I don't want to destroy. I wasn't made to destroy. I was made to create. And now I can—anything I want. There's no limit to what I can do. The walls are down. You helped knock down the last one, here, today. I'm free of you. Free of the tragedy you brought with you. Once I was afraid I was as evil as you are, that no matter what you did, I was capable of doing the very same horrible deed. But I'm not. I know that now."

Pietro lunged at him, but the gesture was feeble. Gino gripped him by the shoulder and led him, almost carried him, to the door. "Goodbye, my brother. God be with you."

Pietro tottered for a moment at the landing, then placing one foot carefully before the other, he made his way painfully down the stairs.

Gino went back into the room and gathered up his things. He glanced into the street before he closed the shutter, but saw no sign of Pietro. He closed the door, locked it, and left the building.

He walked to the promenade below the Sacré Coeur. The sun was setting behind the city, outlining the buildings in sharp purple rectangles.

"The most beautiful city in the world!" he cried aloud.

People turned to look at him.

He smiled. "It's mine," he told them softly, "all mine."

He swung his paintings over his shoulders and started down the steps.

Epilogue

Grazie Mille, Mille Merci

For a moment Gino wasn't certain where he was or what he was doing. Slowly shaking his head to clear the visions and blinking his eyes to get his bearings, he realized that he was standing on a stage in a huge auditorium, and the entire audience, including people on the dais, was also standing and staring at him, in almost total silence. And then he understood.

"Please forgive me," he said, "I don't know how long I've been standing here. The last time anything like this happened, I drove off a mountain road, and after the crash I remained unconscious for three months. I don't suppose it's been that long—most of the men look freshly shaved."

The audience laughed, at first tentatively, and then perhaps excessively, but they were relieved. And soon they began to applaud. Gino raised both hands to stop them and then gestured for everyone to be seated. Somewhat uncertainly, the now restive crowd sat down.

"You have been honoring and rewarding me far beyond my value for a long time now, but especially today." Many in the audience began to disagree, but he went on. "As you were standing and applauding, I thought to myself how unbelievable it is that I, an Italian peasant, should have his work hanging in the Paris Museum of Modern Art, and that great men like Sartre and Malraux, Picasso and Chagall, and so many others, are here today on my account, on my birthday. Yes, as I thought about who I was and who I am and what you have done for me, I began to laugh—not at you—but at me, feeling quite unworthy. And that sent me back over twenty-five years to the day the armistice was signed by the Western Allies and Italy, and I was a bumbling soldier, running down the streets of Bari. It seemed as if I suddenly recalled everything that had happened since that day in one second. I'm sure it took a little longer than that, so I apologize for my day-dreaming.

"I am sad that so many who helped me are not here. First of all, Brother Domenico, who thought I could be a real painter, not just a big kid who drew little curlicues on wallets. I know he's up there watching; I hope he's pleased. Pierre Petit is in heaven, too, repainting the clouds without a scaffold. And Louis Le Temps is giving all the young and talented angels a *vernissage*. There have been others, many others, but my heart is so full that I can't name them all. I hope they know I cherish them."

"Even for those who are here, I have not words to thank them enough." He gestured towards Ariane (and her young man) and Chagall, then applauded them, and the audience joined him.

"I've just made the longest speech of my life," Gino said. "I've spoken too long and not said half enough. *Grazie mille, mille merci.*"

The audience rose and applauded him, and continued to applaud him, and someone yelled "Bravo!" and many others took up the cry and sent it echoing across the Garnier Opera House again and again until even the great chandelier began to vibrate, sending out flickers and flashes of light. Gino could only smile and nod his head and say his *grazie's* and *merci's* over and over again. Sartre and Malraux and the Italian ambassador were shaking his hand and embracing him, and others were climbing the stage to do the same. He hardly heard what was said, and he repeated his thanks and smiled until his face ws nearly frozen. Although people were taller than in his youth he was still able to look over most heads and see Vava and Marc Chagall leaving the hall. He climbed down from the stage, pushed through his admirers and hurried to reach them. Marc turned just as Gino arrived, and Gino lifted the older man off his feet in a strong, but not quite crushing, embrace.

Chagall laughed aloud and playfully swatted at him. "I painted the ceiling," he said, "but I don't want to reach up and touch it." Gino quickly set him down and kissed both his cheeks, but Chagall pulled his head towards him and kissed Gino on the mouth. "My spiritual son and challenger," he said.

Gino embraced him again, tried to kiss the hand of Vava, who also insisted on being kissed on the mouth.

"*Mes amis*," Gino murmured, again and again, locking them both in his arms. Finally, he let them go and worked his way back through the throng, the backslapping, and "*Bonne chance*," "*Félicitations*," and "*Congratulations*," "*Mon cher ami*," and hugs and smiles—nodding and smiling himself again and again—until he reached Ariane and her young man.

Gino bent over Ariane's hand to kiss it, and although she smiled warmly, she did not embrace him. "I never doubted your genius," she said.

He might have hoped for more, but he accepted it, thanked her and turned to the young man, who was as tall as Gino, broad-shouldered, but very slim. "Domenico," he said, and when the young man seemed ready to frown, added hurriedly, "All right then, *Dom! Dom! Va Bene?*"

The young man smiled, perhaps a bit grudgingly. "Congratulations," he said.

"Congratulations?! That's all you can say to your father? Your mother and I never divorced, you know? You *are* truly my son."

The young man was blushing and stammering, "I meant—I'm proud—that is—"

But Gino threw his arms around his son and hugged him to him. "Enough! *Ça suffit! Parfait! Bene, Bene!*"

And then Domenico Bondone was smiling freely, and his

mother was smiling, too. Gino put an arm around each of them, and together they walked up the aisle and into the splendid foyer of the Garnier Opera, where many hundreds still waited. "I never learned to paint a crowd," Gino said.